Taming
Mariah

⋈ LEE SCOFIELD ⋈

HarperPaperbacks
A Division of HarperCollinsPublishers

This is a work of fiction. The characters, incidents, and dialogues are products of the author's imagination and are not to be construed as real. Any resemblance to actual events or persons, living or dead, is entirely coincidental.

HarperPaperbacks   *A Division of* HarperCollins*Publishers*
10 East 53rd Street, New York, N.Y. 10022

Cover illustration by Pino Daeni

First printing: April 1994

Printed in the United States of America

HarperPaperbacks, HarperMonogram, and colophon are trademarks of HarperCollins*Publishers*

❖ 10 9 8 7 6 5 4 3 2 1

To all those who lift my spirits with so precious an offering as encouragement, thank you.

1

She'd made a danged fool of herself!

The dark, very masculine eyes a good ten inches above hers held surprise and not a little questioning amusement. She gulped, dropping her gaze for a scant second to his full, well-defined mouth. Had she really just kissed those lips? A perfect stranger?

Yep. She had. She'd given him the biggest goldern smack, square on, he was likely to see in a month of Sundays. It was certainly the boldest thing in the world she'd ever done regarding the lovin' thing. Only now did she have the sense to blush, and she felt the heat crawl up her cheeks. Hang it all anyway. She could never hide her real feelings for love or money, and she seldom tried because she didn't give a hoot. But this would've been one time when it would've helped if her fair coloring hadn't given her away.

Had Tommy noticed her impulsive actions?

Nervously, she peeked over her shoulder. Nope, she didn't guess he had. Tommy seemed oblivious to her presence, blast him! But the others on the station platform had.

"What a lovely welcome, Miss . . . ?"

Her attention jerked back to the stranger in front of her. Behind him, the train still disgorged passengers. White steam swirled around his gray bowler, adding to her sense that he was extremely tall.

"Mariah," she said. "You by any chance lookin' to meet Elam Taggert?"

By criminy, she fervently hoped so. Her grandaddy had sent her to pick up a cattle buyer—she'd forgotten his name—but she'd been so desperate to appear purposeful and otherwise occupied in front of that bunch of gawkers surrounding Tommy and his bride twenty feet away, she'd done the most stupid thing in her life. Grabbed a hold of and kissed this stranger. A blasted Easterner, too, by the cut of him.

Her heart sank. Most likely he wasn't the cattle buyer. He didn't have the smell of cattle on him. Although she couldn't imagine what she'd have done if he was, her embarrassment was so high. She'd worry later about how to explain her behavior to anyone who asked. Right now it was better that he was a stranger, someone she'd never see again.

Part of her brain noted the merriment dancing from his deeply set, smoky gray eyes. He must think she was loco, for certain. Squeezing her eyes tight shut wouldn't cause either him or herself to disappear, either, though she could try.

Then facing reality, she opened her eyes wide again. She'd made a sure enough blasted fool of herself.

But the hurt she felt went deeper than a three-hundred-foot well, and she reckoned making a fool of herself with what looked to be a foreigner on the train platform in front of half the town of Mead couldn't make it any worse. She might just as well become a blooming idiot, too.

Trilling laughter from the milling party down the train platform caused her to risk another quick glance over her shoulder. The happiness she saw there slammed into her like a blow. Five young women still dressed in wedding finery stood there surrounded by several men. In the center of their gaiety was the bride. And the groom. Tommy. Thomas Harold Bakersfield.

A knifing pain twisted her heart. She wanted to sob wildly, but she'd been unable to choke out anything for days, even speech. Now she felt strangled by all the tears and unspoken words trapped inside her.

In all the long weeks leading up to the wedding, she'd thought . . . oh, lord in heaven, she'd really counted on Tommy coming to his senses. To the last minute, she'd thought it. He had to. How could he marry some other girl when they'd been in love with each other all their lives?

But time had marched on like Sherman through the South and Tommy hadn't changed his mind. Two hours ago Tommy had married Miss Myrtle Alice Sonyers, an Eastern girl who had moved into their little town only six short months ago. The Presbyterian church in the center of town had been packed with everyone who was anyone in the state, come to dance attendance on the new banker's daughter.

Now the wedding party was there to see the blissful couple off on a wedding trip. To San Francisco, she'd heard. Financed, she was sure, by the bride's father, since Tommy didn't have that kind of money.

Oh, look at him! He looked so fine . . . so very fine. The new brown suit made him shine with his good looks. And she had to admit it, Myrtle Alice was a whopping beauty. A blonde, blue-eyed china doll, dressed in the height of fashion, royal-blue plumed hat and all.

Mariah felt like a rag doll half the time, even in her best dress. Here she stood in her *second*-best dress, a made-over garment of black serge, with her cotton poke bonnet bent and crushed on one side where she'd sat on it, and, furthermore, without either proper gloves or reticule.

Flying out of the house to be on time for the train, she hadn't bothered to dress her hair. It lay in the loose braid she'd carelessly done this morning. Loose strands flew about her face, showing more red than brown in the sun. But this morning she hadn't cared what she looked like. She hadn't counted on running into the wedding party.

A pitying glance came her way from Caroline Benton, Myrtle Alice's best friend, and Mariah's worst enemy from childhood. Then suddenly Tommy stared at her, holding a like expression. It nearly killed her, that look. It slashed another death wound deep in her chest. She couldn't, *wouldn't* be an object of pity and secret scorn.

Her head swiveled back to the stranger. Then, her stubbornness evident for all to see, she stood on tiptoe, seized his cheeks in both hands, and tugged his face down to hers. Letting her lips part, she laid her mouth square on his for a second time.

Her mind swirled with a raging need to show the town she didn't care, that she could handle being jilted. To show Tommy her heart wasn't lying at his feet in a million pieces.

So jumbled were her thoughts, she scarcely noticed that the stranger was kissing her back until his long arms wrapped around her waist and lifted her off the wooden platform. Her feet dangled. One large hand slid up her shoulder blade and cupped her neck, his thumb curving against her jaw. Startled, she tried to pull away.

"Ump-mmm, sweetheart," the deep, rich voice said huskily into her mouth in very proper English. "Let them have a real show." Whereupon, his mouth joined hers again in a plundering kiss.

Mariah felt overwhelmed, dizzy. Her stomach sank, as though she'd dropped suddenly from a high place. Her nerves tingled. She thought she might faint.

Scared out of her wits at such a possibility, she circled her arms around his shoulders and held on for all she was worth. She was almost lost to all sense of time and place when a rude voice intruded.

"Gladys, would you look at that shameless little hellion, Mariah Taggert?"

Past her confusion, Mariah recognized Mrs. Patrick from the general store. Gladys would be Caroline's mother.

The stranger let her slide, slowly, down his body until her feet touched the ground. His mouth lingered on hers.

"She hasn't a lick of common sense, has she?" said Mrs. Patrick. "Displaying such . . . such . . . vulgarity! That intensity is indecent! Why, with her wild, careless behavior, her grandfather must be sick with worry about, you know, her getting herself in the family way without benefit of marriage."

"Oh, my dear, of course. I'm sure that's one reason Tom made his choice elsewhere," Mrs. Benton said on a sniff. "Mariah Taggert would have been nothing but an embarrassment for an up-and-coming young man with ambitions. And a finer girl than Myrtle Alice couldn't be found anywhere east of the Rockies, in my book. So cultured, you know. I'm so pleased my Caroline has the company of the Sonyers family."

Mariah leaned weakly against the stranger, her forehead resting against his chest. She knew she was incapable of anything close to a maidenly blush at the deliberately cutting words. On the contrary, still recovering from his kiss, she felt she had no blood left in her body; certain sure, it had all drained into her boots.

The Englishman's firm fingers lifted her chin. Through a haze, she saw his lips move and heard a barely audible, "Smile, sweetheart," and then, louder, "Sorry you have had to wait so long for my arrival, darling. Since I could not persuade you to come to New York . . ." He smiled with a charming twist to his mouth as he talked and slid his arm through hers, then guided her down the platform steps. "I had to stay long enough to make sure my investments are in good hands. Those railroad stocks . . ."

Mariah glued her gaze to his face and forced her lips to stretch. She hoped it passed for a smile. She desperately wanted to see Tommy's expression, for she felt his gaze on her back. She wondered if he felt any of the hurt and sense of betrayal she did. Ready to turn, she felt the steel of the stranger's arm harden. His eyes commanded her to hold steady.

Automatically, Mariah walked toward the spring buggy she'd brought into town today. Behind her, she heard the conductor's voice calling the last of the boarding passengers to get on the train. She waited silently while the noise of the train pulling out of the station receded. Then for a long minute, she stared at the toes of her boots.

That was that! Tommy was truly lost to her. She felt purely flat. Drained. She should thank the stranger for his kindness and go on home.

"Are you all right, Miss Taggert?" the stranger asked at her elbow, his voice compassionate.

She wasn't, but she had too much pride to let any more of her insides show than she already had. And to a stranger, at that. "'Course I'm all right! I'm right as rain. A little stormy weather won't keep me down."

"I think what happened just now was a mite more than a little bit of a blow, don't you?"

Any hint of her gratitude toward him vanished. "Don't go spoilin' it by feelin' sorry for me, mister. I've survived an Indian attack, floods and drought, an' bein' an orphan. Reckon I'll come through this."

"Heartbreak is a different matter, my dear."

"Heartbreak?" She hadn't yet put that term to what she felt. Stunned, she wondered if she wore the brand so big even a foreigner could see it. "Never such a thing!"

A dark brow arched in disbelief. Gray eyes remained thoughtful. She turned away in discomfort.

The train chugged out of sight and the remainder of the wedding party drifted down the station steps. That know-it-all snub-nosed Caroline would try to speak to her, if she could, all smirks and little darts aimed to maim with smiles. She had to get away.

"Can I give you a lift to the hotel, mister?" she offered as she climbed into the buggy. She owed him that much, she figured.

"What makes you think I want to go to an hotel, Miss Taggert?"

She glanced at him, taking in his black wool suit. It

was beautifully tailored. Her gaze paused at the silk shirt beneath the stiff collar before returning to his face. It nettled her a little to find he was amused. "Folks don't much ask your business in these parts, mister, but I reckon you're not the cattle buyer."

"You have 'reckoned' correctly, my dear."

"Then get in the buggy! Before that high-nosed cat, Caroline Benton, gets any closer." He stepped up and she slapped the reins sharply. "Git, you slowpoke Lulubelle."

Lulubelle pranced into a smart trot before the stranger could seat himself. Off balance, he dropped awkwardly onto the seat and took a grip on the side of the buggy as it careened down the street, narrowly missing an oncoming buckboard. "My undying thanks for your gracious invitation, Miss Taggert. Er, might I ask how far this hotel is?"

"Right here, mister," she answered. She tightened the reins to an abrupt halt in front of a three-storied brick building with the sign *POWELL'S* on its front. Lulubelle half reared with the sudden stop, and the buggy swayed.

Paying no attention to it, Mariah glanced warily behind her. Sure enough, there came a buggy which held Mrs. Benton and Caroline. They wore disapproving expressions that told everyone who happened to look at them that they were scandalized. They shook their heads in false pity.

"Blast it!" Mariah muttered. Well, in for a penny, in for a pound. Her reputation was already in shreds.

She jumped down and hurried around to join the dark-haired man on the wooden sidewalk. "Mister," she murmured as she twined her arm through his, "'scuse my bad manners, but would you mind tellin' me your name?"

He tipped her a smile. "So formal, my dear?"

"Could call you tenderfoot or greenhorn, but—" She glanced back to see that Caroline was still gawking. As someone came out of the hotel, Mariah took advantage of the open door and tugged the stranger through.

She had barely returned her gaze forward and sighed in relief when the balding hotel clerk spoke to her. "Afternoon, Miss Mariah. We seldom see you in our establishment. What might I do for you this fine day?"

"Oh, um, nothing for me, thanks, Mr. Zigler. But this gentleman, he—he's a f-friend of m-my grandfather's—um, h-he—" Blast it! She could never tell a straight-out lie. Sidestep the truth a good bit, but not tell a bald-faced lie. The few times she'd tried it as a youngster, her face would tattle on her every time. As she'd grown older she'd found that the stark truth often got her into almost as much trouble as telling a fib, but she'd gotten stubborn about it and usually told it anyway.

She looked helplessly up at the greenhorn.

The stranger took over for her. "I'd like your best accommodations for, ah, let's see . . ." He stared into her eyes, then let his gaze drop to her mouth for a moment before returning his attention to the clerk. "A week, at least, I should think. My luggage will follow," he said smoothly, "and a companion will join me in a day or so."

Mr. Zigler's small eyes, bright with curiosity, scanned the stranger's expensive clothes, then lingered on the small, diamond-studded gold ring he wore on his little finger. "All right, sir," he said. "Would you prefer a room that gets the morning sun or one that gets it in the afternoon?"

"Afternoon, I should think. I prefer to rise at a civilized hour."

"Okay, mister." Mr. Zigler shoved the registration book across the desk. "Sign the register, please."

Mariah ignored Mr. Zigler's inquisitive expression and instead watched as the stranger drew the book closer. His hands were beautiful—masculine, well formed and neatly manicured, and soft. No, she amended, remembering how they'd felt on her back and the bare skin of her neck. Not *quite* soft, only without the calluses she normally saw on the men she knew. Obviously, he was unused to manual labor. Maybe he was a gambler. She'd heard tell of gamblers who kept their hands as soft as a woman's so they could have a more sensitive feel of the cards.

He picked up the pen and wrote in a firm hand, Henry Clayton. A faint pause ensued before he added Surrey, England, beside his name, then laid the pen down.

"Okay, Mr. Clayton. You got number three, the second door in the back. It's convenient to the rear stairs. For privacy, you know," the clerk said, giving them both a knowing look. "Hope your stay with us is satisfactory."

Mariah caught her breath at his implication. Gossip would fly, thanks to the dirty-minded little weasel. Of all the rowdy behavior and harebrained scrapes she'd gotten into as a child and over the years, never had she been accused of—of outright *immoral* behavior. Until today!

Now everyone would believe she was sleeping with Henry Clayton when she'd only meant them to think—what had she meant them to think?

She had half a mind to tell her grandaddy, Elam; but then he would feel honor-bound to come tearing into town to call Mr. Zigler out and she could hardly face such a possibility after what she, herself, had already done today. She'd have some almighty tall talking to do anyway to keep Grandaddy out of town until the latest prattle died down.

And what was everyone to think after today's display? What did Henry Clayton think?

"We can only hope," Henry Clayton answered the clerk disdainfully, then stared at him until the man dropped his gaze and turned away. Then, taking her elbow, he escorted her outside. "I shall see you to your conveyance, Miss Taggert."

They paused beside the buggy. All at once feeling lost and dispirited, Mariah gazed at him.

"Well, greenhorn, I reckon I owe you a heap of thanks for your playacting back there," she said, speaking past a harsh lump in her throat. "Everybody who saw thinks . . ."

She stopped, threatened by tears. Why now, she wanted to know? She'd gone months without crying once! Blinking rapidly, she gulped at the same time.

She'd blocked out everything about Tommy's defection these last weeks and days by mucking out the barn to the last corner of each stall and mending the home fences until each wire and pole set tighter than a church pew. She'd personally inspected every animal in the Circle T's home section, checking for the new calves being born and any disease she could think of, and riding to the far corners of the small ranch every third day merely to prove to Grandaddy she didn't need anyone to help her run the place, ignoring the truth that she did. Even the house and bunkhouse came under her polishing rag, much to Grandaddy's and old Nate's grumbling. She'd worn herself to a frazzle.

Now suddenly, under the dark-eyed, compassionate gaze of this tenderfoot from England, it was all too much. She had no defenses left. Unacknowledged exhaustion mixed with raw emotions to rob her of her resolve to tough it out. She thought if she didn't find someplace utterly private to let out some of her pain, and soon, she'd plumb explode and die on the spot.

Henry Clayton took her hand while he studied her face. His fingers were warm and comforting and she had the unbidden wish to press her face into his shoulder and howl. "There is no need for thanks, Miss Taggert. I assure you, the pleasure was mine indeed."

"I reckon there is, Mr. Clayton, and I owe you," she declared. "If there's anything I can do to repay my debt, you can find me at the Circle T. It's about five miles out of town past the wooded holler."

He raised her hand to his lips and gently brushed his mouth across her knuckles. "I'll take note of your direction, my dear."

"Um, there's just one thing. Would you mind still pretending we're, um, special friends, if someone in town should say something? Mostly, they won't, but . . . after you leave, I'll just say we had a difference of opinion."

"Everyone I meet shall know our friendship is close to my heart."

"Thanks, Hank." She paused, and then her sense of obligation prompted her to add, "I reckon your best bet will be The Golden Rose. . . ."

"The Golden Rose?"

"It's the fanciest saloon in town, two doors down from the hotel. Only caters to the best, so a high-class gambler like yourself would be welcome. High-stake poker games are the rule there, and you don't have to put up with the town riffraff."

There went those arched brows again. Beneath them, his eyes danced. "How astute of you to guess my favorite pastime, Miss Taggert. How did you come to it?"

She looked him over, from his gray bowler with its black ribbon, to his closely shaven cheeks, to his wide silk tie which disappeared beneath the tailored vest of his dark suit.

"You're too pretty and dressed too fancy to be anything else. Besides, your hands give you away."

Henry's eyes gleamed before he let go of her gaze to stare at his hands a moment. "Ah, yes, I see why you would say that. And The Golden Rose is the best pick of the lot, you say?"

"Uh-huh. Of course, you can find poker at most any of 'em and there's always Tillie's—but I'd stay out of Tillie's, Hank, if I were you."

"Tillie's, I take it, is another saloon?"

For the second time that day she felt a heat in her cheeks. "Um, yeah, sorta. It's really a whorehouse. But they tend to cheat a man at Tillie's and serve cheap liquor to boot."

If he was scandalized by her bald explanation, he didn't show it. His mouth quirked into a disbelieving grin. "You know this by personal experience, do you?"

"Yep. Tommy sneaked me in one night a couple of years ago on my seventeenth birthday. I dressed up in baggy men's clothes and nobody guessed the truth. Walked right up to the bar and ordered a whiskey. Wasn't much, though. Too much water in it. Saw the girls, watched them flirt and go upstairs. Lucky for me the town—or my grandaddy, either—never found out about that one."

Henry Clayton's brows no longer arched in amusement. "This Tommy . . . was he the young man with the bride this afternoon?"

"Yes. Tommy's my best pal. Or was." Never to be again. Maybe that's what hurt the most.

"Rather irresponsible for a best pal, I should think. Sounds as though it is an establishment where you could have become involved in real difficulty."

"It wasn't his doin's," she said, quick to defend Tommy. She should have known better than to tell a tenderfoot. "I badgered him into it and he made me leave before half an hour was up. Wouldn't even let me look upstairs, the rat."

"I should think not," said Hank in a supercilious tone.

She was about to tell him a thing or two about being sorry to have confided something she'd never told anyone else before when she caught a suspicious twitch at the corner of his mouth. It did lift her spirits a tad to realize he found her escapade amusing.

"Well," she paused, torn now about leaving. "You know how to find me if you need to. If you run into that cattle buyer, tell him to ride on out to the Circle T. And watch out for a slick cardplayer by the name of Kasey. He's got a wicked reputation."

"Thank you, my dear, I will keep your advice in mind."

Without looking back, she whipped Lulubelle into a trot. But underneath her best effort at a calm exterior, Mariah acknowledged her heartbreak and wondered what she should do next.

2

Henry Clayton Ackerley, third son of one of England's leading families, watched Mariah's proud back until it was out of sight. Still amused at his recent experience with the wonderfully artless young woman, he turned toward the hotel. He had guessed correctly. The comedy-drama which had unfolded before him at the train station was high adventure indeed. It was Mariah's determined display of undefeated spirit which had drawn him into it—plus the taste of her delightful mouth.

And her unusual style of beauty. Although she wasn't, by conventional standards, beautiful. High cheekbones, a mouth too wide, freckles. Too slender for most men's pleasure. Yet . . .

Nothing had tickled his fancy so wildly in a long while. He was beginning to think his stay of a few days in this plain little western town would be an event he would long cherish in the dull future looming before him. It had the flavor of the untamed frontier he had read about. Certainly, he planned on another encounter with the young lady—a much more private one, he hoped. He would make her forget her broken heart.

Two women strolled his way, arm in arm, making an unsuccessful attempt to appear casual. Henry was used to such attention in this country—indeed, anywhere, but especially in these rural, frontier towns. His more formal dress and manners frequently invited curiosity from the locals, and much more than mere passing attention from the ladies.

The younger woman threw him a barely concealed gaze of admiration before whispering to her companion. He recognized them as the two women his little auburn-haired enticement had avoided with striking agility. Mother and daughter, he rather thought. The younger, with her short nose and squared chin, favored the older.

He wondered what irritations or perhaps unkindnesses these women had given Mariah prior to this afternoon to cause her to feel she could not bear to face them. Doubtless, their presence at the train station to witness her humiliation and hurt had added to her acute discomfort.

He tipped his hat and proffered a half bow. "Good day, madam." He offered his most alluring smile to the younger as he added, "Miss."

While the mother watchfully inclined her head, the daughter flushed and fluttered her lashes as she murmured, "Morning."

His smile widened as he left them to stroll the street. The young woman's reaction to his practiced charm was typical of the fairer sex, but it neither set his own heart to a faster rhythm nor caused him to preen with success. Mostly it bored him. To charm, he had discovered at a very young age, was as easy as to breathe and, coupled with good manners, it brought him most everything he desired from everyone, young and old alike. Definitely, from young females.

He used all of it to his own advantage. Too carelessly, according to his oldest brother, Lord Robert Ackerley, who fumed at his extravagant ways. And too self-centeredly, according to his second brother, the esteemed Reverend Anthony Ackerley, who shook his head sadly at what he called Henry's rakish behavior. They both worried over his wasting his youth and small fortune and had lately pushed him to settle down.

A pity, that. He saw no need for it when Robby capably saw to the family estates and Tony took care of everyone's souls. It seemed left to him to have all the fun for the family. But alas, his brothers felt differently. They abhorred his profligate ways, and told him so regularly.

Poking his nose through the swinging doors of the closest saloon, he perused the premises with a jaded eye. A pair of dusty cowboys leaned against the bar, ogling a bosomy barmaid as she poured drinks. Otherwise it was empty. Too early in the day for much of a game, he suspected. He moved on.

He passed a mercantile store, a bootmaker, and another saloon before spying Tillie's, set apart and facing the end of the street. This was the place Mariah had warned him against. It was enough to immediately make him long to see it.

Inside, he let his gaze roam. The room was large and furnished sturdily rather than in the plush style he had observed in similar establishments. It was nearly empty and no one paid him much attention at

first. A man slept against a back table while another
tickled the giggling girl on his lap. Only one man
stood at the bar, along the right wall.

His mouth curled with indulgent humor as he
imagined little Mariah bellying up to the bar in this
place. He wished he could have seen her, the little
rascal. She must have been a sight dressed in men's
clothes—although he thought the men in the town
must have been blind not to have noticed her curves,
for she had them, however slender her body.

Two scantily dressed women descended the back
stairs. The brunette gave him a smile intended for
allurement as she approached. He thought it failed
miserably and resembled a hyena, an animal from
Africa he had once seen.

"My, my, my, aren't you a fancy one," she said
while her dark eyes boldly assessed him. "You just
surely are." She raised a knowing brow and fingered
his lapel. "You like it fancy, honey?"

The woman had not even bothered to ask his
name. Henry felt his humor fading while disgust took
its place. A cheap whorehouse dealing in the lowest
form of human transactions was no place for an innocent girl like Mariah, even on a lark. Tommy was a
proper lunkhead for having allowed her in the place.

But then, he had a sudden image of the headlong,
impetuous little whirlwind and felt a faint pity for
Tommy—and a bit more than a faint gratitude for
the protection he had afforded her. He suspected Mariah
needed a stronger hand than Tommy was able to give.

He shrugged the woman's white, feminine hand at
his lapel away. "Not today, my sweet."

He left Tillie's and directed his step along the other
side of the street, passing The Nugget saloon, Silas
Patrick's general store, a meat market, and the Mead

City Bank before he reached The Golden Rose. He sauntered through the swinging doors and found what he wanted. A poker game. It would fill his time for the present.

He wondered how long it would take James, his valet, to make his way back to this little town. James would have surely missed him soon after the train departed the Mead station when he did not return to their private car. The matter would not put him off for long. James had traced him down on several past adventurous occasions.

He settled into the game.

Mariah sat on a smooth rock at the edge of the stream and choked out her tears of disappointment. Her closed fist beat at the cottonwood tree beside her. It wasn't fair. After all their plans to run the Circle T together, Tommy hadn't even had the gumption to tell her face-to-face about his change of heart. Instead, the dirty skunk had simply let her find out slowly, by way of his absence and Caroline Benton's snide remarks. It would've hurt her less if he'd made a clean, razor-edged cut.

Tommy undoubtedly soaked up Myrtle Alice's adoring blue eyes like the earth soaked up water after a drought. It was something Mariah had never been able to do—look at any man with simpering adulation.

Never mind that Myrtle Alice was prettier than she. That she dressed beautifully. Never mind that Myrtle Alice was more of a lady.

Mariah thought about that again.

All right—Myrtle Alice was *much* more of a lady. Her manners, judging from the two times Mariah had met her, were impeccable. She'd been sweet as sugar and she probably never smelled like the stables or showed her legs, either. Or argued with Tommy.

Sighing deeply, Mariah let her tears and anger subside. She'd always been the stronger between them, she knew, pulling him willy-nilly into all sorts of scrapes when they were younger. Tommy . . . well, hellfire, he'd always been afraid of getting into trouble and hated the resulting censure.

He was afraid of all the work the Circle T would take, probably, too. She had to admit it. There was a lot of work to be done to make the place pay once again, and the size of it would scare most men off. But with only her and two old men, one going deaf and the other with a bad heart, she needed another strong body to help run the place.

Well, she wasn't going to get it from Tommy.

Climbing back into the buggy, she thought of what else she could do to get the Circle T going again. Even selling some of their cattle wouldn't put them back on their feet entirely. Most of the money would go to relieve their mortgage debt and they still wouldn't have enough to carry them through another year. They needed more help, but who would hire on without hope of decent pay?

Mariah pulled the buggy right into the open barn, then hopped down and started to unhitch Lulubelle.

"You come home alone?" Nate asked.

She turned her back and discreetly wiped her face. No good would come of letting Nate guess she'd been crying. She raised her voice. "Looks that way, doesn't it?"

"What happened?" Nate almost shouted.

"Danged if I know," she muttered. All the events

of the day seemed beyond her understanding. She'd never acted so irrationally before.

"What's that?"

She raised her voice again. "Couldn't find him."

"Your grandpappy ain't gonna be pleased," he continued to shout. "He was s'posed to be on today's train."

"Well, he wasn't." At least she didn't think so. She'd been so full of seeing Tommy and all, and then in getting herself entangled with that greenhorn, that she hadn't looked around properly.

Sudden remembrance of the stranger's unusual kiss gave her pause. Would she have seen the cattle buyer even if he'd been there? For a few lost moments she must've been thinking of the moon or something, for all the awareness she'd had of anything around her. All she could distinctly recall now was a pair of strong arms holding her.

"Mariah," said her grandaddy from the barn doorway. His concerned expression made her feel guiltier. "How come you're so late? Did you leave him in town?"

She glanced at him as she slapped Lulubelle on the rump, sending her into the pasture. Grandaddy looked increasingly tired these days, his whiskered face showing the strain and worry of the long winter and low productive spring they'd been through. It seemed he'd grown suddenly old. She hated to give him anything else to grieve about.

"Oh, yeah. Guess I did."

"What did he say? Will he be out tomorrow?"

"Um, how're you feeling, Grandaddy?"

"Fine, I'm jes' fine. Now tell me why you didn't bring Mr. Rhodes out with you? Did you miss the train?"

"No, I made it to the train just as it pulled in, but I—What does Mr.—Mr. Rhodes, is it?" At his impatient nod, she continued. "What does he look like?"

"Don't rightly know, now, do I? Only know him by letter, missy, an' you know it. Ya haven't answered me. Why're you so late gettin' home?"

"Well, the train station was crowded. I didn't see Mr. Rhodes and . . ." She let her voice trail away as she fought the tightening of her throat.

"Crowded, you say?" shouted Nate. "Why? What's goin' on in town?"

"A wedding party was seeing the bride and groom off and a bunch of townies were there."

"A pride an' broom?" Nate asked, cupping his ear.

She tried hard not to let her frustration show. Usually she didn't mind repeating herself, but today it seemed just too much to bear.

Her grandaddy's face softened. "Young Tom an' that Sonyers girl, was it?"

Mariah busied herself by hanging up the harness on a barn post nail. "Yep."

"Mariah, girl, I'm right sorry."

"It doesn't matter anymore, Grandaddy. I've plumb forgot about Tommy."

"Tommy warn't the man fer you nohow," shouted Nate.

Mariah turned around in time to intercept Elam's warning glance at Nate. The two old men worried about her far too much. It saddened her as well as made her feel guilty.

She tried for a cocky grin. "No sir, Nate, he sure wasn't. But wait 'til you see the new fella I got my eye on. Why, he's the prettiest gent I ever saw, and dressed real fancy, even wore one of those fancy bowler hats, and when he got off the train I went right over and introduced myself. Yes sir, I did! Mrs. Benton and Mrs. Patrick were about knocked over, they were so impressed."

Grandaddy gave her one of his disbelieving looks, as though to say, "Quit your imaginations." Her grin became genuine. The old man seldom went to town anymore and the odds were that the greenhorn would move on quickly, before Grandaddy had a chance to meet him. But the next turn of conversation gave flight to that thought.

"I reckon I'd best ride into town after supper an' see if I can locate Mr. Rhodes," Elam said. "With all that commotion you likely missed 'im."

Mariah watched the worry lines deepen in her grandfather's face. She'd have to be the one to go. She hated the idea of seeing anybody again today, but it was her fault for not finding the cattle buyer. Besides, she'd go to any lengths to keep Grandaddy away from the town gossip of her foolishness at the railroad station before it had a chance to fade from people's memory.

"No, I'll go back to town, Grandaddy." She glanced at the lowering sun. "I only came home because . . . because I forgot the money to pay the account at Silas's and I need a new pair of work gloves. I can't very well ask for more credit without paying on it, now can I?"

"No, s'pose not. Well, as long as you're goin', you might as well take that pinto"—he tipped his head toward the corral, where a small white stallion with a few brown patches pranced over to nose Lulubelle—"over to John Truit's like we talked about. He won't pay what the horse's worth, but it'll be somethin'. Anyway, put a little toward the blacksmith's account. Lem got left out last time."

"All right, grandaddy." Mariah agreed without argument, though she had a special fondness for the pinto. She'd found the young range stallion in late winter, fed him until his ribs filled out, named him Patches, and broken him into a good cow horse. But most cowmen didn't care much for pintos, she knew, and they were lucky to find a buyer.

Mariah hurriedly changed into her split skirt, then saddled her roan, Skedaddle. Heeling her mount and leading Patches, she speculated that if she could make it into town in thirty minutes, most everyone would be at supper. Maybe she could avoid running into the Bentons or anyone else who was likely to have seen today's disgrace.

However, the *GONE TO SUPPER* sign at John Truit's livery stable reminded her the advantage was double-edged. She'd have to double back later to collect her money. Luckily, she'd pass Lem's smithy on the way home.

She shooed Patches into the livery corral, then walked her mount past a quiet Tillie's at the end of the street. It was too early on a weeknight, she presumed, for the establishment to be in high gear. She swung down near the hotel and flipped her reins around the hitching post.

The hotel lobby was empty. Glancing around, she wondered if she could find Mr. Rhodes without running into anybody else. After making sure no one was coming, she strode to the desk and pulled the register toward her. Sure enough, Mr. Oswald Rhodes was listed two lines down from Henry Clayton.

Her finger tapped the name, then slid up the page to the beautifully scripted name of the Englishman. How on earth did anyone learn to write like that? she wondered. The bold lines fairly jumped off the page, while the curled ones possessed grace and poise. As he did. It reminded her that her own handwritten scratches appeared to be just that—scratches.

"You want somethin', Miss Taggert?"

She jumped guiltily. "Mr. Zigler. Yes. I'm looking for—for—Mr. Rhodes. Have you seen him?"

"Rhodes, is it?" His expression was one of disapproval. "Short fella from Chicago?"

"Yes, that's him." She refused to be intimidated and answered firmly. "I was supposed to meet him this afternoon for Grandaddy but I missed him."

"Ah-huh. Well, he went out, as far as I know. But if you want to know where that foreign fella is"—his expression went sly—"why, he's playin' poker at The Golden Rose. Stakes are gettin' interestin', I hear. Picked up a bit of an audience. Mebbe your, hmm, Mr. Rhodes is there."

Not giving Mr. Zigler the satisfaction of her irritation, she whirled on her heel, tossing out, "Much obliged."

Outside on the wooden sidewalk, she paused. She should have left a note for Mr. Rhodes telling him she'd return in the morning, but she'd be danged if she'd go back to face Mr. Zigler again tonight. Besides, that would leave her to do this all over again tomorrow, and Grandaddy would have a restless night. He was plumb vexed over their need for cash lately. She was too, she had to admit; they owed money all over town. She really should find Mr. Rhodes.

Excitement coursed through her at the thought of looking for Mr. Rhodes in The Golden Rose. She'd always wanted an excuse to see the place. Built only three years before, The Golden Rose was run by a woman of indeterminate age named Rose who dressed very simply, always in gray, with her gilt colored hair neatly piled high. Mariah had seen her a few times in the course of her trips into Mead.

The stranger was there, Mr. Zigler had said. The image of the tenderfoot's finely sculpted hands dealing, shuffling, and tapping the cards intrigued her. That might be a sight worth seeing. How good a player was he? Pretty darn good, by the way he dressed. She wondered what kind of poker face he carried.

A more practical question, she told herself firmly, was how crowded the saloon might be early on a weeknight. Who would be there to see her? Or to tell about her the next day?

She'd never get away with it. Grandaddy would never in a million years approve of her visiting The Golden Rose. Even the best of saloons was still a saloon, he would point out, and good women didn't go into them. He'd burn her ears with the dressing-down he'd give. And certain sure, the Bentons and the other good folk of the town would be in a twitter.

But she had to locate Mr. Rhodes. And besides, the town already looked askance upon her.

She supposed Myrtle Alice Sonyers would have asked Mr. Zigler to send someone to find Mr. Rhodes while she sat demurely, hands folded, waiting in the hotel lobby. Myrtle Alice wouldn't dream of going into The Golden Rose. No sir, Myrtle Alice wouldn't dare do such a thing. Neither would Caroline Benton.

Three minutes later, Mariah shoved open the frosted, etched-glass double doors of Mead's finest bar. Curiosity won her first attention. She quickly looked over the nearby billiard tables, mostly empty, and the prominently placed faro table, attended by one player. Then she covered the highly glossed mahogany bar, where her gaze finally crept up the flocked paper behind it to take in a huge portrait of a pair of angels. Nude, female angels, with pink and gold flesh tones and prominently displayed womanly . . . parts. Was that why the men liked The Golden Rose best? Sudden embarrassment made her jerk her head away.

Where was the danged poker game?

She spotted Rose carrying drinks through a draped door in the back. Deciding that must be it, Mariah ignored the few inquisitive men at the bar and strode down the room. The doorway was hung with the most beautiful gold-fringed red velvet draperies she'd ever seen, but they were closed. She hesitated a moment. Beyond them, she heard the soft buzz of men's voices and clinking coins.

"I'll take three," said one.

"Gimme two," said another.

"Aw, hell, I need all five new," grumbled another to several chuckles. "Okay, gimme four," he added in disgust. A pause ensued before she heard another voice. "What about you, stranger?"

"I shall stand pat," replied the English-accented voice.

"Again?" asked the first voice. There was an edge to it. "A man might get suspicious of a fancy gent who wins too easily, mister."

"Yeah, mister. Yore luck seems too good ta be true."

Quietly, Mariah parted the drapes and peeked through. The smell of cigarette smoke and stale air made her nostrils quiver. About a dozen men lounged behind the five seated players, watching the game. It was mostly a mixed bunch of miners, cowboys, and farmers, and except for the three or four townsmen, they were unwashed, scruffy, and roughly garbed. It looked as though her assessment of The Golden Rose as riffraff-free had been mistaken. Next to them, the clean-shaven, nattily dressed greenhorn looked like a prince from a fairy tale.

No one paid her much mind as she slipped into the room and peered through a gap in the standing crowd.

Hank laid his cards on the table facedown. "I will remind you, gentlemen, that I can play only what Mr. Carollton here has dealt," he said. Mariah noticed that his gaze held those of his accuser steadily.

"I don't care who dealt them cards," said a husky young man, his heavy jowls set in anger. Mariah thought he was one of the freighters who made periodic stops in Mead. "Ya can't deny you've had a high streak of good luck."

"Yes, indeed I have." Henry appeared to ignore the challenge thrown at him.

He spoke altogether too self-confidently for Mariah's peace of mind, as though he hadn't a nerve in his body. She worried that the English dude, for all his charm and self-possession, might not realize how explosive a situation he was in. Western men didn't put up with much nonsense. They were as likely to draw a gun or knife as spit.

Rose stepped forward. "I run an honest establishment here, Abel. Are you accusing anybody of cheating?"

"Now, now, don't get your feathers ruffled, Rose," said one of the watchers, a man Mariah recognized as the new deputy sheriff, Thorndyke Sands. "Nobody's accusing Carollton of dealing favoritism. Right, Kasey?"

Kasey was in this game? She shifted her weight and leaned to the right to gain a different perspective.

Sure enough, Kasey was there, seated next to the heavyset freighter. Kasey was known as a poor loser, and at the moment, he didn't look too pleased.

The man was a real snake as far as Mariah was concerned. He swaggered around town thinking himself a gentleman and ladies' man, but he could be poisonous if you crossed him.

"Cain't rightly accuse Miss Rose's place," Kasey said as he threw a fatuous, lovelorn glance at Rose. Then his eyes grew cold as he turned to Henry. "But it's been known a card c'n find its way from up a sleeve or from a vest pocket."

Mariah held her breath. She didn't like the way this was going. No one seemed to recognize Thorndyke's attempt to diffuse the growing tension in the room. She edged her way closer to stand at Henry's shoulder.

"And you think I have been supplying my poker hands with additional cards?" Henry's brow lifted in disdain. His voice was as cool as a mountain stream.

"Might be I'd like to see what's inside yore coat," said Kasey. His right hand edged closer to the small derringer lying on the table.

3

A *wave of sudden concern* washed over Mariah. Violence wasn't unheard of in Mead. Kasey's nasty temper was known, too.

Deputy Sands reached out and snatched the gun before Kasey could, but Mariah knew there was a good chance the gambler had another weapon on him.

The other men at the table also looked restless. If there was any real question about the stranger's honesty . . .

Mariah made her move. Sliding her hand along Henry's shoulder—a gesture that would speak loudly to those watching—she said, "Here you are, Hank. Gentlemen, I'm right sorry to bust up your little game"—she smiled, giving them all a hint of playfulness—"but I've been looking all over for Hank. He promised to buy me supper an' then . . ."

Kasey frowned at her. Deputy Sands looked puzzled. The others stared in curiosity and speculation. Normally, no one dared interrupt a poker game.

The heavyset freighter protested. "We ain't finished here."

"Um, you know, meet my grandaddy . . ." she continued blithely, then let her voice drift.

Hank grinned at the company at large as if to say he'd been caught by the little woman and now had to placate her. He rose and spread his hands wide, his eyes twinkling. "Mariah, darling, I am sorry to have kept you waiting. I was merely finishing a little business."

Mariah surreptitiously tugged at his coat sleeve. "Well, can we go now? I'm hungry enough to eat a bear."

"Yes, my dear, in just a moment. I believe these gentlemen and lady"—he inclined his head politely to Rose—"wish to see what I have up my sleeve. Deputy, perhaps you would assist me, please?"

Mariah felt her nerves stretch. What in creation was the greenhorn doing? Didn't he know throwing challenges out to a hair-trigger crowd was inviting danger?

"Reckon I can." Surprised, Deputy Sands nodded, then ordered, "Now, nobody move but the Englishman. Everybody else keep their hands on the table."

Hank carefully took his own small handgun from a pocket and laid it gingerly on the table. Then he removed his coat and handed it to Mariah. "Perhaps Miss Taggert will be kind enough to turn my coat inside out for the perusal of you all."

Hank looked completely sure of himself, Mariah decided. Smug, even. Intrigued, she turned her attention to the garment and pulled the sleeves through, then held it out for the crowd to see.

"Whut's in that there inside pocket?" asked the freighter, pointing.

Mariah took out a leather wallet and a piece of paper. A quick look told her that it was a letter written by a feminine hand, and that it came from Boston, but she didn't take time to think about it. "That's all that's in here."

"You may open the wallet, Miss Taggert. Tell this fine company if you find anything which resembles a playing card."

Curiously, she searched Hank's expression. This stranger was almighty accommodating toward a bunch of barroom know-nothings. There wasn't another man of her acquaintance who would carry things so far to prove his innocence. They would more than likely start a fight.

He gave her a nod of encouragement and she returned her gaze to the wallet. She felt a bit of a shock at the amount of American bills as well as English pound notes Hank carried. She reckoned her question regarding his success was answered, but she hoped to high heaven it was gained honestly.

All she found, however, was the money. "Nope. None here."

"And my vest," Hank said as he pulled out his gold watch and chain, then handed the garment to Mariah. The fabric was the finest wool she had ever seen, or felt. Inside, the silk lining was smooth and inviting to her touch. It gave out a fragrance of something she didn't recognize, a pleasing spicy smell. It sure beat the stuffin's out of the way anybody else in the room smelled, she mused, except for maybe Miss Rose.

She ran her fingers around the edges to assure everyone there were no hidden pockets. "It's clean."

"And now, Miss Taggert, would you be good enough to search my person for the benefit of these gentlemen?" He lifted his arms out and smiled impudently into her eyes.

Search his person? For a moment, Mariah was aghast. How dare he! He meant his body! If she did so, it would completely cinch her reputation as an improper young lady.

But why wouldn't the greenhorn think her either thoughtless or daring enough to do it? She blushed to think she'd given him no reason to think otherwise.

Every gaze was on her, waiting to see what she would do.

At his last request, Henry watched Mariah's cheeks pink as one of the miners snickered and another leered. She looked decidedly uncomfortable.

He had wondered how far his pert little miss would go. It pleased him out of all proportion that her sensibilities balked at the kind of lewd commentary her personal search of him, in public, would create among the locals. It seemed she had her own limits.

Far less flustered than she had been earlier in the day, her behavior nevertheless continued to show an unconventional manner. His gaze roved over her unruly curls and the clean lines of her face. Her eyes were an umber brown and full of intelligence. But a bit of appealing rebellion seemed just below the surface, showing fire and courage and stubbornness. He wondered how often it got her in trouble. If she could harness all that spirit, she'd be quite a woman, he mused. All in all, the womanly package as a whole intrigued him more than ever.

Her sudden appearance at his shoulder did amuse him, indeed, and oddly enough, he felt flattered. But on the other hand, it caused a conflicting protective feeling to creep up. He could not imagine why, for he did not usually feel protective toward females. It was a puzzle he would have to think about later.

"Um, Hank, I don't think this is, um, proper," Mariah said, glancing from him to Rose to Deputy Sands and back. Her brown eyes beseeched him.

"I am sorry, my dear, you are quite right," he acknowledged, letting his grin remain. "I did not think."

One of the crowd hooted. Another laughed.

"You ain't goin' to back down from a little challenge like that, are ya, Miss Mariah?" someone dared.

She pursed her lips against her rising temper. It was only words, she reminded herself. She didn't have to respond.

"Gentlemen, I respectfully decline on Miss Taggert's behalf," said Henry, suddenly very businesslike. He turned to Thorndyke Sands. "Deputy? I have no doubt these gentlemen will be quite satisfied if you tell them I have nothing hidden."

"Sure, I'll oblige," Sands responded. He moved around the table and efficiently frisked Henry. "Nothin' here. You boys ain't got nothin' to gripe about. His wins've been on the up-'n'-up."

"You mean there's someone in this town who's as lucky at cards as ol' Kasey here?" the freighter grumbled.

"Hell, I reckon I'll jest quit now and save myself the trouble of playin' the rest of the night."

"I'm through," said another player as he threw down his cards.

Mariah let her breath go. Thank goodness, nothing had been found. She hadn't known what to expect and was glad that her own nagging suspicion had proved groundless. Now they could leave.

Henry forestalled that notion. "Gentlemen," he said as he donned his vest. "I obligingly disrobed and allowed myself to be searched to prove my innocence. I would like Mr. Kasey to do the same."

"You what?" Kasey said with a snarl.

The room went still.

"Hank," Mariah whispered, clutching his vest's front point. "Let it go."

For the first time since she'd met him, the handsome Englishman ignored her. "I think you heard me quite well, Mr. Kasey. I want you to show the company here that you do not have any extra cards up a sleeve or in a vest pocket."

"You callin' me a cheat?" Kasey roared. He half rose and reached for the derringer on the table. A collective scramble began.

Mariah stumbled backwards as someone pushed into her. She bumped into Henry's shoulder. His hand shot out to grab her forearm, saving her from a fall, but his gaze remained unwaveringly on Kasey. She held her breath again as she realized Hank was not backing down.

"Hold it," Sands commanded. Without Mariah seeing it happen, the deputy suddenly had his gun drawn. "Easy now, folks. Kasey, leave it."

Everyone in the room froze. Kasey eyed the big .45 staring him in the face, then did as the deputy ordered. He slowly raised his hand from where it hovered at the table's edge. Mariah suspected he had a knife in a boot or some such.

"Now then, Mr. Kasey," Henry persisted. "Would you please remove your coat?"

"Hank," Mariah urgently whispered. "Quit while you're ahead."

"Nonsense, my dear. Mr. Kasey has impugned my honor. I demand the satisfaction of his compliance to the same proof of his integrity as he forced on me."

"What'd he say?" asked the freighter as he stared at Henry.

The short man next to him seemed amused. "Said Kasey insulted 'im an' he wants Kasey to prove himself jes' as honest by showin' off the inside of his coat too."

Kasey glared his fury at the implied insult. "No, I ain't goin' to do it."

"Are you refusing to comply, sir?"

"Already said it, didn't I?"

"Then you admit to—"

"I ain't admittin' nothin'."

An older man standing in the crowd offered his say. "Wal, Kasey, it seems to me you been doin' an awful lot o' winnin' at poker yerself fer some weeks now. Ya took a purty good poke from me last week. I reckon I wouldn't mind seein' the inside o' yore coat."

Several voices agreed. Someone grabbed Kasey's collar. He jerked away, his pale blue eyes flashing a warning. "All right, all right."

Angrily, he peeled his coat from his shoulders and then flipped it open for all to see. There was no sign of a hidden device or unaccountable pocket. "Satisfied?" he snarled.

He quickly started to put the coat on again, but Henry lifted his hand. "Sir! The vest, if you please."

Kasey opened his mouth to protest.

"Better do it, Kasey," said the freighter. "I've played plenty when I lost to you, too."

"Yeah, Kasey," insisted the older man. "This here stranger proved he was playin' square. You better show us you was too."

Kasey's face lost some of its color. The freighter, suddenly impatient, shoved himself up from his seat and yanked open Kasey's vest, popping a button in the process. "Nothin's here," he stated, disappointed.

Eyes narrowed to slits, Kasey jerked his chin at Henry. "You happy, Mr. High an' Mighty?"

Before Henry could say another word, Mariah quickly interjected, "Yes, of course. Um, we have to leave now."

"One moment more, Mariah." With lightning speed, Henry flipped his cards to show four kings and an ace. "Anybody beat that?"

No one answered and a couple of players shook their heads. Henry scooped the pile of coins and bills into his bowler, then bowed. "Thank you, gentlemen, for a very enlightening evening."

Exasperated, Mariah grabbed Hank's hand. This dad-blasted tinhorn didn't know when he was truly lucky. She wheeled and shoved herself through the men in back of her, hauling him behind her. She nearly ran through the saloon's long outer room. Outside, she didn't slow down until they reached the safety of the hotel lobby.

"There is no need for such haste, Miss Mariah," Henry protested. "The law is not chasing us."

"You tenderfoot!" She brought him up short barely inside the hotel door and glared at him. Without realizing it, she was still holding his hand. "Anybody ever tell you that you push your luck too far?"

"I have always known my limit, Mariah," he said, his eyes twinkling. "I also seem to have an uncanny knack of knowing when I have a winning hand."

"Luck or not, greenhorn, you don't understand the men in these parts. They don't like a stranger, especially a foreigner, besting them in the kind of showdown you just forced on Kasey. They aren't exactly the civilized type like you're used to dealing with."

He grinned lazily. "Indeed, I am quite well aware

of that, my dear. Nor the women either. And I might remind you, the showdown, as you call it, was forced on me. But I have dealt with rough men before. You need not worry so."

"You could've got yourself killed," she insisted, ignoring his reference to women. "Didn't I tell you not to get mixed up with that Kasey fella? He's meaner'n a double-headed sidewinder."

"And that would have caused you grief?"

Caught by the expression in his gray eyes, she hesitated. Why should she care? "You scared me out of a month's growth. He would've killed you if they'd found anything."

"You suspected they'd find evidence of cheating on me?"

"Well, I—I hardly know you. You're a gambler."

"Yet you stood by my side."

"You did me a good turn."

Mr. Zigler came into the lobby from the hotel dining room. He stared at their joined hands. "I see you found your young man, Miss Mariah. Did you find Mr. Rhodes as well?"

Mariah dropped Hank's hand as though it were a branding iron. Rhodes! Heaven help her, she'd forgotten the man entirely. Again! Embarrassed, she backed a step or two toward the door. "Um, no, I— oh, he—I gotta go."

After all this, she had to find the man. No amount of explanation would cover her tracks with her grandaddy if she went home a second time without even word of him.

Deputy Thorndyke Sands pushed through the door, accompanied by a short, mustached man Mariah had seen watching the poker game. They both looked at her curiously.

"Oh, Mr. Rhodes," Zigler called. "This young lady has been asking for you."

"Me?" said the short man, surprised.

Mariah's discomfiture was complete. How could she have been such a nitwit? She hadn't even asked for the man at The Golden Rose and he'd been there all the time.

Tamping down her chagrin, she did her best to look calm as she extended her hand. "Mr. Rhodes. I'm Mariah Taggert. I reckon you must've expected to meet my grandfather, Elam Taggert."

"Yes, ma'am, I did." Obviously puzzled, he politely shook her hand.

"I'm right sorry I missed you at the train today." She boldly held his stare, hoping to begin on a business note.

Mr. Rhodes awkwardly looked toward Hank. "Uh, these things happen."

Mariah nearly groaned aloud. It was clear the cattleman had been among those who'd seen her kissing Hank at the station. Now she'd gone into the town's leading saloon—after dark, no less—supposedly to look for Mr. Rhodes and instead had latched on to the Englishman once more. She reckoned the whole town would know about this foolishness as well.

Mr. Rhodes was to stay with them at the Circle T for a night or two while he and Elam concluded their business. She didn't know whether to ask him to say nothing about what he saw to her grandaddy or to pretend it didn't happen at all.

Maybe she'd be lucky and the matter would never come up.

Maybe a snowball wouldn't melt in hell.

Grandaddy expected to sell Mr. Rhodes some cattle—although why they just didn't ship them off as they'd done before puzzled her more and more. There was something about the whole matter she didn't understand.

Henry inclined his head. "Mr. Rhodes, I am Henry Clayton. I was about to take Miss Mariah in to supper. Won't you join us? You too, deputy."

"Don't mind if I do, if you don't," Thorndyke said, glancing briefly at Mariah. "We were headed that way ourselves."

"Sure," Mr. Rhodes said.

A protest rose in Mariah's mind, but before she could voice it, Henry muttered for her ear alone, "Mr. Zigler is observing us a bit too close for comfort. The best way to prevent further gossip, my dear, is to pretend that everything is quite normal and you have the highest intentions possible."

Mariah decided she might as well go along. Since she was already in trouble, at least she could suffer the consequences on a full stomach. She pasted on a smile and allowed Henry to steer her into the hotel dining room.

Powell's dining room was the finest their little town had to offer. Mariah had eaten there only a time or two. The last time had been with Tommy. Living so close to Mead, she usually had no call to stay in town for a meal.

A deep longing caught her unawares. She couldn't help but see the contrasts. Hank politely held her chair and deferred to her in her food preferences. He ordered wine with a flair no Western man she knew possessed. Tommy always let her make her own choices, all right, but it was with the "you-can-take-care-of-yourself" air they'd shared.

She had thought she and Tommy had stood on equal ground. But maybe it hadn't been quite equal.

She wondered if that was why Tommy had deserted her. She'd never given him an inch on anything.

The waiter set a basket of bread on the table. Its aroma made Mariah's mouth water. Between all the commotion that day, as well as her emotions being in a turmoil, she'd eaten only a cold biscuit. Now she wanted to put all of the day's heaviness past her. Perhaps after supper she could relax.

She nearly dropped her butter when Hank opened the conversation with, "Deputy, I hope you realize that fellow's vest did, indeed, provide for an extra card."

Thorndyke glanced up sharply. "Couldn't tell, for sure, without a closer look. Have to say I've been a mite curious from time to time about Kasey. He rolled into Mead about the time I took up bein' a deputy a couple of months ago. Seems his luck tends to run high regularly. But after seeing his coat and vest open like that, what makes you so sure he's been cheatin'?"

"It was well hidden, I must admit. There was the faintest line and pucker at the left bottom seam, a heavier thread running through the cloth. I daresay, if given a chance at a more complete search, I could have uncovered it."

He gave Mariah a wry smile, enough to tell her he'd left because of her urging.

"That place was ready to bust open," she defended. "Anything could've happened."

"Quite so."

Rhodes, buttering his bread, agreed. "Saw something like that vest thing back in Chicago once."

"How could an extra thread matter, anyway?" Mariah asked.

"A card or two can be secreted against the vest with a thin run of elastic," Henry explained. "A skillful cardplayer can pull one down and introduce it into his hand without anyone being the wiser."

"But Kasey didn't have any cards in his vest."

"No, he was very clever, I think. He somehow got rid of them before he could be discovered. But he knows I know."

"Why do you say that?"

"There is a certain expression a gambler gets."

"Hank, Kasey is dangerous. Maybe you oughta leave town right away."

Hank was taking the matter all too lightly. Mariah's fingers itched to tug at his coat to make him pay closer attention to what she said, but she refrained. Thorndyke was observing them, and she was determined to keep her behavior unremarkable.

"Reckon I'll just keep a closer watch on him," the deputy said. "Might even suggest he move along. Miss Mariah is right, Mr. Clayton. I wouldn't trust turning my back on Kasey."

Rhodes changed the subject as their dessert was served. "Miss Taggert, I think I'll wait 'til mornin' to come out to the Circle T. I'll rent a hack at the livery."

Mariah agreed and they finished their meal amid talk of the weather and local events. But she knew the deputy had given Hank a subtle warning, too. It would be better for all if he left town sooner rather than later.

"You are to return home after dark without escort?" Hank asked her an hour later. Mariah found his astonished concern downright funny after all they'd been through today. He insisted on walking her to her conveyance.

"I can take care of myself," she said. True, she rarely rode home after dark alone, but the prospect didn't frighten her. The road was as familiar to her as her own corral. "The Circle T isn't that far."

She paused in front of Skedaddle at the hitching post. Far more concerned for Hank's safety than her own, she felt obliged to caution him again. "Hank, I've been thinking. . . ."

Muted laughter came from The Nugget, the saloon across the road. The front door swung open and the sounds of laughter and banjo music rolled out, raucous and loud. Two men staggered out and started up the street.

Hank glanced around. "Where is your buggy?"

"Left it home this time. I'm riding Skedaddle here."

"Mariah," he said as a third man hailed the two. He paused to observe all three turn and lurch down the street. "I think I should accompany you home."

"Much obliged, Hank, but I'll be all right. It's you—"

Mariah caught her breath when she heard the scrape of a boot nearby; it made her edgy after their recent confrontation with Kasey.

The place where they stood was lit only by the lamplight showing from the windows of the dry goods store and the nearby bank. The walkway between the two buildings was very dark. Then the light went out in the bank, further darkening their position. But a moment later a man stepped out of the bank and locked its door before walking away. She sighed in relief.

"Me?" he prompted.

She turned back to the tall Englishman. "Yeah. Hank, don't get into another game tonight." She touched his hand for emphasis. "Lay low, for a day or two. Let Kasey cool down."

"My dear, you flatter me with your worry. But I do assure you I can fend for myself."

Around them, the evening grew quiet once more. She took a deep breath. The cool spring air smelled fresh and sweet.

"I gotta get going. Grandaddy is likely stompin' the ground waiting for me. But don't be a dunderhead, Hank. You made a bad enemy, showing up Kasey that way. He isn't likely to forget it. Please, stay out of sight 'til you can leave town."

Hank's long fingers lifted her chin. "I have no intention of leaving just yet."

His head lowered. His lips hung inches above hers. Mariah thought he might kiss her.

"But gambling in this town don't hold a candle to Denver," she murmured. "You'll find higher stakes there."

"It was you who convinced me to linger here a while. Now what would the good ladies of Mead say if I left you as suddenly as I arrived? Especially after our very loving performance."

"Oh, well . . ." His mouth was so close. She might as well let him. She wanted him to kiss her again. It was unlikely she'd have another anytime soon. This time it would be for real and she could keep the memory against the days when the lonelies crept in.

Her expectation of being genuinely kissed was suddenly blasted by a disturbance from one of Mead's raunchier bars, as several noisy men spilled out onto the street. Someone shouted, "Watch out fer Kasey. He's drunk an' gunnin' fer that there foreigner."

"Hell's bells," Mariah said through her teeth, disappointed. Then, alarmed as the sudden warning sank in, she said, "C'mon, Hank. Reckon we better scat."

"Scat?"

"Yep. We gotta leave, pronto!"

4

Mariah pulled the reins free of the post and mounted Skedaddle in one smooth leap. The horse felt her urgency and danced sideways.

"He ain't at the hotel," a loud voice protested from the small knot of men approaching.

"Well, he ain't in none of the saloons, neither," said another.

"I'm gonna find 'em," said a slurred voice Mariah recognized as Kasey's. "He cain't hide, the two-bit tinhorn. Trying to show me up for a fool."

"Whatcha gonna do, Kasey? Trade vests?" taunted a laughing man.

"He cheated," roared Kasey. "He had to of. Ain't that much luck, natural-like, for any man. Gonna make him tell how he done it," he said, sounding angrier than ever. "Then you boys can help me teach him what for."

"Yeah, I'd like a little of the fun," someone else said.

Trouble always followed that crowd, Mariah knew. Hank didn't stand a chance of staying out of a fight if they cornered him. She briefly wondered where the deputy had disappeared to, but it was no time to speculate. She tightened her grip on Skedaddle's reins and brought the mount closer to the wooden sidewalk, then held out her hand. "Well, don't just stand there gawking, greenhorn."

"Uh, Miss Mariah, perhaps I should take care of this matter immediately," Henry said.

"Hey, ain't that him?" said the first voice. "Let's git him."

The knot of men broke up. Two hurried toward Henry and Mariah, shouting, "Hey, mister, hold up there."

"C'mon, Hank! Don't be a fool!"

"I am no coward, my dear girl. I did not cheat. I shall talk to them."

"You're not likely to get a chance. Those no-goods want a piece of your hide. Save it for when the odds are back in your corner."

"But the deputy can prove—"

A shot rang over their heads and Mariah gave an imperative, "Hank!"

Henry watched the approaching thugs for all of three seconds, then decided Mariah might be right. Those men were in no mood to listen to logic.

He stepped forward and put his toe into the stirrup.

Mariah put her hand under his elbow and yanked. He sprang lightly enough, but the horse shied and he landed awkwardly on Skedaddle's rump. Mariah gave him no time to settle in as she dug her heels into the roan.

Skedaddle snorted and half reared. Hank slid off

the horse's back end and landed on his rump with an "oof," losing his bowler in the tumble. Mud hit his face and squished underneath his hands.

Kasey's voice rose in contempt for all the town to hear. "You blasted yellow-bellied foreigner. I dare you to face me."

Mariah wheeled as Hank shot to his feet. Oozing mud ran down the back of his trousers. Leaving the hat behind, he made a running leap, placed his hands flat on the horse's rear, and lifted himself. Once more he found his seat on the horse's rump. They plunged forward down the road.

Hank righted himself just as Kasey staggered forward, waving a gun in the air. Several mounted men fanned out to chase them.

"Hang on!" Mariah yelled.

Hank's arms circled her slender waist. They dodged the nearest man on foot, his outstretched hands sliding against Skedaddle's muddy rear, then raced past a couple of buildings before Mariah guided the horse in between two, taking them out of sight of the street.

Behind them, a whoop sounded, and a "Down this way!"

It sounded a bit like an English fox hunt, Henry mused. He never thought he would have a chance to experience how the fox felt.

Coming out behind Morton's general store, Mariah galloped Skedaddle around a corner, then backtracked. She slowed the horse and cautiously peeked around the building in front of them. Noise and commotion still hung in the air at the bottom of the street.

"Where are we going?" Hank asked.

"Shh. We—" Behind them the pursuit suddenly sounded imminent once more. "Oh, shucks," she complained.

She put Skedaddle to a run and raced across the road, hoping no one would spot them. When they emerged from the shadows, they faced open ground. She observed it carefully. They had to reach the livery corral to get Patches. They would have a better chance of escape if Hank had his own mount.

Hesitating only a moment, she guided the roan toward John Truit's, hoping to go undetected. Thankfully, only one lamp shone from the house, which probably meant only Mrs. Truit was home.

They eased alongside the wooden fence. "Patches," she half whispered. "Here, boy."

"What are you doing?"

"Getting us another horse."

"Another? What—"

"Shh. Keep your voice down."

Hank clamped his teeth together, but he felt very uneasy.

Mariah slipped to the ground. Hank watched intently as she took a bridle from a post and approached a small brown-and-white stallion. The other horses skittered away, but the horse she was after let her approach. She deftly slid the headpiece in place.

"But, Mariah," he said when she led it through the gate. "You cannot simply take a horse from someone's paddock."

"It's all right, don't worry."

"What do you mean, don't worry?"

"Shh. Mr. Truit will understand."

"But you Westerners take a dim view of horse stealing!" Actually, so did his countrymen.

Swinging lithely, Mariah mounted, bareback, just as a shout came from the house. "Hey, you! What you messin' with?"

The shout was heard and taken up by the hunters.

"Aw, now see what you've done? C'mon, Englishman."

He didn't have time for further protest. He scooted forward onto the roan's saddle, his knees bent awkwardly in the too-short stirrups, and raced after Mariah.

After a long, rough climb, Mariah pulled her horse to a stop in a hillside stand of pines. She patted the heavily breathing mount. "Good boy," she whispered. Hank halted beside her.

The silence settled around them. In the distance, they listened to the chase die out. Finally, Mariah laughed in delight. "Well, reckon we fooled 'em that time."

"Do you think so?" Henry reflected her amusement, his voice low. The round, musical tones of it fell pleasantly on her ear.

"Yeah. They probably think we're holed up somewhere for good and gave up."

"Perhaps Deputy Sands has put a stop to their shenanigans," said Henry. "Or perhaps he is searching for us as well."

"Maybe." She started her horse down the slope, aiming toward the back of Powell's hotel.

"Is this kind of thing a usual occurrence here?" Hank asked, merriment still in his voice.

"Oh, no." She thought about it. "Well," she amended, "not too often. Only about once or twice a month something happens that causes a stir. Usually Mead is pretty tame compared to what we read about events over in Kansas, and Arizona, and New Mexico. Though I hear tell the mining camps can get a mite exciting."

"It surely couldn't be more so than our adventures of today."

Adventure? Was that how the Englishman viewed all that had occurred since morning? She wondered if he always found the unpredictable interesting and alluring. Most likely he was a thrill seeker, she decided. He was a gambler, after all, and according to Elam, gamblers lived from moment to moment, game to game. Town to town. Always in search of excitement.

She could never live such an existence. The Circle T was all she'd ever wanted; she'd loved the place more than anything since she'd come there, an orphan, at ten. Granny had been alive then, and she and Grandaddy had given Mariah all the love her scared and lonely little self had needed. Now it was her turn to give the love and security back. And she would, too. She'd never leave the Circle T or Grandaddy. *Her* gamble and purpose was in making it successful.

Mariah had to admit, though, it had been a pretty eventful day. Her pain and foolish behavior of that morning seemed a very long time ago now.

Which reminded her—she'd better get the man back into his hotel. He may have been having fun, but she had to face Grandaddy yet tonight and explain where she'd been 'til so late and why she still didn't have Mr. Rhodes in tow.

They moved quietly down the back alley. As they neared the rear of Powell's hotel, the darkness beyond the main street loomed suddenly deeper. Patches slowed and his ears flickered. So did Skedaddle's. Mariah blinked against the lack of light. Her breath felt trapped; she sensed danger.

Just as she tightened the reins, Henry's large hand wrapped around hers to halt the horses some yards from the hotel's back entrance. He leaned close and murmured next to her ear, "Stop here, Mariah. Someone is there in the shadows."

The faintest of movements alerted her, too, as a stray gleam of light fell on a drawn gun barrel. She'd never thought Kasey's challenge would go so far. Whoever it was, she didn't plan on challenging him for entrance into the hotel.

Pressing her knees into the pinto's sides, she backed him slowly. Despite her caution, the two horses' hoofbeats thudded loudly in her ears and the leather saddle creaked. But no shout came and she let her breath out in relief.

They halted once more, deep in the shadows.

"If one of those ruffians is at the back door, then you can bet your last dollar one'll be at the front, too," she whispered.

"My dear, I suggest we find Deputy Sands and let him take care of these brawlers."

"Thorndyke Sands is only one man," she said, exasperated. "He can't protect you against half a dozen sneaking coyotes."

"But I have done nothing wrong. I refuse to allow mere barroom louts to intimidate me."

"Greenhorn, you don't understand. Right or wrong, Kasey now has a grudge against you. He's bragged all over town that he's gonna get you. He isn't likely to give up and he most likely won't wait to hear any argument of fancy words."

"You mean he will demand a fight? Possibly a standoff with pistols like those of which I have read?"

"Yep."

"Very well then. If Kasey demands satisfaction we had better find him and make arrangements."

"Hank, are you loco? He's killed at least three men in the last year—supposedly in fair fights, but . . .

Never mind that he was drunk tonight. He's pretty good with a pistol anytime."

"And you think I would lose in such a fight?"

"Are you any good with a gun? Or a knife? Oh, never mind! Unless you're trying to make a name for yourself as a gunfighter, it'd be downright stupid to take such a chance."

"No, I don't wish to be thought a gunfighter."

"Then we'd better get you outa town."

"I do not wish to leave just yet."

She shook her head in disbelief. The man was past stubborn. "If you stay . . ."

He ignored her implication. "Let's approach the front of the hotel, my dear. In plain sight."

"But—"

"They are not likely to shoot us in the back, are they?"

Thinking about it a moment, she said, "No, guess not. That would get any of 'em hung in a hurry. Folks out here take a low opinion of such cowardly action."

"You see? If I simply refuse to fight, Kasey cannot win."

"But then everyone would think you're the coward."

"You find that distasteful, do you?"

"Well, I . . . it . . . you—" she stumbled over her words, unable to explain her sudden disappointment. She didn't really want him to face Kasey in a gunfight and she'd just spent the last two hours helping him stay out of the clutches of the town's worst bullies.

Why should she care if he was a gambler who, despite what he'd said, had a cowardly streak in him after all. He'd be gone on his merry way in a day or two and likely she'd never see him again. So what if people thought him chickenhearted? They already thought her hell-bent. It would only be one more thing she'd have to live down.

But he'd been kind to her in a way no one else ever had. He'd saved her embarrassment and humiliation at one of the worst moments of her life. She didn't want him to get killed.

Looking back on the morning, it suddenly struck her as downright funny. She began to laugh. Riding up the street with the possibility of receiving a bullet in the back at any second was just a different kind of courage than he'd shown this morning, she decided.

"Okay, Hank. Stiffen your backbone, 'cause yours is the one they'll aim for when we're riding up the center of town."

He chuckled in response. "Carry on, my dear Mariah. We have a new kind of citadel to capture."

Not exactly sure what he meant, she nevertheless heeled Patches into a slow walk. She looked straight ahead, but her nerves tensed with her effort to see everything from her side vision. Hank kept pace with her, making her feel they were synchronized.

The saloons were in higher swing than earlier. The glow of more than a dozen lamplighted windows was cast onto the road. A few loungers leaned against doorways, watching them pass. At each step, each yard, she expected shouts or even gunfire. But there was no sign of Kasey or his cohorts.

When they reached the front of Powell's, however, Kasey was there, flanked by three men.

Her heart in her throat, Mariah watched them warily as they stepped forward. She couldn't tell if Kasey had sobered to some degree or was even drunker, but he stood remarkably straight.

Hank slid off his horse and faced them.

"So ya came back," Kasey said with a sneer. "How come? Thought you could hide in the hotel? Or maybe you hoped I'd be gone?"

"I have returned, Mr. Kasey"—Hank tipped his head slightly in acknowledgment—"to accept your challenge to duel. But as the one challenged, I retain the right to name the weapons."

"What are you talkin' about?"

"Mr. Clayton speaks of the correct rules of a gentleman's conduct, Kasey," said Thorndyke as he stepped forward from the shadows. "You threw down the gauntlet."

More men arrived, curious to see what was happening.

The deputy touched his hat brim in greeting. "Good evenin' again, Mr. Clayton. Miss Taggert."

"Gauntlet? What gauntlet?" demanded Kasey, clearly puzzled. "I did no sucha thing."

"You threw out the challenge."

"So?" Kasey snarled.

"So Mr. Clayton here gets to choose what weapons are used."

"Now see here—" Kasey started to bluster.

"It's the old rules of the game, Kasey," insisted Thorndyke. He casually rested one boot on the edge of a watering trough and leaned forward. "Now listen up, folks," he addressed the crowd as well as Kasey. "You all know I like a peaceful town. I could throw these men in the jailhouse for disturbin' the peace. But I'm findin' all this a mite interestin', so I'm gonna let these men have their duel. But I hereby declare myself in charge of it." He turned to Hank. "What's your choice, Englishman?"

Mariah slid to the ground and edged close to Hank. Like Kasey, she didn't exactly understand what Hank intended.

Henry stood straight and proud. "I am quite proficient with a pair of boxing gloves."

"Boxing?" Mariah repeated. An echo of the word rippled through the people close by.

"Yes."

"You want to box?" asked Thorndyke, obviously intrigued.

"Why not? It is a more civilized and less damaging way to settle one's differences. And one man against one man is infinitely more fair."

More men and a few women had gathered and now Mariah felt the crowd's surprised excitement.

"Boxing! Why, I haven't seen a good match since I left New York!" said Ira Morton, of Morton's general store.

"Bare-knuckled fisticuffs. It's a right good idea," said John Truit.

"Actually," said Hank, "I had in mind to use gloves."

"A fistfightin' match? Gloves?" Kasey asked, frowning suspiciously. "What're you tryin' to pull now, dude? You shufflin' the cards again?"

"No, not at all. It is only that many fighters are now wearing padded leather gloves especially designed for boxing. I have a set in my luggage."

"Uh-uh!" Kasey protested. "It sounds sissy to me and it ain't what was intended. I ain't gonna do it."

"Now who's the yellow belly, Kasey?" Mariah called.

Kasey threw her a fulminating glance. His mouth pinched closed as he glanced at the crowd.

"What's it to be, Kasey?" said Thorndyke. "Do you accept or forfeit?

Mariah held her breath. Eyes from the crowd around them were hard, speculative, excited. And unforgiving. Kasey wasn't much liked, and his reputation was on the line. If he backed down now, he might as well snake-crawl out of Mead before first light tomorrow, because the town would never tolerate him again.

And not a little of that speculation and judgment was coming her and Hank's way.

Kasey stretched his neck. Pure hostile nervousness made him sweat and his face shone with it. "All right," he agreed in a petulant tone. "But I choose the time."

Hank graciously agreed.

"Tomorrow. No . . . two days . . . no, wait. Next week. A week from Saturday."

"Aw, hell, Kasey," one of his buddies complained. "Why doncha jes' get it over with now?"

Kasey's eyes glittered. "No. I want at least a week."

"A week," Hank agreed. He turned to Thorndyke. "Will you perform the referee duties, Deputy?"

"I'll certainly be there. But I think Sheriff Tinsdale might be called in for that."

"Then perhaps you would be good enough to act in my behalf to make the arrangements?" Hank asked. "Queensberry rules."

"Sure 'nuff, Mr. Clayton. I'd be glad to do it."

"What's this here Queensberry rules?" demanded Kasey.

"Why, it is the accepted rules of fair play, Mr. Kasey," Hank stated quietly. "Do you have any objection?"

Kasey opened his mouth, then snapped it shut. His fury evident, he finally said, "Reckon I ain't gotta choice. Okay, Manning"—he pointed to one of his sidekicks—"you be 'tother one. You'n the deputy, here, figure things out. But you better look out for my side of things."

Kasey gave Hank one last hard stare, mumbled, "We'll have a real showdown yet," then strode off in a swagger, followed by three of his cronies. Mariah had a suspicion he was no longer as affected by the alcohol as he'd been. Something in that last look made her shiver. She didn't trust Kasey. Not for a second.

Instantly stirred up, the crowd began to discuss the goings-on. "It might be entertaining," commented Ira Morton. He rubbed a finger thoughtfully across his small black mustache. "Good for business."

"Reckon we can use my livery barn fer it," offered John Truit. He rocked back on his heels. "I bet some of them miners wu'd come to town to see it. It'll be a real event."

"I'd be glad to handle the betting, gentlemen," said Mr. Sonyers.

Mariah listened to the male voices behind her agreeing to meet the next day to organize the event. The crowd was dispersing. Once again she thought about starting for home.

A sudden gap opened to reveal the censuring expression of Gladys Benton. The older woman's gaze roamed over Mariah, then over Hank.

What was it now? Mariah wondered. She hadn't used a single cussword all night, nor had she spit in the street.

Mariah looked down. Her faded blue shirtwaist was certainly mud-spattered. Another black mark against her name in Mrs. Benton's mind probably, along with her being in the middle of a crowd of brawling men. Nothing a lady would be caught doing.

Automatically her hand tugged the fabric straighter. Then she saw the more damaging evidence. Three muddy finger marks showed in the center of her torso, right at the place where Hank's hand had clutched her in their first mad dash for safety. They nearly touched her left breast.

This certainly capped her day. Mariah's mouth tightened for a moment as she felt another jolt of defiance assail her. Then, spying Hank's lifted eyebrow and amused expression, she felt a flash of spirit flow through her heart. Not everyone found her disgusting. Casually turning her gaze back to Mrs. Benton, she gave her her most beatific smile.

"Shall we go, my dear?" Hank said as he took her elbow.

Mariah sailed by the woman with her chin high.

5

Henry insisted on escorting Mariah home.

"It is very late, Mariah, and it does not bear contemplating for you to travel home alone. I cannot imagine what your grandfather must be thinking at the moment."

He could not quite grasp the freewheeling style American women exhibited, especially this Western girl. He was certain she had no real concept of either her danger or her reputation. Furthermore, although he had seldom ever worried about another human being, he found himself very concerned about this one. A young woman riding through the countryside alone at night, and rather more innocent than she would like him to believe—the thought was beyond his newfound need to protect.

Mariah, on the other hand, knew her own mind. "Hank, quit fretting. I can get home by myself. I've been doing it since I was knee-high to a grasshopper."

She stepped up onto the wooden sidewalk, prepared to mount.

"But you said the neighborhood has become more noticeably dangerous and you do not trust Kasey."

"I don't. But you're the one he wants to drill holes in. And I thought you didn't want to leave town just yet."

He laid a hand on her saddle horn. "That was before. And your grandfather must be distressingly worried. I shall merely go along to explain—"

"No! No, um, thank you kindly, Hank, I'll do my own explaining. But it's true I have to get home." She couldn't allow him to meet Grandaddy and Nate. They'd ask too many questions and she'd have to think up too many answers.

Thorndyke Sands approached them. "Miss Mariah, I'd take it as a favor if you would let Mr. Clayton here take you on home like he wants to. And it'd be a bigger favor if you'd keep him there 'til this here boxing match is over."

Hank's eyes narrowed. "Oh? Why do you say that?"

"Well, I have a hunch you'd be safer out there. I can keep an eye on Kasey and his bunch easier if I don't have to worry about where you are every minute."

"I see," murmured Hank.

Hank looked happily at Mariah. She returned his gaze suspiciously. He seemed altogether too pleased with the deputy's suggestion.

"That okay with you, Miss Mariah?" Thorndyke asked.

"Um . . . uh," Mariah mumbled over her growing dismay. Neither the mud plastered against his fine suit nor his stubbled chin and tousled dark hair robbed Hank of his natural elegance. He couldn't be taken for just a saddle bum needing a place to sleep for a night or two.

How could she explain his presence at the Circle T for a whole week? How on earth could she downplay her part in what had happened tonight—and after all this, she knew Grandaddy would hear all about it—if Hank was there on the spot?

Mariah wanted to tell both men that no, it was not all right with her, that she had enough to juggle with the two men she had at home. "Well, Grandaddy—"

"Mr. Taggert will be looking to meet your intended anyway, won't he?" Thorndyke asked.

Intended? Mariah frantically searched her mind. Had she actually said that the Englishman was her intended? She'd be in more trouble than bees in a blizzard if Grandaddy thought she'd . . . that this stranger had . . . Oh, boy! She had to point this whole thing in another direction altogether.

"Well, he—"

"Quite true, Deputy. I have yet to meet Mariah's grandfather, and this might be the perfect time to do so."

Mariah folded her lips and gave Hank a "why-did-you-have-to-go-and-say-that-for" look. She'd have to have a little talk with him. This pretense was taking on more legs than a centipede and was fast running away with her.

"I would be pleased with an invitation, Miss Mariah," he pleaded with a great deal of charm. His eyes shone with it. "It would save me from having too much time on my hands here in town. Without you, I could find myself in another, um, disturbing poker game."

Mariah responded to his charm in spite of herself,

but she tried to hide behind annoyance. "Oh, you—you . . . Are you blaming me for getting mixed up in the wrong poker game? You greenhorn! I warned you to watch out for Kasey, didn't I?"

"Yes, indeed you did, my dear. But we all do foolish things sometimes, do we not? This morning, for instance—"

"Okay, okay," she said through her teeth at his reminder. She wondered what Thorndyke thought. His stance was casual as he listened, but she had the uneasy impression there wasn't much that was casual in his attention.

It seemed she'd boxed herself into a corner and might as well make the best of it. "All right, Hank," she said, determined to hide her nervousness. "I'll take you home to the Circle T."

He rewarded her with a fine, wide smile. For the first time, Mariah noticed one of his front teeth was a wee bit crooked. It overlapped its neighbor. The small imperfection somehow appealed to her. She lost her irritation suddenly and grinned back.

But she wasn't about to let him off the hook entirely for maneuvering her in front of Thorndyke and the others. Hank thought he'd have too much time on his hands, huh? A germ of mischief corralled her former flutter of panic. He just might have to get those handsome, very clean hands dirty, she decided. There certainly was enough work on the Circle T to show him there were other things with which to occupy his time besides playing poker. Time on his hands? She'd have him sweating over not having a moment to spare, she vowed.

"C'mon, Hank," she said sweetly as she mounted Skedaddle, then indicated Patches. "You might as well ride that one home."

A mild anxiety crossed Hank's face. "Shouldn't we return the borrowed horse first?" he said, emphasizing the word "borrowed."

Thorndyke's expression sharpened.

"What horse did we borrow?" Mariah asked innocently.

"Um, at the livery. You know."

"Oh, that one. Well, Thorndyke, what do you think? We took this horse out of the livery corral without asking Mr. Truit's say-so."

Thorndyke solemnly shook his head. "Might be in a bit of trouble over it, Mr. Clayton. Horse stealin's a serious matter in these parts."

"I assure you, Deputy, we had no intentions of stealing the horse. Really, I—"

John Truit stepped forward. "Stealing from my place?"

"We had not planned to, Mr. Truit, by any means. Our need was such that we borrowed it in a hurry, but we would not have kept the horse without ample compensation to you. Can we not settle the matter without further ado?"

"Well now, Mr. Clayton, I don't know," said Mr. Truit. He lifted his hat and scratched his head. "Might have to talk to the little lady here." He turned to Mariah. "This the pinto you were bringing me, Miss Mariah?"

Mariah gave up her tease and grinned, only a light pink stain in her cheeks betraying her. "You can relax, Hank. Reckon we were pulling your leg a bit." She turned to the liveryman. "Yes, Mr. Truit, this is Patches. I left him at your place earlier, but then we kind of needed him in a rush. Sorry if we scared Mrs. Truit."

"You had another horse here in town?" Hank asked.

"Said so, didn't I? John Truit trades in horses. I brought Patches in to sell."

Hank gave Mariah a promising look. It held amusement as well as intent of retribution. The corners of her mouth curled in answer.

Turning to Mr. Truit, Hank asked, "What is your price for the horse, sir?"

Astonished, John Truit glanced at Mariah, then looked at Hank in speculation. "Well . . ." He named a sum.

Hank watched Mariah blink in surprise. The price was more than she had expected, he was sure. He wondered if the liveryman planned to pay Mariah a good price before, or would have asked as much for the horse if he were not a stranger. He didn't quibble, though, and pulled out his money. Counting out bills, he placed one in Mr. Truit's hand and said, "I am sure ten percent of the price is ample return for holding the animal for a few hours and acting as middle man."

"Yes sir, that seems fair 'nuff," Mr. Truit answered. He touched the brim of his hat and said, "Pleasure doin' business with you, Mr. Clayton."

"Thank you, Mr. Truit." Hank handed Mariah the remainder of the money. Apparently embarrassed, she barely glanced at it before she stuffed it into a pocket.

"All right, Hank. Let's go," she said as she kicked her mount into a brisk trot without a backward look, leaving the Englishman to gawk after her.

"I suppose I should wish you good night, Deputy," Hank murmured, turning his disbelieving grin into a shake of the head.

"S'pose if you ain't plannin' to get left behind, you oughta," advised Thorndyke Sands with his own grin.

Hank mounted the small horse, its bare coat feeling warm against his backside, his feet dangling long without a saddle, and trotted after Mariah.

Half an hour later, Mariah urged her mount past the small, low building that was her home. She noted its single lit window which signaled that Grandaddy was probably waiting up for her, but she didn't stop until she reached the bunkhouse. Except for Nate, it was empty now. She remembered when it held four or five hands for most of the year.

Two dogs barked, and she hushed them with a word as they came to greet her. She watched Hank glance around. More than a little aware of the way everything on the ranch had gone downhill these last three years since Granny died, Mariah pretended she didn't notice the broken-down buckboard sitting in a patch of weeds or the gaping barn door with its missing planks.

Instead, she stared at the house, mentally running through explanations of what had happened and who Hank was. Grandaddy would demand details.

Sure enough, she heard the slap of the house's front door and Grandaddy's call. Within seconds, a light shone out from the bunkhouse also, telling her Nate planned to get in on what was going on too. Nothing she ever did on the Circle T went unnoticed, or without comment.

"Yep, it's me, Grandaddy," she answered.

"Where in eternity have you been, young woman? You know it's plumb midnight?"

"Reckon so, Grandaddy, but I had more business in town than I'd counted on."

"What kind of business is it that'd keep you this

late into the night? What've you been up to? I was about to saddle up and go lookin' for you."

"Saddle up, you say?" queried Nate. He swung through the door pulling his suspenders over the dingy stockinette underwear he wore. "What's amiss?"

"Nothing's amiss, Nate. I'm home, safe and sound," Mariah said loudly, then more moderately, "Sorry, Grandaddy. I got caught up in town."

"Well, I guess you c'n tell me 'bout it tomorrow. I see you brought back that pinto. Didn't Truit want him after all? And who're you, young fella? You Mr. Rhodes?" The old man ran a skeptical glance over Hank in the dim light.

"This the pretty gent you was ajawin' about earlier?" Nate asked, squinting at Hank.

Mariah shied away from Hank's look. However, it was no good to deny she'd said it, and anyway, the Englishman already knew her at her most witless. She adopted her mildest tone to answer. "Yep. This is the gentleman I met at the train this morning."

"Good evening, Mr. Taggert," Hank said as he politely proffered his hand. "My name is Henry Clayton."

"Didn't reckon you looked much like a cattle buyer," Elam said as he shook hands.

"Mr. Rhodes will ride out in the morning, Grandaddy," Mariah reassured him. "And Mr. Clayton's bought Patches. He's, um, gonna be with us a while. He, uh, he's from England, an' he wants to, uh . . . he's interested in seeing how we run cattle."

She looked toward Hank to back up her explanation. She couldn't tell Grandaddy outright about Hank being a gambler. He hadn't much regard for wasters, as he called them. He was bound to find out about the boxing match, but she thought she could tell him about it later.

"That's right, Mr. Taggert. I am combining a business trip with pleasure. I have been traveling throughout the American West to gather information on possible investments for my family. We have multiple holdings in Scotland and Wales as well as our home ground, but we thought it might be far-sighted to look into something out here. I would be pleased to board with you for a week or two if you have accommodations."

Mariah threw Hank an exasperated glance. There was no need to carry it that far. She should have warned him to keep it simple—Grandaddy wasn't that easy to fool.

Elam looked doubtful. "Well, I don't know. We ain't got much in fancy rooms or beds."

"Hank's gonna stay in the bunkhouse, Grandaddy," Mariah said hurriedly. She gazed at the Englishman with a challenge in her eyes. "He's already agreed to that."

"I suppose it might be all right," the old man responded with a frown. "But we ain't got much in fancy vittles, either."

"He'll eat what the rest of us eat."

"That is correct, sir. I want to experience Western life to its fullest."

"Well, I suppose . . ."

"Also, with your permission, Mr. Taggert, I would like to engage your granddaughter as a guide. I had planned to see something of the mountains before moving on and I will gladly pay a dollar a day, if you find that a fair wage."

Mariah gaped at Hank, her mind floundering with the amount of money he offered. What a taradiddle.

A dollar a day! Why, a full-fledged cowpoke made that much. She couldn't imagine anyone paying her a dollar a day merely to jaunt around the countryside.

Her mind flew to what she could do with seven dollars if he stayed a whole week. It was tempting. Real tempting. But it didn't feel quite right. Then she remembered his face when he'd given her the money for Patches. . . .

His expression had held a touch of bestowal . . . charity.

Funny, she hadn't noticed his autocratic attitude before. Except there'd been something in his voice that morning when he spoke to the hotel clerk and again at the poker game, now that she thought about it. It seemed he could put on a cloak of power when he wanted to, as though it were his prerogative. He was used to service at a snap of the fingers, she supposed.

He could pay for anything he wanted, she knew. She'd seen the amount of money he carried.

And he'd easily guessed she had none.

Pity or charity was something she wouldn't stand for, not from the townsfolk, not from anybody.

Without conscious thought, her back straightened. "You're gonna work for your room and board, Hank," she said. "And I'll guide you round to the places you want to see for free if you have any energy left at the end of a week."

She gathered the reins of both horses and started clipping out orders. "Nate, show Hank where he can bed down. Hank, I'll take care of your horse . . . this time. Morning chores begin at dawn so we'd all best get some sleep."

Hank didn't miss a beat. "One moment, Miss Mariah. Mr. Taggert, I will settle matters with you in the morning, but I must tell you that my fellow traveler, James Moore, will be arriving in Mead in a day or two. I would be very grateful if he could join me here. Unfortunately, we became separated when I left the train this morning and he did not. My luggage was also, ah, inadvertently left behind."

Nate cupped his ear. "What got left? Your behind?"

"All my personal belongings," Hank replied, hiding a grin.

"Don't worry, greenhorn. Reckon we can find you some workin' duds," snapped Mariah. "And when your friend comes, why, I reckon I can find something for him, too. Both to wear and to keep him busy."

A clanging the equivalent to St. Peter's bells in London sounded just beyond Henry's ears. Startled out of what was at last a sound sleep, he jolted to a sitting position.

Immediately, he found himself staring into a pair of beady, glassy eyes. They were sunk into a brown, furry head with small ears. The creature's mouth was pulled into a dangerous snarl, showing large, pointed teeth.

His heart pounded. "What the—!"

"Mornin', son," old Nate pealed out with a gap-toothed grin. Already dressed, he held high a kerosene lamp. It threw dancing shadows against the square room's roughly built walls, along which six cots were lined up. "'At's the mornin' call."

Only inches from the bear's head, whose pelt was tacked against the wall above his cot, Hank let his breath go and ordered his nerves to return to normal.

He had barely noticed the animal hide the night before.

He pressed his hands against his throbbing temple. His head felt as bad as if he had spent the night before drinking. "That thing is loud enough to be heard in Mead," he mumbled.

"Mead? Ya wanta go to Mead? Thought you was stayin' a while."

Hank winced as he raised his voice. "I am staying."

"Well, if'n ya want breakfast afore we git to work, ya better rise an' shine."

"Breakfast? It isn't even light."

"Whazzat?"

"It is still dark!" Hank boomed back.

"Dawn's knockin' on the horizon. Miss Mariah said ya have ten minutes. She's a generous one, ain't she?"

Ten minutes. He blinked sleepily as he mumbled in disbelief, "Uh-huh. Generous." He never dressed in under thirty, although he frequently took the unfashionable view—in London, anyway—of it being perfectly acceptable to dress oneself. One reason James and he got on so well was that James never made the flap about it that other valets might have.

"Any coffee to be had?" he asked Nate. Then, raising his voice, "Coffee?"

"Soon's we sit, coffee'll be on the table."

Hank yawned hugely, then stretched his arms over his head in an attempt to relieve the middle of his spine of the knot lodged there. He hadn't slept well until a couple of hours ago. The thin, lumpy mattress, though thankfully clean, had caused him to roll around half the night looking for a comfortable position. Then there had been the problem of listening to the old man snore.

"Brought ya a bucket o' washin' water, seein' as how you're used to high-class hotels an' this is your first day here an' all," Nate explained, setting the sloshing pail on the shelf beside the door. The shelf also held a tin pan and the old man's shaving gear. "Tomorra ya c'n do fer yerself. Miss Mariah sent ya a towel an' some workin' duds. 'At's them over the cot next to ya."

Hank swung his legs over the side of the narrow cot and grimaced as he examined the clothes. Worn, patched dungarees, a red flannel shirt, and loosely darned wool socks. He put them up to his nose. At least they smelled clean, like lye soap, something he was familiar with from the scullery and kitchens of his family home in Surrey.

They weren't the softest of clothing, nor did they fit. They must have belonged to a man at least six inches shorter than he and a dozen inches wider in girth. He wondered if Mariah had deliberately given him clothing which would make him look ridiculous. He was beginning to understand her impish impulses.

Despite everything, he washed and dressed speedily, pulling the trousers tight with the belt Nate loaned him, combed his fingers through his hair, rubbed his knuckles against his jaw, then shrugged. It itched a bit, but he could do nothing about it until he was in possession of his things again. He pulled on his finely grained leather half boots and grinned at the incongruity of his costume.

All at once the thought of the disbelief in his brothers' eyes if they could see his attire while working as a common ranch hand amused him. And what was James going to think? They certainly would hardly credit it. Neither would he have, had someone told him a week ago. He would not have thought he would be having a great time playing at both a cowboy and a knight to a damsel in distress.

Whistling aimlessly, he followed Nate along the path toward the house. He stopped a moment when he rounded a boulder and realized the sky had lightened considerably. The house was set about a dozen yards in front of him, a hodgepodge of what he thought were three building periods. Part of it was log, chinked tightly with mud. He glimpsed faded blue curtains at the open window; hung immediately under a low sloping roof, it resembled a staring square eye under a perplexed brow.

The next section, the largest and middle part, was built of wooden planks and had a peaked upper story. A large stone chimney rose next to it. The stone room at the end seemed to be an afterthought. It leaned almost precariously against the main portion and showed no windows. Weeds fringed the foundation but could not hide one lonely vine spreading over the stone. Altogether, that end looked as though it had been there a long time.

The smell of bacon and eggs hit him as Nate motioned him through the door. Mariah stood at the stove, cooking, with her back to him. Immediately his gaze slid down to admire the boyish rear end and slender legs in the almost indecently fitting jeans.

There was nothing boyish about the way the shirt clung to her front, he quickly noted when she turned. In fact, she was more rounded than she had appeared yesterday.

"Mornin', Hank."

Today she wore her auburn hair tightly braided and tied with a string. She swung around with the coffeepot in her hand and looked him over. Her mouth appeared trembly, as though she was trying to control the smile that lurked at its corners. Fresh and sweet, she was so appealing that he acknowledged her amusement with a raised brow and a half smile of his own. He couldn't help himself. He knew he looked silly and didn't care.

But he would make her pay.

"Good morning, Miss Mariah," he said, his voice deeper than normal. "So nice of you to find something clean for me to wear."

She ignored his wry remark and instead tipped her chin at a chair. "Sit there. This is your lucky day. It's my turn to cook."

Nate wheezed as he laughed. Elam snorted. Hank glanced at them suspiciously, but said nothing beyond "Good morning."

Elam took a chair at the round table and Nate scraped his along the floor until he reached his place. Hank waited politely beside the one he thought was Mariah's.

She looked at him in puzzlement. Her grandfather and old Nate did the same.

"I will wait until you are ready to be seated, Mariah," he said without censure.

"Oh. Oh, well, if that's all . . ." she said, flushing. She plopped the coffeepot in the center of the table, then dished up the bacon and eggs, and together with a plate of half-burnt toast, pushed the whole array in front of Hank. The bacon was dark brown in places, almost burnt, and yet looked uncooked in others. The eggs . . . he had to assume the eggs were well-done. Or something.

"Now, then, young man," Elam boomed as Hank pulled out Mariah's chair, then seated himself, "we say grace to the Almighty before we eat." Whereupon he bowed his head.

Hank followed suit. It was a new experience, for he had rarely heard prayers outside of church. But Elam's simple offering of thanks and his request for blessings on the day's work touched him. The old man spoke as though he was talking to someone he knew well.

As soon as the amen was done, Nate heaped his plate with food and silently began to eat. Hank watched in amazement while the old man's jaws chomped and his Adam's apple bobbed. Elam, he noticed, ate sparingly.

Hank worked gingerly around his breakfast, chewing thoughtfully on the rubbery egg as though he savored it. Mariah glanced at him a couple of times with an "I-dare-you-to-complain" glint in her eyes. He merely raised a brow and smiled, then shoved a bite of burnt toast into his mouth.

Elam swallowed his coffee before starting a discussion of the day ahead. "Where you goin' to be today, honey?"

"Oh, I 'spect I'd best stick around. You'll need me to ride out to the south range and show Mr. Rhodes the cattle you want to sell."

"Now, not necessarily, Mariah," Elam said with a frown. "I can do it."

"That's a long ride, Grandaddy. Are you sure you're up to it?"

"Reckon I can still get around when I want to, don't you worry about that," he insisted, then plunged in with, "It wouldn't hurt none for you to check out those expectin' cows in the enclosed meadow."

Mariah gave him a puzzled glance. She couldn't understand her grandaddy's insistence that he would take care of the cattle buyer himself. "I checked 'em yesterday before I went to town, remember?"

"Yeah, but this time of year, you know . . ."

"Let Nate go," Mariah said. "If you don't need me to show Mr. Rhodes the cattle, I'd like to ride out to see if I can find the young black mare I saw drinking from the sinkhole last week. That stallion she's with is an old one. I don't think he'll be able to hang on to his harem this year and I'd like to make a try for her before she's herded off by another. Providing I can even get near enough to get a rope on her, she'd bring a nice sum from Mr. Truit."

A quick light flashed for a moment in Elam's eyes. Hank caught the swift glance his way. It was calculating and a bit suspicious, as though the old man was trying to decide what to do. He wondered if Elam thought of him as a young stallion after his granddaughter. Someone he had to protect her from.

"I suppose it's okay," Elam said dubiously.

Henry felt uncomfortable. The old man didn't quite trust him. It didn't help any to realize he had good reason not to.

Nevertheless, he was thoroughly exhilarated at the thought of being alone with Mariah today.

6

Nate tossed an old saddle over Patches. Its worn leather fenders and cracked horn told of long use.

"Reckon this here Texas saddle's the best we c'n offer, young fella. Only extry we got right now. Seein' as how you'll only be here a few days, reckon it won't matter." The old man looked Hank over doubtfully, then offered, "Howsomever, the double cinch might come in right handy."

Nate didn't put too much faith in his riding ability, Hank mused. Hard pressed to keep his amusement from showing, he merely said, "Beggars can't be choosers, Nate. You are most generous to lend it to me."

He stepped into the wooden stirrup and mounted. Bits of frayed leather thong flapped loosely around the horn, and the broken seam gaped, showing the wood base underneath. It felt awkward, but in the short time he had ridden Skedaddle last night, in

Mariah's saddle, he had barely noticed the encumbrance in his haste.

Now he had no choice except to ride it, if he wanted to go with Mariah. His own English saddle was with James and, anyway, he didn't have much time to dwell on the differences because Mariah pushed Skedaddle into a lope and Patches followed on his own.

They rode southwest toward the higher elevations. Within seconds, Hank caught his breath at the splendor of the mountain range. The morning sun sparkled on the snowy peaks, bringing into brighter display the purples and golds.

An hour later, Mariah glanced over her shoulder. She was a bit surprised the tenderfoot had kept up with her pace without a fuss, especially after last night's chase. But then, perhaps his pride wouldn't let him complain. And the climb had been an easy one so far, compared with the next few miles, which would take them into much rougher country before they reached their goal. She wondered if she should take it slower.

He didn't look as though he was suffering, though. He halted next to her and smiled pleasantly before turning to gaze around them. "This is quite spectacular. How far do your borders extend?"

"Borders? Oh, you mean the Circle T boundaries. Actually, we left the ranch about twenty minutes back. We're small compared to some of the ranches hereabouts. Grandaddy and Granny settled here almost thirty years ago, but they never had the money to expand."

"Who owns this, then?"

"It's government land."

"Ah. Well, how much farther to the sinkhole where you saw the mustangs?"

"Another thirty minutes or so," she answered. "You gettin' sore?"

His gray eyes sparkled with amusement. "You jest, surely. Do you think I am as soft as all that? Obviously, my dear, you have never experienced the riding to hounds."

"Nope, reckon I haven't. But I don't guess it could be any harder than chasing an ornery cow or a wild horse."

"Perhaps not, but jumping fences and dodging tree limbs and bramble bushes are no light training. I suppose I could ride any territory put to me."

The challenge was blatant. So was his self-satisfied grin. Mariah couldn't resist it.

"All right, greenhorn, you're on. If you can't stay with me, just holler uncle and I'll come back to get you."

"Cry uncle? Never."

Mariah dug her heels into Skedaddle's flanks and headed off between two boulders. For the next few miles, they climbed steeply through the pine and aspen, crossed a couple of streams, wove their way around boulders, and warily trod a few yards on an animal trail beside a deep drop.

The possibility of a fall didn't seem to faze the girl, Hank marveled. She appeared to take the risks in stride. He wondered if she ever thought about danger or if she simply refused to recognize it. He hoped she never carried things to the point of recklessness. But then, last night's activities had certainly been on the edge.

They pulled to a stop on an open perimeter of hard rock above a small meadow. The air was colder, in spite of the spring sun. Snow and ice still set in the rock crevices. He pulled his collar closer around his ears.

Automatically, Mariah put out her hand to signal caution and quiet. Her face lit up with triumph, and without a word she pointed toward the opposite side of the mountain meadow. There, a small band of mustang mares grazed contentedly, unaware of them. A couple of newborn colts hovered close by.

The wild horses were just as he had heard them described, Henry thought. Smallish, of various dark colors, they appeared thin after a bleak winter. Several were heavy with foal. He wondered where their stallion was.

Mariah studied the situation for a minute. The black mare she'd seen last week wasn't there. One of the horses raised its head, then another. Their ears flickered forward. Nervously, then, they all began to move.

She stood in her stirrups to see if she could spot what had spooked them. They couldn't have caught their human scent, because she'd brought them the long way around in order to stay downwind.

A sudden high, piercing scream rent the air. Mariah whipped around toward the sound. On a rise of land near the other end of the small meadow, the old stallion, its brown coat still showing the remnants of winter, stood stiffly as it faced a challenger.

The second stallion was larger and heavier-boned. By the look of him, he was the offspring of more than the small Spanish remnants. Of a mottled steel-gray color, he stood proudly, his black mane tossing and tail lifted. While they watched, he screamed his decla-ration, pawed the ground, and shook his head with bared teeth.

Beyond, the black mare waited, visibly quivering.

The clash was immediate. The stallions lunged at each other, necks stretched to bite, then reared and kicked and screamed again. The challenger viciously clamped his teeth into the old one's withers, driving him backwards up the slope. The old one broke free long enough to lash out with his rear hooves. He landed a staggering blow against his opponent's shoulder. The younger stallion quickly recovered and retaliated with savage intensity with another bite to the withers. They reared once more, their front hooves striking out. Underneath them, the earth churned to mud.

Mariah watched in fascination as the battle raged. She caught her breath at the force of the clash. This was the first time she'd ever witnessed a combat between two stallions, though she'd heard of them. The elemental nature of it seemed to vibrate the air, filling her with excitement. She was only faintly aware of Hank's tense posture as he leaned forward in his saddle, his gaze glued to the scene.

The old one was tiring. It was only a matter of minutes until the confrontation would be over.

"Let's go." Mariah heeled Skedaddle down the slope.

"Mariah, wait. It could be dangerous."

"We can't wait," she shot back over her shoulder. "Our best chance to get the black mare is while both stallions are still fighting."

She plunged through the underbrush and rocks to the valley floor. Hank raced after her, marveling at her perfect control over her mount. She circled, remaining clear of the battleground, then approached the black mare from the rear.

Their presence added to the mare's nervousness. She shied and turned to face them, her eyes rolling and ears flickering. Mariah slowed her pace to a walk and started to talk with the animal.

"C'mon, now, stay right where you are. I promise I won't hurt you any more than I can help it. You're real pretty. . . ."

Perceiving the double threat, the old stallion screamed again. His nostrils flared as he caught their scent and his eyes seemed to expand with greater terror. Relentlessly, the challenger pursued his advantage. The two foes moved up the slope.

Mariah, meanwhile, unfastened her lariat. Sliding it loosely through her gloved hands, she formed a noose as she rode slowly closer to the mare. Continuing her soft, nearly crooning tone with the mare, she also instructed Hank.

"Ride to the off side. Don't let her back down the slope. She'll try for any opening." ·

For the next three minutes, they tried to contain the mare long enough for Mariah to rope her. The young black ran this way and that, reversing her direction abruptly, wildly frightened. When it looked as though the mare might make it through a sudden opening, Mariah whirled the rope over her head and pitched it.

Amazed, Hank watched the lariat snake out and land easily over the mare's head. Mariah instantly pulled the loop tight as the horse reared and fought. He watched her play out the struggle, observing the fine display of her wiry strength and remarkable skill. He moved closer to her but didn't know what to do to help her. Finally, the horse stood, trembling and petrified.

Mariah dismounted in a flash and swiftly took up the slack on the rope. "We have her! Oh, she'll make a splendid mount." Then as she approached the animal with care, she said, "Mr. Truit can't roll his nose up at you, can he, girl. By the time I train you . . ."

While all their attention had been engaged in the young mustang's capture, Hank was vaguely aware of the other battle continuing. Now he heard another shriek, and glanced toward the stallions.

The old one was down, his form barely moving with loud, heavy breathing. Hank thought the stallion near death.

The young gray faced them, his legs stiff while he snorted and tossed his black mane. He pawed the earth and took a few running steps toward them, then stopped.

Hank was on the far side of Mariah. He called to her softly. "Mariah . . ."

Mariah was busy calming the mare. At Hank's soft call, she barely spared a glance his way. "Hank, pass me your rope," she said.

He started around her and the mare, his intent to put himself between them and the young stallion. He didn't know if the mustang would attack or not, but he thought there was something a little crazed in the turbulent eyes that he couldn't trust.

"Hank?" she asked when he didn't answer. But she kept her gaze on the mare, shortening the length of rope by steadily coiling it.

"Move along now, Mariah, if you can."

"What?"

"Remount. Start back with the mare, please."

Hank's extremely reasonable tone of voice suddenly alerted her. It was the same tone he had used when they were in the saloon and he'd addressed Kasey. She turned to see what made him so cautious.

The young stallion glared at them. His wild stare and the nervous quiver of his nostrils suggested that he might charge at any minute. He stamped and whinnied. The mare answered. Hank edged forward, blocking the stallion's way to Mariah and the mare.

Mariah took a few steps backwards, then whirled and leaped into her saddle just as the stallion issued another challenging call. The mare danced and resisted the rope, nearly jerking Mariah from her seat.

The stallion snorted as he ran toward them.

"Huaah!" Hank yelled as he kicked Patches into a forward lunge. He waved his coil of rope. The stallion suddenly pivoted and dodged, then raced down the valley toward the small herd. But upon reaching them, he turned and neighed loudly as though to issue a warning.

Mariah twisted in her saddle to watch the gray's defiance, then laughed. "That fireball sure didn't like giving up this little beauty, did he?"

Henry glanced at Mariah. Her spirits were high, her face flushed with triumph. He was struck by her sparkling eyes and smile, beaming a sweet encouragement for him to join her excitement.

He flashed a smile in return. The encounter had affected him, too, but he thought his response was very different from what Mariah felt. The excitement rushed through him like a flood tide. While she was ardently happy to have gained the mare, he fully understood the stallion's reluctance to let the mare go. He, like the stallion, wanted possession of the female in sight. And he wanted nothing more at the moment than to make love with Mariah.

His own intensity startled him. His limbs tingled with it, and it pounded through his veins. It spoke to a deep, fervent need he didn't know he had. Mating Mariah, possessing her, was a sudden, overwhelming need. He had never experienced such desire before. Not to this extent. Something basic, primitive.

Mariah seemed innocently unaware of the emotions that waved over him, and with a great effort he clamped down on them. But she must have detected something in his expression, for her artless smile faded while a questioning look crept into her face.

Suddenly, he found a use for his saddle's pommel. His fingers tightened around the curved wooden protrusion until his knuckles turned white. He drew a long breath to control his lust. Still, he had to clear his throat before he could speak. "No, indeed. I do not blame him."

He remained silent as they began the long trek back to the ranch. They stopped at a stream, where they dismounted to allow the horses to drink. He rigidly kept his distance while he wondered at himself. They were alone in this wilderness—a perfect place to make love to her, and oh, how he wanted to. Only years of training in propriety held him back.

Mariah coaxed the mare to a handful of grain, then stood very still while the mare became used to her scent.

"Grandaddy will be pleased." She spoke in a soft voice so as not to frighten the mare. "After a few weeks of training, she'll bring top dollar."

Hank leaned against a boulder and crossed his arms, giving his fidgety hands someplace to hide. "You will train her yourself?"

"Uh-huh. It's my favorite part of ranching."

"How do you go about it? I have read . . . surely you do not plan to—to just climb onto her back and ride her to a standstill."

He had a horrible vision of Mariah doing just that—she had enough nerve—and of the injuries she might sustain from it. It effectively dampened his sensuous thoughts.

Hank had heard such a process described, but it did not sound like an activity in which she should engage. Surely her grandfather would object. Hank would, if she were under *his* care. "Isn't that dangerous? You could break a bone or fall and be dragged or—"

"Don't get into a tizzy, Hank. I don't break horses like that."

"I thought wild horses were broken to ride by spurs and brute strength. And that they were rounded up in bunches for ranch work."

"Most are." Her mouth tightened, showing her disapproval. "A whole outfit usually goes after as many mustangs as they can at one time. As for bronc-busting . . . Ranchers don't want to take the time or lay out the pay to a buster to do it slowly. All they're interested in is gettin' a new remuda as fast as they can. A good bronc rider can break five or six nags in a day. The big ranches need hundreds of horses to run their spreads. But as for the Circle T . . ."

She started to add that they were too poor to support more than a small remuda and that, anyway, they needed the thirty-five or forty dollars in cash money that the mare would bring more than they needed an extra horse. But he already knew all that. Even though it hurt her pride, she hadn't hidden it.

She brought her thoughts back to the subject at hand. "I'd rather gentle a horse into a good cow pony than beat it down. I think they live longer and work better that way."

"Ah, I see. Why did you try for only one horse?"

She shrugged. "No time to work with more than one or two right now. Which reminds me, we should swing over to the north section and check on the cattle."

*   *   *

Dusk was setting in by the time they reached the ranch yard. Hank carried a tiny calf across his saddle, where Mariah had placed it. His reaction had been a mixture of disbelief and amusement, but he'd accepted the creature without complaint. Alone, only a day or two old, and too weak to stand for long, the calf barely made a plaintive call when they'd approached it. Although they'd searched for more than an hour, they couldn't find its mother. Between the mare needing tight control and the delicate calf, they'd traveled home at a maddeningly slow gait compared with the morning's vigorous pace.

Mariah called Nate in the loud voice she used with the old man. "Got another baby for you, Nate. She's gonna need some help right away."

"What happened to its mama?" Nate shouted as he reached for the calf.

"Don't know. Darndest thing, though. None of the few cows we tried to match it up with would mother it."

"Happens, once in a while. Lucky it weren't left out on the range, though. Wolves woulda got it. I'll get some o' Betsy's milk an' see whut I c'n do."

Hank gladly handed over his burden. Secretly, he feared the tiny thing was too feeble to live, but Mariah had fiercely declared otherwise. Then she'd worked for a full fifteen minutes to get the calf to accept water when they'd come upon it. She'd allowed him to help her lift the creature to his saddle, but admonished him about the care it needed on the way back to the ranch. Her passionate need to save it seemed on a par with her zestful approach to everything she did.

Nate carried off the calf and Mariah led the way to the ranch corral. She turned the black mare in to it before they unsaddled, wiped down, fed, and watered their mounts at the barn. Then she returned to the corral and fed the mare.

Hank trailed in her path, observing her as she moved gracefully and with an economy of motion. Again, she kept a running stream of chatter going with the mare as she worked to win the animal's trust. It didn't take long, he noted.

If she gave that much attention to *him,* he thought wryly, it wouldn't take him long to enjoy it to the fullest, either. Not a second longer than instantly.

She gave the mare a last pat and said, "Okay, Hank, that's it for now. Go wash up for supper. It should be ready in about half an hour."

Mariah turned on her heel and headed for the house. He watched her go. She astonished him. Yesterday and last night she had been full of daring and saucy defiance toward the town. Today she had exhibited the same mettle and spirit, but with an underlying seriousness. He wondered which trait was the predominant; he felt a strong pull to the whole package. She certainly kept him guessing as to what would happen next.

Mariah, meanwhile, wondered where her grandaddy was. She hoped to heaven he'd remembered to stir the beans, which she'd placed on the back of the stove this morning. Slow cooking was the least likely way they'd get burnt, but they still needed tending.

The house was empty and almost dark, and the stove cold. That meant Grandaddy hadn't returned all day. It worried her a little. He'd tried to make light of his weak heart all winter, but he'd mostly stopped trying to handle too much heavy work. She hoped he hadn't pushed himself beyond sense in showing the cattle buyer around.

Which reminded her: There would be two extra people for supper.

She lit a lamp and checked the beans, only to find they'd barely cooked to half tenderness. She sighed in disgust. Well, at least they weren't burnt past eating, as they'd been last week. The house had smelled gosh-derned awful for the rest of the night.

There was nothing she could do. Supper would simply be later than usual.

By the time she'd built up the fire, started the beans again, threw in some chili peppers, and put together a pan of corn bread, she decided she'd better feed the chickens before it was too dark to see at all. After that chore was done, she hurried back to the house, hoping to have time for a better wash than just her hands and to change her shirt before serving the evening meal.

The timing was perfect. She was buttoning her last button as the four men trooped through the kitchen door. She rushed down the last step from her little upstairs room, ready to greet a happy gathering.

She looked toward her grandfather. If his deal with Mr. Rhodes was a good one, he'd be all smiles. But his features were quiet and still as he politely listened to what the man Rhodes was saying, and he wouldn't meet her gaze.

Turning quickly to the stove, she hid a feeling of puzzlement and the tiniest bit of alarm. What was the matter? Had something gone wrong?

The big pot steamed. She barely avoided a burn, jerking her hand from the handle and instead grabbing a dish towel with which to hold it steady. Absentmindedly, she salted and peppered the beans.

Had she peppered them earlier? She frowned at the kettle, but couldn't recall. She tried to judge from looking into the pot but the lamplight didn't carry that far, and she couldn't see enough to tell, so she gave up the effort with a mental shrug. Whatever they tasted like, the beans were all she had to serve. Moments later, she plopped it onto the middle of the table, set the pan of corn bread beside it and a full coffeepot opposite, then announced, "It's on."

"Smells right good tonight, Mariah," said her grandfather. But still, he didn't meet her gaze.

"Hope so," she mumbled.

In honor of the guests, she'd also opened a big can of peaches. Now she poured them into a bowl, listening to the scrape of chairs behind her while she silently fretted over the cause of her grandfather's worry. He wouldn't avoid her without cause. She wondered if he would tell her about the problem later without her dragging it from him.

Mariah composed her own features into a bright smile as she faced the table. Caught off guard, she was again surprised to see Hank waiting beside the chair she'd occupied at breakfast.

"Oh. Excuse me." She hurried to join the men.

Hank seated her with little fanfare, then himself, and, at Elam's direction, bowed his head. But halfway through the prayer, he couldn't prevent himself from glancing at Mariah. As he suspected, she was staring at her plate, eyes wide and pensive. He wondered what he really saw, in her mind's eye, beyond the plate. Something was troubling her.

Her lips looked very soft and vulnerable. An instant desire to kiss her rose. He wanted to hold her close, to comfort her, over whatever cause. But it was more than that, he admitted. What he felt was a renewal of the hot desire that had swamped him earlier in the day.

He had the sudden feeling it would never leave, not until he had satisfied his need, but he was beginning to doubt the wisdom of this pursuit. It no longer seemed like just a lark, and he didn't know where it would lead.

A moment later, all of his sensual thoughts of Mariah were wiped from Hank's mind when he put a forkful of beans into his mouth and began to chew. The spicy heat exploded against the sensitive inside tissues of his mouth and nose while sweat popped out on his brow. Even his eyes smarted.

His gaze shot to the others. Mr. Rhodes swiftly reached for the water pitcher, but Nate, Elam, and Mariah seemed not to notice. Hank grabbed the pitcher as soon as Rhodes set it down and, reaching for an empty cup from the middle of the table, poured, drank, then poured again. As soon as he let go of the pitcher Rhodes instantly refilled his own cup.

Mariah looked at Hank speculatively, a little too innocently. "I reckon I did get the supper beans a mite spicy tonight."

"A mite," Nate agreed loudly. But it didn't seem to slow his appetite, Hank noticed. Or Elam's.

"Too hot for you, Hank?" she queried.

"Only . . ." He gulped more water. "Only a tad," he said, loath to admit it. Was it too hot! The girl hadn't the slightest notion of the discomfort she'd put him through.

Something would have to be done to correct that.

7

"Hold it, Hank," Mariah instructed above the noise of the bawling, half-grown bull. "I think we need a rope on the front legs, too."

"Steady, boy," Henry said, his hand on Patches's withers. The horse quit pulling, but the rope tied around the muddy animal's neck on one end remained tautly wrapped around the saddle horn on the other.

The bright noontime sun was warm on Henry's neck, counterpointing the cool breeze against his cheeks. He watched Mariah, jacketless, wade farther into the colder main flow of the standing pool. The pond was fed by a spring runoff, she had told him, and was mostly muddy pockets.

They had been working to free the young bull for twenty minutes, but he seemed well and truly entrapped, having sunk to his belly in the mud. Mariah thought he had been there for a couple of days and had worn himself down with the struggle to get out.

Henry dismounted and untied the rope from Mariah's saddle. Initially, he had objected to her being the one to do the dirty work, but she had insisted. "We can't leave it in there any longer. It'll die. Besides, I'm used to this kind of work and I know what to do," she had said.

Now Mariah rolled her sleeves to her elbow as she waded deeper into the boggy hole in which the animal was stuck. "Okay, tie one end to Skedaddle and throw the other end to me."

Henry followed her directions, then silently watched the spattered denim pants she wore tighten around her bottom as she bent over to plunge the rope into the mud. She was concentrating so completely on the task at hand, she seemed completely unaware of herself. Her slender torso strained as she stretched to accomplish the job. He wondered if she had any idea how her movements affected him.

He suddenly felt an inept fool letting Mariah do the hard, unappealing labor while he stood around hopping uselessly from foot to foot, no matter what she had said. He threw off his jacket and shoved his shirt-sleeves up. "Here, let me help you do that," he urged as he plodded into the mud.

Mariah didn't glance up, but only nodded her acceptance. "Get on the other side of him. We have to get the rope under both hooves. I have the left one. . . ."

He leaned his shoulder into the plaintive bull's side and thrust his hands straight down. By inches, he felt around until at last he found both the rope and the right hoof. "I have it. Now . . ."

They worked diligently for a few moments, using only single-word exchanges, until Mariah gave the horses the command to go forward. In seconds, the young bull was out and angrily bawling, louder than ever.

Mariah slogged out and hurried to free the animal from the ropes. It tossed its head and twisted, attempting to butt her. She swiftly dodged, barely avoiding the animal's horns. A moment later, it trotted a few yards away before stopping at a patch of grass to graze sedately.

"Ungrateful creature," Hank said in mock disdain. He refrained from mentioning the danger Mariah had barely avoided from the bull's horns, and continued to make light of the heavy work they had just completed as he scraped some of the muck from his arms and shirtsleeves. "After putting us to all that trouble he didn't bother to give a backward glance. Hardly said 'pardon' or 'thank you.'"

Mariah chuckled as she stamped her feet in an effort to shake as much of the mud off as she could. "A bit like a greenhorn I know who never appreciated my help in getting him out of a mess just as sticky."

"Oh? *You* helped *me* from a sticky situation?"

"Yep."

"And I never thanked you?"

"Nope."

He gave an exaggerated sigh. "I thought you offered your help in return for the favor of my becoming your fiancé."

"I offered my help because you're a tenderfoot who didn't have any better sense than to get yourself tangled up with a cardsharp like Kasey," she said in both defense and cheerful provocation. "And I never wanted you to be my—my intended, only—only . . ." She trailed away in embarrassment. They both knew the situation had gotten far out of hand.

"Then why did you throw yourself at me at the

train station, where half the town could see, especially that young man? You did want to offset their pity, did you not?"

"Oh! I didn't mean— Well, I know I did, but . . ." This time she really was irritated. He needn't have brought up those embarrassing actions. "Quit misdirecting the point."

"The point being?"

She felt confused for a moment. "The point is we did each other a good turn. Now we can call it quits anytime."

"Not yet." He rubbed his hands against his thighs until they were mostly free of the wet mud. "Since you've pointed out that I have never thanked you for your good deeds, I must remedy my oversight."

"Well, no need to, now."

He strolled toward her, his amusement still evident. "No, my dear, you are quite right. You saved me from a gunfight and possibly an ambush. I should thank you suitably."

Although his movements were slow, there was purpose in his step and a like gleam in his eyes. His amusement dimmed while he held her gaze.

Mariah backed up a step. She wasn't quite sure of his intention, but there was something about his expression she recognized. A light, an emotion. She had glimpsed it fleetingly the other day in the mountains after they'd caught the mare.

"And anyway," she murmured, "I wasn't much help after everything went loco. You still have to face Kasey down."

He stopped in front of her and slid a hand against the side of her face. Traces of mud gently scratched her cheek as his warm palm caressed her skin. His touch was both erotic and sweet, bringing every one of her nerves to attention in a way nothing else ever had.

"Let me worry about my match with Kasey. I suspect you, too, still have your demons to face." His voice was low and rumbling, the distinctly round British tones coaxing.

"My demons?" she said, so confused by her own racing response that she could barely answer.

His head bent, his thumb tipped her chin up, and his mouth hovered over hers. "The Mead town matrons."

"Oh, yeah . . . my . . . demons."

His lips touched hers in slow, soft pressure. She didn't breathe, only assimilated his touch. It was wonderful.

He felt so familiar as his other arm went around her, lifting her to her toes. Her mind vaguely recalled they'd kissed before, yet this was infinitely different. Beyond the smell of mud and cow was the faint fragrance of lye soap, while a two-day-old beard felt far softer than she would have imagined. The heat of his body radiated into hers, warming her against the cool spring air; she hadn't realized she'd felt cold. She shivered, realizing it wasn't the cold that caused it, and slid her arm around his waist and leaned into him.

He gathered her yet closer in response.

The kiss intensified as slowly as the flow of cold honey, yet it sent a searing message of desire which couldn't be mistaken.

Suddenly frightened, Mariah pulled away and stared at him in shaky surprise. Unlike the kisses at the train station, this one had been fully shared by them both. With mind as well as body. But unlike then, no amusement shone in the smoky gray eyes that returned her gaze and there was no recognition of a part being played out. This kiss had been completely real and Hank's desire was stamped on his face in bold terms.

She wondered if her own desire was as clearly reflected in her features.

The thought made her reel. She couldn't, shouldn't feel this way! She still loved Tommy. Didn't she?

How could she suddenly be overcome by the attentions and attractions of another man? According to what Granny had told her long ago, a good woman didn't know this . . . this *emotion* until she married. Nor should she entertain thoughts of it. Only men felt a continuous lust, Granny had said. That was why places like Tillie's existed.

But Mariah felt it. The passion in Hank's kiss had exploded something in her, something hot and needy that hit her with all the force of a thousand-pound bull. Maybe Mrs. Benton was right—maybe her unruly streak was unhealthy and shameful.

"Put me down," she said, her voice crackling. She pushed against Hank's chest and when he complied with her order, she took a determined step backwards. His eyes fairly sparked with desire as he watched her withdraw. The response running along her nerve endings scared her out of her wits. She had the unmistakable self-knowledge she wouldn't put up much of a fight if he insisted on making her his; that realization frightened her even more. How could she respond this way to a near stranger?

Mariah knew what it meant, too. She wasn't ignorant about that part of it; she'd watched the animals mate more than once.

Moving toward a nearby aspen tree, Mariah shakily tried to get her feelings under control as she absentmindedly grabbed a few leaves and began to scrape the mud from her boots.

She had to end it, right now. There was no use in starting something that had no future. Hank was the most handsome and charming man she'd ever meet in a month of Sundays, and he'd made her toes curl just now. But Hank was also a traveling man, an irresponsible gambler. His world, his expectations in life were so different from hers. She had no business getting all worked up over him, no business at all, no matter how he made her feel. It would only cause her a mountain of trouble if she gave in to it, and she already had enough problems to fill a canyon.

His shadow loomed over her. "Mariah?"

"That mustn't happen again, Hank," she said, keeping her head down.

He was silent a long moment before gently replying, "I can't promise it won't."

She glanced up at him swiftly. For a fleeting second, Mariah was sure he felt as confused as she did. Then it was gone, covered by his usual pleasantness.

His expression changed, and a subtle, neutral kindness came to the fore.

"Come along," he said, offering her a hand. "Isn't it lunchtime? Didn't you promise me some of last night's, ah, *delicious* corn bread?"

Mariah laughed nervously. Her corn bread could be called edible, but never delicious.

Late the next day, as Henry and Mariah rode into the ranch yard, Nate told the Englishman his friend had come. They'd been gone since early morning, the same as the day before, riding the western line and checking on the main herd and new births in the enclosed meadow.

"Mr. Moore's waitin' in the parlor," old Nate said. Then in a loud aside to Mariah, "He's got one of them there bowler hats like you was talkin' about, an' he's jes' as fancy an' proper as Hank here. What ya gonna do with the two of 'em?"

Henry turned away to hide his grin and began to unsaddle Patches.

"Um, I reckon I can find enough work for them to do," Mariah said. "Where's Grandaddy? Did he finish his business with Mr. Rhodes?"

"Yup, reckon so," Nate said. "Went back to town with 'im."

"He did?" Mariah felt a rising panic. "Why?" It was too soon after her misbehavior at the train station and the incident with Kasey for her to be comfortable with the idea.

She glanced at Hank. The corners of his mouth turned up and he winked at her. She glared, then turned her back. *He* wasn't the one who had to make excuses or worry about what people would say to upset her grandfather. *He* would move on in a week or two, but she had to live with the repercussions. Grandaddy would hear about it from a dozen people and he wouldn't like her part in any of it.

"What in blue blazes did Grandaddy need in town that I couldn't have taken care of?" she mumbled to no one in particular.

Surprisingly, Nate heard her. "Don't know. Said somethin' 'bout arrangin' things. Supplies, I guess. Here, I'll feed the horses an' rub 'em down fer ya."

"Thanks, Nate," she said unenthusiastically. "Hank, you might as well get your friend settled at the bunkhouse. I'm going to work with the new mare."

Henry hurried to the house, passing a hitched buggy parked to the side of the rutted drive. The sorry-looking horse had all the earmarks of a rented nag. James must have hated having to be seen driving it, he thought with a chuckle. His man was rather proud of the horseflesh Henry owned in England.

When he entered the parlor, he found his valet sitting primly on the edge of the lumpy sofa. Around him was the normal chaos of a room where no one had the time to worry or care about neatness. Tumbled, dusty cushions, worn boots, and old periodicals cluttered the floor, while on the table at his elbow was a dirty, coffee-stained cup.

Henry found James's expression of stoic patience amusing, but even more so as he watched James's brown eyes widen at the sight of him. He laughed, then said, "James, I was never so glad to see you as now."

James lowered his eyes to cover his unspoken disapproval and near shock as he stood. "Quite, sir."

"Did you have any difficulty in finding me?"

"No, Master Henry, you left a broad trail."

Again, Henry laughed. "How much gossip did you hear in town?"

"Enough, I should think. You are believed to be a—ahem—close personal friend of one Miss Mariah Taggert, a—a 'highfalutin' gambler, I think was the term, and finally, sir, engaged to perform a fisticuffs exhibition with a local bully called Kasey. On Saturday week, I believe."

"Exactly." Henry rubbed his hands together. "Where are the trunks?"

"At Powell's hotel. It seemed the reasonable thing to do to leave them, since you had paid for the week."

"Yes, yes, indeed. But I must have some of my

things brought out here immediately. Did you rent that rig for only the day?"

"Ah, no, I took the liberty of renting it until the end of the week. I thought—"

"Right. Well, James, I must fill you in. But come along to the bunkhouse. We can talk there in privacy for the moment. It is where we will be sleeping for the duration of our stay. And one other thing . . ."

"Yes, Master Henry?"

"You must call me Hank. No Master Henry. Just plain Hank."

"Sir?"

Grandaddy was quiet again during supper. Mariah didn't know what to make of it. He was never garrulous, but he plowed through Nate's onion-heavy stew without a word, as though he didn't taste it. He did, however, glance toward Hank several times, and took a couple of thoughtful stares at Hank's friend Jim.

Mariah wondered if Jim had a voice at all. He sat very straight in his black suit with his dark hair slicked back, wide-eyed, politely passing the stew and biscuits, but saying nothing after a "How do you do."

After three days at the Circle T, Hank appeared more at home. He looked refreshed, too. Newly shaven, he wore a set of clothes just as richly tailored and fine as the suit in which she'd first seen him, but his posture was casual and he seemed to enjoy the lively thoughts running through his head, for she frequently noticed a corner of his mouth curving into a half smile.

What Grandaddy made of their two guests was a puzzle. He hadn't once discussed Hank's presence with her after the first introduction. She'd waited nervously to get an earful ever since his return from town just in time for the evening meal, but he didn't mention hearing any gossip, either.

Elam finally pushed his empty plate back and Nate filled the coffee cups for the last round, the signal that usually opened conversation.

"Is Mr. Rhodes coming back out tomorrow to help round up, or is he sending his own outfit for the cattle, Grandaddy?" Since she helped run the ranch, it seemed a normal question. If she could get him talking on cattle, maybe she could distract him from the touchy subject of her troublesome ways, and she'd also find out what was bothering him.

"Mr. Rhodes had to get along back to Chicago, honey," Elam replied, fishing in his pocket for his tobacco pouch.

"Oh." She reached for a kitchen match from the table's center. "When can we expect the cattle to go?"

"Don't rightly know. Mr. Rhodes had some unexpected changes in his plans."

"Well, did you shake hands on the deal?" Mariah thought he was hedging his answers.

"No, honey, reckon we didn't."

"Well, then," she said as she struck the match and held it toward Elam's pipe. "I think we should look to another buyer. Mr. Waters, that dealer from Kansas City, will be coming this way in a few weeks, surely."

"I'll think on it," Elam said. He tipped the flame to his pipe, drew on it to get it going, then narrowed his eyes at Hank.

Mariah puffed at the blue flame. It died, sending a tiny spiral of smoke curling into the air. Elam cleared his throat. Her grandaddy was ready to talk.

Silently, Mariah rose and began gathering up the dirty dishes, turning her back to the men. She nearly winced with impatience, biting at the inside of her mouth as she worked. Here came the questions.

Grandaddy would recount what he had heard and then ask what she had to say for herself—and ask Hank what he had to say for himself, and what his intentions were. Then he would shake his head as though deeply disappointed in her and sadly remark that she was too old to be gallivanting around the town in such a harum-scarum way and doing things so thoughtlessly that it caused an upset.

What he *wouldn't* say was what Mrs. Benton had said last summer, that no decent man would want to marry her if she kept up her wild ways. But there would be a tiny frown of worry between his eyes.

"Hank, I heard in town today that you plan to fight Mike Kasey on Saturday?" Elam finally said around his pipe.

Mariah slowly let out her breath. That blasted fight.

"Yes, indeed." Hank bent to light the cigar Jim handed him. "His challenge could not be ignored."

"A boxing match, that right?"

"Yes, sir. James, er, Jim and I have trained for some years in the art. It is quite popular in England, you know."

Elam nodded. "Smart action on your part, from what Thorndyke says. Right nimble. Sidestepped what could have been a bad gunfight and turned Kasey's game inside out. Even drew the town into sponsoring the match."

"As to that, the townspeople have made their own arrangements," Hank responded.

"Well, Kasey can be a wicked foe. I'm glad to hear you know how to protect yourself, son. And you, too, Jim. But you know, if you win this fracas, other men will likely want to take up the challenge. And there's no guarantee Kasey still won't try to goad you into a gunfight."

Hank shook his head. "I've no designs on a boxing career, Mr. Taggert. People will forget me when I move on. As for Kasey," he said with a shrug, "I'll cross that bridge when I have to."

"And when do you plan to move on?"

Elam's steady gaze asked a deeper question than the verbal one. Hank was loath to give an answer, for he didn't know it. Yesterday he could easily have said he would probably have his fill of the place in a few days or a week or two. Now he couldn't say.

He glanced toward the dry sink where Mariah stood washing dishes. He noted the way her shoulders moved and the slender bones of her wrists as she worked, and the delicate, unutterably soft, curve of her cheek. A long strand of auburn hair trailing across her shoulder reflected the lamplight, stirring his senses.

The sight of her now made a vast contrast to the picture of her working with the cattle that morning. Yet she tackled both tasks with the same vigor. Both pictures were Mariah.

Then he thought of the lively miss of the train station with the kisses, courage, and vulnerability. It stirred his heart.

The women from home carried a Victorian veneer of simpering flirtatiousness and beneath it they were ever conscious of themselves. But Mariah had a naturalness, a giving without guile. It stirred his mind.

Was he ready to leave this place yet? He should leave soon if he cared not to break Mariah's heart. But he knew he wouldn't, yet. He couldn't.

"I sincerely hope you will allow me to stay a while,

Mr. Taggert," he replied slowly. "Perhaps a month or so. I find the Western country here worth studying. Mariah tells me you have fought not to overgraze your land as other ranchers have. Jim and I can learn a lot about your methods of cattle raising—for my family's possible investment, of course."

Elam hesitantly nodded. "Very well. If you want to learn, I reckon we can share what we know. Nate and I, and Mariah, too, have put in some hard years together. It would be good to know someone can gain experience on it."

"Thank you, sir. Naturally, I will pay you for your training as well as our room and board. And I would be very grateful if Jim and I could use a portion of the barn to spar in the evenings."

"Done. Are you needing anything else? Extra blankets? Pillows? Reckon you've got your shaving gear back."

"Yes, Jim brought all my trunks out just before supper. But I think we shall have to make a trip into town to buy some things."

"Sure 'nuff," Nate put in on a snort. "Workin' clothes. Some decent boots an' not them there sissy half boots you've been awearin'. An' hats. Nothin' marks a man faster'n his boots 'n' hat."

Mariah jumped in. "You shouldn't risk going into town before Saturday, Hank. Thorndyke said Kasey might try something funny. Or one of his cohorts. He might be sneaky enough to shoot you from ambush, even."

"You don't say!" James spoke for the first time, his eyes wide. "You mean this chap wants to *kill* Mr.— Mr.—" He caught himself at Henry's warning glance and said, "Hank, I beg you to be more cautious."

"I can't very well hide forever," Hank said mildly.

"And I think it a better strategy to show myself so that Kasey will know I am not frightened."

"Then I'll go with you," Mariah said. "You might need me."

"Now, Mariah, I don't know as that's a good idea," Elam protested. "Hank might not want a woman along. Might look like he was standing behind a woman's skirts."

"Oh, but—"

"Hank said he could take care of himself, Mariah," Elam said, this time more firmly.

Mariah finished the dishes, knowing she couldn't argue with Grandaddy any further when he used that tone of voice, but still wondering how she could help protect Hank if he went wandering into town without her.

"Perhaps you should ride into town with us, Nate," Hank said. "We could use your advice on clothes and equipment."

"Why, sure, Hank, don't mind if I do. We'll get you fixed right up."

That did it. Whenever Nate went into town, he always brought home an explosion of rumors. Some of them would be disturbingly, wildly false.

She had to find a reason that Grandaddy would accept for her to go along. She had to find out what people were saying about the events of the other day.

8

In the end, they all went into town. Mariah insisted she needed to talk to Lem Harrington, the blacksmith, about shoeing the black mare and a few of their other horses. Hank and Jim, besides wanting to buy work clothes and equipment, apparently had an agenda of their own. Nate said he'd been missing out on all the fun going on in town and it made him feel old. And Elam, without saying much, seemed determined to chaperon.

Surprised, Mariah wondered why her grandfather should take a sudden hand in the game, for she'd been going to town by herself to run errands since she was fourteen, and he'd seldom objected to her going off alone with Tommy. She'd only received a scolding when their pranks and her outsized curiosity caused a stir—like the time she and Tommy had lit firecrackers under Mead's Fourth of July celebration speaker, or put a mouse in the teacher's desk, or when, at twelve, she'd asked the Reverend Higginbotham, in front of the church ladies, if God made little babies because he liked them, and everyone else thought it was pretty fine, too, then what was the matter with the one Sally Harrington had had all by herself?

Yes, she'd certainly caused a stir that Sunday morning. But she had to hand it to Granny. Her grandmother, the most righteous woman Mariah had ever met, but the most loving as well, had looked beyond the ladies' snit at her innocent inquiries. In fact, there had been a look of gentle pride in her eyes, Mariah remembered. A few days later, Granny took her to see Sally and the new baby, ignoring the continued gossip about who had fathered the child.

Mariah sighed at the memories as she sat next to Elam in the buggy. She'd grown up considerably since then, but it seemed she nevertheless couldn't stay out of trouble. She suspected her grandfather had come to town with them because he wanted to keep her under his wing. He didn't know what to make of the rumors flying around town, and with her loss of Tommy still so fresh, he wasn't yet ready to face her square on about them, which was fine with her. She wasn't exactly ready to face them square on, either. However, mindful of how her reputation sat on a narrow line, she'd dressed more carefully than usual and put on her best Sunday dress and bonnet, a blue-gray serge trimmed with black braid.

They split up when they reached town. Elam parked the buggy next to Jim's rented one in front of Silas Patrick's general store, then said something about an errand of his own. Hank, after giving her an infectious grin and salute, followed Jim and Nate through the store's wide doors. Hazel Patrick, from her place behind the counter, stared out at her with frosty disapproval through the store's front window before turning a merchant's smile on the new customers.

Mariah started down the main street toward Lem's on the outer edge of town. There seemed to be more traffic than usual, even for a Saturday, she thought as she made her way past the saloons and merchants. She glanced warily down the side street where the Benton house stood. Thank goodness, neither Caroline Benton nor her mother was anywhere in sight. She didn't think she'd recovered enough patience or self-control to rebuff the honeyed sympathy Caroline would feel duty-bound to dish out. Certainly, she didn't want to listen to Caroline rhapsodize about the beauty of Myrtle Alice and Tommy's wedding.

Stubbornly, neither did she want to answer any snide innuendos or questions about Hank. But she had to face the town again sometime, and she didn't mind so much as long as she could put off a personal encounter with the Bentons. There would be time enough for that when Tommy returned from his honeymoon.

To Mariah's relief, as she strolled over to the smithy, the general excitement seemed more centered on the coming fight rather than anything she'd done recently.

"Good morning, Miss Mariah," said Sheriff Tinsdale, a slightly heavy man of medium height, touching the edge of his wide-brimmed hat. "My, you look fetching this morning. Must be that English visitor that's bringing out the roses in your cheeks."

"Thank you, Sheriff." Mariah smiled tentatively. It was rare that the sheriff had ever given her more than a nod of greeting unless she was with her grandfather.

"This boxing match is shaping up as quite an

event. Thorndyke says Kasey is gettin' into a regular lather about it. Been practicing in the Last Chance's back room. Won't let anybody in unless it's one of his cronies. Tell me, is your young fella any good at this boxing stuff?"

"I really don't know, Sheriff. I've never seen Hank fight, or a boxing match at all."

"Oh, well, I guess not. Didn't think about the propriety of it. Reckon we'll all have to take our chances on who to bet on, won't we? Good day, my dear."

Mariah found the same curiosity at Lem Harrington's smithy. There were a couple of cowhands lounging against a wall there, one a youngster with straw-colored hair named Billy and the other a Mexican named Jose, from one of the outlying ranches. She'd gone to school with Billy and he'd been a sometime pal of Tommy's.

Lem looked up from his bellows. "Howdy, Miss Mariah. What can I do for you this morning?"

"I came to settle our bill, Mr. Harrington," she said as she handed him the money Hank had paid her for Patches. "And I have some work for you out at the Circle T one day next week."

"Why, sure 'nuff. Pleased to help ya."

"Morning, Mariah," Billy said. "That foreign dude of yours come to town with you this morning? You didn't waste no time gettin' yourself a new beau after Tommy, did ya? Sure would like to get a gander at that fella. Heard he's a real fancy dresser with real polite manners. Heard how he put Kasey's nose outa joint." His tone held an edge of derision. "Also heard Thorndyke told 'im to stay outa town 'til the fight on Saturday."

"He's here. So's my grandaddy," she told him.

"That so? Well, where is he?"

"Minding his own business," she said pointedly.

"Well, hell's bells, Mariah," Billy said, coming away from the wall as he reverted to the eagerness of boyhood. "What are his chances? Ya think the tenderfoot's strong an' mean enough to take Kasey?"

Mariah didn't know whether to be defensive, irritated, or simply amused. To be honest, she felt a bit of all three emotions. She didn't dislike Billy, but he was entirely too nosy. Besides which, while she felt it was all right for her to call Hank a tenderfoot, she didn't like to hear the slightly derogatory term from anybody else.

And Hank wasn't mean at all.

Letting her exasperation show, she said, "Hank's strong, you can bet on that. And too smart to let Kasey beat him in a *fair* fight. As for mean enough, I reckon you'll just have to wait to find out, won't you, Billy."

"S'pose so. Should be excitin', whatever the odds. Too bad Tommy's gotta miss it."

"Yeah." The proposed boxing match was something she and Tommy would have discussed excitedly and mulled over between them, and she would have badgered Tommy to take her to see it. "Too bad."

It suddenly dawned on her that she might not be able to watch the match. Grandaddy would object and, without Tommy, she'd have trouble sneaking in to see it on her own. Her attending an event that was considered out-of-bounds for a respectable woman, especially without a male protector, would really raise eyebrows. And there would be plenty there to note her presence.

She left the smithy, waiting for the thought of her loss of Tommy's companionship to invade her with pain. But she felt more annoyed than sad. Those days were gone, and she didn't have time to think about them any longer anyway, because by the time she got over her encounter with Billy, she was stopped by Mrs. Kelly, who had been one of Granny's closest friends. After discovering Elam was also in town, the older woman decided to walk along with her.

Mrs. Kelly dived right in. "Lots of excitement in town lately."

"Uh-huh. Seems to be."

"This new beau of yours is from England, isn't he?"

"Yes, ma'am."

"What's his name?"

Mariah knew very well that Mrs. Kelly had heard, but she answered evenly, "Henry Clayton."

"He's extremely handsome, and most charming, I hear."

"Yes, ma'am." Charm was Hank's main attraction, Mariah suspected. His smile alone could light up a Christmas tree and invite you to sit in its glow. Mariah had felt the strong tug of that invitation and it was getting stronger every day. It felt strange and powerful and full of more passion than she knew how to handle, and she wanted to give in to it.

But the season for Christmas trees lasted such a short time and Mariah suspected that Hank's charm would be short-lived, too, but without the holiday's depth of meaning. If she accepted only what Hank offered, if she indulged her sudden, unexpected fancy for the greenhorn, then when her season to receive the Englishman's charm was over, she'd be lonelier than ever. It was better to keep their friendship light and let the whole thing blow over.

"By all accounts," Mrs. Kelly continued, "Mr.

Clayton is well-to-do. You'll have a comfortable life, I suppose. Your grandfather must be very pleased."

The ladies of Mead had worked mighty fast to know all that, Mariah mused. They had her married and well situated quicker than a blink of an eye. This cleared up what Grandaddy may or may not have heard; he would have had an earful by now. She hated to think of how Elam would be affected when he found there was to be no marriage between her and Hank. With his weak heart, she'd have to gently ease him into the truth.

Her guilt took a giant step forward. She'd really done it this time. The whole situation was more tangled than a can of worms.

Mariah hid her own doubts and discomfort as she watched Mrs. Kelly's blue eyes sparkle with warmth. The older woman was a sweet soul, with none of Mrs. Benton's malice or Mrs. Patrick's constant disapproval, and Mariah wanted to soften her misconception. She felt it would almost be the same as talking to Granny. Perhaps if she set the record straight with Mrs. Kelly, and the word trickled through the town, then Elam wouldn't end up getting too hurt.

"Um, Mrs. Kelly, there's nothing official, you know, between Hank and me. We haven't had time for a proper courtship or to think about anything very serious."

"Sometimes marriage shouldn't wait too long, my dear. When love strikes, you have to act. I knew Mr. Kelly only a few weeks when I married him. You've heard of 'whirlwind courtships,' haven't you, dear?"

"Yes, but—but Hank and his friend Jim are only staying a while to learn the cattle business. He's looking for possible family investments."

Hank had given Grandaddy the best explanation possible last night and Mariah was grateful to have it now, although privately she didn't quite believe it. She thought Hank was only having a good time at her expense.

Still, it seemed like a fair exchange. If he wanted to pretend he was a wealthy businessman and to play cowboy for a while instead of gambling, then she'd go along with it. It served to detract everyone's attention from her less-than-ladylike behavior. Meanwhile, she'd have time to get over Tommy's defection in her own way without the whole county watching her grieve, and then by the time Hank became bored with his adventures and left, everyone would have forgotten her old heartache.

"Mmm. Well, Mr. Clayton didn't waste any time making a name for himself, did he?" Mrs. Kelly commented.

"He had no choice. Kasey didn't like losing at cards."

"Yes, dear, I've heard all about it. A boxing match, I believe?"

"Yes, ma'am." Mariah's thoughts switched back to her chances of attending it.

"Does your Hank know what he's doing?"

Mariah sure as shootin' hoped so. She hated the idea of him getting beat up, more now than she did the other night when they'd been on the run from those bullies. Funny—she seemed to have developed a squeamish side to her nature.

If she could only be there . . .

"He must," she said, hoping she sounded positive. "He's the one who suggested it." Her voice lifted with a sense of pride. "He sure turned the tide on Kasey when Kasey wanted a showdown. Hank made it go his way. Twice." After a moment, she added, "Hank's a good talker."

"Hmm. Well, I hope it all comes out the way it should, dear." Mrs. Kelly patted her hand. "Your grandmother would be pleased to know you had married and settled down."

"Yes, ma'am."

Reminded that she'd lost the only man she'd ever expected to marry, Mariah fell silent. She wondered what Granny had wanted most for her, to settle down or to marry. It didn't seem to her to necessarily be one and the same thing. She wanted to run the Circle T for the rest of her life, and maybe that would be enough. She didn't know about marriage, now. Perhaps in a few months or a year or two she would have to consider it anew, but at the moment she had too many other problems to worry about.

Mariah heard Nate's near shout the minute she entered Morton's general store. "Them chaps'll keep yer legs from gettin' cut up an' such while yer out tendin' the cattle. Now this kerchief c'n be a lifesaver in sev'ral ways. It c'n protect yer mouth 'n' nose in a storm, or ya c'n tie it around yer forehead on a hot day to catch the sweat. Even use it as a bandage or tourniquet if needed."

Mrs. Kelly stopped to talk to another customer while Mariah made her way past the display of dry goods to the wall of stacked shirts and jeans. She spotted Nate's back as she went down the aisle, his gnarled hand waving to make his point as he talked. Hank's bent head was beyond. Then Nate stepped aside.

Hank straightened slowly and, catching her gaze, smiled. His good looks stood out like the evening star, even in working clothes. A light of mocking self-awareness and fun shone from his gray eyes. More of his charm, Mariah thought.

Have mercy, she silently begged him. She couldn't seem to keep her heart from fluttering like a bird learning to fly, although she did her dead level best to hide it.

He wore a light gray shirt tucked into blue denim dungarees, over which was a tanned leather vest and chaps. With even the slightest move, the fringe of the chaps fairly danced down his long legs. Barely showing beneath the jean hems were the shiny toes and higher heels of his black Western boots. A bright red bandanna was knotted around his neck and a set of gloves stuck out jauntily from his belt, the fingers slightly bent as though to wave.

In a gesture of showmanship, Hank bowed, then placed a stiff new plainsman hat on his head.

Yessiree, he was outfitted in typical range-hand style. As working clothes went, they were unadorned and made for heavy action. But on the knightly Hank, the garments took on all the romance of a suit of armor.

"Howdy, ma'am," he drawled in his best imitation of the local speech.

"Howdy, mister," she answered in kind, her own laughter bubbling up. "You look as fresh as a newly minted gold piece. Are you sure you want to get them duds all messed up by hiring out as a cowpoke?"

"Reckon these duds were made for hard work, ma'am. They should stand up to a little mud and water now and again. Especially when I end up in mud or water 'most every time I'm in your company. And they fit me better than the ones you provided. No offense to you, ma'am, but since you're proving to be rather a hard taskmaster, I reckon it's better to have clothes that fit."

"Are you saying I'm a tough boss?"

"Yes, ma'am, reckon I am."

"Well, if you're not up to it . . ." Mariah casually shrugged to indicate she didn't care much if he was or wasn't, but she couldn't prevent the corners of her mouth from curving into a response.

Hank reverted to his regular speech. "*I* not up to it? Darling, have I not followed your lead? *Every time?* Have I failed to fulfill your, um"—he raised an eyebrow expressively—"expectations?"

Mariah blushed at the endearment, even knowing that Hank was teasing. Quickly looking to see who was around to have heard him, she felt relieved that Mrs. Kelly was still at the front of the store talking with Mr. Morton.

Glancing in Nate's direction, she wondered how much of their conversation the old man had followed. His avid expression of approval told her he'd understood the gist of it even though he'd probably missed many of their words. All this playful trifling with Hank wouldn't help her cool the fires of gossip or the old men's expectations any, and would only add flirting to the list of her sins.

"Yes. Er, no. I expect you're having more fun than a family of fleas on a mutt at the moment, Hank. But so far, you haven't faced a steady diet of hard work." Mariah let her gaze rove from the top of his hat to his booted feet; then she struggled to retain her amusement as her thoughts turned more serious. "Or Saturday. Hank, are you gonna be okay?"

"So that's it. You're worried about Saturday."

"Some."

"You needn't, you know."

"Word is, Kasey's been training every day. I don't know about your Queensberry rules, but Hank, I wouldn't count on him following them to the T. Kasey'll probably try any dirty trick he can."

"You still doubt I can take care of myself, don't you."

"Well . . . well . . ." She wanted to deny it, yet couldn't bring herself to lie. For all the fun he was having, he was still a tenderfoot. "You're not exactly a hard case, now are you?"

Hank studied her face. "You think I'm soft?"

"I think you might've bitten off more than you can chew. But if you want to get all beat up, I guess it's your business."

"I suppose you need proof that I know what I'm doing."

"No, not if you're sure. It's your . . . game." She'd started to say "funeral."

"Quite so."

"Only time will tell what kind of stamina the boy has," Nate said loudly. "But ya haveta give 'im marks fer not runnin' scared."

Mariah chuckled. "True. Hank here doesn't take to runnin'." She had to give the greenhorn that. She glanced around, then asked, "Where's your pal Jim?"

"He had business to take care of," Hank replied. "Don't worry, Nate and I have him all fixed up with the proper clothes. We'll be ready for work at first cockcrow tomorrow."

"That's good, because tomorrow we have to ride to the canyon corner of the Circle T and look for strays."

Mrs. Kelly wandered back to where they stood and Mariah dutifully introduced Hank.

"My, my, Mr. Clayton, you have surely set the town abuzz," Mrs. Kelly remarked good-naturedly. "I hear this boxing match is drawing attendance from even the mines and outlying ranches."

"I hope the men won't be disappointed in my skill, Mrs. Kelly. More importantly, I wonder if I've done Kasey a bit of an injustice. I have trained with the best fighters in England, after all."

Mariah felt a gentle touch on her arm. "Mariah, dear, why don't you spend Saturday afternoon with me?" asked Mrs. Kelly. "We can wait out the fight results together."

"How nice of you to ask," Mariah responded as she scrambled for an excuse to refuse. She wouldn't have a chance to sneak into even the outer edges of the attending crowd if she was stuck at Mrs. Kelly's house. "But—"

"Excellent idea, Mrs. Kelly." Hank gave one of his most winsome smiles. "Miss Mariah would love your company, I am sure."

Mariah stared daggers at Hank before she turned back to Mrs. Kelly. He knew very well how much she wanted to see that match. She had a vested interest, after all, didn't she? They'd been partners in their chase the other night.

"We'll make an afternoon for ourselves," the older woman added.

"It sounds lovely, but—"

"Might haveta deliver her there yerself, Hank," Nate said in his loud voice, then laughed. "And tie 'er in a chair to keep 'er there."

Mariah gave the old man a disgusted look, which made him laugh even harder. It seemed she couldn't win.

"Mariah," Elam called from the front of the store. "I'm ready to leave. Got chores, you know."

"Yes, Grandaddy, I'm coming." Her grandfather's

call reminded her that she'd recently made a vow to think before she acted. She turned to the older woman. "Thank you for inviting me, Mrs. Kelly. I'd be pleased to visit with you on Saturday."

But as she passed by Hank, she let him see she was annoyed with him. Maybe she couldn't openly go to the fight, but he needn't think he'd gotten away with maneuvering her.

Hank merely smiled. Murmuring something about further business to take care of, he and Nate strolled away, leaving her to her grandfather's company. It also left her feeling purely flat, for the moment.

But only for the moment. On her way home, Mariah delighted herself by imagining all the things she planned to tell one Mr. Henry Clayton, of Surrey, England, about what he could do with his attempt at playing her suitor. And with his telling her what to do. She simply wouldn't put up with his shenanigans. Not a jot.

9

Near sunset, a buckboard arrived at the Circle T, bearing two men as well as Nate, and piled high with sacks of flour and grain, crates of vegetables, canned goods, and gear. Two new sets of bits, bridles, lariats, and saddle blankets rode loosely in the wagon bed, as well as two Western saddles. A stack of rich leather luggage, two trunks, and one large crate sat alongside them.

Ira Morton's young helper, Sammy, hopped down from the buckboard. "Where you want all the foodstuff, Miss Taggert?"

"Why, in the house, I guess," she answered automatically. They hadn't used the cookshack in three years, the last time they had more men than only Nate for an outfit.

Nate climbed down slowly, favoring his aching joints. "Evenin', Mariah. I ferget how tiresome town can be. Look whut we brung home."

"Who bought all these supplies, Nate?"

"Whazzat?"

"All this food," she said, raising her voice.

"Food? Oh, yeah. There's 'nuff vittles to feed a outfit three times our size."

"I see that. Who paid for it?"

"Hank, of course."

Mariah sighed. She supposed they did need additional supplies, but it nettled her that Hank had to pay for them. It was hard to admit their credit was down to the last dollar even though the Circle T was in no different shape than a dozen other small spreads. The spring cattle sale ought to help matters.

She turned her puzzled gaze toward the third man on the wagon. The small figure moved with agility as he climbed over the wagon wheel, then bowed deeply in her direction. Mariah recognized him as the son of a former miner, who now owned a small bar in town, and a Chinese woman. His dark eyes snapped with pleased excitement as he introduced himself.

"How do, Miss Taggert. I'm Brown. I'm to cook."

"Cook?" Mariah replied in astonishment. She half turned toward the staircase, worrying about her grandfather hearing. At her insistence, Elam had been resting in bed since their return from town. He'd seemed a little overwrought and she hadn't liked the tired lines around his eyes. Hearing sounds of stirring from upstairs, she stepped to the edge of the porch and lowered her voice. "Did my grandfather hire you?"

"No, ma'am," replied Brown. "Mr. Moore hired me."

"Mr. Moore?"

"Yes, ma'am. If you'll just point out the cookshack, I can start supper right away."

"Now wait a minute here. Mr. Moore had no

business in taking you on as cook. I can't afford a cook and I'm the ramrod of the Circle T."

Unconcerned, Brown gathered a bundle of clothes from the wagon bed and tucked it under his arm. "Don't know about that, miss. Mr. Moore said the Circle T needed a cook and Mr. Clayton paid my wages in advance. Three months' worth."

Hank! She should've known he was behind this. Her temper and her alarm at his takeover attitude rose instantly. Where had she lost control of the situation? Perhaps it was the other day when she allowed him to kiss her as though he truly was her intended. "Where are Mr. Clayton and Mr. Moore now?"

"There." Brown directed her gaze into the distance, where the rented buggy she recognized as Jim's approached at a sedate pace.

Mariah flung herself down the path toward the outbuildings. She stopped short, waiting in the middle of the road in front of the barn with her arms crossed. All but tapping her boot, she stood her ground and stared while Hank brought the two nags to a halt.

"Good afternoon, my dear Mariah. I see you are waiting for me. Did you miss me that much?"

"I didn't miss you at all, greenhorn." She was so angry, she nearly sputtered. "I want to talk to you."

"I thought you might," Hank returned calmly. "Jim, take care of the buggy, please."

"Yes, certainly, Hank."

Mariah narrowed her eyes as she observed Jim obeying Hank's directive. Jim did that a lot, she had begun to notice. Any task Hank wanted done and didn't want to do himself, Jim was right there to perform it, almost as if he were a personal servant.

The suspicion brought her gaze back to Hank. Surely not; she was only being fanciful. She'd never heard of a gambler, even a rich one, who won consistently enough to pay for more than his own travel expenses, never mind a servant. As Grandaddy always said, she ought not let her imagination run away with her. Jim was merely a friend of Hank's who liked to be helpful, as he was being now.

Hank, meanwhile, faced her with a mere foot of space between them. He unhurriedly removed his gloves and tucked them into the back of his belt, all the while watching her face.

"Wouldn't you prefer to remove to a quieter place or do you wish to berate me here in front of everyone?"

Mariah's awareness swiftly returned to the object of her anger. That solemn, evenly toned question didn't quite hide Hank's amusement at her. She felt no answering merriment.

"What in blue blazes do you find so all-fired funny, anyway?"

"You." His voice held an intimate huskiness while a knowing smile stretched his mouth.

That only served to fuel her feelings of frustration, and her teeth clamped together against an immediate explosion. Hank was altogether too charming, too at ease with everything and everybody, and too autocratic. And he wasn't taking her seriously. Didn't the dolt realize he was getting the two of them deeper and deeper into this pretense of being engaged by hiring help for the Circle T, and accepting invitations for her? She'd have the devil of a time getting out of it all when he left.

Mariah wanted to stomp her foot, only she'd given up the childish habit at fifteen. Instead, she opened her mouth to give him a sharp piece of her mind, but noting Brown and Sammy curiously looking their way pointed up the need to find some privacy. She was learning the value of that commodity.

"All right, greenhorn. Follow me."

She led him away from the buildings—the dogs, Barney and Mutt, at her heels—and down the path toward the stream, then stopped at its bank by an outcropping of aspen trees. It was a pretty spot. Spring grass added a bright color against the gray boulders that tumbled into the water. It caused the rushing mountain stream to eddy and swirl into a pool.

Mariah turned around, her hands balled at her hips in an attempt to keep a cool head. Waiting for him to give her some indication that he felt guilty or sorry for his actions seemed fruitless. He felt neither sorry nor guilty, she realized. He gave her a nod, as if only mildly interested in what she had to say. Angrily, she firmed her resolve and began to pace.

"Hank, we have to get a few things straight."

"Yes, my dear?"

She ignored his amiable response.

"Now, I know I owe you a debt, and I appreciate your help these last few days in pretending to be my beau and all. The whole county will be talking for weeks about our, er, greetings at the station and your later altercation with Kasey. Which has replaced the talk about Tommy marrying Myrtle Alice and not me, thank goodness. But you can relax your vigilance. You don't need to protect me all the time."

He had the audacity to raise that telltale brow at her. "Protect you? Why do you think I would do a thing like that?"

"Well, you—" She paused in her pacing. "Don't pretend you don't know what I'm talking about. Wasn't that what you were doing today when you pushed me into accepting Mrs. Kelly's invitation to visit?"

His mouth compressed and his eyes twinkled, but he said nothing.

"Are you making fun of me?"

Hank cupped her neck, kneading her back muscles with strong fingers. The contact felt sweet and soothing.

"Not at all, my dear Mariah. Only teasing you a bit."

"Oh." She ought to move away, but his massage felt too good. After a moment, much of her ill humor drained away. No one had ever called her a poor sport, and she had to admit she'd been tense all afternoon. "Well, I reckon I can stand a little teasing," she mumbled. "How did I give myself away, anyway? You know very well I'm itching to see that boxing match. Can you truly read my mind?"

"Your face."

"My face?"

"It speaks for you. Didn't you know?"

Mariah sighed. Hadn't she said the same thing herself a hundred times? "I suppose so. Anyway, I want you to stop it."

His hand dropped. "Stop what?"

She hadn't wanted him to stop his ministration to the back of her neck, but she didn't have the nerve to ask him to continue. It felt too intimate and she had the mixed reaction of wanting his hands on her and being frightened away altogether. Pacing seemed easier to handle.

"Protecting me. Keeping me from the match. Since my reputation for unseemly behavior is already as high as a mountain, I figure I won't lose much if I go." Besides that, she didn't see why she couldn't join the fun. "Are you any good? I suppose so or you wouldn't have used it to throw Kasey off. What's boxing like? I've never seen a planned-out fight and I've been trying to think of a way . . ."

"Let us deal with one issue at a time, Mariah."

"Which one?"

"Protecting someone. I suppose you were only passing the time of day when you rescued me from unknowingly walking into a gunfight the other night? Or when you rode down the street at my side even though either one of us could have been killed by an unseen assassin?"

"What's that got to do with anything?"

"You were protecting me."

"Oh. Well, don't let it go to your head. I told you, one good turn deserved another. I knew what I was doing."

"And I know what I am doing. This is a preserving action—you do realize that, do you not? You want to counter the town's opinion of you. To do that, you must take an interest in the way the good ladies behave and happily join them in their activities, however much you may dislike it. Put a good face on it and ignore the fight—if not for yourself, then for your grandfather's sake."

That reminder made her conscience smart. Half of her had already conceded that she needed to consider Grandaddy's feelings. She wasn't ready to give in so easily, however.

"Yes, but you're beginning to act like my intended, Hank, and I want you to stop. You sound like my great-aunt Harriet, Grandaddy's sister from Ohio."

"God forbid, I don't." Hank was astounded at the accusation. He, the veritable ne'er-do-well of the Ackerley family, being likened to someone's great-aunt?

"Mm-hmm. You want to dictate my behavior. You have to promise me—no more pushing me into a corner, making it impossible for me to refuse something, like Mrs. Kelly's insistence on my spending the afternoon with her in order to keep me from going to the fight. We're not engaged, Hank, even if people think we are. And I'll be the one to decide who I can visit and where I can go."

"My dear, it is only for your own best good. . . ." Hank suddenly closed his eyes. He could not believe he had espoused that old saying. He had stomped away from Robby a hundred times while it rang in his ears, to immediately find something to do that would not be in his "own best good."

"For my own good? Are you piling on that wagon, too?"

"Forgive me, Mariah. I had not meant to, ah, sound like Great-Aunt Harriet."

"Well, you did."

"Hmm. I humbly apologize. Is that all?"

"What do you mean?"

"Is that all that is bothering you?"

"No. I don't want you fooling my grandaddy with your pretenses of possible investments anymore. I didn't mind it when it explained things, like your being here for a few days. But now you want to stay for a whole month. It's all too much. His hopes are up too high. I can't allow anything more to upset him."

"You are worried about Elam?"

"Yes," she said with a sigh. "The doctor says his heart is wearing out."

Hank studied her a moment. "It is no less than I have guessed."

He turned aside and watched the river pond. The evening breeze rose against his cheek, a nighttime nip in it.

Mariah was fighting for far more than the average nineteen-year-old girl of his acquaintance usually had to—the extension of her grandfather's life and the salvation of their livelihood. He wondered how long she'd struggled alone, without anyone to relieve her of her worries, and what she expected of her own future. He suspected she hadn't looked farther than marrying Tommy, which would explain her underlying desperation at the train station. Her pride had been mixed up in her pain.

He wondered what she would do after Elam died. She worked far too hard already. Old Nate tried, but he was not enough help. The Circle T, even though small by Western standards, was more than one woman could manage profitably unless there was money to hire the help it would take. And there was none.

She should sell the place, but he knew instinctively that she would never do it. The ranch held the only security she knew.

That brought his thoughts back to the problem at hand. Regardless of his sounding like her dictator, he wanted Mariah to choose the safe course of action, which in this instance was avoiding the censure of the people who might help her in the future. Eventually, she would find a man she could marry to help her run the Circle T.

Disregarding his twinge of jealousy at the thought of her marrying, Hank strolled back to her and approached the subject seriously for the first time.

"Mariah, you make my point for me. Don't you think your attendance at that fight will upset Elam? The place will be swarming with rough men, and what few women are likely to attend won't be the kind Elam would approve of. Your grandfather worries more over you than anything else on this ranch, and the ranch worries him quite a lot. His concern is for your future, your place in this society after he dies."

Mariah sighed deeply. Losing Grandaddy frightened her more than she wanted anyone to know, and Hank had gone right to the crux of the matter. She had to mend her childish ways and quit vexing Grandaddy.

"Heavens, don't I know it." She turned to look away from him, fighting tears. "Okay. I'll mend some fences by acting like the perfect lady and pretend I'm not interested in the fight. I'll drink tea with Mrs. Kelly next Saturday and be polite as can be with the ladies she invites. Probably Mrs. Patrick and Mrs. Benton and Caroline," she said in disgust.

"Excellent. That should lift your level of esteem in the minds of the town matrons."

"I suppose." She faced him once more. "But I won't like it."

"No, I suspected you would not. Undoubtedly it will be as dull as similar teas at home. But since you've agreed to moderate your behavior—for your own best good, of course," he said, and grinned with a mischievous gleam in his eyes, "you may watch Jim and me spar after supper."

Mariah smiled. "I'd already planned to."

"Oh, you had, had you?" He took her arm companionably and they began to stroll toward the house.

"You bet. You didn't think I'd allow something to go on at this ranch that I didn't personally take an interest in, did you?"

"I can very well imagine that you wouldn't," he replied. "All right then, Mariah. Shall we see what Brown has for our supper? Then, after we've given it time to settle, Jim and I will be ready at the barn."

"Oh." She stopped and frowned up at him. "That's the other thing. Um, about the cook."

"Brown?"

"Yes. He told me you paid him three months' wages."

"I did. What are you objecting to in that?"

"It's only that I can't afford a cook and you, uh, seem to be spending your money pretty freely."

"Oh, is that it? Do not worry about it."

Totally exasperated, she pointed out, "Hank, I know you won a lot in that poker game, and I appreciate all you've been doing to help, like buying Patches and offering to pay me for a guide but, hang it all, you're not going to have a penny left at the rate you spent it today. You can't be so—so . . ."

Hank studied her earnest expression. He had heard a lot of the same argument from his brothers—for his own best good, of course—but this was the first time a woman had pleaded with him on the side of prudence about how he spent his blunt. Mariah could not know how much money he had. She believed him a gambler, and probably thought he had nothing more than what she saw in his wallet. Granted, he did not own what Robby did, nor receive even a quarter of the income, but the annuity he had from his grandmother was a nice figure and had always been enough. By American standards it would be considered quite a lot. This sweet girl who found pleasure in the simple things in life would undoubtedly be staggered if she knew the amount.

"How would you have me spend my money, Mariah?"

"You ought to save some of it for a rainy day. You never know how your fortune can change in the wink of an eye."

"True. But hiring a cook is a little thing, Mariah, and eating well is necessary to my continued state of good health."

Hank had the funniest way of joshing sometimes, Mariah thought. It delighted her. He could redirect her dismals into new ways of looking at a thing and make her laugh at the same time.

"You don't like my cooking?" she asked innocently, and watched for the way his half smile uncovered the crooked tooth.

"No, my little prickly pear, I do not."

"Criticizing the cook can get you into lots of hot water out here in the West, you know. Cowpokes who do often end up with a, um, oh, coffee grounds in their soup or sand in their biscuits. Or worse. Besides which, going over the ramrod's head can be dangerous in the extreme."

"In this case, Mariah, you must bow to the wishes of your paying guests. If Jim and I continue to chase after you and the cows all day long, we deserve to do it with decent meals at the beginning and end of the day. So do you. Think of all the added work you can accomplish if you have no cooking duties to attend to."

"I hate it when you're so logical and practical."

Logical? Practical? He, Henry Clayton Ackerley, described as logical and practical? His brothers would laugh their heads off at the thought.

Mariah slipped into the barn on silent moccasin-clad feet to stand quietly on the edge of the pooled lamplight. The sounds of thwacking and occasional grunts filled the air at the rear, where the planked floor had been cleared of animals and clean straw distributed. Grandaddy and Nate were already leaning against a stall railing, watching with obvious fascination.

Both Hank and Jim were naked above the waist and barefoot. Their skin gleamed in the soft light. Their chests and arms were more muscular than Mariah would've credited, their shoulders broader. Their bodies were finely toned and looked strong. Both chests were covered with dark hair, Hank's straighter than Jim's brown curls. Although Hank was the taller, Jim's weight was almost equal.

Granny would have said Hank was a fine figure of a man, and Jim, too. They seemed much the same, yet Mariah's eyes kept returning to Hank. He was very impressive. There had been a lot hidden under that fine suit, she mused.

It was clear by watching the men move that they had worked at this together for a long time. They wore the padded gloves—mittens, actually, for they had no separate fingers except for the thumb—Hank had described. They circled and feinted, then lightning-fast, Hank's right glove shot forward and connected with Jim's jaw. Jim's head snapped back, but his retaliation was swift. He landed a punch to Hank's ribs.

"Keep your elbows in," Jim muttered.

"Watch your own," Hank replied, snaking a right thrust to Jim's shoulder, then a left.

The sparring continued. Their hits would undoubtedly leave troublesome bruises, but neither man seemed to notice the blows. Faces set in concentration, they warily watched for openings. Mariah silently wondered how much punishment they were prepared to take in the name of sportsmanship.

She watched Hank's face intently. Beyond his absorption, there was a hint of savagery which startled her, made her uneasy.

Hank had called boxing a civilized way of dueling. It seemed barbaric to her, this standing toe-to-toe and hitting another human being. If this was sparring, how would it compare to the real thing? The blows would be harder, more designed to do damage, she imagined. She wondered how much of Hank's previously hidden savagery would come to the fore then.

Kasey's brute nature was seldom hidden. The town had talked of it and he didn't care anything about keeping a control on himself. What if Kasey was good at fisticuffs—better than Hank?

She felt ridiculous, for up until now, she hadn't thought of Hank really getting hurt. But it had been Hank who suggested the fight as a means to settle Kasey's anger, and his own need for satisfaction. He had said it was a civilized alternative to gunplay.

Her stomach tightened. Danger was not new to her, nor was violence. But never before had she felt ill at the thought of the possibility of such deliberate damage being inflicted on someone she knew. The very sounds of the punches ringing in her ears made her shake. She wanted to yell at Hank and Jim to stop, and she wanted to demand Hank call the match off. It didn't seem to her that boxing was any more civilized than the roughhousing that was considered play in town. Furthermore, it could do a man real harm. How could he subject himself to it?

She wanted Hank to return to being the gentle, considerate man she had thought him.

Mariah turned to go. She had to think about this new side of Hank. All at once she was glad she'd agreed to have tea with Mrs. Kelly on Saturday afternoon. Now that she knew what boxing was about, she had no desire to see it.

There was no understanding men. There was also no understanding herself. . . .

10

Sunday morning brought a change in the ranch routine. The day was dark and dreary, with intermittent rain. Hank found himself wakened, suddenly, much later than usual.

"Have I overslept? I did not hear your call," he said apologetically as he watched Nate pull his dungarees on over his red stockinette underwear. In the bunk next to his, Jim stirred and sat up.

"Whazzat?" Nate shouted.

"We are late," Hank shouted back.

"Naw, ya ain't. It's Sunday. Elam's a religious man," Nate told him. "Him and Mariah goes to church. Ever'body else's on their own on Sundays."

"Ah, yes. I should have thought of that. What time do Mariah and Mr. Taggert leave?"

"Already gone."

Hank shot out of bed, grabbing his shaving gear. "Hurry, Jim. I must have my gray suit. And I want you to come, too."

Hank and Jim dressed hurriedly, to Nate's amused interest. "Ain't ya gonna take time fer Brown's flapjacks?"

"Nope," Hank replied.

"Reckon the young bulls always have to be chasin' the good-lookin' heifers."

Hank merely grinned as he wiped some lingering soap from his face. When it came time to don his footwear, Hank happened to catch the old man's gaze. Nate screwed his mouth into a pucker and reminded him, "Hats 'n' boots."

Hank instantly put aside his best pair of patent-leather ankle boots and instead stamped into the calf-high cowboy boots. With a glance, he saw that Jim had done the same. He slapped the wide-brimmed plainsman's hat on, and pulled it forward as Nate had showed him. Then he and Jim were out of the door with giant strides.

At the unpainted clapboard Trinity Methodist Church in Mead, Mariah stepped down from the buggy and straightened her bonnet while her grandfather secured the reins to the hitching post. They made their way inside slowly, to many greetings. Grandaddy was popular. Men respected him and there were a couple of widows who, since Granny died, always made their presence known in some way or other. Mariah didn't mind Mrs. Kelly, but she purely couldn't abide nosy old Mrs. Reed, who had attended only irregularly until Grandaddy was suddenly wifeless.

Happily, the little gossip circles wouldn't begin until after the service when, in fine weather, everyone congregated on the steps or in the front yard while the children raced around the building. The goings-on of Mead would be discussed then, social invitations given and accepted, and courtships begun, carried on, or ended.

Until lately, she frequently had enjoyed the social chatter. At least she wouldn't have to face the Sonyers family with all of the postmortem news of the big wedding, because they belonged to the brand-new Presbyterian church in the center of town. Neither would she have to see Caroline Benton, as she and her parents had changed their church allegiance soon after Caroline had become Myrtle Alice's best friend. So had Tommy.

But the Patricks were staunch members of the Methodist church. They would think it their Christian duty to visit with Elam. And there were the Whitlocks and other ranchers—although she liked Amity Whitlock and her children.

The morning weather was dull, which would discourage many of the talkers, thank goodness. Mariah planned to corral Grandaddy to leave quickly this morning. She just didn't feel up to more suppositions or suggestive questions.

Now, counting herself lucky to have been slowed down by only three "Good mornings," she slipped into a pew on the left. She kept her face forward and held on to the hymnbook as the service began. Beside her, Elam cleared his throat.

The first hymn was announced and she flipped the pages until she found it, then stood and lifted her voice to enter into the music joyously. The music was always her favorite part, especially the rousing tunes. Quietly, she tapped a foot. Say what she would about Mrs. Patrick, the lady knew how to pump that organ.

From the corner of her eye, Mariah noticed that

someone wanted to enter their pew. She nudged her grandfather and he moved down a seat. She followed, then sensed a tall presence slide in beside her.

"Move down another one, please, Mariah."

She looked up swiftly and stared. It was Hank, with Jim trailing. What in blue blazes were they doing there?

Hank merely gave her a gentle smile and the barest of winks. It was all she could do not to explode. Had he no sense? Whatever the speculations had been about their relationship, Mariah had held on to the belief that she could explain, after Hank left, that they had not suited each other after all. But sitting beside her in church, along with Grandaddy, was almost the same as a public announcement of intentions to wed.

Mariah felt as caught as a beaver in a steel trap. If there had been any hope at all of explaining Hank away to Grandaddy, it had just gone to hell in a hand basket.

The second stanza lead-in started. She missed it. Hank gripped the corner of her book, his long fingers nearly touching hers where they splayed against the back, and began to sing, his baritone ringing out as strongly as Grandaddy's, on her other side.

Mariah felt wedged between the two of them, although not touched by either. She had a sudden urge to climb to the top of the pew and make a mad leap down the row to escape. Now wouldn't that create a humdinger of a hullabaloo. A giggle nearly got away from her and she shook silently. Hank's fingertips touched hers, imparting their warmth and calm. Making every effort to cover her agitation, Mariah took a deep breath and caught up with the song in the middle of a phrase.

Mariah sat quietly, barely taking in the gist of the

sermon. An hour and a quarter later, the last amen rattled the rafters and the service was over. Hank stood and left the pew behind Jim. She followed.

"How do you do, Elam? And you, too, Mariah," Mrs. Patrick said. "Nice to see you at service, Mr. Clayton. I do hope you are enjoying your stay in our county."

Mariah returned the greeting politely while Hank introduced his friend Jim. And so it went, down the aisle. Either she or Elam made introductions until they finally shook the minister's hand and passed to the churchyard.

Outside, the weather had cleared considerably, much to Mariah's disgruntlement. She gave up the idea of leaving quickly when Elam stopped to talk once more, this time with Captain Whitlock and his wife Amity, and waited patiently, with Hank and Jim by her side.

The tall, handsome duo certainly attracted the ladies, she admitted in disgust. Betty Shoemaker and Laurie Franklin, both sixteen, sidled up to them for introductions. Mariah made them, barely hiding her impatience and amusement. Hank, she noticed, was unfailingly polite.

Amity broke away from Elam and her husband and approached them with the younger of her two sons, Adam, on her hip. Evelyn, her ten-year-old daughter, trailed behind, hand in hand with John Charles, the older Whitlock boy. Again, Mariah made introductions.

"Are you really gonna fight in a box, Mr. Clayton?" John Charles asked, looking up from his four-year-old height. He had dark brown eyes and dimples, like his mother, which played in his cheeks as he talked.

"Not exactly, John Charles. It is a sport called boxing."

"But is it in a box?"

Betty and Laurie giggled, and the rest of the adults smiled.

"Er, no. It is commonly called a ring."

John Charles frowned. "A ring? But—"

"That's enough now, John Charles," Amity admonished him. She turned to Hank and Jim with a smile. "I do hope you're successful, Mr. Clayton, Mr. Moore, on Saturday. I think Thaddeus plans to attend, and some of the others. So, Mariah, I'll see you at Catherine's?"

"Yes, I'll be there."

The group broke up and Mariah breathed a sigh of relief. She started once more toward the buggy, Hank cupping her elbow to escort her, and Jim a step behind.

"Mariah. Oh, Mariah, dear."

Mariah stopped short and squeezed her eyes tightly shut for a second. She should have known her luck would have run out by today, given all the times she'd been in Mead this week. The sugary voice behind her belonged to the one person she had laboriously avoided all week: Caroline Benton.

Mariah flashed a warning glance at Hank before the three of them turned around. Caroline, caught in the act of smoothing a dark blonde curl against her neck, blushed prettily. There was a suspiciously rapid rise and fall of her chest, as though she had rushed.

"Why, Caroline, what brings you down our way?"

"I had a message for dear Mrs. Patrick from Mother. About the Ladies Mission meeting on Thursday, you know. We are sewing for the poor, unfortunate orphans over in Denver, the dear, dear little things." Caroline flashed a sweet smile toward the men, her pale eyelashes fluttering only a little.

"It's dreadful, don't you think?" she said, applying for a masculine involvement by widening her eyes at the men, her hand limply resting against her cheek. "How the cities are overrun with waifs?"

"Indeed, ma'am."

"Quite."

Hank squeezed Mariah's elbow and she pasted on a smile while telling herself she had to do this up right rather than rattling off a "This's Hank and Jim."

"Caroline, may I present Circle T's guests from England, Mr. Henry Clayton and Mr. James Moore. Gentlemen, this is one of Mead's prime spin—" She felt Hank's fingers dig into her flesh. "Um, leading young ladies, Miss Caroline Benton."

Caroline arched her hand into the air in front of her and smiled. Sweetly. "How do you do. I'm so pleased to meet you."

Hank touched her fingers and bowed formally, giving an impish smile calculated to melt the most hardened heart. Jim took her fingers more firmly and bowed deeper, placing his lips for an instant on the back of her hand, which almost sent Caroline into the boughs. Mariah could practically see her swoon.

As soon as Caroline had breathlessly recovered, she went right on with what she wanted them to know.

"Also, the ladies are planning a spring dance to raise funds for our town hall. It will be a social event of great importance. I do hope you will extend your stay, gentlemen, until then. My dearest friend, Myrtle Alice, suggested it before she and her husband Tommy left on their wedding trip. She's very clever, don't you think?"

Mariah made a sound in her throat which she hoped would pass for a noncommittal agreement and not the snarl she wanted to emit. Caroline fluttered her lashes over her puzzled blue eyes, but when Mariah said nothing, she continued. "Well, I should pass along the word about the women's meeting."

Caroline turned away with obvious reluctance, then glanced provocatively over her shoulder. "Oh. Would you like to come to our meeting, Mariah?" She asked the question as though the thought had only just occurred to her, then answered in the same way. "No, I suppose not. You are always so very busy at the Circle T, aren't you? And the dance . . . oh, I'm *so* sorry, my dear. I forgot. Your grandfather doesn't approve of dancing, does he, being so straitlaced."

"Well, I—"

Once more, Caroline fluttered her lashes at the men. "But that shouldn't exclude you gentlemen. Mead would be very honored if you would attend."

"You are most kind, Miss Benton. We shall give all consideration to your invitation," said Hank.

"Indeed," Jim added.

Grandaddy broke away from the men he'd been talking with and climbed into the buggy. "Gotta go," Mariah muttered. "Nice seeing you, Caroline."

The two men bowed their farewell and followed her.

Mariah fumed all the way home. But at least her first meeting with Caroline after Tommy's wedding was over. It hadn't been nearly as painful as expected, only infuriating. Caroline's sweet pity had been spent more on trying to make headway with Hank and Jim than on wounding her.

"Why don't you purchase a new hat for Saturday, Mariah?"

"Don't need one," she replied shortly.

Hank had made the suggestion in an effort to lift her

spirits as they bunched a dozen cows together and drove them toward the lower grassland. He wondered what had put her out-of-sorts. She hadn't said more than was absolutely necessary all morning, snapping out orders as though she had a toothache. He and Jim had been hard put to keep up with her, too. If a cow or calf bolted or straggled, she bolted after it as though shot out of a cannon, throwing them a directive to guard the rear of the small herd. They were eating dust.

Hank moved a few yards to the outer edge of the herd, where the air was clearer. While they were learning a lot about cattle driving, Hank had the distinct impression he had lost ground somewhere with Mariah. He wondered if it had anything to do with the night before. She had come by so quietly again while he and Jim were engaged in sparring that by the time he had become aware of her, he'd seen only her back as she was leaving. It puzzled him, after her earlier enthusiasm.

Or her upset could have had something to do with yesterday morning, though he had been the epitome of politeness and attention and could not imagine what she could have objected to. But she had disappeared right after they arrived home from church and he had seen nothing except that glimpse of her back until this morning.

Now he tried again. "You would look wonderful in something which required an upswept hairstyle. Perhaps in a royal blue, to enhance your hair."

She gave him a curious look. Royal blue was Myrtle Alice's color. "Haven't the time to shop," she said, then dashed after a feisty heifer. She herded the animal slowly back into the bunch.

Hank didn't understand Mariah's reluctance. A new bonnet had always cheered his mother, and she never turned down an opportunity to buy one. And a new bonnet always necessitated the purchase of a new dress to match. Every woman of his acquaintance liked purchasing new clothing.

Perhaps Mariah was unsure of herself. Then again, she hadn't shown much interest in fashion. He assumed it was because she was low on funds.

That was it, of course.

His female friends had frequently commended him on his good taste in women's fashion—especially when he paid for them—and he had never minded visiting the women's shops. "I will help you choose one," he said, assuming she would understand his subtle offer. "I saw a hat and sempstress shop in Mead."

Mariah was politely firm. "I'll wear what I have, thank you."

Hank let the matter drop for the moment; he would have to approach it from another direction. Meanwhile, he wanted to find out what was troubling her. He had thought they'd addressed all her concerns the other night, but when they'd met at breakfast this morning, she had retreated into spare responses to his conversation.

"Miss Mariah certainly rides well, doesn't she, sir?" Jim said with admiration as she galloped after two more cows.

"Like a female centaur," Hank answered absently while following her with his gaze. "And remember to call me Hank, please."

"Sorry, Hank." Jim glanced at his employer. They had been adventuring together going on ten years, and he had seen Master Henry through difficulties and triumphs alike. But this was the first time the gallant had pretended to be a plain bloke. It was for the girl, of course. Henry had had a normal interest in women and gone to great lengths for one or two in the past.

This was also the first time Henry had entered into a completely different life, and Mariah was nothing like his usual choice in women. Furthermore, there was a look in his eyes when Mariah was about that Jim had never seen before. It was more than a casual sexual interest, he thought, although that was certainly present. One couldn't help wondering.

They rode along in silence. At a distance, Mariah was waving her lariat to get the cattle to move in the direction she wanted them to go.

"Jim, did you notice Mariah watching us spar last night?" Hank suddenly asked.

"Yes, I saw her."

"Was she upset, do you think, or put off in some way?"

"Actually, I thought her very quiet, which I understand is rather uncharacteristic of her."

Hank nodded. "That's just it. Mariah is rather a hoyden, albeit a charming one. It is unlike her to withhold her opinion on anything."

"So it would seem."

"And she wanted most earnestly to attend the match on Saturday," Hank continued. "I barely convinced her it would be in her best interests to stay away—you know, to stay in the respectable ladies' good graces and all that. As a substitute I invited her to watch the sparring. I thought she would almost be under our feet and overflowing with questions after, but . . ." He trailed off, shaking his head.

"I don't think she liked the sport much. She looked somewhat upset when she left."

Hank shook his head. "That is odd. Mariah, unlike most women, is not a shrinking violet. She neither pulls away at unpleasant tasks nor scares easily. You should have seen her stand beside me, Jim, when I faced off with that hooligan who calls himself a gamester. I am convinced she would have fought like a tigress that night if it had come to blows."

"But you know, Master Henry, uh, Hank, almost anyone would fight in a fit of passion. For something or someone they deeply care about. However, a cold, deliberate round of fisticuffs is very different. Many would find it unpleasant. Do you recall my sister? I offered to let her come with me to a match once and she said it was the most repulsive thing she could imagine, two men beating on each other for sport."

"Ahh . . . Quite so. I had not considered it in that light. Thank you, Jim."

Mariah rejoined them and pushed the new beeves into the herd. "When we get this bunch down to the river we'll go up the other draw. No telling how many we'll find there. As it is, Grandaddy will be pleased that there're more than we estimated. We'll start branding in a few days."

"Make it after the fight," Hank said. "After Jim and I are done sparring at night." He deliberately brought the subject up to catch her reaction. She flashed him a glance that puzzled him, one of question and doubt, and it dawned on him that Jim was right. Mariah hadn't liked what she saw last night. For some reason it had caused her to regard him differently.

"There's no need to wait," she insisted.

"I would like to learn the process so I may help, Mariah. But right now I have to concentrate on the match."

"So do what you have to do," she snapped. "But I'm going to begin branding as soon as possible. Nate and I will do it."

"Look at me, Mariah. What's the matter? What is bothering you?"

"I thought you could read my mind."

"I can guess at a lot."

"Then you have no need for me to tell you." She kicked her mount into a lope and moved toward the ravine.

Telling Jim to stay with the cattle, Hank followed.

Mariah knew he was behind her. She ignored him as she entered the wide vee cut in the earth. Brush and small trees filled the back end and she was sure cattle could be found there.

Hank rode up beside her. "All right, give over. What have I done to upset you? Are you still perturbed about the coming match?"

"I guess I am." More than she wanted to admit, and it had nothing to do with missing out on an entertainment. But she couldn't tell him of the other thing that had thrown her for a loop. She'd been jealous of Caroline yesterday, of all people. She hated the feeling, but there it was. First Myrtle Alice and now Caroline.

"I thought we agreed it would be better if you did not go."

"It's all right. I don't want to go anymore."

"What changed your mind?"

"You did. Last night."

Hank quietly reached out and took her reins. The horses slowed, then stopped.

"You didn't like the sparring, is that it?"

She shook her head.

"What was it that distressed you?"

"I don't know, really. I—I think I expected . . . It wasn't anything like I thought it would be. I've seen fistfights a time or two. I thought it would be something like that. The other day when I was in town, someone asked me if you were mean enough to hold your own against Kasey. It made me right peevish, for I thought you wouldn't know how to be mean. But when you and Jim were practicing, you . . . you somehow changed. A look in your eyes . . ."

There had been a look in his eye for Caroline, too, she thought.

"Mariah, after watching last night you must realize I have been trained to fight. And by some of the best in England and Europe, I might add. Part of that training is to divorce yourself from all of your emotions at the time of your contest. A man has to concentrate all his ability and power on what he can do to his opponent and at the same time protect his own body. It is actually an artful sport."

"It's a blood sport, no better than a shootout and likely just as damaging!" she cried passionately. "Someone could be hurt badly or killed. How could you think it would be better to—to indulge yourself with this 'boxing' than to face Kasey with a gun?"

"Had you no notion of what I had been talking of, then?"

She shook her head. "Not 'til last night."

"I am sorry, my dear, for not warning you. You see now why most women find it distasteful."

"I suppose I do." That, at least, was something she most likely held in common with Caroline. "I sure wish we'd never run back into Mead after we slipped away from those coyotes. Then we could've avoided all this. But Kasey would've hunted for you the next day, probably."

"Either way, it looked as though nothing less than a standoff would do to appease him. I realized I would more than likely have the advantage when I turned his challenge back on him. Shall I call it off?"

"No! No. You have to finish it. Only I wish . . ."

Hank felt stirred by her wistful murmur. "What?"

"It's too unpredictable. Anything could happen." Mariah pulled her reins free and kneed her mount to move forward. "And you like it too much."

Her voice floated over her shoulder with a sigh. Hank wasn't completely sure he had heard her correctly, but the concern in her tone was evidence of more than a casual caring. He frowned in thought, then hurried after her as realization hit him. Mariah's feelings for Tommy must have been only childhood emotions. He was certain of it, for now he was just as certain that she was falling in love with him.

He breathed deeply of the elation that that knowledge sent roaring through him.

Mariah climbed halfway up the slope, trying to concentrate on watching for cattle. She heard a snort and a piercing whinny and lifted her gaze. There stood the wild gray stallion with the black mane. She pulled to a halt and stared.

The rascal was after more mares. The horse she rode today, a four-year-old mare named Flirt, danced nervously at the stallion's call.

Hank caught up to her, ready to spill over with something else he wanted to say. She diverted him with, "Shh. Look, Hank, there."

He stilled and followed the line of her gaze. "The gray! What is he doing here? And where are his mares?"

"Don't know where his mares are, but it's normal for a mustang herd to have a territory. Guess this fella's curious about what's over the mountain."

The gray pawed the earth, half reared in challenge, then raced away. Hank watched the animal in fascination. "He sure is a wild one."

"Uh-huh. He'd be the devil to tame."

"He has some beautiful lines. Wonder if we could go after him. I have thought of it ever since we saw him the other day."

Mariah stared at Hank. "You want that horse?"

"I wouldn't mind owning him. Would you train him for me? Or teach me how to do it?"

"I'm not sure he'd ever gentle down, Hank. Might be he would need a professional bronc buster."

"I would hate to see his spirit broken."

"Once in a while you find a horse that can't be broken. Fireball there might be one of them."

"Fireball. You have named him, have you? Well, it is appropriate. Mariah, I will pay you to try your hand with Fireball. You can take as long as you need to gentle him. We can go after him next week, after the fight."

Mariah's gloomy mood fled. Going after the gray would surely be more rigorous than finding the black mare, and more exciting. They'd have to prepare well, for she suspected the stallion was a great deal more cunning than most.

No one before Hank had ever offered Mariah a wage for her work and though she had refused his similar offer the first time, all her earlier objections now fled. The reasons for them were becoming far too confused in her mind anyway.

"Providing we can catch him, it's a deal. But it'll have to wait 'til after branding."

"All right," Hank readily agreed. "And after the fight."

The longer he had an excuse to remain at the ranch, the better.

11

The days that followed were the stuff of routine ranch life. Hank and Jim tumbled out of bed at the crack of dawn, then rode out with Mariah for most of the day. The Western saddle, with its horn, felt familiar to them now, and both Hank and Jim discovered its real purpose.

On Tuesday Mariah led them a merry chase in rounding up extra horses from their previous remuda, which had run free over the winter. There weren't many, and three mares were in foal. Mariah felt that what they had was not enough to make up a real string for a full-scale working cowhand. However, three mounts for each man for trade-offs, to allow the horses to rest between use, would have to do. As long as Hank and Jim were there for only the month, she figured they could get by.

The days were lengthening, so after supper that night, Mariah began gentling the horses anew. Hank sat on the corral fence and watched, fascinated. Mariah didn't mind.

He was impressed by her easy movements and tender care. When full dark descended, he walked her back to the house, wanting all the while to pull her into his arms and kiss her. It was the only time he'd had her alone since those first two days. But Elam walked up the path from the barn and reminded him that Jim was waiting on him, and his opportunity was lost.

Mariah busied herself with the fresh horses again on Wednesday, and Hank and Jim helped where they could, to Nate's cackling cheers and gleeful instructions from the sidelines.

Hank had sometimes assisted in the care of his blooded stock at home, but only casually. Now his respect for his own employees went up several notches. At one point, when both he and Jim had hung on to one particularly rambunctious mount for Mariah, Hank caught Jim's impish grin, his formal demeanor completely gone now. Hank chuckled in return. They were both dirty, sweaty, and thoroughly disheveled. The two exchanged jokes about applying to be stable boys at the family estate, Ackerley Hall.

The blacksmith came on Thursday and spent the entire day shoeing horses. Afterward, Elam stated he would take care of the remuda, and although Hank could tell that Mariah wanted to argue with him, she didn't. Nate didn't seem to mind being relegated to the chores closer to home, like caring for the cow and chickens and mucking out the barn.

For Mariah, since Brown had taken over the cooking chores, the days had become more manageable, as they had for her grandfather, also. Elam tired easily, though he denied it most of the time. Mariah instructed Nate to keep an eye on him the next day when they started plowing the two fields set aside for planting grain. Nate promised not to let Elam do too much.

"But I reckon atween us we can get 'er done, Mariah. Plowin' was always a challenge anyways. Hated it in my younger days. Now I don't mind so bad. Elam an' I c'n spell each other. "

Hank, behind in his correspondence, went immediately after supper to dash off some needed communications. Jim would go into town the next morning to finalize all the arrangements for the boxing match and to take care of other business.

"Are you sure you don't want to go to town yourself? Aren't you missing the sight of all those people?" Mariah asked him at breakfast on Friday with a teasing gleam in her eyes.

Brown set a platter of plate-sized flapjacks on the table beside the one of evenly crisped bacon, and Mariah helped herself liberally. She might have complained about hiring Brown, but she wasn't fool enough not to appreciate what he could do with the old cookstove in the room next to the bunkhouse. That was where all the meals were taken now.

"A big-city tenderfoot like you must be getting bored with the wide-open plains by now, with nothing but animals to see and the same faces each day," she added.

"The country has its compensations, and it depends on the faces," he replied, gazing at her. "But I do miss a good poker game now and again."

Mariah flushed, uncomfortably aware of the whole table of men listening, but tossed back, "Huh! What you miss is trouble and 'adventure.'"

"There are adventures, and then there are adventures," he said enigmatically. Something in his expression made her think of the kisses they'd shared.

She took refuge in a healthy bite of her flapjacks.

"What's on your mind fer today, Mariah?" Elam asked.

"Well, as you agreed to wait on the branding," she said, flashing a half-vexed glance at Hank, knowing he'd elicited that promise from her grandfather behind her back, "I think I'll ride line fence. I haven't checked past the halfway point yet this spring."

"Good idea," the old man agreed. "Nate 'n' I'll finish the plowing so we can afford the day off tomorrow."

Underneath his composure, Hank was elated. That meant he would ride with Mariah. Alone. For the whole day. He had missed it, being with her without a chaperon. Those first two days of freedom already seemed too distant.

He didn't question his intentions too closely, and for the moment buried any conscious thought about the possibility of doing harm. He merely recognized that he had to have a taste of her again, to feel her body pressed into his. His desire for this auburn-haired slip of a girl had tripled.

His thoughts brought him to such an entanglement of urgent eagerness that he suddenly had to look down at his plate, lest anyone guess them.

Later, Mariah led him along the one line of fence the Circle T boasted, explaining it had been put up two years previously when they'd had trouble with one of the big ranches overrunning their land.

"Grandaddy worked mighty hard toward keeping peace—for two long years he tried reasoning with the Triple Bar X before we put up the bobwire fence," she told him. "Ranchers don't like bobwire as a rule, but if it's necessary, they'll put up with it."

"We use fencing in England, but not barbed wire. However, we too have had our troubles over fencing."

"Grandaddy likes to get along with everyone. The Triple Bar X used to belong to Tommy's uncle, and everything was fine between him and my grandparents. That's how Tommy and I always had so much time together. But then, Tommy's uncle died and his aunt sold the place and moved east. Left Tommy flat. Tommy was plumb disappointed down to his boots not to have inherited it, and mad as a hornet, too. He'd been led to believe . . . But he and his aunt didn't like each other much.

"Anyway, Tommy had a little money from his father, but not enough to buy out his aunt, so when the new owners came in, he moved to town and invested in the hardware store there in Mead, with Matthew Logan. Then last fall he went to work for Mr. Sonyers at the bank."

She fell abruptly silent. Hank remained patient. Underneath her recounting, he sensed the pain of her own abandonment. Mariah had thought Tommy would join her on the Circle T.

After a moment, she returned to her story of how the fence came to be put up.

"Then the Triple Bar X's new owners, the Brills, started running more cattle and we couldn't keep them from pushing onto our graze, mixing with our herd. Took time to separate them, and our man-power was already low. Grandaddy couldn't get much cooperation from Brill; the only time I ever saw my grandaddy that mad was when he discovered Brill's men branding some of our calves, and when he complained, Mr. Brill merely shrugged and said, 'So I got a few of yours—you probably got a few of mine.' I thought Grandaddy would explode."

"I take it you could never arrive at an appropriate accounting?"

Mariah gave a sigh, signaling her sense of defeat. "No. Grandaddy didn't argue anymore. Granny had just died the year before, you see, and Grandaddy didn't have the heart to take on a fight. I heard him tell Nate it wasn't worth a range war. We just borrowed the money to put up the fence."

"Did that solve the problem?"

"Not altogether. We have to watch that back end. It's where the Circle T strings wire along its deepest border, north of those breaks we were in the other day. Sometimes mysterious things happen in that back corner."

"Why hasn't Elam applied to the law?"

"Oh, he has, right enough, and we have high hopes that things will straighten out now that Thorndyke Sands has come to Mead to back up the sheriff. But what we need is more men to ride line often enough to discourage freewheeling ways. I just can't get to it every week."

They reached the crest of a low rise, where a small tree looked as though it were growing out of the wire. Beside it lay a scattering of rock. Mariah looked at it in disgust before climbing down. "See? This is pure mischief. I piled these stones myself last fall, right after first frost. Now somebody's gone and toppled my mark."

Hank dismounted and helped her rebuild the small mound. "What do the stones signify?"

"It's our halfway mark. Doesn't mean anything to anyone but us—no one has anything to gain by pulling it apart. But since the fence went up, little things like this have happened."

They rode on, tightening the wire, checking post stability, and hammering new staples against the wire into posts where extra security was needed. Twice, they found a break. Mariah grimly paced for several yards along each side of the downed fence, looking at the ground for clues as to how the breaks had happened.

The first one, Mariah decided, an animal had pushed too hard against a weak post, thus taking both post and wire down. She studied the second break a long moment.

Hank picked up a curled wire string and fingered the end. "It looks as though it was cut with wire cutters," he remarked.

"Yep, reckon it was, but months back. In the winter sometime, I think. Those Brills are nothing better than double-dealing wolves. They know we've been shorthanded at the Circle T this year." That was putting it mildly. They'd had only old Nate with them since Granny died. "If we find their brand on our graze . . ."

"What will you do?"

"Get mad and stomp the ground some, I suppose. Then quietly drive them back to their own range."

"That doesn't sound like you, Mariah."

"I didn't say it was what I'd want to do. But if we bring it into the open, a fight would be hard to avoid. We don't have the resources to stand up to a big outfit like that." She didn't know what she would do if it did come to a showdown. Certain sure, Grandaddy wasn't up to it.

When she remounted, Mariah set her mouth against the blue language she wanted to explode into the air. She'd have to find a way to get out to this corner more often. She didn't think their neighbors would be foolhardy enough to try cutting her fence again if they thought they'd get caught at it. They couldn't claim innocence, then, in not knowing whose cow a baby suckled from.

"But we haven't found any brand other than the Circle T's, Mariah."

"That's not to say we won't."

From then on they took time to check brands on every cow they saw as they rode. Fortunately, all belonged to the Circle T. Even though puzzled and still suspicious, Mariah's mood lifted when she realized they'd routed more cattle than she'd counted on from this section.

Through a few clouds, the sun rose to stand straight over them, and then started its descent before they reached the end of the wire, where it was anchored in a mammoth rock formation.

Hank watched the work of nature as they approached. The long gray stone ascended at a slant to about thirty feet in height and extended south about a hundred yards before sloping again to meet the rolling plain. Stunted trees grew from cracks in its surface and a few thin streams of water flowed from unseen sources. Mostly the stone was stark and bare.

When he twisted in his saddle to view the entire expanse, he realized they were above the series of breaks and ravine area where they had hunted cattle before. He wondered how the land lay beyond what he could see, for the mountains seemed to curl close against the rock formation's back.

"Let's rest here, Mariah." He brought Patches to a halt.

"All right. We can water the horses there, at the base. It's plentiful in spring."

"Mmm. Can we climb it?"

"The Lizard's Tail? That's what we call it."

"Appropriate."

"Uh-huh. As to climbing it, Grandaddy said he did it a couple of times. Tommy and I always wanted to, but we never had the time or the chance."

At last, something she hadn't done with Tommy. "Has your grandfather or anyone else explored the area?"

"Oh, yes. A time back. The stone drops a bit on the other side, then the land levels a mite before the real mountains start. Grandaddy said there's a patch of grass in the level spot, but it wouldn't pay to try putting cattle on it because it would be too small for the effort of getting the cows to it. And getting them down would be even harder, maybe."

"I see. Still, it would be fun to explore it, don't you think?"

"Yes, someday."

"We'll do it," he said emphatically.

Hank amazed her. He talked as if he were going to be around for a long time and there were no obstacles to doing exactly what he wanted to do. Furthermore, he assumed everyone would jump to do it. The habit was sometimes annoying. "We're pretty busy in spring. Too much to do to take time off for a jaunt."

"We'll plan our days carefully. Besides, you promised to show me around, remember?"

"I suppose I did." She admitted to herself that she'd wanted to do it for ages, and the prospect sounded exciting.

They walked their mounts to where a tiny ribbon of water made the rock glisten and glitter as it tumbled to the ground. They followed it to where it joined a larger flow, then dismounted, and let the horses drink.

Mariah wrapped her reins loosely around her pommel and walked a few paces upstream before dropping to her knees. Filling her cupped hands, she drank. Hank knelt beside her and did the same.

"It tastes of minerals," he remarked.

"Yeah. Copper and iron, Grandaddy says."

Hank gently swished another gulp around his mouth before swallowing. "Ever have it analyzed?"

"No, I don't think so. Grandaddy was never interested." Assuming that he was wondering about all the gold and silver that had been mined in the state, she said, "All the Colorado pay ore has been found higher and deeper in the mountains. I don't think there's any here."

"Mmm. There are the obvious precious metals, and then there are others," he said slowly, "less glittering but no less valuable." It was the same way he'd said that funny thing about faces and adventures, Mariah thought.

The afternoon breeze held the promise of warmer days ahead. Mariah removed her hat and ran her fingers through her hair. Hank seemed to like the place, she noted. He reclined, folding his arms behind his head, and stared at the blue sky, appearing relaxed and perfectly content.

She sat beside him, her arms circling her knees. After a moment she spoke. "Are you worried about the match tomorrow?"

She no longer thought him soft, but she still doubted he was aware of how unscrupulous Kasey and men like him could be. All week she had suppressed her worries over what would happen if Kasey ignored all the rules Hank was used to. A snake like Kasey could be counted on to be underhanded.

"No," Hank replied.

"Aren't you . . ."

"What?"

"Oh . . . scared of getting hurt?"

"I have taken my share of licks. I heal. Do you still think I can't hold my own against Kasey?"

"No, I don't think that anymore. Unless it would be with a gun or an ambush, like sneaking up behind you, or five against one, as it was that night."

He turned onto his side and propped his head in his hand. "Do you think I am so naive I would not be on guard for that? Or that I am so pudding-minded as not to prepare for such a possibility?"

"I think . . ." She wasn't sure what she thought. She pulled a blade of grass and started to strip it apart with fierce strokes.

Possibility or eventuality? The distinction made little difference to her insides; they tightened into a tidy knot just from her thinking about it. Hank was a gambler, and a daring man as well. Sooner or later, hanging about in saloons, looking for adventure, he'd get himself hurt or killed—if not by Kasey, then by someone like him.

Hell's bells, there she went again, letting herself fret over a man. She tossed the shredded bits of grass down, thoroughly disgusted with herself. She wished she could either pack him off immediately so she could forget about him entirely or keep him safe under her eagle eye.

"I think you won't believe in me until I win," he murmured, watching her action with the grass.

She said nothing, but snatched another blade from the grass clump in front of her.

"Mariah?"

She wouldn't look at him, either.

"Mariah."

The huskiness in his voice was soft and telling. The sound of it brushed along her nerve ends gently, with enticement as its siren melody. Then his fingertips began an accompanying light touch on the back of her hand while his thumb circled the soft skin at the juncture between her thumb and forefinger.

She should pull away. Yes, she should . . . but she wanted it to continue. She wanted the soothing, seductive feel of his hands touching her.

"Mariah . . ." He opened her palm, gently blew the grass from it, and brought it to his mouth. She felt the soft heat of his lips, a tiny scrape of his teeth, and finally the quick stroke of his tongue. The erotic sensations shot all the way through her body.

She told herself once more that she should stop it, should avoid letting herself give in to these feelings which Hank so easily called forth. But she didn't. She couldn't.

Then he leaned forward and kissed her mouth. She received it with a mixture of joy, wonder, and . . . guilt. She had wondered if she would feel the same as last time, experience the same intense flooding of desire. Now she knew it could be even more. She had scolded herself for thinking too much about it. And now she knew she was truly a fool, for his lips and hands were capable of making her forget herself totally—or rather, become more aware. She felt on the edge of falling into a great canyon of passion.

"Hank . . ." she mumbled when he went to pull her completely into his arms. She barely had the strength to protest.

"Don't pull away, love," he said, tightening his hold.

"Please."

"Yes, please."

The plaintive urge in his voice trapped her. Or maybe that was only an excuse. She gave in to his hands—warm on her back where they had slid between her jacket and thin cotton shirt—and his mouth, which gave her the sweetest, most reckless thrill of her entire life. Even his nose, pressed into her cheek as he pulled her down to lie prone against him, was a contact she welcomed.

His hand slid slowly lower and cupped a buttock a moment before he lifted her, his fingers locked around her thigh, to fit along his length. Through her jeans, she felt his heat clear to her bones, felt his arousal.

Mariah broke the kiss and rested her forehead against his chin. "Hank, please don't," she choked out past the constriction in her throat.

He slowly lifted his hand from her leg and returned it to her waist. Then he tightened his embrace around her. She felt so right this way, molded into his arms, slender yet womanly. And this place in the sunshine, underneath the towering stone, was a perfect setting for loving. "You know I want to make love to you like crazy. . . ."

She nodded, her forehead rubbing against his chin.

"You want me, too." He said it as if it was a statement of fact, not a question.

Again, she nodded, her nose brushing against his jaw.

Even that small motion felt like a piece of heaven. "Then why do you stop me? Why won't you let me make love to you?"

"Because I . . . I couldn't bear it if you . . . we . . . um, made love . . . when you're going to be moving on soon. It would be shattering."

"But I am here now. I want you now." He held his fierce need to smother her objections and strip her bare under tenuous control. His body cried out to feel hers without barriers. Instead, he removed one hand from her back and brought his knuckles up to caress her cheek coaxingly. "You are so vital, so full of life. I need you. . . . Don't turn me away, darling."

"I can't, not now. It's too soon. In time . . ."

"Time . . . If we lose this time it may never come again. We can't know what will happen in the future."

Her reaction wasn't quite what he expected. She raised her head swiftly, her eyes wide. "Don't I know it. I gave Tommy my first kisses and then he up and married another woman. It hurt too much and made me feel like a fool."

Tommy! That damned interloper. Hank stilled his hand, furious that he hadn't banished the man from her mind. But it brought forth another thought, one he didn't like. "Are kisses the extent of what you gave Tommy?" he asked cautiously.

"The extent of— Why, of course." Mariah pushed herself away, looking down at Hank in astonishment. His eyes reflected strangely, a darker gray than usual. They asked questions. "What? Did you think I had done, um, everything a husband and wife do with Tommy?"

"Well . . ."

She jumped up, scowling. "I loved Tommy and I wanted and expected to marry him but I wouldn't have shamed my granny or grandaddy's teachings like that. Or myself."

He stood up to face her. "Calm down, Mariah, I didn't mean to insult you. There is no shame in giving yourself to someone you love. You wouldn't be the first to, er, anticipate the wedding vows. Many a bride has gone to the altar with a babe already in the womb."

"I know that. It happens, right enough, and I think folks ought to be more forgiving when young couples can't hold out. But—but I did. . . . Hold out, I mean. Oh, shucks and damnation. I didn't *do that* with Tommy. And anyway, what about the women who do give in and then get left high and dry when the man just ups and walks away? What happens if there's a baby? What happens to them then?"

"Is that what you expect from me?"

She went on as though she hadn't heard him. "It might've happened to me if I'd made love with Tommy. He—he didn't w-want m-me in the end."

"Would he not have married you?"

"Who knows, now. In any case, he didn't, did he?"

"He did not love you," he stated with some satisfaction.

"Reckon not enough." Her tone was forlorn. "Not as much as he loved Myrtle Alice Sonyers, anyway. But he once said he did."

"But, Mariah, that is not me."

"How do you know? Have you never made love, or promises, lightly? Knowing you'd never keep them and didn't *truly* care about how the woman felt, and then walked away without a backward glance?"

He looked at her in astonishment. He could not answer such a question. A gentleman never divulged information of love affairs to a young female of good standing. Of course he had . . . well, perhaps one could not call it making love. He'd had liaisons. But his women all knew the game; he had been honest in his dealings and they had been satisfied with the money and gifts he gave them along with his loving. They knew he had never . . . *loved* them.

But Mariah . . . She was a different kind of female from the ones he knew. She expected not only the loving, but love.

"Don't you see? If we made love . . . if we gave in to this passion and then you left, what would I do?"

"I don't suppose . . ." Again, he could not answer.

She shook her head. "I don't want to share only a few days or weeks of a man's life. I want to share a lifetime, as Granny and Grandaddy did. Face it, Hank. When your adventuring in Mead is done, you'll leave. Maybe you'll leave this country altogether to go back to England."

They stared at each other, he unwilling to admit the truth of her statement and she wanting to hear above all things the denial of it.

The moment stretched. It was the first time Mariah had ever seen Hank stumble with uncertainty.

"I would never leave without giving you my direction."

"Is that what you've done with that girl from Boston? Did you make love to her and then leave a forwarding address? Were there any promises, or anything else, left behind?"

Half promises, he admitted to himself silently, for he had let it be known he was looking for a rich wife, and had courted the wealthy heiress. He could not offer a title like his brother, but his family name was worth something. After all, it was one of the reasons he had come to America. It seemed shameful, now, to admit it to Mariah, but by English and European standards it was the thing to do for a younger son. Marry for wealth and position.

But no, he had not made love to the stiff, very correct, very *cold* Edith.

"Boston?" Hank asked with a slight frown, a delaying tactic. He was on shaky ground. "How do you know about Edith?"

So that was her name. Only now did Mariah admit even to herself that she'd had any curiosity about it. "That letter in your wallet. When I searched it for the poker crowd."

"Mmm. Edith and her family are among those I visited in the East. Do I have to account for every young woman I know?"

Mariah began to roughly brush loose dirt from where it clung to her denim pants, her eyes lowered to her task. "Not to me, Hank; we've never exchanged a real 'I'll-be-yours-if-you'll-be-mine.' Everything has been playacting. You don't owe me an accounting of the women you've, um, um . . ."

"Made love to," he supplied with a slow return of his humor.

"That too. Most of what you men do I think is . . . is . . ." She felt the heat climb her cheeks. This altogether honesty was getting her into more than a little trouble. Again. She should have shut up five minutes ago.

"Lust?"

"Uh-huh. I guess I know now that girls can feel it too. Or at least that *you* can make *me* feel . . ." Mariah worked hard to lighten her tone. "But let's you and I agree to only be friends for the rest of the time you're here, Hank. That way, when you leave, it will be with no regrets for either of us."

It might be with no regrets, Mariah thought, but

she would be left with a mountain of might-have-beens. However, if she didn't hold on tight to her emotions now, she'd be worse off than ever she was after Tommy's defection.

Hank watched her mount her horse with a graceful leap. She seemed totally ignorant of his unsettled emotions and regrets—regrets he already felt in the here and now. "Friends," she'd said? Not likely. Never merely friends, with all that laughter, fire, and passion between them, ready to burst into flames.

However did she think that would be so easy to ignore? He didn't plan on allowing her to put him aside so blithely.

12

Little was said at breakfast the next morning. It seemed that everyone was thinking about the big event in front of them—the boxing match. The men rushed to finish chores, even Grandaddy. By midmorning, Mariah felt deserted, but no less excited. She had agreed to go to Mrs. Kelly's tea party, but that didn't mean she had to be ignorant about what eighty percent of the town would probably be doing.

As for the match itself, her feelings were ambivalent. She already knew she didn't like the nature of the sport, especially because Hank might get hurt, but at the same time she wanted to see him in action. He had said he knew what he was doing and assured her he could hold his own. She wanted to see Hank win, and beyond that, she couldn't stand the thought of missing out on anything.

After the men cleared out, she took her time in bathing and dressing. Her blue-gray outfit, freshly washed and pressed as a courtesy from Brown, was laid out on her narrow bed in the tiny upstairs room which had been hers since she was ten. After she dressed, she turned this way and that in front of the old, cracked mirror, wishing the dress were more the color of spring grass than the dull hue it was. But the only other dress she had that was decent was the made-over black and it wasn't a bit flattering. No, she'd make do with this one.

She should try to do something different with her hair, though. There was a lot of natural curl in it, if only she knew how to make it work for her. Usually it had a mind of its own. On Sundays, she pulled it back and piled it all under her bonnet for church, which was usually the only place she had to dress up for.

Mariah leaned over from the waist, twisted her still damp hair into a long rope, and flopped it forward. Rose, who ran The Golden Rose saloon, wore her hair up kind of like this, with curls dripping down her forehead, and Hank had suggested an upswept style when he wanted her to buy a new hat. It must be the fashion.

She straightened. A foot of hair dangled in her face. It mightn't look too bad. Now where had she seen Granny's curling iron?

By the time she was ready to leave, Mariah felt quite proud of her efforts. She'd burnt herself only once, and the resulting curls were, if not as perfectly round and dainty as Myrtle Alice's, at least bouncy. The problem was, they wouldn't stay in their pins. She needed the bonnet.

Carefully, she eased it onto the back of her head and pulled the narrow brim forward. It pushed the curls forward, too, and one of them fell just at her brow. She turned her head as she tied the ribbons. Yes, this should do it.

She tripped out of the house and down to the barn and stopped dead. Lulubelle and the buggy were gone.

Grandaddy had obviously taken them. He had begun to use the buggy quite frequently, because it was an easier ride and he was so often tired. Mariah didn't mind—not usually, anyway. But today she had planned to arrive at that danged tea party as a lady.

Well, there was nothing else but Skedaddle, and she was already late.

She ran down to the corral and whistled. Skedaddle hadn't been ridden in a few days and snorted in disdain. The five other horses in the enclosure moved to the far side. She put her little finger between her teeth and gave a sharper command. But Skedaddle tossed his head as though to say he simply wasn't in the mood to be cooperative. "Are you going to make me sorry that you're my favorite, you dad-blasted animal?" she scolded.

It took her another fifteen minutes to climb through the rails, separate the roan from the others, saddle him, and mount. She stood in the stirrups to arrange her skirts. They were full enough to cover most of her legs, but she was reminded of how Granny had frowned on her riding astride. So would Mrs. Benton and Mrs. Patrick. She leaned sideways to look. Yep, a fair amount of ankle did show. She should've worn her boots.

So much for putting her best foot forward. Her black slippers did look nice, though, and her apparel shouldn't embarrass Grandaddy or anyone.

Mariah put Skedaddle into a lope to make up for lost time, then slowed to a sedate walk as she approached town. The moment she neared Mead she knew the boxing match had to be the shindig of the spring, at least for the men. The town looked as good as on the Fourth of July, and teemed with men of all types—cowboys, ranchers, farmers, freighters, hunters, and miners. The stores and saloons had their doors open and the sidewalks looked festive with signs. Even the horse races last year hadn't drawn this much interest, Mariah thought in amazement.

She wondered what the crowd was like around the livery stable, where the match would be held. It couldn't hurt anything to ride that way, merely to take a peek.

Directing Skedaddle down a side street, she circled the long way around the center of town to come up to the livery from the back. The place was already surrounded with horses, buckboards, and buggies, and men stood around in clumps, waiting. She strained to see if she could spot Grandaddy or Nate. Or Jim . . . or Hank. But none of them was in sight.

Sighing with disappointment, Mariah reckoned she'd better continue on to Mrs. Kelly's before someone paid her too much attention. The ladies would be watching for her.

The small house that Mrs. Kelly occupied already held a dozen women and various children. Mariah dutifully smiled, returned greetings, and made her way to the hostess's side to accept a cup of tea. She stood awkwardly and sipped the scalding brew, wishing for all the world that she could walk right on through the house and out the kitchen door. She'd rather be training the black mare than drinking tea.

Confound it, she'd rather attend that dad-blamed boxing match.

Pulling herself in sharply, Mariah was reminded that she was there to build a reputation for ladylike behavior. She gazed around the room and tallied her choices for company. Five older women, three under thirty, and a handful who could be counted as girls of marriageable age. Most of them would be either bored with her conversation or scandalized. She didn't seem to follow many feminine pursuits.

Caroline was engaged in conversation with young Betty Shoemaker and Laurie Franklin, no doubt talking of their various gentlemen callers and who would be married by summer. Mrs. Patrick sat on the sofa with Mrs. Sonyers, probably discussing the latest missionary project. Mariah decided she would be better off to remain by Mrs. Kelly.

"What a lovely tablecloth, Catherine," Mrs. Benton said as she joined them. "Where did you find just that shade of blue embroidery floss you have used in it?"

"Thank you, Gladys," Mrs. Kelly replied. "It is a beautiful shade, isn't it? My young friend Evelyn Whitlock gave it to me for a Christmas gift."

Mariah smiled at the golden-haired girl who stood nearby and Evelyn beamed back. Too bad they couldn't go strolling. She liked the child.

"I so often have difficulty finding the color I like," Mrs. Benton said. "I am working a piece now that is less than what it should be for the lack of the right ruby red."

Amity came over to join them. "It's nice to see you, Mariah. How is your grandfather these days?"

"Oh, he's a bit tired now and again," Mariah replied, relieved to have someone talk to her. "The winter was hard for him this year, but he seems some better this spring."

"I'm sure having more help is easing your worry for him."

"Yes." The remark made her realize it was true. However, it was a good time to start spreading the word that Hank wouldn't be staying. "Yes, it is, but my help is only temporary. Hank is only visiting, you know."

"Oh. Does that mean that nice gentleman, Jim Moore, will leave too?" Caroline asked at Mariah's elbow. Mariah hadn't noticed her join them.

"I reckon so. Jim and Hank travel together."

"Rumor has it that they plan to make investments in Colorado. Is that true, Mariah?"

"I haven't really asked Hank his business, Caroline."

"Oh. I only wondered about . . . well, I had hoped Mr. Moore might return and settle down in our town. He seems such a pleasant man." Caroline's eyes grew wide as she asked, "He doesn't have a family, does he?"

"He hasn't a wife that I know of, Caroline."

"Oh." Caroline's cheeks turned pink. "Don't you find those gentlemen's accents delightful, Mariah? So refined."

Actually, she did. Especially Hank's. When he spoke in precise tones while imparting his wisdom, or relaxed into a drawled laughter, or when his voice was morning-husky. His voice always pleased her. Even so, Mariah found it hard to agree with Caroline.

"Mr. Clayton surely has brought extra excitement into the county," Amity remarked. "I swear, this boxing match is all our men could talk about for the last ten days."

Mrs. Benton, although engaged in conversation with Mrs. Kelly, overheard. "Humph. Brawling all over town and then setting a specific time for such a thing seems shameful to me. I cannot understand how our menfolk could sanction such a thing and then call it sport! The only good I can see to come from it is to cause Mr. Kasey so much humiliation he will leave town."

Mariah stared at her with stark wonder. How had

it happened she actually shared an opinion with Mrs. Benton? Something very strange had to be happening to her.

"Indeed, I agree with you, Gladys," said Mrs. Patrick as she joined the group by the tea table. "I cannot approve, however much I appreciate the patronage of the English gentlemen. It would be best for Mead if they moved along soon."

Mariah felt her hackles rise. The old hypocrite. As merchants, the Patricks had helped promote the boxing event as much as the others.

"Gladys, about that embroidery thread you mentioned," Mrs. Kelly put in hastily, "I have a skein of deep ruby. Would you like to see it? It might be just what you need."

The three older women moved away into the bedroom, and Mariah turned back to Amity and Caroline.

"No matter what Mrs. Patrick says," Caroline said, nearly under her breath, "I think the two gentlemen are prodigiously elegant. And when I chanced to meet Mr. Moore in town while shopping on Friday, I thought him especially sweet-natured."

Mariah looked at her longtime enemy-friend closely. Caroline's color had grown even pinker. Why, saints preserve us, as Granny would've said, the girl was actually enamored. A smile tugged mischievously at Mariah's mouth.

"Yes, indeed, Caroline. Jim is more help than a wagonload of cowhands. And you wouldn't credit that gentlemen so refined would be engaged in fisticuffs, would you? Why, watching them spar at night—"

"You saw them? Mr. Moore, also?"

"Uh-huh. They're quite a pair." Mariah lowered her voice. "And both of them cut quite a figure. Why,

when they strip down to only their trousers, they look
. . . very . . . masculine."

At this, Caroline, Mariah would swear, was on the
verge of palpitations.

"Well, it does seem unfair that the men are having
all the fun of a sporting event while we women are
relegated to a tea party," Amity said. "I always think
it most unequal when men are allowed to do things
which women aren't."

"I knew there was a reason I have counted you a
friend, Amity," Mariah said, smiling broadly.

Caroline blushed more furiously than ever. "I know
it is wrong of me, but I do wish we could attend."

Mariah's mouth nearly dropped open. What was
her world coming to? Twice in a day, a Benton lady
had shocked her.

"I almost went regardless, but I promised Hank I'd
behave myself," she admitted. It was the closest she'd
ever come to exchanging a real confidence with
Caroline.

"If we only could," Caroline said wistfully. "But
without a doubt, my mother would be greatly dis-
pleased at even the suggestion."

Caroline lost the points she'd just gained with
Mariah. "No, you mustn't disobey your mother."

"Oh, she didn't command me not to go. It merely
never occurred to her I would wish to. If only more
women wanted to, then we could go quite respectably
in a crowd."

"Or with a chaperon," Amity put in lightly.

When Mariah's glance flew to Amity's, she spied a
suggestive gleam there. "Would you? Would you
really dare?"

"If I can find someone to keep an eye on my children and we can leave without comment. Only for a

few moments, though. It wouldn't do to stay longer than ten minutes."

Caroline's mouth was framed around an invisible O, her eyes full of shocked excitement and doubt.

"Caroline Benton, don't you turn chicken, now, or I'll tell your mother it was all your idea," Mariah said under her breath. "You sneak out first. Nobody will notice if you say you want to go home to—to, um, fix your bloomers or something."

A moment later, Mariah practically pushed Caroline out the door, then watched her scurry up the street. She didn't know how long the girl could be trusted. It had usually been Caroline who told on her and Tommy when they were children.

She turned to find Amity speaking to another woman. "All right, we'll be on our way. I'm sure I can find just the pattern I am thinking of and return in half an hour. Come along, Mariah. I need your opinion."

The two of them walked along sedately until they reached the corner, where they found Caroline.

"Are you sure we should be doing this?" Caroline begged.

"You are already doing it," Mariah told her and took a firm hold of her wrist. Caroline looked altogether too dainty in her pink dress, light cape, and spring straw hat for a sporting event that was likely to be a little rough, but it was too late to think of that now.

"Stay together, now," Amity admonished them. "We mustn't be separated."

The three of them increased their pace until they were practically running. When they neared the livery, the men's shouts and cheering met them long before they reached the door.

Out of breath, Amity put her arm out. "Since I will

be held responsible for this escapade, let me poke my head inside the door first and see how things look."

Caroline rolled her eyes. "Mariah, perhaps we shouldn't, after all."

"You're not going to desert me now, Caroline."

"But—"

"But nothing. If I get a scolding from your mother or Mrs. Patrick, so will you. Even Grandaddy can't be too upset if we're in this together."

Amity waved them through and the three linked arms. The men they pushed past barely glanced at them as they elbowed between them and made their way forward. Someone clanged a cowbell as they squeezed into a tiny space just behind the first row of men. With all the men standing, hanging from the loft and beams, and sitting on the makeshift stands against the walls, Mariah couldn't find Grandaddy or Nate. Amity, she noticed, was looking around too, probably for her husband, Captain Whitlock.

Mariah leaned sideways to peek past a beefy man's shoulder. Before them, a space was roped off in a square. In the near corner, Kasey and his cohorts rested. She saw only his back, but his head hung against his chest. One man poured a bucket of water over Kasey's head. It splattered everywhere and out onto the front row of men.

"Hey, watch it," the man in front of her shouted. Mariah ducked around him to try and see Hank.

On the far side of the roped square, Hank was bent over from the waist, his hands on his knees, taking deep breaths. Jim was wiping his face with a cloth.

"Is the fight over?" she questioned the man next to her.

"Naw, t'ain't over yet, Miss Mariah. It won't be over 'til somebody gets knocked out or calls it quits."

"Oh, Mr. Truit," gasped Caroline.

"Doesn't it go rounds or something?" Amity asked.

"Yep. Three minutes a round."

Thorndyke Sands rang the cowbell and Hank straightened and came to the center of the ring. Kasey did the same, weaving a little. Both men raised their padded gloves.

Mariah wanted to hide her eyes, but at the same time she felt compelled to watch. Hank took on the single-minded stare she had objected to and began his feint-and-punch. Kasey defended himself in the same way, but it was soon obvious that Hank was superior in this contest. Even so, the air was deafened by men hooting, jeering, and cheering.

The cowbell clanged again and the men stepped apart. Hank, it seemed, had landed more punches than Kasey, and Mr. Truit muttered that it wouldn't last too much longer.

Mariah heard Amity say it was time to leave, but she had a hard time tearing her gaze away. When she finally did, she noticed Caroline's glazed eyes were also riveted to the scene. She glanced back to Hank's corner. Jim, although not fighting, wore the tight jersey top he sometimes did when he and Hank sparred. It was he who seemed to be the object of Caroline's focus.

Amity started to work back through the crowd, and she urged Mariah to follow her. It was a moment before Mariah turned to grab Caroline's arm. But all she found was a jumble of men.

"Amity!" Mariah yelled. "Where's Caroline?"

"Isn't she on the other side of you?"

"No." Lord have mercy, they'd lost Caroline.

Mr. Truit bent to her ear. "Miss Caroline went round the other way."

"Drat that girl," Mariah muttered. First she wanted to come, then she was too scared to come. Now it seemed the whole packed barn of men didn't frighten her.

Mariah tipped her head, indicating to Amity they had to go the other direction if they expected to find Caroline. They began to elbow their way through the crowd. At one point Mariah thought they were locked in by solid male bodies, but Amity calmly raised a knee and kicked. That broke the deadlock.

Another round began and the men surged forward in excitement. Mariah felt her bonnet jerked off her head; it hung down her back, barely held by the ribbons. A second later it was gone for good, but she made no effort to retrieve it. Behind her, she felt Amity stumble and she stopped, gripping her friend's elbow tightly.

Amity righted herself and they moved forward again. Suddenly, both of them were shoved. Mariah, blazingly angry, used a sharp elbow and heard a grunt. A space opened up, and all at once, there was Caroline.

Caroline stood immediately behind Hank's corner, behind Jim. She appeared enthralled, not only with Jim, but with the fight itself. She practically leaned on the rope in her zeal. One fist pounded the air. She was cheering. And hooting. And jeering.

Moving swiftly, Mariah and Amity reached the girl.

"Caroline Benton, what do you think you are doing?" Amity scolded her. "We have to leave now."

"Not yet, Amity. Our side is winning."

"That's not the point, Caroline," Mariah said. "We've been here too long. The ladies at Mrs. Kelly's tea party will be suspicious." And outraged, she was sure.

"Just a little while longer," Caroline begged.

"Especially your mother," Mariah added.

Caroline pouted. "Oh, very well."

"Let's leave by that door there," Amity said, pointing. "Oh, oh. There's Thaddeus."

Captain Whitlock, with a scowl on his face, reached them through the crowd. "What are you ladies doing? You shouldn't be here. Let's go this way."

Caroline turned for one last look. Mariah grabbed her, but she couldn't resist one last glance at the ring herself. Just at that moment, Hank's concentration seemed to break, for he looked right into her eyes. And Kasey landed a heavy punch to his jaw.

But Mariah saw no more, for Amity pulled her through the crowd. A moment later, they reached the outside. All of them gasped for fresh air. Captain Whitlock began to fuss over Amity, while she merely laughed.

"See, you've torn your dress," Thaddeus said. "You could've been badly mauled, Amity."

"But I'm fine, Thaddeus, and we three women stuck together. Besides, now you're with us everything is all right."

"Oh, Mama will be so furious," Caroline said.

"Hush, Caroline," Mariah responded. "We're in Captain and Mrs. Whitlock's company. How could anyone object to that? Besides, you look perfectly unruffled. I, meanwhile, lost my bonnet and all my hairpins."

"So you did. Oh, Mariah, your hair is really flying all about your face. We must do something with it."

Mariah gathered it as they walked, finger-combed it as best she could, and quickly braided it.

"Have one of my ribbons," Caroline offered as she removed a pink one.

"Thanks, Caroline," Mariah said, surprised at the uncharacteristic generosity. She accepted it and tied the end of her hair. The front curls, however, continued to bob over her forehead.

Amity, on Thaddeus's arm, entered Mrs. Kelly's house first. Mariah noted that Caroline's color was high as they walked through the door and that the girl began to fidget instantly. Mariah remained as calm as possible, but when she intercepted a suspicious glance from Mrs. Benton, she couldn't help herself. She smiled sweetly. Then giggled. If only Mrs. Benton could have seen her dainty little daughter, hooting and cheering in the midst of that mob of unruly men.

Caroline kept twisting the strings of her tapestried reticule into a knot. "What will I say to Mama when she finds out?" she whispered.

"Was your father there to see you?" Mariah asked.

"No, of course not. Papa is probably still at his law office. He doesn't care for those things."

"Well, then, don't tell her until you have to. Anyway, you wanted to see Jim, didn't you?"

"Oh, yes, wasn't he divine-looking?" Caroline sighed, enraptured. "So strong, and . . . and forceful."

"Uh-huh," Mariah answered absently. She was already thinking about how she would answer the Circle T men, for it was certain sure they'd probably seen the commotion they'd made in getting out of the livery. "Listen, Caroline, just blame it on me if your mother scolds too hard. It's what she'll believe anyway."

Soon the tea party broke up. The Whitlocks collected their children and left. Mrs. Patrick stated she had to get back to the store to tend to customers and Betty and Laurie went with her, chattering about new dresses for the spring dance. Mrs. Benton gave Mariah a frosty look but said nothing.

Mariah glanced through the windows. A man on horseback, then another, then a buckboard, moved down the road beyond the corner from the direction of the fight. Heading for the saloons, probably. It must be over. She thought perhaps she ought to start home before the mob of men burst the seams of the livery barn and spilled all over Mead's streets. That way she'd be home before Grandaddy and Hank.

She started searching for her tan gloves and realized she'd lost them. Sighing in irritation, she then tugged at the front of her dress. For some reason, it felt funny. Then she saw why. A hook was completely gone at the waist and two more hung loosely by a thread, leaving a gap. They must have been pulled free when she'd struggled to leave the barn.

"Dang."

"Mariah!"

"Oh, sorry, Caroline." Mariah looked the other girl over. There wasn't a blonde hair out of place, nor did her dainty pink clothes show the least bit of wear and tear. No one, including Mrs. Benton, would ever believe that Caroline had just been shoved and pushed in a rowdy crowd of men.

"I must go." Mariah said her good-byes quickly and left the house, then swung astride Skedaddle with deliberate flair for the watchful eyes. At least six inches of her white-stockinged legs showed. In an added gesture of defiance, she pulled the pink ribbon from her hair and let it flutter away as she galloped out of town, her tresses flying behind her.

13

She'd done it again, thumbed her nose at being a refined woman, and this time she thought she wouldn't even try to redeem her reputation or defend herself. It was all too tiresome.

Halfway home, she heard racing hoofbeats behind her. Already having pulled Skedaddle to a slow walk, she turned to see who it was.

"Wait up, Mariah," Hank called. "I want to talk to you."

Hell's bells, she hadn't counted on seeing him so soon. She'd assumed he would have gone with Jim and his other pals to celebrate. "You mean it's over?" she asked in mock innocence.

He came up beside her, slowed Patches to the same easy gait as Skedaddle's, and looked her over. Curls rioted down each side of her face and onto her shoulders, framing her face and neck in auburn gleams from the setting sun. It was lovely, the way he had imagined it would be when loose.

His admiration warred with the anger he felt toward her for violating their agreement. "It was over three minutes after you left."

"Oh," she said. "I thought it might go on a while longer."

"I tired of the game and put a quick end to it."

"What happened?" He was annoyed about something, she was sure. It was unusual for him to show his anger. "Did Kasey—"

"I knocked him out."

"Well, I hope this puts paid to the whole thing," she said with asperity. "You have a bruise forming on your cheek, did you know that?"

"Mmm, I'm not surprised. The one real blow Kasey landed was when I heard a commotion and looked up to see you," he said, throwing the accusation back at her. "I was defending myself quite nicely until then—completely in control of the whole blooming match, in fact, including Kasey. What the bloody hell were you doing there? I told you not to come."

Startled, Mariah caught her breath. His anger was directed at *her,* not at Kasey. She pulled her mount to a halt and faced him, her mouth tight in the very defense she'd hoped she wouldn't have to mount. He'd been the one male of her acquaintance whom she had thought wouldn't take her to task for anything.

"Now wait just a dad-blamed minute. I wasn't there alone. Amity Whitlock and Caroline Benton wanted to go and I—"

"You just couldn't stand being left out, could you?" he railed. "I don't care who you were with, it was no place for a lady. You promised not to come."

Her temper flared. "Well, you forget something, Hank. I'm not a lady. But the two women who came with me are. And they wanted to see what was going on just as much as I did. You did see three of us there, didn't you?"

His answer was a continued scowl, and she prompted Skedaddle to move on. They rode into the ranch yard and dismounted beside the barn in silence. Still irritated, Hank wasn't ready to give up the argument. He rested an arm on his saddle and looked across at her.

"The fact remains, you broke our agreement."

He had her there. Remorse set in. "About that . . . I'm sorry. I don't normally break a promise. I haven't any excuse, really. I couldn't help myself when Caroline expressed—" Mariah looked at Hank in amazement. "She actually wanted to go! It was like a dare, almost. You see, Caroline seldom got in trouble when we were children. She never got into scrapes or got dirty or lost sight of who she was, the lawyer's daughter. It seemed like fate when Amity offered to chaperon, and I knew she really wanted an excuse to go too, and suddenly I couldn't help it. Anyway, Amity made us promise we wouldn't stay more than a few minutes."

"Thank God for that. And thank heavens Captain Whitlock arrived by your side when he did to hustle you girls out of there."

"More's the pity," she said. "Caroline would've climbed inside that rope in another minute. I'd give my new black mare to have seen that."

"You could have been crushed in all that throng. Your grandfather was very worried."

"Where is Grandaddy? He's all right, isn't he? That mob . . ."

"A fine time to fret about him now, Mariah. Don't worry, he is fine, just fine. He is resting at the widow

Kelly's, who assured him you had returned all in one piece. Although by the look of you, I wouldn't quite agree with her."

Mariah suddenly grinned. "I lost my bonnet."

"Yep," he answered, imitating her speech, while his gaze traveled down to her toes and back. A hoyden, indeed. Mariah appealed to him mightily at that moment, her hair wild down her back and with that saucy, inviting smile. He had to rein in his mad impulse to grab her and kiss her until his need was eased. But he thought she'd had enough flouting of convention for today.

And there was a limit to what she would or wouldn't do, he knew that well enough. She might not like the limits which society placed on her—by damn, he shared that trait—but she had her own standards of acceptable morals and behavior.

Yesterday she'd put on an armor of wariness against him and against what he made her feel. At least he had the satisfaction that he was driving her as loony as she was him.

He raised a brow and grinned. "And a fastening or two?"

Mariah flushed and slapped an open palm across the gap at her waist. The white stuff of her undergarment poked out.

"Oh, heavens." She backed up a step. "Excuse me. Um, I'll change and be back in a flash to unsaddle. Meanwhile, why don't you see if Brown has a piece of raw meat to put on that bruise. It looks as though it might puff up your eye."

She turned and ran.

Indeed, she was back in a flash, joining him in the barn, where he'd led the horses. Hank decided she had to be the least vain, most unpretentious woman of his acquaintance. He knew of not one other who could change without primping. Now wearing a faded dress that once had been green, she had not bothered to even braid her hair. He admitted to himself that he liked it free. It brought up images of what it would look like if—when—they made love. It was all he could do not to fill his hands with it.

Hank turned away to the animals. He'd unsaddled them while Mariah was gone and given them some feed. Now she picked up a cloth rag and began to wipe down the roan. They worked side by side companionably for several moments, then walked the animals out to the home corral. The barn cat followed, scampering ahead, while old Barney and Mutt fell into step beside Mariah.

Mariah rested her arms along the rails, her chin on them, and watched the sun sink lower behind the distant mountains. The two foals that had been born last week peeked adorably at her from behind their mothers. Next to her, Hank leaned, too, with one booted foot on the lower rail. Around them, except for an occasional snuffle from one of the horses or a cat mew, all was peaceful and deeply quiet.

"Well, Grandaddy should be getting home soon," she remarked for something to say into the silence.

"Perhaps not. I suspect he will be invited to supper at Mrs. Kelly's."

"Oh. Well, regardless, he won't stay late. He likes to be home by dark. What happened to Jim?"

"He decided to celebrate with Thorndyke and a few others. Nate went with them."

"Mmm. We won't see them until late, then, if at all. Saturday night all the hands go to town. I thought you would go with them."

"I had other things I wanted to do."

She noted his cryptic glance, a hooded look of promise covering his mild response. "Oh. And where is Brown?"

Hank seemed surprised. "I don't know."

Mariah sighed and teased, "Reckon our supper is up to me, then."

As though he understood her need for lightness, he made a mock shudder. "You don't say so!"

"And that leaves the chickens to be fed and the cow to be milked."

Again, he seemed mildly surprised. "I had not thought of those chores."

She shook her head, pulling the corner of her mouth into an amused grimace. "Even for a green-horn, Hank, sometimes you're a total washout."

"No, how could you say so? You think I am ignorant of the mundane chores, is that it? Or that I could not do them?"

"Yep, that's what I think. You've been almighty spoiled, it seems to me, by too many people around you willing to wait on you hand and foot. Why, even Jim jumps to do what you tell him. The poor man hardly calls his days his own. It's almost shameful the way he kowtows to you. It's a wonder you haven't grown so lazy you refuse to bathe and dress yourself, like those fancy Easterners and European aristocrats and such."

Hank continued to stare out at the distant mountains. Was he spoiled? he wondered. The way she said it made him sound so.

Mariah had no idea she'd hit so close to the truth about the kind of life he had been born into—huge family estates that were filled with all manner of fine furnishings, with nannies and servants, then tutors and the best schools and elaborate holidays with his brothers. They all had wonderful toys and clothing, abundant food, and as they grew older, the very best in horses, carriages, and equipage.

Yes, the three Ackerley brothers had always had anything they wanted—except the attention of their parents. Henry had loved his grandmother better, and it was she who gave him his small inheritance.

And when he had finished his schooling, like his brothers before him, he had taken the Grand Tour of Europe with a tutor and Jim, his valet. After that, he had drifted through the years living, as had been expected by the English upper crust, an almost profligate life.

For the first time in the whole of his existence, it made him feel uncomfortable. He'd learned very little about attaining or appreciating the basic necessities of life. He hadn't even cared to think about it.

Now he faced a simple way of life every day, one that demanded his mental capacities as well as hard physical labor and, the wonder of it was, he liked it. He liked the uncomplicated girl standing next to him, and her grandfather, and old Nate. He liked this small ranch nestled at the foot of the Rocky Mountains, and even liked his valet calling him Hank and working with him as an equal. But it was a far cry from the life he'd led in England. He didn't know what to do about it all.

"Which reminds me," he began, to cover his discomfort. "I did not have a chance to bathe after the fight as I usually do. If you wait for me, I will help you, er, feed the chickens."

She pushed away from the rail, and strode toward the cookhouse to fetch the milk pails. "Ha! Much obliged! But I'll be done by the time you heat water. If you're in a hurry, though, you might try the river pond. But one warning. It's cold yet, this time of year."

She turned, walking backwards, still taunting him. "I now know you can take a punch, tenderfoot, but are you man enough for that icy mountain water?"

He hurried to catch up with her. "Now what are you accusing me of? Cowardice of the cold? Or is it a challenge you are offering?" The sudden vision of her bathing there was almost enough to make him try it. But already, the evening breeze had risen and the air had cooled. "How often do *you* bathe in that pond?"

"Never, until it warms up."

"Then I will wait for you. You may let me know when you are ready to brave it."

She laughed as she picked up the milk pails. "I'll milk and feed the chickens, then I'll come see what we can scrounge for supper."

"No. *I* will tend to supper."

Mariah laughed once more, disbelievingly, as she left. But when she returned with the heavy pails, Hank met her at the door dressed in fresh clothing, his dark hair still wet and combed close against his head. He must have bathed in cold water after all, for there hadn't been enough time for water to heat.

He relieved her of the pails, setting them on the dry sink. Mariah set about straining the milk. From the stove, something smelled good. It reminded her she'd been too busy to eat a noon meal and too nervous to eat any of the refreshments at the tea.

She glanced over her shoulder. One end of the huge planked table, which could easily hold a dozen men, was set cozily for two with the preciseness of Powell's dining room. Large serving bowls sat on tin service plates and Hank ladled a thick soup into them.

"The cupboard does not boast of soup bowls. These will do."

"Where did you find that?" she asked in wonder.

"There was enough of last night's roast left. Meat and vegetables. I added a little barley broth and rice."

Hank seated her. On the corner between the table settings sat a small, carved wooden box, its lid gleaming in the lamplight. "What is this?" she asked.

"It is a small gift for you."

A gift for her? Shocked, she stared at him. A gift. It wasn't as though she'd never had gifts . . . only very seldom. At Christmas or on her birthday.

"It isn't my birthday," she protested lightly.

"Lift the lid," he suggested, an expectant smile tugging his mouth.

Tentatively, she did. The box began to play "Yankee Doodle," its tinkling sound delicate and lively.

"That tune usually brings a gnashing of teeth to the English people, my dear. But I thought it quite descriptive of one saucy American miss's 'thumb-your-nose' attitude."

One look at his gleeful face and Mariah burst into laughter. "You never expected me to stay at that dad-blamed tea party, did you?" she said when she was able to speak.

"Not altogether, no."

"Then what made you so angry?"

"I don't know, exactly. It was seeing you suddenly in that rowdy mob which was barely hanging on to whatever thread of civility it possessed. For a moment, it scared the living daylights from me."

He spoke in a light, self-deprecating, conversational tone, leading her to believe he was only joshing and hadn't really been worried at all. After all, he liked adventure and danger.

Then she realized he was serious, and that something about his admission embarrassed him. He turned his back suddenly, for a moment, before he brought thick slices of buttered toast from the oven to the table.

Hank took his place. He lifted a spoon, then stopped. Mariah was staring at him. Elam always said grace.

Between them, the music wound down.

"Er, do you want to, er . . . grace?" he asked.

Hank didn't know what to say. He had never in his life talked to the Almighty outside of the Church of England's formal prayers. He felt awkward; he could never match Elam's simple elegance.

Grandaddy had given thanks and asked the blessing at every meal since Mariah could remember. It would seem sacrilegious not to have one just because he wasn't there.

"I'll do it," she said. Then, bowing her head, she offered up the simplest of words. "Thank you, Lord, for the food, and for the fine weather, and for Hank's success in his contest. And, please, keep Grandaddy safe on his way home. Amen."

Her hand rested near the music box on the corner between them and Hank's hand reached out to cover hers gently. The gesture felt warm and natural to them both.

When Mariah raised her head, Hank's smoky gaze was on her, and there was an intimacy there. As she watched, it deepened into a look of stark hunger.

When his fingers stroked hers, her heart began a double rhythm. She wanted to say something. She should withdraw her hand, her gaze. Where was her resolve to remain just friends? She'd sworn to guard herself, and she needed to break the entrancement.

Her mouth felt dry. His dark lashes flickered down, then slowly up again.

A shuffle at the door swiftly caught her attention. It swung open and Grandaddy was there. "Good, Mariah, you're home. Was a mite worried, but Hank said he'd see to you. Didn't want to stay in town, but Catherine insisted you were all right and she had to give me supper."

Elam's gaze fell onto their joined hands. Mariah flushed and jerked hers free.

"Uh, would you like a little soup, Grandaddy?"

"No, I've had plenty to eat. But I'll set a spell, then walk you up to the house," he said.

Thereafter, they ate while Elam talked about the match and other things going on in town and Hank and Mariah gave disjointed answers to his questions. When it was time to go, she picked up the music box and clutched it against her. "Thank you, Hank."

Mariah remained quiet on their stroll back to the house. Grandaddy didn't exactly lecture her about what she'd done today, but merely said that she had acted unwisely. Then he changed the subject to the future of the cattle business and mentioned, in passing, what he thought the ranch might be worth. Then he launched into the fact that her great-aunt Harriet, his sister, had written with a request for them to visit her in Ohio before the year was up and that he'd been seriously considering it.

Mariah's thoughts spun while she digested the information he was giving her, and she felt more than a little hurt. It all smacked of giving up. Grandaddy was thinking of selling the Circle T and moving back east.

*   *   *

Hank lounged on his bunk with a book loosely in his hand, every now and again attempting to read it. The bruise on his face had spread. It was sore, but he thought little of it. He couldn't sleep, and he wondered when Jim and Nate would wander home.

Elam entered the bunkhouse quietly. Hank sat up immediately. "Elam . . ."

"May I come in, Hank?"

"Certainly, sir. Please sit down." He offered the edge of his own cot, for the bunkhouse boasted no chairs, and then swung over to sit on Jim's. "What's on your mind?"

The old man dug into his vest pocket for his tobacco pouch before he sat, then gave full attention to filling his pipe. He lit it, drew on it, then snuffed the match flame out before settling his gaze on Hank. He sat straight, belying the tired lines in his face. His eyes, a soft golden-brown color, reminded Hank of Mariah's, full of honesty and straightforwardness. "I thought it was time we had a talk."

"All right," Hank replied and waited.

"You've made a reputation for yourself in this territory right fast, you know that?"

"Yes, I suppose I have."

"Mostly, the town likes you."

"I am glad to hear you say so," Hank said, a little dryly.

"Yeeup. They think you're a mite peculiar, but they'd think the same of any foreign fella. You proved yourself honest at poker without takin' undue offense, then while defendin' yourself you were willin' to give the town some fun at the same time. And you spend your money freely with the Mead merchants."

"I see."

"Thorndyke Sands thinks you're some clever."

Hank didn't know how to reply to that one. He wasn't sure if Elam meant it as a compliment.

"The ladies like you."

"Thank you, sir." At one time he would have felt smug about that. Charming the ladies was one of his easy talents. Now it only made him feel restless and impatient—it seemed unimportant. He waited for the old man to get to the point.

"I want to know what you intend toward my girl." Baldly put, there it was.

Hank remained silent a moment, forming his thoughts. He didn't know what he intended; he only knew he couldn't pick up and leave her or this place just yet. He'd never felt responsible for another life before, never felt as though if he left a woman without resolving the growing feelings between them he'd be making a huge mistake that would haunt him forever.

"I do not wish her harm, sir."

"But do you wish her best good?"

"Of course." How could he have answered anything else? But was *he* her best good? He yearned for her fiercely and would not have scrupled to take her the other day, there in the shadow of the Lizard's Tail. If she had let him. She had charged him with wanting to love and leave and he was guilty. He would have loved her, and he would leave, eventually. His family would demand it.

"I have a bad heart, you know." Elam touched his chest. "Doc says it don't sound good most times. Had a spell in the winter. . . ." He drifted off, shaking his head.

"I am deeply sorry, Elam. Mariah has expressed her concern about you often."

"Yes, yes, I know." He puffed a moment, then looked at Hank through his shaggy white brows and pipe smoke. "You remember that Rhodes fella?"

"Certainly."

"He wasn't just a cattle buyer. He came to look over the Circle T itself. But it wasn't what he had in mind. Too small, I'm guessin'."

"You want to sell the Circle T, then?"

"Thought it best 'til you came along. Thinkin' of Mariah's future."

Mariah's future. She loved the Circle T. A future for Mariah, without her grandfather or the Circle T?

Or him?

"But now I reckon I can rest easy, knowin' you'll do right by my granddaughter. She's a good girl, you know, in spite of her bein' a bit coltish now and again. She'll take to tamin' with the right handlin'."

Elam rose and clapped a hand on Hank's shoulder in an affectionate gesture one man makes to another when congratulations are in order. His face looked content; his eyes held a soft glow. "See you in the mornin' for church, son."

Astounded, Hank opened his mouth to deny the assumption the old man had made. Words rushed through his brain and his mind boggled at the box he had so easily stepped into, mostly of his own making. But alongside those thoughts were ones of free-spirited, impish Mariah, a coltish girl, a prairie beauty, a cowgirl sprite.

And Mariah's future.

And the impossible, unthinkable thoughts of any other man but himself doing the taming.

14

She should have expected all the flat-out hullabaloo Hank and Jim's attendance at church would cause the next morning. Dressed in their English-made clothes, they rode into town behind the buggy, looking as handsome as any two men in the territory as far as Mariah was concerned, despite the discolored bruise on Hank's cheek. She felt very proud to be seen with them.

As soon as the service ended, the women flocked about them like hens lured with precious corn. But the men, as well, greeted and talked to them with deep respect. Most of them wanted to discuss what had happened yesterday.

"That Kasey went down like a ten-ton stone," said one laughing man. "The bettin' went haywire just before that."

"That was a helluva—beg pardon fer my language, ladies—right hook, Mr. Clayton. If you could hit that hard, how come ya didn't do it in the first place?" asked another.

"Had to give the fellow a fair chance, you know," Hank replied.

"Sure was a pleasure, Mr. Clayton. I reckon you made lotsa people happy, showin' that skunk Kasey up. He crawled outa town first thing this mornin', head bowed," said Mr. Truit. "Didn't even say good-bye."

Mariah broke into the circle. "Kasey's left Mead?"

"Yes, ma'am. Saw 'im leave myself."

"Thank goodness," she mumbled under her breath. Kasey was the joker, the wild card. Her secret worry that Kasey would try to get back at Hank lifted. It was unlikely, now, if he was shamed enough and out of the game.

"Won some money on you, Mr. Clayton," Mr. Morton told him. "You looked like the sound side of a bet."

"Happy to oblige, Mr. Morton. I won some myself," Hank answered.

At that acknowledgment, Mariah glanced at her grandfather. He didn't hold with gambling. Surprisingly, Grandaddy took it all in stride, saying only, "Hope you folks were generous when the church plate came around."

The women, matrons and girls alike, flattered Hank and Jim with smiles and invitations. Hank charmed them even when he politely refused. Jim, standing a few feet away with his own admiring twosome, the two sixteen-year-olds, Betty Shoemaker and Laurie Franklin, seemed to have the same ability.

"All this needs is for Caroline to show up like she did last Sunday," Mariah muttered. "And we'd have three of a kind."

"Did you say something, my dear?" Hank asked her.

"Uh, no. . . ." Nevertheless, she found herself craning her neck to gain a view of the street leading to the Presbyterian church. Way up, there was a suspicious flutter of pink.

"I'm ready to go home, now, Grandaddy."

"Just a minute, honey."

"I do hope we've seen the last of your sport, Mr. Clayton," Mrs. Patrick said, the one dissenter in the praise chorus. "I believe it brings out an undesirable animal instinct in our men, as well as drawing the worst elements to our town."

"Hush, Hazel," her husband admonished her.

"Well, really!" Mrs. Patrick gave him a freezing stare.

Mariah, still loath to admit that she shared an opinion with Mrs. Patrick, sidled away from the crowd and viewed the road from a better vantage point. Uh-huh. A female figure walked toward them so fast her pace was almost a gallop. And a step behind her was a second, a more buxom figure. It was Caroline, she was sure, and her mother.

"Grandaddy . . ."

"I'll be right there, Mariah."

She climbed into the buggy on the driver's side and picked up the reins. She directed Lulubelle forward a few yards to be closer to her grandfather. The horse turned to look at her. "Oh, hush, Lulubelle," she said under her breath, "I don't want any complaints from you."

Up the road, Caroline's features could be distinguished.

Hank looked Mariah's way, then followed her gaze. His lips broke into a slow smile. Suddenly, he said, "I really must be off, gentlemen." He gallantly tipped his hat. "Ladies."

"I'm ready, Grandaddy," she said one last time.

"What's your hurry, Mariah?" Elam asked, finally climbing into the buggy. Hank and Jim mounted their horses.

"I just wanted to, um . . ."

"Mariah promised to teach me to rope this afternoon, sir. It seems there's a knack to capturing exactly the, ah, heifer you've got your eye on."

Mariah made a tight horseshoe turn and headed out of town.

Thank heavens, Grandaddy only harrumphed.

They started branding the following week. Nate, in spite of his "rheumitiz," still threw a pretty good loop and taught Hank and Jim the rudiments of the skill. Elam worked the iron the first morning, showing the Englishmen what to do, then turned it over to Jim with gratitude at noon. After the first morning, Mariah persuaded her grandfather to return to the house in the afternoons.

"These cowpokes will learn fast enough with Nate and me," she insisted. "They'll earn their keep by the end of the week."

Hank, helping to drive and rope, made every effort to follow Mariah's and Nate's directions, which were often yelled at him over the noisy herd. It was necessary to learn fast, as Mariah had predicted, and he did, picking up the tricks of roping while on the run. He often missed, but then he began to get the hang of it, and eventually learned to wrestle a balky, bawling calf.

It was a far cry from any romantic view he may have held of Western ranching, but oddly enough, he loved every minute of it.

On the fourth day, it was he who worked the fire and iron, until he felt as if the heat had welded his hand to the iron's handle and sweat ran down his face and soaked his shirt. He straightened from his haunches to work a kink from his back and wipe his forehead with a sleeve while Mariah dragged another small, feisty beast toward him.

"Git it by the leg there, Hank," Nate instructed him. He did so and put his body into throwing the creature on its side. Instantly, Mariah moved her horse back, making her rope taut as Nate looped the opposite hooves and backed his horse in the other direction.

Hank leaped to grab the iron, then pressed the white-hot Circle T brand firmly against the calf's rump as it bawled and the stench of burning hide permeated the air. They were quick to release it, and Jim herded it back through the corral opening so it could find its mama.

Hank stood straight again, his eyes smarting, and looked around to see what was left of the milling herd. Lifting his hat, he used his neckerchief to wipe his face and neck. The day wasn't that hot, but the heat of the fire caused him to seek a cooling breeze.

The sun hung about midway in the western sky—hours, yet, 'til sunset. They'd worked 'til near dark each day. Bone-tired, Hank again marveled at Mariah's strength and the long, hard hours she worked. She shouldn't have to do so much. No wonder she had no extra flesh to her. Perhaps selling the Circle T would be the best thing after all, for her and Elam alike.

Mariah suddenly called it quits. "Okay, boys, that seems to be all for now. We'll work on the stragglers next week."

Hank had no desire to argue the point. He stamped the branding fire out and gathered up the tools while Nate brought the buckboard around. They'd had Lem repair the wheel and Jim had helped Nate put it back on the wagon. Mariah caught Baldy, the gelding Hank had ridden that morning, and brought him up.

"Hank, help me get the herd moving back toward the north range. If we don't, they'll bunch up around here too long."

He responded by mounting Baldy and joining her in waving his lariat and whistling sharply. Slowly, the cattle began to move. He was glad when he realized Mariah didn't intend to take them far.

"That'll do it, I think." She rode her small mare, Flirt, up to him and they turned toward the barn.

"Righto."

"You had the hot job today."

"Uh-huh."

"Wanta take that swim?"

He looked at her in puzzlement. "Swim?"

"In the river pond."

"Won't it still be ice cold?"

"Yep, it sure will. I'm game if you are."

Hank couldn't resist the challenge in her sparkling eyes. She had that impish innocent expression she sometimes wore when she thought she was getting away with something.

"You bet."

"If we hurry we'll have time for a quick dip before supper. We don't have to stay in too long. It'll feel good, after."

"All right."

"Okay. You and Jim meet me there in ten minutes."

Mariah raced ahead, leaving Hank to follow when he would.

And Jim? she'd said. All of a sudden the visions he'd had of having a few moments alone with Mariah after nearly a week of work vanished. But the swim sounded too good to pass up. He kicked Baldy's flanks, sending him into a gallop, and he arrived at the barn as Jim and Nate were unloading the tools.

"Jim, we're going for a swim down at the river pond. Hurry and change."

"Whazzat?" Nate shouted.

"A swim!" shouted Hank.

"A swim, you say? No, don't b'lieve I will. That dern water'll be colder'n Pikes Peak in January. Too old fer that kinda frolickin'. You and Jim go ahead, though, iffen ya need to."

Hank nodded, a grin tugging at his mouth. "Okay. Jim?"

Jim looked up with a question in his eyes. "Sounds invigorating," he said. "Thank you, I'll come."

Nate shook his head. "Young bucks do some crazy things. Wal, don't fergit blankets. Fer after. Y'all likely to catch yer deaths as 'tis. An' wouldn't hurt to take the buckboard. You c'n ride back when you're cold."

Hank hurried through unsaddling and rubbing Baldy down, then turned him into the corral. Then he unbuckled the cinch on General, Jim's horse for the day, and pulled the saddle free. Jim approached as Hank was applying the rag to General.

"No need for you to care for my animal as well as your own, Mr. Henry," he said in a low voice.

"You were engaged in helping Nate," Hank replied. "It seemed faster to take care of General right away rather than wait for you to be free to do it.

While I finish this, why don't you dig out the bathing costumes. Mariah plans on joining us."

"Ah, then perhaps you would prefer I didn't?"

Hank gave him a wry look. "Remember, Jim, we're on equal footing here. What I prefer doesn't always go my way. Mariah expects both of us."

"I see. Well, in that case, Hank, let's go!"

After that it was a scramble to finish their chores, don bathing clothes under their regular ones, hop onto the buckboard seat, and hurry Lulubelle and Lena, the second horse in the wagon team, down the path to the river pond. Hank heard the dogs barking before they reached the place, signaling that Mariah had arrived before them.

She was already in the water. Barney yipped at the pool's edge excitedly while Mutt ran up a large boulder, jumped in, and swam out to Mariah as she laughed. She gave no indication she knew the men had arrived. Her hair was tightly braided into a top-knot and she wore something white.

Hank peeled off his outer clothes in almost as much frenzied excitement as the dogs displayed. His boots thudded as they hit the ground, his hat flopped on top, his denims he left where he stepped out of them, and his shirt was flung wide as he reached the water.

He ran in, in three steps, the cold water shocking his heated system immediately, then plunged into the deep with a skimming dive. He came up stroking hard. Jim followed him, only half a stroke behind.

"Good boy, good boy," Mariah praised the dog paddling around her. She ignored the men as she swam closer to the center, and then dived, the white material of her overdress billowing a moment before she submerged. Hank was treated to a glimpse of slender ankles and feet, pink and white under the clear blue water. She shot up to the surface again, gasping for breath in the icy water.

Hank was there, a mere foot away from her. "No wonder you . . . said a quick . . . dip, you . . . little rascal. This temperature would . . . rival an ice floe."

"I did . . . tell you." Crystal water drops dotted her face, making her skin look dewy, and spiked her brown lashes. Her mouth, normally a soft pink, had paled to a cream with cold.

"So you did. Are you . . . trying to freeze us all?"

"Quite refreshing, Miss Mariah," Jim commented. "But I think I shall decline further enjoyment."

"One race," she begged. "Across and back . . . from the boulder. Then we can go have supper."

"Mariah, it is really too cold," Hank protested.

"Cluck-cluck." She clicked her teeth as she would to call the chickens, turning her head to look at him sideways. "Cluck-cluck."

"Very well. But if you catch influenza, I shall not sympathize. And if I catch it, you must personally nurse me back to health."

When Jim gave the signal they plunged forward. Mariah was a good swimmer, but it was soon obvious she was no match for Hank. His reach was farther and stronger.

Nevertheless, she continued on, refusing to give up. Hank touched the point of return long before she and started back.

"Give in," he muttered as he passed her.

"Never," she replied through gritted teeth.

"Stubborn . . ."

"Uh-huh."

Hank reached the originating point and hauled himself out, standing on a rock that jutted out over the pool. His muscles tight with cold, he shivered in the breeze. He turned to observe Mariah. She was still halfway out.

"Come along," he muttered. She'd been in the freezing water too long.

Jim, wearing a blanket closely wrapped about himself, had already pulled on his shirt, socks, and boots. He held out a blanket to Hank. Hank took it, but let it dangle while anxiety built as he continued to watch Mariah. She was slowing down.

Mutt climbed out and shook himself all over, panting hard. Hank barely noticed.

Arm over arm, she came, but he wondered at what cost. She looked as though she could barely lift her arms into the next stroke. At last she stood, but her feet didn't want to hold her. Her knees buckled and she fell.

"Mariah," Hank breathed on a near groan. All at once he couldn't stand there watching her struggle the last few yards. He dropped the blanket and rushed into the shallow water to meet her, feeling the shock of the icy cold all over again. When he reached her, he swept her into his arms. It was a mark of how tired and cold she'd become when she didn't protest.

"Foolish girl," he said through his own chattering teeth. "Wouldn't admit . . .you were in trouble."

"I-I'd-d-d h-have m-m-made it," she insisted.

"Nearly dead."

Her thick white cotton dress streamed water all over him, and clung to her skin and him. They added pounds to her weight, but even so, she felt as light as down in his arms.

Jim was ready with a blanket. Hank shot him a glance of gratitude and held Mariah tightly against himself, hoping to impart some warmth to her as Jim placed the blanket around them both. She snuggled into him, pushing her face against his shoulder.

"Let's get back to the house," Hank ordered gently, but with urgency as he headed toward the wagon.

"M-my c-clothes . . ." she mumbled.

"Damn the clothes."

With Jim's help, he placed Mariah in the back of the buckboard, then climbed in beside her, swiftly cocooning her in the remaining blanket. She pulled herself into a ball as he cradled her back against his chest.

Jim whipped the team into action and they thankfully arrived at the house in mere minutes. Hank swung himself over the wagon side and then reached for Mariah.

"P-put m-me d-down, Hank. I c-can walk."

"Time enough later, Mariah," he said as he shouldered through the kitchen door.

Elam entered the kitchen from the parlor. His gaze flew to the girl in Hank's arms; the paper he'd been reading slipped from his fingers. Hank saw the old man's face go white and cursed himself silently. He should've called out an assurance as they arrived through the door, before Elam spotted them.

"Mariah!" Elam's voice was a croak. "What happened?"

"G-grand-dad-dy. I'm-m all right. J-just c-cold."

Hank hooked a kitchen chair with his foot and scooted it close to the stove before settling Mariah in it. Even though they seldom used the stove for cooking these days, Elam frequently kept a fire going.

"It's my fault, sir. The water was far too cold and we stayed in it much too long." Hank dropped to his haunches and began rubbing Mariah's feet with a corner of a blanket. "Find a towel, please, Elam, for her hair."

Mariah moved inside her cocoon to accept the towel Elam handed her. Her fingernails looked blue, her skin too white. "Wasn't H-Hank's fault. . . . I w-wanted . . . to race."

Elam opened the stove door and threw in a couple of wood sticks. "Where's your head, Mariah?" he scolded. "You know that stream stays cold even in summer. This time of year . . ."

"Sorry, Grandaddy," Mariah apologized sincerely. There was worry in the old man's eyes and she had caused it. When would she learn?

She leaned back wearily. Hank had progressed from her feet to her calves, rubbing gently to help the circulation return. He glanced up at her frequently through the fringe of his black hair, which lay scattered across his forehead. His gray eyes were serious in a way they seldom were. In the back, his hair clung wetly to his neck. The striped bathing costume, looking foreign and strange, seemed a second skin against him. He was as wet as she.

Without thinking, she wiped a trickle of water from his cheek and gently stroked the back of his neck with the towel. It seemed natural to do so. The air around them was warm, but they both had been chilled to the bone. "Oh, Hank, you should take care of yourself. You're cold too."

"I'm fine," he said, dismissing her concern with a slight frown. "You need to remove these wet things immediately."

"I reckon so." She started to rise.

"Where's Mariah's room?" Hank asked Elam.

"Upstairs," the old man answered, pointing to the tiny staircase in the corner.

Hank only nodded, then bent to Mariah.

"Oh," she said, caught by surprise. "You don't have to carry me. I can walk."

"I want to make sure you're warmed right away."

Mariah looked in puzzlement toward her grandfather. He wasn't protesting this high-handed, very personal treatment a bit. It was unlike him. She fleetingly wondered what her grandfather was thinking to allow a man into her bedroom, but at that moment Mariah found herself in danger of bumping the walls as Hank juggled and shifted her in order to maneuver her up the enclosed stairs. She pulled in her toes and elbows and hugged herself against him.

"All right, Mariah, which one?" he asked as he faced two doors in the small upper hall.

"That one," she said, pointing. "But I—"

Hank paid as little attention to her impending protest as he had a few minutes before. He shouldered through the half-opened door and took two steps to the bed, which was flush with the wall. Only then did he lower her to stand on the braided rug.

"Do you have something warm, a robe or something to put on?"

Hank glanced around the room, noting its whitewashed walls, sloped ceiling, and diminutive size. It held only the single bed and a narrow, six-drawer chest. The only real color in the room was a bright quilt made of many colors, plain and print, its pieces jumbled and mismatched in sizes and shapes. It was an unequal balance of no pattern at all that he could determine. Nevertheless, it blended into a strange appeal to the eye.

"I can manage on my own now, thank you."

"Certainly," he said, but without concession. He spotted a few pieces of clothing hanging from hooks against the wall and started searching among them.

"You may leave now," she said in a stronger voice.

"Uh-huh, in a minute." He found what looked to him to be a robe, though there was nothing feminine about it. It was faded and probably old, but he guessed it would keep her warm. Underneath it, he found her nightdress.

It was of white flannel, washed so many times it was ultrasoft to the touch. He lifted it free from the hook and held it up against the fading light from the tiny window. Around the neck was a single piece of narrow lace, unpretentious and spare.

Hank glanced at Mariah, who clutched her blanket around herself protectively like a child. Pink crept up her cheeks. Here was another facet to her personality, a hidden one, and one which he thought she didn't want him to know. Amazed, he could only look at her in wonder. Her lashes, looking darker in the gloom, fanned her cheeks; she could not return his gaze. It was one lonely concession to femininity, a piece of lace she never expected a man to see, and it embarrassed her.

"I'll take that, please," she said stiffly, almost painfully shy.

Without a word, he handed it to her and left the room. He descended the stairs, remembering all the lacy, flimsy things the women he knew wore to enhance their beauty. Someday, he would give Mariah some pretty things, he silently vowed, but not because she needed them to become more beautiful. She didn't need anything more than herself to attract him. Like that quilt, she was different parts and pieces, but the whole of her came together in a crazy kind of way to make her unique, like a piece of art. And he wanted her all the more.

Yes, by heaven, he wanted her like he'd never

wanted another woman. All through the swim and after, he had wanted not only to care for her and warm her against the bitter cold, but to hold her close in a loving embrace.

It caught him by surprise how much he had hated to leave her just now.

He frowned as he entered the kitchen. Brown was there, pouring hot coffee. Nate loudly asked how Mariah was feeling, as Jim pushed through the door carrying dry clothing for Hank.

Elam, still a bit pasty-looking, hovered around the stove as though he had been chilled, too, and needed the warmth. "Mariah all right?" he asked quietly.

"Yes, Elam, she will be fine. Why don't you sit down," he suggested calmly. "She will be down in a moment, I'm sure."

"You should change into dry clothes, too, Hank," Jim said, indicating the bundle he held. "I didn't think you would wish to linger in those wet things."

"Good thinking, Jim." He turned to Elam. "May I change in there?" he asked as he tipped his head toward the parlor.

"Yes, of course, son. Tend to your own needs now."

Hank saw the quiet speculation behind Jim's outward demeanor at Elam's affectionate designation "son." Jim's eyes widened with a deepening compassion and understanding.

Hank acknowledged it with a gentle smile before he turned to the cook. "Brown, perhaps we could have supper here tonight. I would not like Mariah to have to go out again."

"Sure, Hank. Pot of stew. I'll bring it right away." Brown handed him a cup of coffee, swiftly covering his own curiosity.

Nate stared openly, his gaze shooting from Elam to Hank, while Elam sat very still, letting Hank take charge.

It then dawned on Hank that he didn't want to explain or make excuses to anyone. He wanted the right to make these commands, to bring order out of the jumbled situation. Who better than he to do it? Elam had been strong and hearty, once, Mariah had told him. Now it didn't take a doctor to see Elam was ill.

In the parlor, Hank peeled off his wet bathing costume and rubbed himself vigorously, then dressed as quickly as possible, all the while wondering what to do.

Elam seemed to think he would marry his granddaughter. Now, so did the other men. A shaft of pain shot through him. He couldn't marry Mariah, no matter what he wanted. His life was vastly different, and his family still expected him to marry Edith, or at least someone else of her type.

He had to leave here soon. Soon . . .

But he couldn't leave Mariah with no future. After the discussion the other day, he simply couldn't. Something would have to be done to see that she had more resources. But loving this ranch as she did, he didn't think she would willingly leave it. He hadn't figured it all out yet.

"Hank!"

He heard the sharpness in Jim's voice instantly, and then, Mariah's soft cry.

"Oh, please God, no! Grandaddy . . ."

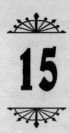

15

Mariah bent over her slumped grandfather, desperately feeling for a pulse. Her heart beat painfully, fearfully, the thrumming loud in her ears. She didn't hear Hank speak her name but heard only a murmur in her ear as he gently pushed her aside.

Hank knelt down and slipped his hand inside the old man's shirt. Mariah couldn't tear her gaze away from the scene; she seemed suspended while everything around her rocked.

Oh, Grandaddy . . .

She clamped her teeth down hard on her trembling bottom lip. Then Hank looked up at her, and faintly, she saw an expression of hope there in his gaze.

"Is he . . . ?"

"His heart is still beating, Mariah. Let's get him to the sofa," Hank murmured softly. He carefully lifted her grandfather and carried him into the parlor.

Jim was there before them, straightening pillows and smoothing cushions, an afghan in his hand. Elam began to stir when Hank laid him down. He muttered Mariah's name.

She took his hand in both of hers, trembling with emotion and her effort to hold in her tears, using sheer willpower to remain calm as she knelt on the floor beside him. "I'm here, Grandaddy."

Please, God, let this spell pass like the other one did. I'll be so good, I promise. I'll work triple hard to make Grandaddy proud of me. I won't even hate Myrtle Alice.

Granny had always told her she couldn't bargain with God, but she thought He had to listen if she was truly contrite.

"I'm right here," she whispered again.

Elam nodded faintly, and seemed to relax. His eyes remained closed. Hank covered him with the afghan while Jim pulled off his boots. No color at all softened his features, making him appear waxy and ancient.

"Does he take anything, Mariah?" Hank asked.

"Oh, yes, he does. Grandaddy, where's your medicine?"

"By . . . bed," Elam breathed out.

Mariah murmured encouragement and Hank was back in a moment with the brown bottle. While he lifted her grandfather, she spooned some of the liquid down Elam's throat. "Rest easy, now, Grandaddy. This should help."

Elam made another faint nod, but reached once more for her hand. Mariah settled down on the floor, her long robe tucked under her, and leaned against the sofa, her fingers wrapped around her grandfather's.

"Would you send Nate for Dr. Canton?" she asked Hank.

"Jim's already gone."

"Thank you."

She remained quiet after that, waiting. After a few moments, Hank placed a quilt around her. She looked down as he tucked the corners across her raised knees. It was her bed quilt, the crazy patch her grandmother had made just before she died.

Hank knelt before her and, without comment, pulled one of her bare feet toward him. He had her stockings in his hand, the ones she had carried down from upstairs, intending to put them on in the kitchen. She'd dropped them somewhere when she saw Grandaddy. Now Hank slipped them onto her feet.

She accepted his ministrations gratefully, but didn't seem able to say another word.

Nate came in with an armload of wood. Quietly, he built a fire in the fireplace, and the room began to feel warmer.

Finally, the doctor arrived, and shooed her out. Hank took her arm firmly and led her into the kitchen. He insisted she drink some coffee, heavily laced with sugar and a shot of whiskey, then sat beside her. She didn't question the whiskey, though she knew it must have been Hank's. Grandaddy, being a staunch Methodist, never drank and wouldn't, under ordinary circumstances, even have it in the house.

"Ol' Elam's gonna be all right, Mariah," Nate said, awkwardly patting her hand. "He ain't agonna die without me. We been together too long, an' I ain't ready to go." She accepted his bravado with gentle thanks, but they both knew how weak Elam had become in the last year.

And she had upset him—three weeks ago, last

week, and today. She'd behaved unseemly, which made gossip for the town to chew on, thereby embarrassing him. Selfishly, she had caused him worry. Mariah cringed inwardly with all the guilt she felt. It was her fault her grandaddy was ill.

The other men crowded the kitchen. The stew Brown had put on the back burner filled the room with the fragrance of meat and onions and spices she couldn't name.

"You men should eat supper," she said. But no one did.

Darkness fell, but Mariah hardly noticed the light fade. Then the doctor came out of the parlor. She watched him steadily, her chest tight, and gathered all her courage to hear what he might say.

"Elam's heart took a bad turn, all right," he told her. "But I'm not sure if it was a full-blown attack or not. I suspect he's been working too hard. I told him last fall to slow down," he said, compassion in his deep blue eyes.

"Wh-what should I do for him?" Mariah asked.

"Keep him quiet and in bed a few days, don't feed him anything heavy, and we'll see what happens. I'll try to get out tomorrow and the next day if I can." He rummaged through his black bag, then handed her a medicine bottle similar to the other one. "I'll leave some more of this. See that he takes it on time—no more of this 'when I think of it' stuff. And no more excitement for a while, understand?"

"We'll see to it, Dr. Canton," she assured him.

She allowed Hank to see the doctor out while she returned to the parlor. Grandaddy was struggling to sit up.

"Now what d'you think you're doing, Grandaddy? You heard what the doctor said."

"I know, honey, but . . . have some business. . . ." he said in a near-whispered breathlessness.

"What business? If it's the cattle you're concerned about, well, I'll just ship them off next week to the Kansas City packing house. With Hank and Jim here, we'll get them to Mead in no time. We've had a better spring than we thought; we can pay our note and some of our other accounts."

"Other business. . . ." he insisted.

Hank spoke from the doorway. "There is no business you need to worry about, Elam, that Mariah and I can't take care of between us."

Elam stared at him a long moment. "You . . . sure?"

"I am sure."

Elam nodded, seemingly satisfied, and lay back. He said nothing further and Mariah watched his face as he settled again. She felt rewarded when his coloring returned to almost normal.

The sounds from the kitchen were muted as the men ate their belated supper. When her grandfather finally slept, she gently kissed his forehead and tip-toed out to the kitchen. Brown spotted her first.

"Here, Miss Mariah, sit down and eat."

"I'm not sure I can."

"You've had a double trauma today, Mariah," Hank told her firmly. "You would benefit from some food."

She'd forgotten all about becoming too chilled. "All right."

Nibbling from a corn cake, she thought about how to manage during the next few days. Someone would have to stay with Grandaddy at all times. She would be there at night, but what about during the day? Nate could sit with him some of the time, but he couldn't hear well enough to always understand Grandaddy's whispers.

Brown had been paid to cook, although she thought he would be willing to do a few extra chores.

Hank and Jim . . . They had come as paying guests, wanting adventure and to learn the ranching business. Hank had said they'd help take care of Circle T business, but they hadn't bargained for illness and nursing duty. In fact, they might want to leave sooner now, after the cattle were shipped. Her grandfather was no kin to either of them, and with so many other things Hank wanted to do, it seemed reasonable for him to want to move on.

But, oh, how she dreaded the idea. She would miss him. His grin with the slightly crooked tooth, his ability to make a statement just by lifting one eyebrow, the uncanny way he seemed to know what she was thinking, and how his actions often dovetailed with hers. She would miss the way he laughed at her antics most of the time and could make her laugh in return. She would miss his warmth, and his . . . oh, hellfire, she would miss his *kisses*.

She pulled herself up short. This would never do. How could she feel so attached to Hank when she'd only known him a few short weeks? It was stupid. Especially now, when she felt even more vulnerable with her grandfather ill. She'd better find a dad-blamed giant-sized padlock to guard her heart or she'd end up being the biggest danged fool of the county yet.

Putting her fork down, she placed her head in her hands and stared between them at the oak table. It did seem that while Grandaddy had the worn-out heart, she actually carried the weakest one in the family. To have tumbled for the wrong man again . . .

Ruthlessly she pushed that weakness aside. She refused to allow any more feelings of loss and abandonment to take root. After all, it wouldn't be like losing Tommy if—when—Hank left. Hank had never planned to stay and she hadn't expected him to remain even this long. She would just have to get along without him.

Mariah jerked her thoughts back to the problems at hand.

"Nate," she said, her voice raised to gain the old man's attention, "would you ride into town tomorrow and ask Mrs. Kelly if she would come out to the Circle T and help out for a few days?"

"Why, shore I will, Mariah. Good idea. Elam'll perk up fer certain, then."

Feeling some relief at the thought, Mariah swallowed a last bite of her supper, surprised that she'd managed to eat almost half of it. Mrs. Kelly had been one of Granny's closest friends and cared a great deal for Grandaddy. It would be a wonderful blessing to have the older woman helping to sit with Elam.

"What else is needed, Mariah?" Hank asked.

"Well, I'd like to make Grandaddy more comfortable than he is on that lumpy old sofa, but I don't want him too far from the kitchen. We should move a bed down from upstairs. It'll have to be mine because his is too big to move without taking it all apart."

"Where will you sleep?"

"Oh, on the sofa or . . ." She glanced around the kitchen. There simply wasn't enough room to put a cot there. "The sofa will do," she said firmly. "I want to be close enough to hear him if he calls."

Brown and Jim went after the bed while she searched for clean linens in the huge chest that sat in one corner of the parlor. Elam seemed to be sleeping, though how soundly, she couldn't tell. At her direction, Hank and Jim rearranged the room, and when it was time Hank once more lifted Elam carefully. Elam remained silent, but she thought the move was, at the very least, uncomfortable for him.

"Thank you, son," he murmured when Hank laid him back on the fresh pillows Mariah had placed for him.

Mariah began to gently unbutton the old man's shirt. "Can you sit up, Grandaddy? I have your nightshirt here."

"Allow me, Miss Mariah," Jim said, bending to her side. "I have had experience in these matters."

"Oh, but I should take care of Grandaddy myself."

"Let Jim help Elam into his nightclothes, honey," Hank said, his voice low as he placed a hand on her shoulder for reassurance. She twisted, raising her gaze toward Hank's. His gray eyes, soft and mellow in the subdued lamplight, held only concern. "Your grandaddy knows you love him. But it will serve his dignity better to have a man help him change."

Mariah looked at her grandfather's drained face. The face that had, all her life, been strong and wise, a face she loved dearly. Now she needed to be the strong one. "All right," she agreed after a long pause.

She left the room and went back upstairs for a few of her things. When she returned to the kitchen, she found Hank dipping into a kettle on the stove's rear iron plate. "I sent Brown and Nate to bed, but before he left for the night, Brown brought some broth he had saved. I thought a little nourishment would be good for Elam about now."

"Yes, I'm sure it will, but I'll do it, Hank."

"Fine." He set the bowl he'd filled on the table.

She picked it up. "You and Jim can go to bed anytime."

"Thank you, my dear. Jim will go. I will stay."

"Oh, you . . . you can't. It . . . it would look . . . you can't stay."

"I can and I will."

"Hank . . . thank you for all your help. I don't know what I would've done without you and Jim tonight. But I'll get through the night with Grandaddy by myself, and tomorrow, hopefully, Mrs. Kelly will come to help."

"Nevertheless, I will stay with you tonight." His face was set into inflexible lines as he went about unrolling a blanket onto the floor by the stove.

"Okay," she said with a sigh. She took the bowl of broth and left him.

Elam sat up with Jim's help, and Mariah slowly spooned liquid into his mouth. After a few spoonfuls, he murmured, "'Nuff, honey."

Mariah helped him resettle, propping his head and back with pillows. After that, Jim left. She heard the kitchen door creak closed as she lay down on the sofa. She thought she wouldn't be able to sleep, and indeed, she did lie awake for a long while, her spirit and mind overly active.

What would she do without her grandfather? His heart continued to weaken and she thought him worse now than in the fall. How much longer would he be with her?

Grandaddy had given her more than one lesson on the way life moved along from birth to death, and dealing with animals had reinforced those lessons frequently. Already, she'd experienced the loss of her parents to cholera, and more recently, the loss of

Granny. Grandaddy believed death was only a doorway to a better place. She had to hang on to that.

Closing her mind to worries, she listened to the night sounds around her. From the bed across the room, her grandfather began to snore gently, and from the kitchen she heard a slight whispering of movement from time to time, as though Hank were restless, also.

She should sleep. Tomorrow would be demanding. First off, she'd establish Mrs. Kelly in the house, then she'd search Grandaddy's correspondence for who to contact in regard to selling the cattle. Then she'd make a head count of the herd, cull the ones she wanted to sell, drive them to Mead—she yawned—plant alfalfa and . . . wheat if the earth had warmed enough . . . check fence . . . train the black mare, she'd neglected that lately . . .

She finally fell asleep by thinking of all the things that needed doing over the coming days. It was the same defense mechanism she'd used just before Tommy's wedding.

Hank tiptoed into the room to check on Elam. He lifted the low-flamed oil lamp high, noting with relief the old man's even breathing. He couldn't resist the temptation of padding over to see if Mariah was comfortable. She lay on her side, facing the room, one hand tucked under her cheek. Her features looked pale, the light freckles receding into nothingness in the lamp's glow.

One small glistening patch lay beneath her eyelid. With the lightest touch possible, he used his forefinger to wipe away the tear. He brought the moisture up to his lips and tasted it. Salty. Like Mariah. She tried in every way possible to hide all her sweetness. And she had a deep well of it.

He bent over to kiss her, pressing his lips tenderly to a corner of her mouth. She didn't stir. Probably exhausted, poor darling. And little wonder. She was more industrious than any other female he knew, and as hardworking as any servant. Now she had the added worry of caring for her ailing grandfather.

Well, he would be there to help her. The thought of leaving anytime soon didn't even raise an argument in his mind. Tomorrow, he would send his brothers notice of where he could be reached.

The days settled into a new pattern. Mrs. Kelly arrived with Nate and took over the household as well as any majordomo Hank had ever seen. It made him chuckle, and he caught no less than a half grin on Jim's face as well.

Catherine Kelly began by fluffing Elam's pillows and ordering Hank to push the sofa into a corner and place the rocker closer to the bed.

"I'm sorry, Elam, you have taken ill. Now, now, no need to try to talk. You must keep quiet and rest, Nate says. Doctor's orders. I brought the *Rocky Mountain News*. I'll sit and read to you after I get things squared away."

She turned to Mariah. "We'll take turns at night nursing. Meanwhile, Mariah, you must have a regular bed in your own room." She emphasized her meaning by looking from Hank to Mariah, and back again.

Mariah agreed. Nate must have told Mrs. Kelly that Hank had spent the night in the house, alone with her except for a sick man. Oh, this would really scald the cat, Mariah thought, if people heard that!

However innocent or necessary it was, there would be some who would consider it scandalous. At least she could trust Mrs. Kelly not to spread spiteful gossip.

Catherine Kelly continued. "Hank, dear, will you and Jim please haul one of those extra cots from the bunkhouse up here to the house? It will do well enough. And I think for a time I will do the cooking for Elam. . . . Tell Brown, please. Elam needs specially cooked food, while the cowhands need heartier fare. Also, have Brown find the fattest hen he has in the flock and bring it, cleaned, to me here. I'll make chicken soup.

"And Mariah, I can see your laundry has piled high; I'll tackle it first thing tomorrow morning, if Elam continues to improve. Meanwhile, please gather anything you have hidden that should go into the wash. Oh, my, I do hope we have a sunny day for it. This overcast weather is no help."

Mariah threw her arms around the older woman. "Mrs. Kelly, you're a godsend."

"Nonsense, my dear." She patted Mariah's back as she talked. "There were many times when your grandmother was my angel of mercy. I am pleased to return some of her generosity. Now, I'm sure you have things to do, and I will entertain Elam for an hour or so with the Denver newspaper. Go, my dear, go."

Mariah did as she was bid. With Hank trailing behind her, she set about her tasks, pushing her day's horizons even farther than usual. Everyone, even old Nate, strove to keep up with her, and the work went forward. Mariah realized she would have faced impossible odds without the extra men.

While Hank remained at Mariah's side, Jim was the one who took care of the errands in town. When, three days after Elam's attack, Hank suggested sending a telegram to the Kansas City meat packing company as opposed to a regular letter, Jim sent it. Mariah was pleased when Jim returned to the Circle T the following day with an agreement of terms. They were to ship the week following, so they immediately went about culling and gathering. This task had been made easier, Mariah told Hank, by the preparation work they'd done earlier.

During the evenings, Hank often strolled to the house to sit with Elam for an hour or two. Mariah listened, sometimes from the kitchen with Mrs. Kelly, and frequently from the parlor corner, happily silent, sitting Indian fashion on the sofa. She found it restful.

The men talked of world events, business, railroad expansions, the current status of mining, and the local cattlemen's concerns. Hank amazed her with all he knew. He seemed well-read, and his interests were obviously broad. Her knowledge stacked up against Hank's like a splinter to a full-grown tree, she mused. Her education had been limited, and consisted only of basics: reading, writing, and arithmetic—and ranching, of course.

Hank came from quality, a good background. Despite his spontaneous spirit and his love of gambling, his breeding showed through. Instinctively, she'd known it all along. He was so much more than a mere adventurer—though the love of adventure was still his driving force.

That was another reason for him to move on soon, Mariah reminded herself. What could hold his interest any longer in this small community? Nevertheless, she was grateful he had chosen to stay and help see her through this difficult time.

The other men came, too, speaking to Elam quietly under Mrs. Kelly's eagle eye and stern admonition to keep their visits short and their talk bland. The doctor, when he returned, approved of the patient's condition. Thank heavens, Elam seemed well on the mend.

Hank, like Mariah, filled the jumbled days with action, with whatever needed doing next. In spite of his concern about Elam, he enjoyed every day. He dug into the work with great satisfaction and stayed close to Mariah.

Then, on Saturday night, Jim broached a subject he had been avoiding.

"I've brought mail from town, Hank." He handed his employer a stack of letters.

Hank leaned back on his bunk and shuffled through them, noting two from his brother Robert, one from Tony, and another from Edith. Until a week ago, all his mail had come through to him from a New York solicitor he had engaged. He had not wanted anyone to know exactly where to find him. Soon, though, his brothers would receive his communication which contained his exact address.

"Mmm. Robert's will be the same recounting of the doing in town or what the estate is costing in repairs." He chuckled as he unfolded his letters. "He would be shocked if he could see the repairs we've made to this place, wouldn't he, Jim? What we could do for the Circle T with a fraction of what he spends. Uh-huh, as I predicted . . . I wonder . . . oh, hell, he is going on again about Edith."

Hank tossed the letter on top of the unopened one from the Eastern girl.

"Master Henry," Jim said, "you should tell Elam about your family. After all this, leading the poor man on to believe you will take over running the Circle T with his granddaughter is pure falsehood. It can only lead to causing him greater harm when we leave."

"I've told you, Jim, I can't explain it all to him just now. Mariah and I . . . we got into this by accident. It was a little adventure, and she needed me. She still needs me, and not only because of her grandfather's illness."

Lord, he knew it sounded idiotic. But having gotten into the pretense, he found himself wanting to live it. It was fun to be someone else beside Henry Clayton Ackerley. He didn't want it to stop, although he supposed the fun had ceased when Elam had his attack.

And he still wanted Mariah. Every day, every night.

"I don't really understand this arrangement you have with Miss Mariah. Master Henry, haven't you thought how she will be hurt by all this pretense, more than ever she was before you came along?"

"Of course I've thought of it. Do you see me as that selfish and thoughtless? I'm working to prevent that from happening, to give her alternatives."

"Yes, sir, but—"

"There is really little harm in Mariah not knowing I come from a titled family, or that I have a little money. Why would she care? She thinks I am a mere gambler, someone seeking a new adventure at each turn of the corner. Or turn of cards. Don't you see, James? She sees me as a man alone—I stand or fall on my own merits, in her eyes. Not for who my family is, but for who *I* am."

"Yes, I do see that. But, Master Henry, don't you see what else her eyes hold? The girl loves you. What will she do when she learns you intend to marry Edith?"

"I am not going to marry Edith."

"No? Then your brothers . . ."

"Hang my brothers. I don't wish to talk about this any longer. And please leave me to tend my own business, James."

Hank stalked out of the bunkhouse, sudden anger riding him hard. He didn't want to be reminded of what his family expected of him, or what Edith and her family expected. This journey had been meant to be his last adventurous fling before he "did his duty" by marrying and settling into a society life which would enhance both families. He no longer wanted any of it.

He paced away, then back. Jim was right—he had been deceitful. But if he told Mariah and Elam the truth about his background, they would look at him differently, treat him differently. He couldn't leave them without help, but he knew they would never accept what they would see as charity. Himself, his help, they could accept.

He didn't know what was best to do, he only knew he couldn't leave this place yet. Circumstances had become so scrambled, so complicated. He had been here, what, a month? A month of hard work, living close to the land. Land which was still half wild, where he felt free with a girl who made him feel . . . everything.

He wanted Mariah, and he wanted this freedom for a little while longer. Only the summer. At least the summer.

In the distance, he saw Mariah come out of the house, a slim figure in an old dress, swinging a pail on her way to feed the chickens. Her hair tumbled down her back, secured only by a ribbon. He stared, his heart longing, until she disappeared from view.

Would she ever let him make love to her? She had responded to his kisses, and he knew she had been as eager as he. But her will was strong and she had determined not to give in. He admired her strength, but, oh, Lord, he wanted her!

He whipped about, suddenly needing diversion from the Circle T.

"Jim!" he called through the door. "I am going into town."

16

That Sunday, Grandaddy wouldn't hear of Mariah not attending church. He insisted he was well enough to be left alone for the morning, with only Nate to keep him company. Anyway, Mrs. Kelly mentioned she needed to pick up a few things in town, so Mariah hitched Lulubelle to the buggy.

"I expect we shall have a few visitors this afternoon, Mariah," the older woman remarked on their way home after they'd made a stop at her house to gather the things she wanted. "To pay respects to your grandfather."

"Oh, do you think so? We haven't had many since Granny died. I'd planned to work the mare this afternoon."

"It might be best if you remained in your good dress, my dear. I know for a fact that Reverend Higginbotham will attend to his calling duties."

"Oh . . . well, he won't care about my company as long as you're there to offer tea and cookies," Mariah said with a smile. Mrs. Kelly had baked three kinds of cookies earlier in the week. "Nobody need see me."

True to Mrs. Kelly's prediction, the pastor came at about three, not so early that he'd had to miss his big Sunday dinner, Mariah noted. He spoke to her stiffly, keeping his eyes on her face, then went on to the house.

Dressed in the tight-fitting dungarees she wore for work, Mariah ruefully returned her attention to the mare. So much for approval from that quarter. He definitely disapproved of women in pants. She should have followed Mrs. Kelly's advice on her dress.

"I say, Mariah, what have you decided this little lady is to be called?" Jim asked from the sidelines as he climbed to sit on the corral fence.

Mariah glanced beyond him to see if Hank was also in the vicinity, but he was nowhere in sight. The two men had disappeared late Saturday afternoon, and she hadn't seen them all morning. They had gone to town, she suspected, as most cowhands did, to have a good time after a hard week. For most men, that meant a saloon and whiskey, a card game, or keno or roulette. Or—she suddenly despised the thought—a woman.

Her lips folded tight. It was no business of hers. Hank and Jim were free agents. It was only . . .

Hang it all, Hank had every right to seek his pleasures like any other man. Just because he'd stuck to her like a burr these last weeks, it didn't give her any claims to him, none at all to protest his activities. She only wished her heart felt the same.

"I haven't a name for her yet," she answered Jim. "There hasn't been enough time to work her lately, and she's become skittish again." It had taken her an hour to calm the mare enough to take the bridle, and now she was removing it once more. "What d'you think I should call her?"

"Oh, nothing mundane or common, even though she is only a mustang."

"You like her, then?" She put a nose bag of oats on the mare, then picked up a brush and began to curry the black coat.

"Yes, ma'am, I do. If I thought . . ."

She glanced at Jim over her shoulder. His soft gaze rested on the mare. But he was staring inwardly, Mariah decided, seeing something beyond his vision.

"If you thought?"

"Well, miss, I would like to purchase the mare. That is, if I thought we would be remaining the season . . . that is, if Hank decided . . ."

"Must you do everything Hank tells you?" she said in exasperation. Her brush strokes became firmer. "Seems to me you have a mind of your own, if you'd but exert yourself a little. There's lots of opportunity for an enterprising man around here. What's it to Hank if you wanted to stay in Colorado?"

"What, indeed?" Hank said from behind Jim.

Mariah whirled. Hank gave her that amused smile, which, at the moment, only served to heighten her irritation at him, rather than charm her.

"Jim may choose his own destiny, my dear Mariah, at any time. If he wishes to establish himself in an occupation here in Colorado, he is free to do so. Right, Jim?"

"Ah, quite so, Hank. I only remarked about not knowing how long we planned to remain in the area."

Hank crossed his arms against the top corral rail. "Hmm . . . Is there something in particular that hangs on when we leave or how long we stay?"

"I was admiring the black mare. I wouldn't mind owning her if we are to stay through the summer."

"By all means, Jim, make your purchase. You will need her, especially when we go after Fireball later in the summer."

"That's it! That's part of what I mean. It seems to me Jim always waits on you to make up his mind for him," Mariah said with asperity. But her heart sang with joy, for Hank still wanted his wild horse and he'd mentioned the summer—a reason to stay longer, and a length of time stated. They were only in late spring now. Anything could happen in those months.

Suddenly Jim let loose a bark of laughter. "Not in every case, I do assure you, ma'am. There has been a time or two—"

"Careful, Jim, you don't wish to give away our secrets," Hank said with a laugh of his own, his mouth edged in teasing self-derision.

"No, of course not," Jim returned. "But you must admit there have been occasions when I have been the one to take charge of an, er, ah, exhibition, or redirected an excursion. Much to your brother's gratitude, I might add."

Mariah's hand stilled. Hank had a brother? This was the first she'd heard of his family. She wondered if he had parents or other siblings, back in England. If Jim mentioned pleasing Hank's brother, that meant Hank's family ties were important to him.

"True enough, but those were in my salad days, before I had gained a command over my own affairs. You should not mislead Mariah—"

The sound of a carriage coming up the drive interrupted them. Mariah glanced that way. "Hell's bells," she muttered in near shock. "It's Caroline and Mrs. Benton. Wonder what they want."

Caroline had been to the Circle T only once or twice in her life. Mariah had always appreciated their close location to town, but now she fervently wished they were back of the beyond.

"Very likely they have come to pay a call on your grandfather, Mariah," Hank said. "Come along, I will escort you to the house."

"If they came to see Grandaddy, it won't matter—"

"It does matter, my dear." He was firm. "You can't skulk out here and ignore your social obligations."

"But—"

"Remember what you promised the night of Elam's attack? You said you would be very good and mind your manners."

Her mouth opened. Had she prayed aloud? She must have, though she thought it very unkind of Hank to remind her of it at a time when she wanted to tell him to take his manners and go jump in the lake. But she had promised. . . .

She threw the brush down and gave Hank a mulish answer, squinting her eyes at him. "All right, but they'll have to accept me as I am. Here, Jim, if the mare is to be yours, you can finish grooming."

"I think Jim should come along with us. Caroline will be expecting to see him."

"So she will." Mariah sighed, catching some of Hank's wry amusement. She climbed through the rails and the three of them started toward the house. "You do know, don't you, Jim, that Caroline has set her cap for you."

"I had rather suspected as much, ma'am. I must say, I am a bit flattered."

She stopped. "You aren't," she said in disbelief. "Hank, did you know Jim felt this way?"

"I had noticed the signs." Hank chuckled, giving his friend a long glance. "He spends a long time at his errands in town."

"Oh. So that's the way the wind blows, huh? Well," she said as she grinned widely and tucked a hand through both men's arms, "let's give her something to think about."

A moment later, Mariah gazed around the small, crowded parlor—Mrs. Kelly had moved kitchen chairs in to accommodate everyone—and greeted the women visitors. She maneuvered Jim to a seat next to Caroline, then took a seat next to him, leaving Hank to lean against the door frame. She ignored Mrs. Benton's expression of distaste at her clothing, and politely chatted up a storm. She was doing fine, just fine . . . until the subject swung to the newlyweds' return.

"Mrs. Sonyers has planned an 'at home' next Sunday afternoon, a reception for Tommy and Myrtle Alice on their return," Caroline said. "I am so looking forward to it. Mrs. Sonyers and Myrtle Alice have such savoir faire, I just know it will be wonderful. Their home is the largest, finest one in Mead. Why, they had furniture brought all the way from Europe, and crystal and china, too! It is exquisitely lovely."

"How nice," Mariah dutifully murmured. Her body grew stiffer as Caroline went on. And on.

"Very nice," Elam echoed.

"Tommy and Myrtle Alice are going to live with the Sonyers family, you see. Can you imagine living in that elegant house? Mrs. Sonyers intends to put in a garden this spring, a real one like they have in England and Europe. She's even hired a gardener."

Of course Tommy would live with the Sonyers

family. Myrtle Alice could never be expected to live in the tiny room above the hardware store where he'd lived before the wedding.

Mariah sighed. She shouldn't fault anybody for that, least of all Tommy. She'd expected him to live with her, here, when she thought that she'd be the bride. But Tommy enjoyed the finer things. Yes, oddly enough, Mariah could imagine Tommy there, in that huge brick house with three servants—or so Caroline had said—and its own carriage house in the rear of the property.

"And Mrs. Sonyers has engaged a musician, a fiddler, to entertain at the reception," Caroline's voice chimed on.

"A violinist from Denver," corrected Mrs. Benton. "Yes, indeed, the addition of the Sonyers family to our little town last year has been a wonderful boon, don't you agree, Catherine?"

"Yes, they have a fine sense of . . . society," Mrs. Kelly replied. "Have some more tea, Gladys."

Caroline continued. "I'm sure the Sonyers family would want to include you, Mr. Moore and Mr. Clayton, if you but say you would come. A chance to be introduced properly, so to speak."

"You are most kind to say so, Miss Benton. But I do not have an acquaintance with the family," Hank answered.

"Oh, I can arrange for you to come. You too, Mariah," Caroline added, her eyes shining. "I just know, now that you have another beau"—she slanted her eyes at Hank—"and Mr. Clayton being so fine a gentleman . . . well, anyway, you don't care about Tommy anymore, and I'm sure Mrs. Sonyers will be quite open to the suggestion."

Go to a party for Tommy and his bride? Watch

him coo over that delicate piece of . . . What did Caroline think she was made of, steel and iron?

"I don't think, with Grandaddy having been ill, I could."

"Don't say no on my account," Elam said. "I'll be up in no time."

"Oh." Caroline rounded her eyes as her hand went to her mouth. "I am so sorry. How clumsy of me, how unthinking. Of course you wouldn't leave your grandfather. Sorry, Mr. Taggert, I am so-o sorry you've taken ill. But really"—she turned to Jim—"that should not keep Mr. Moore at home."

Once again Mariah felt caught between laughter and irritation. Caroline was closing in on her target. "Sure, Jim. Why don't you go . . . I'm sure Caroline would appreciate your very elegant escort."

Caroline blushed to her hairline. Hank's hand came down on Mariah's shoulder with a hard clasp. She shouldn't have put Caroline on the spot that way. It had been an unkind thing to do, but Mariah had had all the sweet poison she could stomach.

"You really ought to attend, Mariah," Mrs. Benton said, rolling right over the byplay. "I'm sure you'll wish to be there to welcome Tommy and his bride home. It would mitigate, somewhat, the unfortunate results of your most recent . . . ah . . . circumstances."

Mariah's hackles not only rose, they stood on end. "'Unfortunate results'?" she murmured. "I don't understand—"

"Elam is greatly improved, Mariah," Mrs. Kelly interrupted, glancing at her sharply. "I think it would do you a world of good to get out with the young people."

Hank leaned forward over her chair, his hand grazing her arm, making it appear they were indeed a twosome. "I think we should go, Mariah." He smiled his slow, charming smile at Mrs. Benton, then Caroline. "If you can arrange an invitation, Miss Benton, we would be most happy to attend."

"What the hellfire do you mean, you cussed greenhorn, pushing me into that—that crock of an invitation? You're the one they wanted to invite, not me!" Mariah stomped up and down the cookshack, waving a fist at him. They'd gone there to talk in private as soon the guests had left. "You and Jim. Why didn't you just let me have my excuse of staying with Grandaddy?"

"Mrs. Kelly offered to stay with Elam. It was she who said you needed to see some young people," Hank said mildly. He leaned against the door, his arms folded across his chest. "And I happen to agree with her."

Mariah ignored his logic. "Well, I won't go."

"You will."

"No, thank you. I won't go and watch Tommy . . ."

"That's why we will go. *We,* my dear. And Jim, of course."

"Fine. You and Jim go. I'm sure the finest society of Mead will enjoy your presence."

"Mmm-hmm. Jim, and I, and . . . you."

"Not in a month of Sundays." She stomped past him.

"Your grandfather wishes it."

"Grandaddy won't insist. It's only a party."

"My point. So why not go?"

"I don't like parties." She would feel totally vulnerable, watching Tommy dance to Myrtle Alice's tune.

"There's nothing of which to be frightened. I will be at your side the whole time."

"I didn't say . . . I'm not afraid. Y-you—" She was only a little frightened. Only to her back teeth. Hank could escort her, but there was no guarantee he would remain at her side, what with all of the notoriety he'd gained. Now he was sought after by the town's elite.

"I do think you should have a new dress, though, and a bonnet and gloves, too."

"No, I don't need—"

He paid her protest little heed. "In royal blue, I think."

Royal blue? Royal blue. The memory of the train station and Myrtle Alice standing there, under Tommy's admiring eye, in a beautiful royal-blue costume, complete with hat to match, flashed across her mind.

"No! Not royal blue!"

"Oh? Why not? You would look lovely in that shade."

"It's Myrtle Alice's favorite color. She wears it all the time."

Hank pursed his lips and narrowed his eyes, his gaze running from the top of her head to the tips of her boots. "All right, then . . . a buttercup yellow. Yeesss . . . buttercup yellow will bring out more of the red in your hair. A square neckline, to emphasize the lovely length of your neck . . . and navy-blue trim. Down the front bodice points, too, along the stay lines."

"I don't wear stays."

A sudden gleam appeared in his gray eyes while a grin tugged at his mouth. "I am well aware of that, my darling girl, but they are fashionable."

"Well, I won't wear them."

"In the practical daily life of your ranching duties, I

would agree. Besides, you don't need them. But this is a social occasion, in which you want to show yourself at your best."

"I haven't said I would go."

"And I have a feeling that, dressed for the occasion, you will be quite stunning."

Stunning? Did he really think so? She stopped her pacing to stare at him. His gaze roved her hair.

"Cascading curls down your back, I think, with only a bit of a hat atop. The hairstyle is out of fashion, I know, but it is one you will look wonderful in—I think we can accept it."

Mariah looked at the floor. It all sounded like a dream, but one she had to wake from to face reality. There wasn't enough money to pay for new duds, and she couldn't justify the expenditure on credit, since they still had bills to catch up on from last year.

"Hank, I don't think all this planning is any good." She bit her bottom lip and shifted her weight from foot to foot.

"Nonsense, my dear. Planning is essential. And while we're about it, when we go to the dressmaker, I think we should order an evening dress for that spring affair Miss Benton has talked of, too."

"Hank, you're not listening to me. I can't go."

His eyebrows rose. Both of them. "My dear, I thought we had finished with that argument. What is it now?"

She hated to admit the truth—she hated it like poison—but it would be decidedly worse if she were to go into debt over her vanity.

"I appreciate what you're trying to do for me, Hank, but I—I simply can't afford new clothes."

"Is that all that worries you? Well, rest easy, my

dear. I had planned on taking care of the dress-maker's bills."

"Now how would that look to everyone? Besides, I can't let you spend any more money for me. Or the Circle T."

It embarrassed her that the credit for a great deal of Circle T's current improvement could be laid at Hank's door. His generosity had been deep, even though he pretended he was getting something in return. But pride wouldn't let her accept more.

"And anyway, you're not going to have any money left after the way you've been spending it," she teased in an effort to cover her feelings.

"Didn't I tell you? Lady luck sat on my shoulder last night."

"What do you mean?"

"I spent the evening at poker, my dear. And won. I have enough money to pay *three* dressmakers."

"Poker!" That explained his absence from the Circle T the night before. But it didn't ease her concern. "You didn't play with any of Kasey's ilk, I hope."

"Didn't see a familiar face except for Rose and Thorndyke. It was a very quiet evening."

"Oh. Well, I . . . I guess . . ." She fumbled to a stop. She wanted to scold him about playing poker—especially when it carried the possibility of great loss—and she wanted to complain that he'd gone to town without telling her, leaving her purely flat without his company. Most of all she wanted to cry, because she couldn't match him for—for that *thing*, that "savoir faire" Caroline kept on and on about.

She spun around and walked away, reverting to what she could express. "But didn't you hear what I just told you? I can't afford a new dress, and it wouldn't look right for you to pay for it."

"Mmm. I shall have to remedy that." He waited until she had made her turn before saying, "How fortunate that bustles have dropped this year, leaving the top of the skirt fitted. We can show one of your best assets."

"What are you talking about?"

"Your derriere, my dear. You have an extremely wicked walk-away."

"Oh! Oh, you—you dad-blamed . . . *Englishman!*"

In his study at Ackerley Hall, Surrey, England, Lord Robert Bertrand Ackerley, sixth duke of Stroud, rocked back in his desk chair as his brother, Anthony, was shown in.

"You sent for me, Robby?"

"I did. Sit down, Tony. Finally got a letter from the scapegrace that hasn't been posted from New York," Robert said, frowning slightly. "Been annoying, having all my mail cleared through a middleman."

"Henry, eh? About time. Where is he?"

Both brothers were tall, well-set-up men with a certain look of power and prestige about them. Neither one had ever doubted his position in life, and both had lived up to what was expected of them. Robert had married well and fathered two children. Tony had chosen not to marry; his scholarly work with the church was enough, he always maintained. Their biggest worry in life was their brother, Henry.

"Someplace in Colorado. He never made it to Denver."

"I see. Was it a girl or a poker game? Or perhaps he's panning for gold?" Tony asked, only half amused.

"He merely says his plans have changed about the

buffalo hunt at this time, and he hasn't had a chance
to see any Indians . . ." Robert reached for the two
sheets of brief correspondence. "And he is no longer
interested in the Boston heiress . . . and is making
investments of which we would be proud."

"Investments? What kind of investments? He cannot afford to squander what little money he has left."

A long-suffering sigh escaped Robert. "No. And I
cannot understand how he could set aside his opportunity to wed into that railroad family. It would be
most beneficial to him. Most beneficial. And to our
interests, as well."

"Is that all he says? He isn't asking for money, is
he? I know you told him he could not have another
penny if he overspent on his Western trip."

"No, he hasn't asked for money. . . ."

"That is surprising. It is a good thing his inheritance from Grandmama is tied up so he can only
withdraw semiannually."

"Yes, yes, it is. Tony, there is something very odd
for which Henry does ask."

"Oh?" Tony frowned, sitting forward. "What is
that?"

"He asks what wool is bringing per pound these
days. And he wants all the information about sheep
and their raising, and wool, that I can get my hands
on to be sent to him at the address he lists. A place
called Mead, Colorado."

"Sheep! He must be joking."

"I don't think so," Robby said, as he steepled his
fingers. "Not in his usual flavor of jests."

"But sheep? I don't understand. Henry has never
in his life exhibited any interest in farm animals,
although he does spend a fortune on his racing stock.
The only other things that seem to excite him are his

harebrained adventures in racing, gambling, and women. And his boxing, of course."

"I know. Tried to interest him in the estate in Wales a few years back. Thousands of sheep there. Would've given him a go at managing, but he would hear none of it."

"What do you think is behind it all?"

"Don't know." Robby shook his head. "He says he'll be there through the summer."

"You've heard nothing from James?"

"No, not a word."

"Ahhh." Tony relaxed. "Well, I think if Henry were in any real trouble, James would let us know forthwith."

"Yes, yes, James is a good man. Still . . . do you think one of us should go out to see what is going on?"

"Tempting, I must say," Tony replied. "And I do plan to take a holiday myself this summer. But let us wait yet a while to decide. Surely we will hear more from him soon. But imagine . . . he has not asked for money. . . ."

17

On Sunday afternoon at about four, Mariah came downstairs into the kitchen, where Grandaddy, Nate, and Hank were waiting. In spite of herself, and though not without some dread, she was excited about the reception. She felt confident in her looks. In fact, she felt positively, stupendously, if shyly, pretty. For the first time in her life.

The look in the men's eyes confirmed her confidence. She gave a tenuous smile. "It is all right, isn't it?"

"More than all right, honey," Grandaddy proudly told her. "You look beautiful."

"Ya look like ya come from Noo Yawk or Denver," shouted Nate. "Never seen a yella dress look so grand."

"I would say she looks like a fashion plate from Paris," Hank said. "Your local seamstress has turned out to be quite adequate to the request. Turn around slowly, Mariah."

Mariah did. She felt their gaze go from the tiny hat which crowned her cascading curls to her hem, where heeled, navy kid-leather shoes over almost sheer stockings peeked out. The buttercup-yellow dress, true to Hank's vision, sported a modest square neckline, trimmed in navy, and the tight sleeves ran all the way to her wrists. From one hand dangled a reticule made from the same navy material of the dress trim. The bodice hugged her long waist before following the sudden flare of her hips. The upper skirt was tight, and the bustle flirted at just above the back of her knees. As a result, she could walk only in small steps.

She came back around in time to catch a totally impertinent glint in Hank's eyes. He had the outrageous audacity to give her a cocky grin and a knowing wink, right in front of everybody. She flushed, fighting the impulse to put her hands behind her back, a purely reflexive intention to protect her rear as she remembered his remark about her backside. She gave him an "I'll-get-you-later" glance, and turned to kiss her grandfather's cheek.

Mrs. Kelly came into the kitchen with a proud smile. She carried a fingertip cape that matched Mariah's dress. "Our Mariah is going to make an impression today, wouldn't you say?"

"Amen," said Elam.

"She'll turn ev'ry head from here ta Denver, I'll bet," Nate said.

"No one would bet against you today, Nate," Hank agreed. He wore his city clothes, looking handsome and urbane. "Let us be on our way, Mariah."

They rode into town at a spanking pace, with the top of the buggy pushed back. Hank parked it along the street neatly, then handed Mariah down. He tucked her hand securely through his elbow and laid a hand gently on top of it.

"Ready, my love?"

"I suppose so," she said. She wondered if Hank knew how quivery she was. After all the years she'd known Tommy, she all at once felt very nervous at confronting him again. It wouldn't be the same. Tommy wouldn't be the same. And Myrtle Alice's superior stare sure did beat all, from what she remembered.

"Chin up, Mariah." Hank looked at her through lowered lashes, and patted her hand. "Remember, I am your most devoted beau. In fact, I will tell one and all, including Tommy, that I think you are the most beautiful girl in Colorado, that I adore you, that I won't wait long to make you mine, and that I have every confidence that my family will take you to their hearts, especially my grandmother"—he barely paused for breath—"the Lady Patrice, who, having been the toast of London in her day, is known for her spirit of adventure, like yours."

Mariah giggled. "Hank, stop it. You can't say all that."

"Why not?" he answered with a straight face and raised brows. "Am I not supposed to divert the company's attention from the fact that you once fancied yourself promised to the bridegroom, and also to make him sorry now that his choice went awry?"

"Yes, but if you talk all flummery like that," she said, leaning closer to avoid being overheard by people arriving behind them, "folks will put you down as a pure fool, besides not believing such nonsense."

"They have already concluded I am a very strange duck, anyway, have they not?"

"Oh, not any more than any other . . . tenderfoot."

"Come, now, Mariah. Truth."

"Well, yes, but they like you anyway. The boxing did it, I think."

"There. So if I look at you with languishing eyes and yearning smiles, they will only put it down to the fact that I am a strange interloper who is hopelessly in love with you. And if anyone calls me a fool, I will simply call him out. Challenge him to a duel—in the ring." He lowered his brow to a heavy scowl. "Do you think my temper fierce enough to send others running for cover like Kasey did?"

They had strolled along the newly laid brick path while they talked, ascended the wooden stairs, and walked across the porch to the open front door. A maid let them into the foyer; Tommy and Myrtle Alice stood ready to greet their visitors, Mr. and Mrs. Sonyers beside them, talking to a couple whom Mariah didn't recognize.

"Like Kasey—" Mariah's laughter bubbled out. "Oh, Hank, you are an idiot."

Myrtle Alice looked around in affronted puzzlement, while Tommy appeared more than a little surprised. Shocked, actually, Mariah thought. She didn't know whether to be pleased or offended as she saw his eyes widen. She let her laughter subside into a smile.

"Mariah!" Tommy muttered. A bit guiltily, she noted.

"Hello, Tommy. Welcome home."

Tommy quickly scanned her costume in dazed disbelief, flashed to her companion, then returned to her. The grudging admiration she saw in his gaze reassured her self-confidence. A heap. Her smile grew impish.

"Mariah, uh, h-how nice to-to see you. I didn't

realize you . . . uh, oh, you know Myrtle Alice, don't you?"

"Yes, how do you do, Myrtle Alice?"

Myrtle Alice wore an exquisite, watered silk baby-blue dress to reflect her large blue eyes. Her golden hair, a few shades lighter than Tommy's, rose smoothly from her neck and temples to a full knot on top. She looked a picture, holding a nosegay in one hand while she extended her other. "Miss Taggert. How very nice of you to come," she said in a reed-high voice.

"It was so kind of your mother to remember me, don't you think? And I'd like you both to meet my guest from England, Mr. Henry Clayton. Hank, this is Mr. and Mrs. Thomas Bakersfield."

Hank did his bowing thing, to Mariah's amusement. He held Myrtle Alice's hand the correct three seconds, murmured, "Very happy to make your acquaintance, madam," and gave her one of his most devastating smiles. Myrtle Alice seemed to lose her poise momentarily while searching for the correct response. Her cheeks flushed while her eyelashes fluttered like the wings of a butterfly.

Tommy's face stiffened. He glanced at Mariah suspiciously as though to accuse her of doing something underhanded. Or of being about to do something to embarrass him. She took a lesson from Hank and merely raised her brows. "Did you have a nice wedding trip, Tommy? San Francisco, wasn't it?"

"Um, yes. San Francisco."

"Oh, it was divine. Simply divine," said Myrtle Alice. "One could never tire of the splendid hills, you know, or the city's ravishing beauty. Thomas insisted we have a cab for every excursion. So-o-o romantic, you understand. The mansions there almost rival the ones in New York, Thomas says. I didn't care much for that smelly wharf, but our hotel was so-o-o elegant, and the meals in which one is able to indulge . . . Thomas insists we must go again in a few years."

"It sounds lovely, Myrtle Alice," Mariah murmured. It was time to move along and she spotted Caroline, proudly holding Jim's arm.

"Oh, yes . . ." Myrtle Alice's gaze almost met Mariah's before returning, enraptured, to Tommy.

Mariah moved away a step and Hank offered his hand to Tommy. Tommy practically sprang forward to take it. "Clayton. Oh, *Mr. Clayton!* You're that fellow everyone's told me about, the one that came up against Kasey. First poker, then boxing, huh?"

"It was not difficult."

Myrtle Alice puckered her pretty brow. "Thomas darling, must you discuss that disgusting man, Kasey, in my parlor?"

"Sorry, Myrtle Alice." Tommy's attention returned to Hank. "Wish I'd seen it, though. Kasey can be a mean son-of-a . . . sorry, dear. I'm surprised the devil didn't try to pull something funny."

"Thomas, really."

"I do apologize, Mrs. Bakersfield." Hank directed his remark to his hostess, along with another charming smile. "How rude we are to impose our vulgar men's talk on such a genteel and lovely lady. I hope you can forgive me."

Mollified, Myrtle Alice sniffed her nosegay and regally nodded in acceptance of the apology. "Tommy, dear . . ."

"Perhaps we can talk later," Tommy nearly whispered before turning back to his guests.

Mariah dropped her gaze. It was almost more than

she could take without comment; she clamped her teeth together to avoid giggling at the look of resignation in Tommy's eyes. Poor Tommy. Myrtle Alice was a very pretty young woman, but there wasn't much more to her than that.

Mr. and Mrs. Sonyers were next. Mariah greeted them in her most affable manner and introduced Hank. Mr. Sonyers, his hazel eyes keen underneath bushy brows, seemed to take a particular interest in Hank.

"Ah, Mr. Clayton. So glad you came, sir. Glad to make your acquaintance, at last. Heard much of you, of course."

"How do you do, Mr. Sonyers. How kind of you and Mrs. Sonyers to include us in your festivity."

"Happy you accepted. Perhaps we could talk later, after some of this crowd gets through," Mr. Sonyers said. "Please, enjoy the party."

Hank bowed low over Mrs. Sonyers's hand, made pleasant conversation for a moment, then took Mariah into the parlor.

"There, my love, that wasn't so dreadful, was it?" Hank asked her.

"No," she replied with a sigh. But she wasn't sure she could have done it without him.

Hank tucked her hand into his arm, and they strolled to the tea table in the dining room. Both rooms opened onto the side porch, where people spilled into the spring sunshine. Mariah looked around, listening to the strains of a violin from the hall balcony and taking in the furnishings and wallpaper, the pictures and ankle-deep carpets.

They mingled with the best of society from Mead and its environs, ranchers and leading merchants and prominent townspeople.

People spoke to them. Most of them asked after Elam. If Hank hadn't yet met them, Mariah made introductions, then later explained to him in an undertone who they were.

As is usual with such a gathering, the young and single among the company eventually congregated in a corner. Today, it seemed to be a back section of the porch where a wide swing was located. Caroline and Jim were already occupying one side of it by the time Mariah and Hank drifted there.

"Ooh, Mariah, your dress is so stylish," Betty Shoemaker said. The pretty little brunette wore all white and sported a parasol. "Wherever did you get it?"

"Mrs. Dolan made it," Mariah told her.

Betty's father had made a modest success in mining, Mariah whispered to Hank. Now he invested in other mines, she thought.

"Mrs. Dolan. Imagine that!" Betty said.

"I didn't know Mrs. Dolan dealt with Paris patterns," Caroline remarked. "She positively rose above her usual offerings in your dress, Mariah, don't you think? You know, Myrtle Alice sends to Denver or New York for her clothes."

"Mrs. Dolan is good enough for me," Mariah said.

"Yes, Mrs. Dolan is rather a find, I must say," Hank threw in. "It is wonderful, isn't it, how one can discover these little treasures in out-of-the-way places."

As Hank spoke he bestowed a worshipful gaze onto Mariah's profile. He sat just behind her, his back against the porch post while Mariah stood inches away. When he saw her mouth twitch, he couldn't resist another sally. "In fact, Mariah was so pleased with Mrs. Dolan's work, I believe she ordered several new frocks. From the Paris fashion plates, to be sure."

Caroline's eyes went round in poorly concealed speculation. "You did? Why, how—how curious. Mariah, I would never have guessed you to be interested in fashionable clothes."

Mariah didn't know whether to laugh or slug that scalawag Hank! She turned enough to slant him a look that told him he was stacking up a list of offenses for which he would later pay. "It is a new idea of mine, Caroline."

She practically choked on the fib, but she couldn't very well tell everyone that Hank had ordered and paid for the dress.

Thorndyke Sands wandered into the group. "Afternoon, there, Hank. Haven't seen much of you in town lately."

"True enough, Thorndyke. We have been very busy at the Circle T."

"Yes, I heard old Elam took a bad turn." Thorndyke continued to make small talk until, under the general chatter, he said in a low voice, "Got a bit of business to discuss with you, Hank."

"Yes, certainly."

Thorndyke moved down to the end of the porch. Hank casually rose and followed.

"Don't want to alarm you, but Kasey's been seen around town again. You know, he's got it in for you, since you first showed him up."

"I settled my quarrel with Kasey the day of the boxing match," Hank protested.

"Yeah, and that's just it. Heard from a fella I know in Denver that Kasey's been spreading tales of how you're a peacock and figure to make yourself king bull of the range. He's challenging one and all to beat you in the ring. Inviting all the meanest bastards around to Mead."

"It does sound as though he is carrying a grudge. Has anyone come to Mead looking for me?"

"None that I'd noticed yet. But, I'll tell ya, Hank, I don't like the situation. Could get ugly."

"I'll be on my guard, Thorndyke. Thanks for the warning. But I doubt anyone will pay much attention to a little pip-squeak like Kasey."

"You're probably right, Hank. But just in case, I'll try to ferret out more of what he's up to and let you know."

"Good enough."

As Hank strolled back to the party, Tommy came out on the porch. He didn't wait past greeting everyone before he said, "Mr. Clayton, there's a rumor going around that someone from Denver has challenged you to another boxing match."

"You can't always count on rumors to be true, Mr. Bakersfield," Hank replied evenly. "I have not offered to take on another challenger."

"You mean it isn't true?" asked a young lad leaning against the house. "Shucks. I was looking forward to it."

"I have no plans for it."

"Would you take on another match? You would, wouldn't you?" Tommy asked. "You'd want to defend yourself."

"That would depend on when, mostly."

"Thorndyke, you can arrange another match, can't you?" begged Tommy. "I missed the last one."

"Could if it was agreeable to all parties involved," Thorndyke answered, pursing his lips.

Myrtle Alice came to the door. "There you are, Thomas darling. Mother needs you. Mrs. Reed wants

to go home and Mother said you would escort her.
Mrs. Truit wishes to stay."

"Why can't your father do it?" Tommy's tone was
almost resentful, Mariah noticed.

"Please, Thomas. Daddy is talking to Mr. Powell
about the expansion he is talking of doing."

"All right, I'll be right there." Tommy excused
himself, but Mariah could tell he didn't want to leave.
He threw her a brief smile, a harried expression that
gave her a world of information. She knew Tommy so
well.

Clearly, Tommy wasn't exactly happy with the way
things worked in the Sonyers household. Mariah felt
a little sorry for him. Then she realized the oddest
thing: she wasn't in love with him anymore. She
didn't even hate Myrtle Alice, and suddenly, she
knew she never had. It had only been a case of petty
jealousy, she was honest enough to admit. Her real
hurt had been from Tommy.

That was gone now, too. Only a sadness remained.

What had happened to her? It was as though time
had tripled its passing since Tommy had been gone.
Her life had definitely taken a turn, and she had no
desire to go back to the old ways.

Mariah was still quietly thinking when Hank suggested it was time they started for home.

"Yes, I'm ready," she answered and gathered up
her cape and reticule. Jim remarked that he would be
along shortly, after he saw Caroline home. Mariah,
surprisingly, felt quite in charity with Caroline—she
hadn't heard one "Myrtle Alice says" from her all
afternoon—and smiled her good-byes in genuine
fashion.

The crowd had cleared out quite a bit, Mariah
noted as they walked through the parlor to thank

their hostess. She no longer heard the violin. They bade farewell to Mrs. Sonyers, but were stopped by Mr. Sonyers in the hall.

"Mr. Clayton." He held out his hand and Hank shook it. "I want you to know, your account has been satisfactorily established at our bank."

"Thank you, Mr. Sonyers. I had no doubt of it."

"Yes, yes. Mr. Moore took care of everything. But I was wondering if you, personally, might call on me, one day soon. At the bank, of course. I think that as a man of business you may be interested in an investment possibility I have recently come across."

"Most intriguing, I am sure, Mr. Sonyers. However, I am assessing my options very carefully at the moment. Don't want to be overweighed in one direction, you understand. Perhaps in the fall . . ."

"Excellent, Mr. Clayton. And may I say again how happy we are to have your business."

After their final good-byes, Hank steered Mariah toward the front door. "How much money did you win?" she asked, very softly through her teeth.

"Enough, my love," he replied in the same way. "Enough to buy you the wardrobe you need."

"Oh, yes. That is something we have to talk about on our way home."

"Hmm. This should be interesting."

They quarreled happily all the way while the early-evening stars came out. Mariah felt totally lighthearted for the first time in days. Seeing Tommy had released something in her. She realized she could let it all go.

And she enjoyed her verbal sparring with Hank; he had a glib tongue and, though she knew much of what he said was pure foolishness calculated to make her either fuss at him or laugh, being with Hank was never boring. She was still giggling at something he'd said when they reached the turn into the Circle T.

Hank suddenly pulled the buggy to the side of the road.

"What's wrong?"

"Something very serious."

"Oh?" She glanced around the road to see if there was anything there of which to be afraid, but found nothing. "What is it?"

"This." In a swift move, he slid his arms beneath her and unceremoniously lifted her onto his lap.

"Hank, what are you doing?"

"Holding you. Kissing you."

His mouth showed no gentle beginning; it took hers in a hot joining, his lips searching for all he could find, his arms wrapping her closer to his chest. Mariah didn't resist. She didn't want to—the tension between them had been building all day. Hell's bells, it had been stalking them for weeks.

Her hands slid around his shoulders. The back of his neck and the line of his jaw felt both strong and sensuous. Her thumb stroked against the faint grain of his whiskers, the scant stubble adding to her tactile pleasure.

Slowly, reluctantly, his mouth lifted.

Hank leaned back into the corner of the buggy, propping one foot on the front while gently guiding her head to rest on his shoulder. They sat for a long time in silence, allowing their breathing to ease. He kept stroking her shoulder.

"You smell so good," she finally said. "What is it you put on?"

The rumble of his laughter vibrated all through her. "I am happy to know you admire my cologne. It is a concoction which comes, I believe, from Paris."

"Why is it funny that I asked?"

"My darling Mariah, most women do not compliment a man in such a personal way."

"Oh. Oh, well, I . . . I never learned much of perfumes and such. Granny gave me some for Christmas the last one she was alive. Lilies of the Valley. But it was all gone and Mrs. Kelly loaned me some of hers. It smells really nice, doesn't it?" She arched the side of her neck in offering.

"Oh, yes, it smells lovely," Hank responded between a laugh and a groan as the cheap fragrance filled his nostrils. "You smell even better than the cologne," he muttered as he took advantage of her invitation and began to kiss her neck, moving up her jaw with his lips and tongue until he captured her mouth once more.

Mariah eagerly responded, allowing him to teach her what a pair of lips and a tongue could do, fleetingly wondering how just a kiss could make her toes want to curl. Her hand lay against his cheek, her fingers lightly brushing the area just under his eye.

Hank thought he might not be able to control himself if she continued to kiss him in such a way, but she curled up in his lap so sweetly he ceased to question it. One of his hands was free to roam.

Nothing of her small breasts had showed above the dress's modest neckline, but his glance had returned to her throat and bare skin more than once over the course of the afternoon. He had seen hundreds of women, better endowed, who wore much lower dresses. Now, in the dark cocoon of the buggy, he could not see her at all, but the thought of her exposed skin drove him crazy. Why this particular woman should have such an effect on him was beyond his reasoning. He only knew he wanted to touch her, to feel the shape of her.

Gently, he stroked her throat. The fastening of her cape came apart with only a flick of his fingers; he didn't think she even noticed.

His fingers brushed lower, his wrist resting momentarily on her soft roundings without causing protest. But when his palm cupped one wonderful mound, she stirred, her body drawing tight.

"Hank, this is wicked. . . ."

"It certainly is. You are wickedly enticing, wickedly tempting." He continued to kiss a corner of her mouth.

"I'm not. What we're doing is." Mariah ran the old arguments of shouldn'ts through her mind, but she couldn't bring herself to pull away from the warmth of his hands. Her whole body responded, unwilling to wait on shoulds and shouldn'ts.

"No, what we are doing is the result of what happens when two people are wildly attracted to each other."

"Well, tell me how to stop being attracted."

"I cannot. God, Mariah, don't you know that!"

Neither of them could have stopped the following kiss even if a herd of buffalo had thundered down on them. It was a passionate, total mating of mouths, and Hank knew he had never experienced this kind of emotional upheaval from only a kiss. And not even from much more.

The only thing that pulled them apart and prevented Hank from upending Mariah right there on the buggy seat was the soft whinny of Lulubelle answering an approaching horse.

For a moment Mariah didn't know what had disturbed her. Then she heard Lulubelle snuffle as a single horse and rider rode around them.

"James, by damn." Hank said, pulling in great gulps of air, as though he'd been running uphill.

"I-I think we-we should—"

Hank abruptly shifted her back to the seat. "Yes," he said. "I'll take you to the house."

Five minutes later, Mariah was let out at the door to the house. Hank hadn't helped her down and he'd barely said good night. He wasn't usually so rattled, she thought. She watched the buggy go down the drive, trying to understand her own state of confusion. But it was hopeless to even try to figure it all out when she could still feel his kiss on her lips. Simply hopeless.

18

"You wanted to talk to me, Elam?"

"Yes, son, I did." The old man sat in the rocker, pillows at his back, next to the parlor window. "Sit down, Hank."

Hank sat on the edge of the sofa, evaluating how Elam looked today. The doctor said he'd improved, yet the old man didn't seem interested in getting out and about much. It was as though he had no energy left. The only bright spot in his days was seeing Mariah, Hank had observed. He watched for her comings and goings. "Would you like me to bring Mariah to you?"

"Not yet. Been wantin' to talk to you. Privately. Can't get a minute alone anymore. Mrs. Kelly, God love her, has been very kind, but I'm glad she's gone home for a while."

"Yes, the household has been crowded, I suppose."

"Wouldn't be too bad if it was all family."

"What do you mean, sir?"

"Gettin' to that. Gettin' to that. Now, tell me. How did you and Mariah make out at the party?"

"Very well, indeed, sir. Mariah received her share of admiration."

Elam's face brightened. "Always thought her pretty, myself, but I'm partial, naturally."

"It is a fault which can easily be excused for the truth. Mariah is quite lovely."

Elam nodded. They sat quietly for a time before he spoke again. "I need to ask a favor of you."

"Yes?"

"Know you've been somethin' of a rollin' stone, but do you like it here, in Colorado?"

"Yes, as a matter of fact, I think it one of the loveliest spots I have ever seen."

Elam was visibly pleased at his answer. "I was hopin' you'd see it that way. You see, Hank, I was wishin' you'd settle down here for a year or two. Know I'm pushin' it, you and Mariah only knowin' each other a few weeks. But you're strong in the right way. Been watchin' you."

"Thank you, sir."

The old man held up a hand. "Also know you ain't had the same kinda raisin' Mariah's had. Some differences, there."

On this last remark, Elam's voice took on a shade of doubt. Hank, afraid of where the conversation was leading, tried to take it in another direction. "Yes, that is true. I have known far more of big cities. I am out-and-out ignorant of many of the things with which you ranchers deal. The cattle diseases, for instance—"

"Don't make no difference what you don't know or Mariah don't. . . . You can learn them things," Elam's voice grew stronger. "Thing is, Hank, even though I don't hold with some of the things you do, I think I can trust you with my girl."

"Uh, Elam . . ."

"And I'd like you and Mariah to get married right away, without waitin'. You can finish your courtin' after."

There it was. Hank stared at him, noting the shock of white hair framing his leathery, lined face. Elam's earnest, questing eyes were the same brownish-hazel as Mariah's, and like hers, they had a powerful effect on him.

And he, Henry Clayton Ackerley, with a world of charm and a ready answer always on the tip of his tongue, didn't know what to say. He dropped his gaze and cudgeled his brain for a way to answer. A long moment of silence hung between them.

"Ya see, son, I ain't gonna get well, not to be the man I was. I might linger a while, another year or two, but"—he shook his head—"I ain't gonna be any good to Mariah. I want to see her married soon, lest I don't get to see it at all."

Hank, looking awkwardly at his hands as they hung between his spread knees, finally raised his gaze. He should have thought more of the inevitable moment of truth; Jim had warned him. By all the saints, he had warned himself.

But if he had told Mariah all about his family, its position and wealth, she would have placed a canyon between them. She would have held him at such a distance he would have had no hope of anything, not even an embrace or a kiss. And he had only to look at her to melt any resolve to tell her, for her kisses would be the only real treasure he could take into his future.

He had to make an explanation now. He opened

his mouth to begin an accounting of his background and future expectations. Elam would understand it; he was wise to what the world expected of men such as him.

Elam's old brown eyes waited.

Hank's heart wrenched; it was almost a physical pain. If he gave his own history it would be the end of it, he would have to leave. What, then, was he to do with this grand thing that had been growing, this tentative emotion he was only beginning to recognize as love? How could he leave Mariah behind? How could he bear living for the rest of his life with no hope of ever again watching those bright, spirited eyes tease and challenge him? And love him? And make him crazy with passion?

Hank heard himself say, "When would you like the marriage to take place?"

"Right off. Soonest is best."

"Have you . . . um, how does Mariah feel about this?"

"Don't *you* know? Thought the two of you were champin' at the bit to get blessed. You do want 'er, don't ya?"

His heart was in his throat. "Yes, I want her."

"Well, then, no need in waitin'. You can have a little ceremony on Saturday. Has to be in church, though, as long as we got one. Ain't like the old days when there weren't none. Then you an' Mariah can move into the big room upstairs—I ain't ever wantin' it again. Ain't been the same anyway, since my wife died."

Hank found himself in need of activity. He rose and paced to the fireplace. An old photograph of a young couple stood on the mantel; they stared at him stiffly, a tiny girl between them, plump-cheeked, with curls poking beyond the bonnet she wore. Mariah and her parents. Next to it was a picture of Mariah's grandmother. Studying it, he saw the same determined look Mariah often wore.

"Mariah might not agree."

"Why wouldn't she? Because of her heartbreak over Tommy? She'll get around to knowin' he wasn't the man for her; give 'er time. 'Sides, that was childhood stuff."

Even the mention of Mariah still holding a soft spot for Tommy set Hank on edge.

"Mariah doesn't like to be pushed into anything," he said.

"You seem to have the knack of bringin' her round to your way of thinkin'."

"Won't a sudden marriage cause more gossip to be heaped on Mariah's head? It might be better to wait. . . ."

"You really want to wait, son?" Elam asked softly.

Hank fingered the old photograph. "No," he replied, barely above a whisper. In fact, he thought he might die, waiting. All reason told him this was the chance of his lifetime for true happiness. If he let it go, it would be gone forever. "No, I don't want to wait."

"Good. Hoped you'd see it my way."

Hank swung around and stared at the old man, his mind awhirl. He felt a freedom, an elation that he'd never imagined would be his. "There's another matter to settle. The Circle T."

"The Circle T will remain Mariah's," Elam said firmly.

"Agreed. But I want some rights in running it."

"What d'you mean?" The old man frowned, but Hank saw a spark flare in his eyes. "What kinda rights?"

"An investor's vote. Elam, you know the Circle T needs money poured into it. I want the right to hire a couple of men and buy some"—Hank paused, not ready to tell the old man his thoughts on bringing sheep to the ranch—"additional stock. All your buildings need repair. And I'd like to purchase that section on the western edge to expand the Circle T's boundaries. We need the grassland. And all of it should be fenced."

"That's a big bite you're offerin', son. You sure you can afford all that? What'll you be gettin' outa it?"

"It might take a year or two, I won't deny that." Hank's smile slowly spread as he stared at Mariah's grandfather. "But I'll have Mariah."

"And you don't want no partnership?"

"The Circle T's ownership will remain in yours and Mariah's hands—and our children, should we have any—but you have to give me the freedom to do what's necessary to make it a paying property."

"All right." Elam spoke slowly, but the excitement in his eyes seemed to wash years from his face. He rose from the rocker and held out his hand. "Done."

The two men shook hands solemnly, yet their eyes smiled.

Then Hank had a sobering thought. "Mariah won't like it, if she should ever find out. Being bargained in with a piece of land."

"That's true, son, but I'd never agree to it if you didn't love her. 'Sides, I have faith you'll know how to calm 'er down. Told ya she'd take to tamin' with the right man."

Mariah rode out very early to check the fence. She wanted the solitude to think, because she couldn't do it with anyone around, especially Hank. He seemed to have the knack of making her forget everything but him, and she couldn't risk another episode like the other night.

She pounded on a post and then tested it for stability. It held steady, but she slammed the hammer down on it once more for good measure. The action helped relieve some of her pent-up feelings. Then she moved on to the next post.

That dad-blasted party, she fumed—the hammer made contact with the top of the post with satisfactory force—had lulled her from her guard on her emotions, and given her too many new ideas to worry about, too many directions for her wayward feelings. She never would have let Hank kiss her again, much less touch her, if she hadn't let her guard down.

She went to the next post, where the wire was sagging. Tugging on it, her hand slipped, and a barb dug painfully through her worn glove into her right thumb. Reflexively, she jerked it away and clamped her good hand around the injured one.

For a moment, she squeezed her eyes closed and stood very still to let the worst of the pain pass. Tears threatened. She silently forced them to retreat while telling herself she'd been entirely too careless with everything lately.

This would never do. Her grandaddy depended on her, the Circle T depended on her, and soon she would have only herself to count on to take care of chores and things. Because, she firmly decided on the spot, Hank was leaving. She'd send him on his way as soon as she returned to the house. That would put temptation out of her path and she could get back to concentrating on what she had to do.

Opening her eyes, she saw blood running down

her hand. The barb must have gone deeper than she realized.

Skedaddle whinnied, and she turned at the sound. A rider approached. It was Hank. "Dang it!"

Mariah showed him her back while she peeled the glove down. When it reached her torn thumb, she hesitated, biting hard at her bottom lip. Then she jerked it off.

"Mariah. What's the matter?" Dismounting, he ground-reined Patches and strode forward.

"Nothing."

"You made a funny sound."

"I make sounds all the time. People do, you know."

"Yes, but—"

Something about the way her shoulders hunched made him suspicious. He rounded her and stopped. She was trying to wrap her kerchief around her thumb. He reached for her hand. "What happened?"

She tried to pull away. "Just a little accident with a barb. Nothing to worry over."

He pried her hand open and pulled the kerchief free. Immediately, blood pulsed from the wound.

"Nothing, bloody hell! How deep is it?"

He didn't wait for an answer. Moving swiftly, he dragged her to his horse, removed his canteen of water, then poured water liberally over the thumb. Carefully, he examined it again.

"Deep enough. Hold still, honey." He poured more water onto it. "Wish I had that pint of whiskey with me," he muttered. "For disinfectant."

Taking the bandanna from his neck, he tore a strip from it. "Clean one this morning," he mumbled as he wrapped the cloth around the injured thumb. "There."

"Thanks." Mariah looked at her neatly bandaged

thumb before glancing at him, then dropped her gaze. Darn him for being so kind and sweet. Why did he have to be so tenderhearted? It was going to be so hard to ask him to leave the Circle T.

But she'd come to know he was too often pure flat-out enchantment, and she couldn't afford another bout like the other night. She'd come as close to mindlessly giving in to a mere sexual lure as a woman could and still have any shred of self-respect left.

Needing to move away, she opened her mount's saddlebags to return her hammer.

"Why didn't you call me to come ride fence with you this morning?" Hank asked.

She shrugged, struggling to find the courage to ask him to leave the Circle T. He had to leave. She'd be lost if he didn't. "I needed to think."

"Well, I don't like the idea of you riding off by yourself. You could get hurt. Like now."

There he went to fussing again. Once more, Mariah didn't know whether to laugh at his assumption that she should be a helpless city miss or complain that he wanted to take charge of her.

"I've been doing it for years, Hank. Whenever something needs to get done."

Independent little rascal, Hank thought. She had had too much lonely freedom, and too much responsibility for her young shoulders. It would make her old before her time. He could lift much of the heavy load from her, and he would; together, they'd whip this ranch into shape. And when they married, he would see to it she was never lonely again. He had plans for her time. All of it.

He turned her and held her gently by the elbows. He smiled in anticipation of her coming sweetly into his arms.

Mariah bit her lip, wanting to move away before she fell all over him. But she was caught between her horse and Hank.

Now was as good a time as any, she decided, to say good-bye and send him on his way. She drew a deep breath and called on all her fortitude. She'd tell him now. Please, Hank, move on to Denver, farther west, or wherever he wanted, only please, please leave her be.

They spoke together.

"You know, Hank, I think the time has come for you to move back to town." Town wouldn't be far enough! she added to herself.

"Sweetheart, I think the time has come for us to be married."

A silence fell between them.

"Why should I move into town?"

"What did you say?" Mariah finally asked, blinking rapidly. Something was out of kilter. Surely she had heard amiss. "I didn't fall on my head, did I?"

"No. Why?"

Hank, who was seldom serious, stared at her in positive solemnity.

Maybe he was inebriated and was one of those men who looked perfectly fine when they weren't. She'd never noticed him drinking, but maybe he did it in secret. She raised to her tiptoes and sniffed his breath, but it smelled only of tooth powder and coffee. She asked anyway. "You haven't been drinking, have you?"

"Why would I be drinking when I have yet to reach my cause to celebrate?"

"What cause?"

"Us. You and me. Our being together."

"We aren't together, Hank. That's something we need to get straightened out."

"Finally, we agree on something."

"Uh-huh. Now, about the other night . . ."

"Yep, that's it."

"I think we . . . that is, you should move on. . . ."

"And I said we need to get married." Hank emphasized each word carefully.

She stared at him openmouthed. He *had* said it. "M-married? Are you funning me?"

Hank felt a little insulted. He had never proposed marriage to a woman in his life and certainly had never expected it to be taken as a joke. But their history together had never led Mariah to take him seriously, he remembered. For an answer, he slid his arms around her waist and lifted her clear off the ground, then kissed her soundly.

"Now what do you say?" he asked, his voice husky.

"I don't know. What about all your plans to go adventuring?"

"I'll take it as it comes. Right now, if you don't say yes, we might be in big trouble."

"Why so?"

He kissed her again. "Does that answer? Lord, Mariah, I almost had your skirts up the other night in the buggy. In the middle of the road."

"In the end, you remained a gentleman."

"Scratch any man very deeply and you will find a barbarian, my darling. I practically ravished you. I could easily throw you down and do it right now without a moment's remorse."

She gave him a sideways look. "Now you are joshing."

"Not by much," he whispered next to her ear. "I think I deserve a prize for remaining a gentleman up until now. I want you so badly I can't sleep at night. So you see, my darling Mariah, we need to marry very, very soon. Because if we don't, we'll end up fulfilling Mrs. Patrick's direst prediction and raising Mrs. Benton's brows beyond her hairline, as well as disappointing two old men."

"Oh, Hank, put me down. I have to think this through." She began pacing as soon as her feet touched ground. "What will Grandaddy say?"

"He is planning on walking you down the aisle Saturday night."

"Saturday night? This is no joking matter, greenhorn." She turned at the fence post and started back toward him. "Grandaddy can't take any sudden, um, excitements. Remember how we sent him into a heart attack when you carried me into the house? I can't risk that again."

Hank agreed nonchalantly. He leaned casually against Skedaddle while she paced, his arm curled around her saddle horn. "Makes sense. No surprises for Elam. We'll have a private ceremony. I wonder if that lavender dress I ordered for you from Mrs. Dolan is finished."

"Hank!"

"Yes, darling?"

He was still playing a part, still playing games. What would happen when he tired of it all? Of her? "I don't think we should get married."

"Should I give you another illustration of why we should?" He moved toward her steadily, purposefully, all humor gone from his face. "If I began kissing you now, if I caressed you now, undressed you and laid you on the ground, would you stop me?"

Mariah swallowed hard while her heart began to beat in double time. Maybe it was true. Perhaps Hank did have a primitive streak beneath his surface.

"Would you?" he whispered. This time he didn't

touch her, only stood and held her gaze. She couldn't look away. All the excitement that had been building in the weeks past, the passion that had never dissolved between them, remained.

"No," she practically croaked.

"Then do you want to wait past Saturday?"

"No." She almost couldn't speak at all.

"I'll make the arrangements with your grandfather." He started back toward Patches, then turned once more. "Oh, and I . . . I have one more thing to tell you."

She tipped her head. "Yes?"

"My last name is Ackerley. For legal purposes, you'll be Mrs. Henry Clayton Ackerley."

"Oh. Oh! You're not running from the law, are you, Hank?"

His gray eyes took on their usual merriment. "No, my darling Mariah. Rest easy on that. Truly, I am not wanted by the law. I merely liked shortening my name."

Mariah nearly slumped in relief. Thank God for heavenly graces, as Granny would've said. Then she realized she would have wanted him even if his answer had been different.

To Mariah's complete amazement, Elam approved. As did Nate. And Mrs. Kelly. And Jim. The many congratulations and happy grins poured over her and Hank like syrup on pancakes.

Didn't anybody see how nervous, how out of control she felt about it all? Hank was nothing like the kind of man she had once envisioned herself being married to. But on the other hand, she wanted him so much that the thought of backing out of the marriage, of never having Hank at all, made her shake with fright inside. She had only to experience one of his good night kisses to discover that undeniable truth.

It was puzzling, because Tommy had never made her scared of her own feelings the way Hank did. And Grandaddy seemed genuinely happy, as well as relieved. He looked more like his old self every day.

Everyone was in agreement about the need to hold a quiet ceremony. When the arrangements were made with Reverend Higginbotham for a Saturday wedding, Mrs. Kelly put it about town that the private nature of the plans was due to Elam's illness, which was true enough. Mariah complained that everyone would count the months ahead anyway, to see when she came up in the family way. "Let them," Hank said flippantly, and plowed his way through any further objections.

Hank suggested Mariah invite Caroline to be her maid of honor. "Who better?" he asked when she looked at him as though he had lost his mind. "She will lend her approval if she is a part of it. Besides, Jim will attend me."

Mariah sighed and gave in. It was true, Caroline was the closest thing she had to a female friend of her own age. And lately, she hadn't been so much a goose. In fact, Mariah had noticed that Caroline had begun to behave with far less starch than usual, which gave her hope for Caroline as a person.

At Mariah's invitation, Caroline went to Mrs. Dolan's with her to fetch her new lavender dress. Mariah asked her then.

Caroline rhapsodized about how romantic it all was—almost as good as an elopement. She was very honored to be included, she said, and nothing could convince her that anything her dear Jim would agree

to, and dear, dear Mr. Clayton, could in any way be
thought of as, oh, you know, Mariah dear . . .
impetuous.

Not impetuous? Mariah could only laugh at that.
Of all the things she'd ever done, this was definitely
one of the most impetuous, and one of the riskiest, as
well, because deep down, she continued to wonder
how long Hank would remain content with her and
the Circle T. How long would he be content with
marriage?

Saturday afternoon arrived. Mariah dressed at
Mrs. Kelly's house with the older woman's help, and
Caroline's.

Her dress was designed more as an evening gown,
in a rich satin with big sleeves and lots of tiny pleats
below the knee. Above the deeply-cut neckline, a silk
tulle had been added for the sake of the church wedding. Her hair was arranged as before, the way Hank
liked it. Curls cascaded down her back and her head
was crowned with a wondrous concoction of lavender
satin and tulle.

Jim arrived in a rented buggy large enough to seat
all three women and drove them the two blocks to the
church.

Elam waited for her at the front of the church. He
handed her a package just before it was time to begin.

"What's this?" she asked.

"Don't know. Hank sent it. Said he was sorry he
couldn't get you no proper flowers."

"Oh." She opened the brown paper with nervous
hands. A fan lay there, of ivory and delicately painted
paper, so lovely that even she recognized its rarity.
When she spread it, the painting was of pink and
white roses. Lavender ribbons, matching the exact
shade of her gown, streamed from its handle. Tucked

into the center ribbon were tiny wildflower blossoms, found only at this time of year, late spring. "Oh, it's beautiful."

Minutes later, Mariah walked down the aisle on her grandfather's arm to meet Hank at the altar while Mrs. Patrick pumped the organ into a hymn. Caroline and Jim stood on either side of her and Hank. When the correct moment came, she kissed her grandfather's cheek, and he sat down beside Mrs. Kelly in the front pew.

Mariah gave her vows in a low voice; Hank's tone was deep and solemn and strong. He held her arm firmly, as though he was afraid she might dash away. When she glanced at him shyly, his eyes shone.

Maybe it would be all right.

Oh, please, God, let this be right.

Then it was done. Faces beamed. Nate, Brown, Jim, Thorndyke, Caroline, Mrs. Kelly, and Elam. Even the minister smiled. Mrs. Patrick nodded her approval.

Congratulations flowed. Hugs and blessings were given. And the party retired to Powell's for a wedding supper.

19

At the hotel's dining room, Mr. Powell himself ushered them to a quiet corner, where screens had been placed around a large table for privacy. Hank had ordered the best from the menu: a mock turtle soup, sirloin of beef, Yorkshire pudding, quail, wild rice, scalloped corn, boiled potatoes, peas, carrots, fruit, cheese, and of course, a wedding cake. In deference to Elam's strong conviction against drinking alcohol, the bride and groom were toasted with fruit punch.

Mariah allowed Hank to seat her—she'd become delightedly accustomed to that polite attention—and let him place food on the plate in front of her, but she found she could barely taste anything. The diamond-and-gold ring on her left hand, the one which had graced Hank's pinkie finger that first day, felt strange. It hung heavy and loose.

She was a married woman.

Mariah stole little glances at him. Her husband,

Henry Clayton. Henry Clayton *Ackerley*, she corrected herself.

He was even better-looking now than two months ago, tanned and fit. His gray eyes frequently twinkled at her, with more than mere amusement. The promise and anticipation reflected there sent her heart into wild expectation. After their dinner, the two of them, just they, were going upstairs to Powell's best room. Openly, without shame.

The sudden memory of Mr. Zigler's sly expression when she had stood by Hank's side as he checked in once before caused a giggle to spring up. The hotel clerk had been so certain she planned to sneak into Hank's room.

Hank turned to look at her. "What has struck your funny bone, Mariah?"

She glanced at their guests, saw that everyone's attention was elsewhere, then opened her fan and spoke behind it. "Um, d'you remember Mr. Zigler, the clerk who was on duty at Powell's front desk the first day you were in Mead?"

"I suppose so. Why?"

"You never stayed in that room."

"No. As it turned out, I had a better offer," he said, grinning wolfishly.

Mariah's gaze dropped to Hank's one crooked tooth. Oddly, it increased her fanciful thoughts. It seemed to represent the small wild streak he occasionally exhibited, the part of him that wasn't always in control. Why, she didn't know, but she liked the small imperfection.

"Um, yeah. Well, Mr. Zigler's suspicion is finally going to be proved right."

"How so?"

"We are going to occupy one of Powell's rooms together."

Hank threw back his head and laughed while Mariah blushed. Everyone at the table stared, wondering what the joke was, but Hank merely shook his head.

Underneath the table, he took her hand. He leaned toward her, smiling. "You haven't eaten anything. Aren't you hungry, darling?"

"Lost my appetite, I reckon."

"I haven't lost mine, my love," he whispered in her ear.

She blushed again. Around the table the talk buzzed, and she listened. To Caroline—"Everything is just too, too wonderful, so elegant"; to Mrs. Kelly—"My, everything is lovely,"; to Nate—"Ya sure 'nuff know how to put on a fine spread, Hank"; to Grandaddy—"Son, you have done me proud. My granddaughter is a fortunate young woman."

And Mariah did feel fortunate. She smiled at Grandaddy. He looked well, for the moment. She thought it funny that he was pleased with her choice for a husband, even with all their differences, and all at once felt he wouldn't have been nearly as pleased with Tommy.

The dinner ended. Thorndyke wished them well once more and took his leave. Jim left to escort Mrs. Kelly and Caroline home, while Brown brought Elam's buggy around. Mariah could see that Elam was tiring, and she walked him and Nate to the buggy. She kissed Nate's cheek, then Elam's.

"Thank you, Grandaddy. It's been a lovely day. You rest easy now, and I'll be home tomorrow."

"Know you will, honey. Don't worry none about me. You take good care of her, Hank."

Hank slid an arm around her shoulders. "I give you my word on it, Elam."

Mariah watched the buggy until it turned out of sight against the sinking sun.

"Would you care for a stroll, love, before we go in?"

"Yes, that would be nice."

They walked the one long street and two short ones, passing the commercial section as storekeepers closed for the night and saloon music sounded brighter as business picked up.

They reached Tillie's and turned to go back on the opposite side of the street. Then they heard loud voices roaring from The Nugget, and a moment later saw Thorndyke Sands hurrying that way.

For the first time in her life, Mariah had no desire to run and find out what the commotion was about. She must have finally left childhood behind, she mused, because suddenly she didn't think she'd be left out of anything exciting by ignoring a saloon fight. She felt distinctly separate from it, and gratefully so.

"Shall we sneak into the hotel's rear door?" Hank teased as they neared the hotel once more. "Mr. Zigler is on duty at the front desk, I believe."

"Nope. I want to parade through the hotel's double doors on your arm and right up those stairs under his weaselly eyes."

He chuckled. "All right. Come, my dear, let's parade."

Mariah sailed into the lobby, her head high. She barely kept her smile under control as Mr. Zigler bowed to her and asked if there was anything more he could do, anything at all, to make their stay a pleasant one. He handed Hank a key with a flourish.

Hank had inspected the room the day before and made his arrangements with Mr. Powell himself. "No, I expect all will be in order."

"Yes, sir, yes, indeed." The balding clerk bowed again.

Mariah was still giggling when they reached the third floor. Hank led her to the end of the hall and opened the door, before he scooped her into his arms. He carried her into the room, kicked the door closed behind them, then deposited her on the bed.

The room was dim, so he lit a lamp.

Mariah's eyes were huge when he turned toward her. In spite of the times they'd shared kisses, and regardless of Mariah's previously eager responses to him, she seemed a little nervous now, he thought. He reminded himself that this was her first actual experience—which pleased him enormously—and he needed to take it slowly.

He turned toward a table by the window. A bucket, packed with ice around a bottle of champagne, sat there with a tray of fruit, cheese, crackers, and tiny slices of wedding cake. He poured the white wine into two goblets and handed her one.

He sipped and watched her reaction as she did the same. She wrinkled her nose, then smiled at him over the brim of her glass. "What is this?"

"Champagne. Do you like it?"

"Uh-huh. Tastes better than sarsaparilla."

"I should hope," he said. He lifted his glass in a toast. "Well, my darling Mariah, this isn't San Francisco, but I assure you we will make wonderful use of our honeymoon bed regardless. No bride, no matter how lavish the setting, could appear any more beautiful to her groom, than you do to me, right now, right here. And someday, I will take you to Denver, New York, San Francisco, London, Paris . . . anywhere you want to visit."

Mariah thought Hank must be referring to Myrtle Alice and Tommy's boasted-of honeymoon. She didn't count it against him that they couldn't afford such a trip. Besides, they'd agreed that Grandaddy shouldn't be left for a long period of time, or the Circle T.

"Those places sound nice, but honestly, Hank," she said, sipping more of the champagne, "you shouldn't be spending money foolishly. Besides, I'm plumb happy right here in Mead. I've never stayed in a hotel before."

Mariah only wished she were less nervous about being a married woman. In spite of her new status, she felt flat-out sinful, being alone, in a hotel room, with Hank. She wanted what was coming, their love-making—in fact, she'd been near loco all week with the thought and excitement of it—but now that it was perfectly legal and preacher-blessed, and everyone would say it was her duty to be a responsive wife, she suddenly wasn't so sure if she could be. Everything was too strange, as if she and Hank didn't know each other at all.

Mariah wished he would kiss her, one of those gentle kisses he sometimes gave that turned into one of those "forget-about-everything-until-the-toes-curl" kind.

"Never?" Hank asked.

She shook her head and swallowed the last of her wine. "Never had reason to before."

"Are you enjoying the experience?"

"Uh-huh. The room's just as pretty as a picture, don't you think?" She gazed around at the blue-and-gold decor while running her hand against the velvet-cut blue bedspread. "I've never seen any prettier."

Hank thought Mariah was pretty as a picture, sitting very primly on the side of the bed in her lavender gown and hat. But she was beautiful in anything she wore. Or in nothing at all, he suspected. He yearned to find out.

He hoped the champagne had relaxed her. She wasn't

frightened, exactly, he thought, only nervous, and maybe uncomfortable in these strange surroundings.

Perhaps they would have been better off going home to the Circle T, to what was familiar to her. But there, they would be occupying Elam's old room. Somehow Hank didn't think it would be any better for Mariah to experience her first sexual encounter in a room she associated with her straitlaced grandfather.

When they had time later in the summer, he vowed, he would take her to that huge stone formation, the Lizard's Tail. He had a fancy to make love to her in the grass below it, and he thought that there she might respond to him in the way he imagined. Without restraints.

But for now, they had one night in a small-town hotel.

Hank had held himself in check for so long, he was afraid to touch her just yet. If he began kissing Mariah now he would ruin the lavender dress in his eagerness to get it off her.

He swallowed hard, and finished his wine. That was the last thing she needed, him tearing her dress off. He hadn't felt so wildly impatient since he had been a lad.

"Would you like more champagne?" he asked.

"No, thank you."

"Then would you like to get into your night things now?" he said, hearing the huskiness in his own voice. He willed her to say yes, though it was early.

"All right." Mariah didn't look at him. Instead, she glanced about the room for the small bag she'd sent with Jim to be deposited at the hotel earlier today.

"Perhaps what you are looking for is behind the screen," Hank suggested, waving at the folding screen in one corner.

"Oh . . . I suppose . . ." She scooted behind the screen. A gold-rimmed washstand held a pitcher and bowl, with thick white towels and an oval of scented soap beside them. She recognized the fragrance of Lilies of the Valley. A woman's hairbrush and comb also lay on the stand, a lovely new silver-backed set which included a hand mirror.

There was no sign of her bag, but lying across a chair were a cream-colored silk gown and robe. She held them up. The robe was almost nothing except see-through lace—at least the top part was.

It wasn't hers. Or rather, it wasn't the one she'd brought with her.

"Um, Hank . . ." she called, peeking around the screen, letting him see only her eyes.

"Yes, Mariah?" He gazed at her innocently and raised his brows.

"Do you know where my bag went to?"

"Your bag? Why, I don't believe I have seen it. What is it you need from it?"

"My night things."

"Ahh, yes, well . . . I believe you have a gown and peignoir there. I chose them for you myself."

"Uh-huh. What if I wanted my own things?"

"Those are your things."

"I meant my other nightdress."

"Well, it is not here. Don't you like the gown? If you do not, you may choose another on Monday."

"No, it's not that. . . ."

"Or you may choose nothing . . . to wear nothing. . . ."

"Um, no . . . no . . . I'll . . . put this on."

Hank waited patiently for her. After a couple of minutes in which he heard no movement, he called, "Do you need anything, Mariah?"

Another pause went by before she answered. "The

buttons on this dress are in the back," she told him in a muffled voice.

Hank needed no second invitation. Moving swiftly, he rounded the screen.

Mariah glanced at him, saw that he had removed his shoes, coat, and tie, bit at her bottom lip, and then, without another word, turned her back for him to undo the buttons.

His fingers made quick work of the task, but his hands lingered, kneading her shoulders.

"Thank you," she mumbled.

"A husbandly task I shall always take delight in, my love." He reluctantly retreated from her tiny space behind the screen.

Moments later, Mariah shyly left her haven and went forward into the room. She didn't know where to look, didn't know what to do with her hands. The robe's deep lace yoke over her bare shoulders left her feeling very vulnerable, for underneath, the gown was a whisper of almost nothing.

Hank felt he could barely breathe as he watched his wife approach. Her golden-brown eyes glowed with expectation while her mouth gently parted, looking soft and tender.

His body tightened in anticipation.

Her hair tumbled freely, as he'd seen it once before. He liked the way it framed her face. Beneath the silk and lace, he could discern her slender lines; she wasn't overly voluptuous, yet he had no complaints. Not one.

Mariah stopped in front of him. Her breath came in shallow drafts. She glanced upward, through her lashes.

Hank observed her through his own lowered ones. To slow himself down, he drank from his wine, then placed the goblet to her lips.

Dutifully, she sipped. When he removed the glass, she pressed her lips together and ran her tongue along them, seeking a remaining drop.

He thought his body would explode with need. His mind silently chanted, *Slowly . . . slowly . . . slowly.*

Suddenly, she spoke. "Hank, if you don't kiss me now, this very instant, I'll purely flat-out faint from skittishness," she burst out. "'Cause in this . . . this lovemaking thing, I'm the tenderfoot and I don't know what to do, exactly."

Hank began to grin. Then chuckle. He carefully set the goblet down, scooped her into his arms, and twirled with her until they fell together on the bed. He felt like whooping with joy.

"Honey, I'll kiss you breathless each and every chance I get, if that will take away your nervousness. And I will teach you all you want to know."

And he did.

Tenderly, with little kisses to help things along, he caressed her skin as he brushed the peignoir off her shoulders and threw it aside, then directed her to remove his shirt in the same way. Next, he stroked her shoulders and arms while kissing her face—her nose, her eyes, her chin, her mouth. Eagerly, she followed his pattern.

After that, he lowered the top of her gown and ran a finger over one of her breasts, gently, feather-light, swirling around and around until he reached the tip.

"Oh . . . oh, Hank . . . that feels . . . it feels . . ."

"Uh-huh. And it's going to feel even better." He lowered his face and nuzzled the skin between her breasts, then kissed his way to where his finger had been.

After that, Mariah found it altogether necessary that every remaining barrier between them be removed as speedily as possible. Impatiently, she helped Hank remove the rest of her gown and his trousers and underthings.

She sighed deeply when his clothing was gone. "Oh, Hank, you're so beautiful."

Busily exploring her navel, he laughed. His breath felt warm and ticklish against her skin. His hand was hot where it wrapped around her hip. It excited her, wherever he touched.

"Men aren't beautiful, honey."

"You are," she insisted.

After that, there was no speech left, for Mariah could say nothing as her husband taught her what her desires had meant and what it was to be a wife. His wife.

And Hank was nearly mindless in his own passion, as well as feeling the fervent need to make their first joining as good as he could for Mariah.

He had always heard that virgins felt some discomfort or actual pain the first time. Mariah didn't whimper or cry out, but instead held him all the tighter. When, afterward, he whispered that the lovemaking would be better next time, she only nodded against his chest. Trustingly. Without question.

Hank felt his heart swell with pride.

Just after dawn, Hank woke to Mariah's caressing hand. It didn't take long to prove himself truthful, for this time, she did cry out . . . in the throes of ecstasy.

They slept again, totally entangled together.

20

"He did what!" Robert jumped up from behind his desk at Ackerley House in London and banged his knee painfully on an opened drawer. "Damnation." He limped from behind the desk to face Tony better. "You can't be serious."

"Quite serious, as a matter of fact," Tony replied, his own face showing his concern. "Henry says we're to wish him every happiness."

"But . . . but . . . who *is* she? Why weren't we informed beforehand, as is proper? And does he say nothing about this girl's family? Her, er, lineage, her dowry, so to speak?"

"No. What he does say is, she is of fine moral character and Grandmama would have loved her."

"I do not understand it. Why this slapdash rush to marry? Is the girl, er, pregnant, do you suppose? Does he say? And why did the scapegrace write to you this time, and not to me? I am the head of the family."

Tony frowned. "I don't know why he wrote to me,

exactly. Must have something to do with my being a clergyman, I assume, albeit a nonpracticing one. He seems to think I would approve. Here," he said, and shoved the letter forward, "read it for yourself. You can see he says very little about his wife, and nothing at all about expecting a child yet."

Robert took the missive but didn't look at it. "How can any of us approve when Henry goes tearing off on one of his little adventures—which was supposed to be his last, blast it, before settling down—then nearly gets himself killed, as I understand it, and now marries an unknown girl. How are we supposed to approve of that, I ask you. What is her name?"

"Mariah."

"Well, this Mariah must think she's come into a cushy position, I imagine, and married for money." Robby began to limp around the room. "One of those fortune hunters. But if she thinks I will support them in high London style, then she will find she is very much mistaken. Henry should not have led her on. He should have been honest with her—his income simply won't stretch to cover such a life."

"Don't know, Robby. Henry has successfully eluded that kind of trap before," Tony said, shaking his head. "Besides, he has never pretended to have more money than he has. I wouldn't think if the girl was looking for wealth and position that she would settle for Henry."

"Well, I don't suppose we will know the right of it until we see her. But if her character is totally hopeless . . . How we will ever get him out of this tangle I don't know. Can anything be done, do you think?"

"About the marriage?" Tony thought for a moment. "Not likely, if it was done properly."

"I suppose one of us should go out there and see."

"Yes, I agree," Tony said with a nod. "With Elmira

increasing once more, I thought I should be the one to go. Thought you would wish to stay home with your wife."

"Good. Good. Very kind of you, Tony." Robert finally sank onto a leather sofa, in apparent concession. "Does Henry still not ask for money?"

"Now that is a puzzle. . . ."

"Aha! I knew there would be something." Robert's interest perked up once more. "What does he ask for?"

"He asked if we would sell his racers and place the money into the hands of Mr. Murchinson. In fact, he wants to liquidate his entire stable except for his stallion, Ebony."

"His entire stable? Murchinson! That man we employ to oversee our sheep farms in Wales?"

"Yes. It seems he wants a pair of our best merino rams, three dozen ewes, two of our better-bred sheepdogs, and a sheepherder who knows all about sheep. And he wouldn't mind a few of the cheviots as well, if we will trust him to repay the loan. All at the speediest transport."

"My God, the boy's gone mad. Is our own black sheep going to *raise* sheep, then? That settles it. Someone has to go out to that . . . that Colorado, and see what Henry is up to."

"That is why I have already booked passage," Tony said. "I leave tomorrow."

In the following month Mariah settled into a hazy pattern of bliss. She found her husband's company a great delight, which had been true from the first day they met. Yet now, since all the restraints were removed, every day was a new kind of adventure. Hank kept her so busy at night, she frequently rose late to begin work the next morning, apologizing to Grandaddy and Nate with a pretty blush. Whatever tasks were laid out for the day, Hank rode at her side and they worked as a team.

In the evenings, Hank included her in his and Elam's great discussions of what they read in the Denver papers and what they heard was happening about the countryside. He began to receive periodicals—among which was one written especially for women—and Eastern papers, so that they knew what the rest of the world was doing as well.

Things began to change on the Circle T. Hank, she noticed, often wanted matters his own way, and nothing was exempt. The surprise was that Grandaddy seemed in agreement with him. Actually, she found no reason to object, since the changes appeared all to the good.

When workmen arrived the week following the wedding to begin repairs on the barns, she didn't question Grandaddy's nod of approval. Heaven knew, the repairs were needed. So was the new equipment that seemed to just appear out of the blue . . . a new buckboard, new kitchenware, and new mattresses for the bunkhouse cots.

Downstairs, the parlor became a permanent bedroom for Elam. Brown removed the old sofa, and Hank purchased a new, comfortable sitting chair for the old man. The carpenter built shelves and made a door so that the room could be closed off from the kitchen.

A man came to whitewash the walls of both the upstairs rooms. Hank ordered new curtains, and new sheets and counterpanes, and helped Mariah polish the old furniture until it shone.

To Mariah's former little room, he not only added a thick new mattress to the cot there, but huge bolsters he had ordered to make it comfortable for sitting, and two new lamps. In effect, it became their own tiny parlor.

Hank often treated Mariah to little surprises from town—books, candy, perfume, hair ornaments, the sheerest of stockings, a new pair of work gloves, new boots, a new saddle blanket for Skedaddle. His gifts were given with a teasing sense of fun; he'd hide them someplace for her to stumble over, or put them under her pillow.

He taught her to dance. She felt stiff and awkward at first, but Hank assured her she would be ready by the time of the scheduled dance. They started in the tiny six-foot square of free space in their bedroom. He had her put her bare feet on top of his and then he moved into a slow waltz until he felt her body relax. Humming the tunes, he gave precise instructions of how to stand, how to hold her head and arms, how to keep her eyes on him and not on her feet.

"You're too tall to dance with," she complained, her head thrown back.

"Too tall? The art, my love, is to be able to dance with anyone, no matter the size."

Mariah rose to her toes on the top of his feet. The skin and muscles underneath hers were firm, but the slant of his arch made her perch precarious. She lost her balance. His arms tightened to steady her, and brought her closer to his body. As always, it started a heat between them.

Mariah wore only her nightgown. The slight friction she felt against her breasts had her breathless in moments. "I'm not sure I should . . . dance with . . . just . . . anyone."

"I'm not sure I will allow you to. . . ."

And the lessons were forgotten for that night.

The next evening they continued down at the barn, in the space Hank and Jim used for sparring. By the time they attended the Mead dance, Mariah was confident. Indeed, she held her own in every dance.

Only her one dance with Tommy marred the pleasant evening for her. He made a sarcastic remark about how she had learned to dance quick enough with her greenhorn but had refused when he'd asked her to years before. Mariah merely gave him a level stare and said, "That was then."

She avoided Tommy and Myrtle Alice after that, and Hank asked for no explanations.

But the best gift, Mariah thought as the weeks went by, was Hank himself. He continued to share the work and the ranch's concerns. It definitely lightened her worries, and she couldn't help but bask in her husband's attention. She felt like it was Christmas every day. But privately, she couldn't help but fret over the money he spent.

One night Hank laid out plans on their bed for a new ranch house. It was triple the size of their present home. Mariah was astounded and petrified. How would they ever pay for it?

"But, Hank, we don't have money to build this," she protested.

"Not right now, maybe. But next year, we will."

"I'm happy you're so optimistic, but there is no guarantee the Circle T will do well next year. We barely held our own this year."

"True enough, but we may be lucky."

"You have to trust in more than luck, Hank."

"Yes, but I told you once, love, I always figure my odds and chances. You have to, you know, when you play poker. And I say our odds of making a go of the Circle T are very good."

"Odds! Odds! I hope you don't plan on risking our income on poker. From what I know of it, a player loses more than he wins."

"Most do, I have to agree. The trick is to never play more than you can afford to lose." He slanted her a dare with a flash of his eyes. "Would you like to learn the game?"

She caught her lip between her teeth in an effort not to smile, then raised her brow. "What makes you think I don't already know how to play?"

"Do you?" Hank stared at her curiously. Was this something else she'd done with Tommy?

"I know the rudiments of the game," she admitted.

"Learned, no doubt, in less than correct company."

It seemed Hank always pulled her secrets from her without half trying. "When I was about fourteen we had a young cowhand who taught me. I lost my best bridle and two bits before I knew it. Granny was so all-fired mad when she found out, she took out a switch."

Hank thought her granny probably had been more frightened by what else the young cowhand had been aiming to win, and he was thankful she had held a careful vigil on his young Mariah. At the same time, he instantly felt sorry for Mariah. "Oh, my poor darling. Was it a bad whipping?"

"Well, not for me. See, she took the switch to that cowhand. But I got the biggest, longest gol-dern lecture like you've never heard. It lasted longer than a three-day July celebration. Scared me so that I never played again."

Hank chuckled. "I don't think your granny would object to you playing with your husband."

"No, but I don't think Grandaddy would like it. He abhors gambling, you know."

"Hmm. And you married me thinking me only a gambler?"

She spoke thoughtfully. "Well, you've shown all the signs of settling down, haven't you? And there's not a lazy bone in your body—you don't shrug off any of the work, no matter how hard or dirty. Besides, there is more to you than just . . . a gambler."

Touched by her trust in him, Hank ran a finger down her cheek. "I am flattered, my dear, that you think so." He kissed her lightly, then reverted to the teasing. "Now. We can play only for our own amusement. For something other than money."

"Like what?" she asked in suspicion.

"We'll think of something."

The idea intrigued her. If she could keep him entertained at home, he wouldn't want to run into town to play the game. Not that he had, since they'd married. "You're on."

After that, they sometimes retired upstairs even earlier than usual.

Then came the afternoon Hank returned home from town and announced he had purchased the section of land that joined the Circle T beyond the breaks. It was wilder, higher country, but had some good grazing, too.

Mariah sank into a kitchen chair while he proudly laid the deed on the table in front of her. She read it, stunned speechless, then handed it to Elam to read. It was made out in her name, Mariah Taggert Ackerley. Her gaze lifted to Hank. "I . . . that . . . that adds considerably to the Circle T. Hank, can you cover the debt? How—?"

He smiled the gentlest smile she'd yet received from him. His gray eyes were tender. "It is completely paid for, Mariah. Must admit, though, love, I am almost broke now."

Mariah was startled to hear him say so, for he never told her anything about his business affairs or how much money he had. She rose again, a frown in place, and walked to the stove and back, slapping mugs on the table.

"Just as I suspected. You've been spending far too much money on me. Really, Hank, I don't need that new dress you ordered from Mrs. Dolan, or any more presents. It would be better to conserve now."

"That's right, son," Elam added. "Better to save against a rainy day."

"There is no need for extreme measures yet," Hank replied. "I am only low on funds until next month. July first, as a matter of fact."

"What do you mean?"

"Oh, I have a little inheritance that is paid to me semiannually. From my grandmother."

Hank felt a little shamefaced for not having told Mariah and Elam of it before. Elam had accepted his word that he could support Mariah, without asking for details. But he was still loath to tell of how wealthy his brothers were, and of what kind and how many estates the family owned. The Ackerley holdings overshadowed the Circle T like a mountain over a foothill. Why, Ackerley Hall alone was filled with treasures that would pay for three Circle T's. He didn't want Mariah to feel ashamed of her piece of land in any way or think he patronized her. In her pride and independence, he worried, she just might think that.

However, he wanted to set her mind at ease. He didn't want her feeling guilty about accepting his small gifts, and he had no intention of stopping them. He enjoyed surprising Mariah with feminine things, especially because she expected so little in the way of material goods, unlike, say, his sister-in-law, who'd complain bitterly if she had to do without. She had dozens of dresses and fripperies—and carriages, thoroughbred horses, diamonds, pearls, and other gems.

Hank suddenly wished he had the wherewithal to drape Mariah in pearls and sapphires. Yet, it wouldn't enter her mind to want them, he realized. She was content with what she had in the Circle T. It made him ashamed for all the times he had foolishly thrown his money away, and extremely grateful for the few very wise investments he had made.

He slid an arm around Mariah's shoulders and tipped her chin up. "You do not need to fret, my darling wife," he told her. "We will always have enough income to lead a modest style of life."

She stood in the circle of his strong arm with the coffeepot in one hand and a creamer in the other. "You never told me of it."

"No, I . . . Sit down, Mariah. I will tell you now."

Hank waited until she poured coffee, then seated her before he began. It gave him time to think for a moment, in order to couch what he wanted to say in terms that would be truthful, yet protective. He knew she had no concept of the kind of background he came from.

"You see, darling, in England, the family's oldest male inherits the family . . . farms. Any younger siblings have to be provided for differently."

"Yeah, I've heard of that. Leaves the younger ones purely flat, don't you think?"

"It can, if the family doesn't help out."

"That's what families should do, I say."

"Yes . . . yes, and I have been fortunate in that regard. Let me explain. My oldest brother, Robert, as expected, inherited our family land when my parents died. Anthony, just two years younger than Robert, has . . ." Actually, Tony had a very nice income from a lesser estate near the Scottish border, but he seldom took up residence there. "Tony has become a . . . um, what you would call a scholar. He studies a great deal for the church. But Tony also has a private income and can do as he pleases. I am the last son. My grandmother provided for me."

"Oh, yes, I see." Mariah continued to stare, puzzled, into her husband's eyes.

Elam nodded. "Suspected something like it," he mumbled. "Like to hear more about your land sometime, an' what kinda crops you raise."

"Uh, all right. Sometime," Hank answered.

Mariah realized Hank was uncomfortable with talking about his family. Maybe there was something shameful about them, something he couldn't yet face. She consoled herself that in time, he would tell her.

She had always known by his education and manners that he came from good breeding stock, and by his dress and taste in choosing her clothing that he knew about the fine things money could buy. Somehow, it had never occurred to her that he might have a private income.

Mariah looked at her husband in wonder. Was it true or only more tall tales? When he first came to Mead Hank had airily thrown about statements of owning railroad stocks and making investments in the West for his family. She even remembered ordering him to stop telling Grandaddy such whoppers. She'd thought it merely part of the game they were playing and she'd assumed he made his living by playing poker.

She looked at the deed. If nothing else, this was legal. Her name was there just above the signature of the town's lawyer, Caroline's father. She felt ungracious to question it further.

"Thank you, Hank. I reckon we can start moving cattle on it later this week."

"Hold off on that for a while, if you please, Mariah. I have some new stock coming. It should arrive in another few weeks."

"New stock? But Hank, we just sold a bunch."

"I know, honey, but this is a special breed. When it arrives, I'll tell you all about it."

He had just told her he was almost broke. "You didn't go into debt for it, did you?"

"No, not exactly. . . . It is a special, um, circumstance."

"I don't understand. What do you mean, 'special circumstance'? You didn't *steal* them, did you? Oh, Hank, I love you, I do, but, please, please say you didn't . . . Rustlers! Is that it? Is a rustler gang bringing stock onto our graze?"

Hank threw back his head and laughed. "No, no, and no." He caught her up and swung her, then set her down again. "Would you really love me even if I were a thief?"

"Yes, but you're not, are you?"

"No, my little love, I swear to you I am not a thief."

She laughed with him then. She didn't really think him a thief, yet just for a moment, she had an awful feeling in the pit of her stomach. There seemed to be so many little mysteries surrounding her husband, and a story about a private family income would cover a multitude of questions.

"You can get a notion, Mariah," Elam said, shaking his head indulgently.

Regardless of Hank's confession of having little money left, a few days later he insisted they hire another hand. It immediately created another argument.

They were out by the corral, where Mariah was feeding a new colt by hand. She'd lost sleep the night before, helping the little fella come into the world.

"Hank, we don't have the money to pay another

man. And speaking of money, how much longer can we keep Brown? And what about Jim? I know he is your loyal friend, but you can't expect him to stay on, working as a cowhand with no pay. Why should he?"

"I have been giving Jim some thought of late. Indeed, I should talk with him soon. But that has nothing to do with our need for another experienced cowhand. Or even two."

"Hank . . ."

"Relax, Mariah. I have money coming along soon, you know. And with a couple of new cowboys under Nate's direction, you won't have to work so hard."

"I've always worked hard."

Hank looked at her in amusement. "Do you think that by having enough help so that you are not exhausted all the time, you will then have nothing left to do?" he asked, his eyes twinkling.

"There's plenty to do, right enough."

"Uh-huh. And I will remind you of your promise."

She looked at him over her shoulder. "What promise?"

"You promised me, did you not, that you would become my guide if I stuck it out here for a mere week or so?"

"That was before . . ." she broke off into laughter. "I thought I was safe."

"Uh-huh. Well, my darling wife, after we get another couple of men and things are running smoothly, I am calling in that promise."

"What do you want to do?"

"Oh, I would like an excursion to see more of the plains. To see buffalo. They are dwindling, I understand. And we can go hunting in the mountains. I heard in town the other day there is a big grizzly roaming the area. And we can take a few days off to climb the Lizard's Tail and explore what is beyond. Then there is Fireball. . . ."

Mariah made no more protest about their need for additional help. After discussing the matter with Elam, she and Hank went into Mead the following Saturday with a "help wanted" notice to post at Morton's general store.

She and Hank had different errands, so they parted in front of Morton's, with plans to meet in a few hours at Powell's dining room.

In the store, Mariah weaved her way past the dry goods to where Mead's post office was crammed into a corner area, separated from the larger merchandise space by a counter. On the wall there, she tacked her notice among a dozen other such messages and business inquiries.

"Morning, Mariah," Tommy said just behind her.

"Oh . . . Good morning, Tommy." As she turned, a rush of gladness overflowed her at seeing her old chum. He looked spiffy, dressed in a dark suit, a fine linen shirt, and a wide tie. His gleaming hair lay closely brushed against his head. "Haven't seen much of you lately."

"Reckon not. You haven't been in town much." A touch of wistfulness laced his speech as his admiring gaze took in her new leaf-green dress and hat. Mariah wondered if he missed their friendship.

"No, I . . . the ranch keeps me pretty tied down, you know, and Grandaddy hasn't been himself. Hank and I don't like to be gone for long. . . ."

"I've seen your husband a time or two. Without you."

She nodded. Hank had come into town on several occasions lately, alone or with Jim.

A moment passed.

"How . . . how is Myrtle Alice these days?"

"She's fine. Just fine." He looked down at the floor.

"And the . . . the bank. Is business going well?"

"Yeah. Look, Mariah, I . . . gotta get back there." His gaze met hers again. He seemed troubled. "I only came over to pick up the mail, but . . . but I'd really like to talk to you. Something's been on my mind. Meet me later, before you go home."

Old habits die hard, Mariah thought, for her first unspoken reaction was to immediately agree to meet him. Tommy hadn't questioned that she would. Indeed, there had been a time when she would have run to their meeting place without a second thought. Now she had more than one second thought about doing so.

She wanted to find out what bothered Tommy, yet she didn't think it wise to conduct a private meeting with him. Hank wouldn't like it. And she wasn't about to start lying to her husband over anything. Furthermore, she thought a personal friendship with Tommy would only lead to problems. Especially in this town.

"I shouldn't, Tommy. I don't think Hank—"

"Please, Mariah. We always . . . Please!"

"I don't know if I can."

"Meet me at noon. At . . . at, um, behind Truit's livery."

"Well, I suppose—"

"See you there." He turned and hurried away.

Behind the livery? Now what the devil? What was so all-fired important that Tommy had to meet her on the sly?

She bit her lip. What if Tommy was really in trouble? Could she turn her back on him?

21

Mariah checked the time at Mrs. Dolan's Fine Fabrics and Fashion. It was almost noon. Hurriedly, she thanked Mrs. Dolan and picked up the brown paper package that held two new cotton shirt-waist blouses and brightly colored print skirts that Hank had ordered for her. Ranch wear for the warmer weather, he'd said. Hair ribbons had been added to the package, Mrs. Dolan told her with a smile.

Mariah was again thinking of Hank's generosity as she lengthened her stride. Even knowing he had a steady income, she worried about his continuous spending, but he'd teasingly told her that she'd lived too many years pinching pennies until they cried "ouch." He made her laugh over the problem of where to put all the clothes he kept buying her.

She came upon Tommy waiting at the livery's corner.

"Mariah." He grabbed her arm. "I wasn't sure you'd come."

"Well, I can't stay long. I have to meet Hank. Now, what is it you couldn't wait to talk to me about?"

"Let's walk down to the gully, there." He nodded toward the rolling dip in the land beyond the edge of town. It was unlikely anyone would see them down there.

"I'm not sure that's a good idea, Tommy. Just tell me what you want to, okay?"

He gave her a disgusted glare. "At least come around to the back of the building. You don't want the whole town to see us. . . ."

Mariah sighed. "Hang it all, Tommy—"

"All right, all right. Don't get your temper up."

She waited, her mouth compressed.

"Hell, Mariah. I just don't like what you've gone and gotten yourself into."

"What are you talking about?"

"Well, that foreign dude you married. I don't like him."

"I don't understand your concern, Tommy. Has he done you a wrong? Or been rude to Mr. Sonyers? Or you?"

"Not exactly, no. But he puts on all these high-and-mighty airs when he comes into the bank, like . . . like we're a bunch of inferiors."

"I admit Hank sometimes has an autocratic attitude, but there are a lot of people in this town who like my husband just the way he is, Tommy, including me."

"But I'm not sure he's on the up-and-up."

"What do you mean?"

"People are talkin'. Half the time, this . . . this Jim friend does business for him. It's a little odd for him not to take care of his personal finances, don't you think? And where does he get his money? He doesn't work at nothin' that I can see."

At Mariah's affronted stare, he amended his statement, but not by much. "Criminy, Mariah, it isn't like the Circle T earns much, you know. This dude has money pouring into his account, and I don't see where any of it comes from. Besides all that, word around town is he's nothin' but a high-stakes gambler. Is that so?"

"It might be. So what?"

"Well, for Pete's sake, Mariah, I know you married the greenhorn on the rebound, and I'm sorry about hurtin' your feelings and all that, but I can't believe your grandfather allowed you to do such a locoed thing as marry the man."

"Is that what you think? That I married Hank on the rebound?"

"Well, didn't you? Everybody in town knows you're stuck on me."

"Well, for once, Tommy Bakersfield, everybody is double-barreled dead wrong."

"Wrong, huh? After you made such a doggone fool of yourself the day Myrtle Alice and I got married? Criminy, Mariah, you embarrassed the you-know-what outa me."

"Well, that's too bad, Tommy, because I didn't embarrass Hank at all. He liked my kissing."

"Huh. He was a sittin' duck. I heard all about it. You latched on to the first raw tenderfoot you saw and chased the bastard all over town 'til he finally had to marry you! What'd you do, Mariah, give 'im what he wanted so that your grandaddy forced him to do the right thing?"

It was just like Tommy to exaggerate everything he heard and twist it with his own brand of insult. At one time, she would have launched herself at him, fists flying. Now she only stared at him with contempt.

"You know what, Tommy? You're a downright silly, homegrown, king-sized jackass. You and I went trailing all over this territory for years by ourselves. Talk went around about us, too. Did I ever let you do more than kiss me once or twice? Did Grandaddy ever take a shotgun to your back? Nope, he didn't. Know why? 'Cause he knew you were no threat to my virtue."

Tommy's face went red as a beet. "I was too much of a gentleman to—"

"Gentleman be damned. You never had a chance. I whopped you once for trying, remember? Hank and I, on the other hand, married quick because we couldn't keep our hands off each other for another minute. And we wanted it legal fast because we weren't about to shame Grandaddy."

As she spoke, the truth of it hit her square on. She had loved Tommy. But she was flat-out crazily *in love* with Hank.

Behind her, a loud clapping began. She turned swiftly. Indeed, they had an audience.

"Bravo, Mariah." Hank stood at the corner of the livery barn, looking tall, handsome, and very masculine. Dressed in his town suit and with his wide-brimmed hat pushed casually to the back of his head, he was every inch a gentleman—yet he had a gun strapped to his hip, Western style.

She had noticed it before—there was little of the Eastern dude left. In his face or in his bearing. At the moment, Hank wore a watchful, languid half grin, but that didn't cover the spark of danger behind his eyes.

Several men stood listening.

Mariah pursed her lips as she calculated how much of the argument they had heard. Enough, she thought. Now it would be all over town what she'd said to Tommy, especially about how wanton she and Hank were.

Well, hell's bells, she didn't care a hoot. She loved Hank too much to care what anybody thought.

Hank dropped his hands and strode forward to take her elbow. "Shall we go, my darling?"

She raised her chin to a haughty angle. "Yes, I'm ready."

"Lord a'mighty, Mariah, you're as harebrained as you always were," Tommy muttered low.

Mariah heard him. And Hank heard him.

Very calmly, Hank turned back to the younger man. He spoke quietly, yet no one doubted his sincerity.

"Mr. Bakersfield, I give you fair warning but once, so I advise you to listen well. If you ever, *even once*, offer my wife an insult again—and you know that with the way this town loves to talk I would hear of it—I will take you apart piece by piece. Every bone in your body will suffer. Separately. One after the other.

"And if you ever *approach* Mariah again, unless it is merely to offer a polite greeting in my company, I will take delight in breaking your head."

Tommy, suffused with anger, fright, and humiliation, stood rooted. He opened his mouth to protest such treatment, but he was cut off.

"I wouldn't, Tommy, if I were you," Mr. Truit said from the small crowd. "Ya ain't got no rights, nohow, to insult a man's wife."

"Tommy, you're a sore loser," added Billy, the cowboy Mariah had gone to school with. "Seems to me you're feeling real sorry you picked the wrong gal an' now that you're miserable with that little stuck-up banker's daughter, you want to spoil things for

Mariah. Saw you do that when we were kids. Well, this time"—he cast an admiring gaze on Hank—"you can't do it."

Hank escorted Mariah to the buggy and handed her in. Both of them were quiet.

"Do you want to eat at Powell's?" he asked.

"No . . . let's go home."

Hank skillfully drove Lulubelle and Lena through Mead's Saturday traffic, then headed the team toward home. Mariah remained silent.

He turned down the broad path that led to the river pond. The buggy could go only so far over the rough growth and boulders, so he halted the team halfway down the slope. From there, the view was pretty and they could see the river bend.

Mariah sat with her white-gloved hands tightly laced. She looked charming and town-smart in the leaf-green dress with the bonnet to match. With her head turned just so, Hank saw only her lovely profile, but he didn't need to see more to know she was upset.

"All right, Mariah," he began. "When you become quiet it signals that something is wrong. What is it?"

"I don't know."

"Come on, honey. You don't usually run from a problem."

"I haven't figured this one out yet. I have to think on it a while."

"Let me help you, then. Tell me what's bothering you."

"Something Tommy said."

"I didn't doubt it." He waited patiently.

Hank thought he knew what Mariah was getting at. He had arrived upon the scene around the time that clod Tommy was filling her ears about being suspicious of his money, then accusing Mariah of marrying him on the rebound.

The idea had crossed Hank's mind, early on, when Mariah had kissed him so enthusiastically in the mountains. But it didn't take him long, as time passed, to disregard it. Mariah and he shared something satisfyingly deep that had nothing to do with her childhood attachment. The timing had been purely coincidental, that was all. He wasn't surprised that some of the townspeople would put the wrong conclusion on their marriage.

But Mariah tugged and pulled on another idea. She was troubled by a hurtful thought and lifted her gaze to meet his.

"Did Grandaddy . . .?"

"Yes?"

"Did Grandaddy make you marry me?" She said it all at once, her voice unusually breathless.

"Make me? *Make* me?" Hank raised a brow and gave her a gentle smile, trying to tease her out of her concerns. "Did your grandfather use force, do you mean? Now Mariah, darling, I know you consider me quite inept at some things, but really . . . How would that old man make me marry you if I hadn't wanted to?"

He slid a palm against the back of her neck, his thumb making circles just below her ear. She seemed all tied up in knots.

"Did he ever, uh, offer you something to marry me?" she asked, insistently pursuing it. "Like the Circle T?"

"No, he did not," he answered firmly. "In fact, he made it very clear . . . that is, we both agreed the Circle T is to remain yours."

"You agreed." She homed in on a delicate point.

In the depths of her brown eyes, Hank read the

same mixture of vulnerability and courageous determination Mariah had exhibited the first time he met her. She was fighting an impending wound with all the inner strength she had.

"Then you did talk. The two of you."

"Yes, of course, love." He gentled his voice and leaned nearer. "It is the proper thing to do, you know, in England and Europe. Most of the world, in fact. A suitor approaches his prospective in-laws to apply for permission to marry his chosen woman."

He felt the sharp edge of her tension begin to fade.

"Oh . . . I hadn't thought of that. Then you didn't . . . that is, Grandaddy didn't bribe you in any way?"

He started to chuckle and laid his lips against her jaw. "Why would Elam need to bribe me?"

"Oh, you know . . . to get something else you wanted. A prize or something."

He moved to her chin, feeling its roundness under his lips. "If you must know, my sweet darling, you are the prize."

"Me?" she whispered.

He nibbled his way up to her soft lips, where he rested a moment. "I wanted you more than anything else in life. I want you now more than anything else this day could offer. Do you suppose we can find a soft spot under a tree down by the pond?"

Mariah let the tiny remaining doubt drift away as he carried her from the buggy. He shed his coat, spread it on the ground, and drew her down to lie on it. There, he made her feel the gentlest, sweetest love she'd ever known, giving her long, precious moments of pleasure, deriving his own in an agony of whispered passion.

In being held and loved, Mariah thought she might have drifted into the boundaries of heaven.

And in giving himself completely, loving whole-heartedly, Hank finally believed there was one.

They hired two men the following week, and a boy. Hank hung back and watched Mariah make the final decision while Elam looked on.

The first was an experienced middle-aged man by the name of Chad Elkton who rode up to the cook-shack one morning in time for breakfast and with whom Mariah and Elam were acquainted. He had worked for people they knew, and they hired him without question.

"He's a good hand," Elam said.

Nate agreed. "Yep. Reckon we c'n count on Chad."

Randy Potter applied a day later. Neither Mariah nor Elam had ever met or heard of him. He was young, hadn't reached his potential growth yet, and had hiked out from town.

He was a total novice. Mariah looked at the skinny youth in sorrow. "Um, Randy, I'm sorry, but we need an experienced cowhand."

Randy shifted from foot to foot. One of his boots was separating, the sole flapping from the upper leather. His shoulder blades looked sharp underneath the bare threads of his shirt. "Need the work, ma'am. I learn fast. I'll even clean out the privy for ya if you hire me."

Mariah knew that hungry look he wore. She hated to turn him away, but she couldn't hire someone she'd have to take the time to teach when the purpose was to free her from some of the work. She was about to send him to Brown to get a meal, and then on his way back to town, when she caught Hank's expressive eyes. He gave the faintest of nods.

Mariah returned her attention to Randy. "All right, you're hired. You missed the noon meal, but Brown always has extra. Go eat, then report to Nate, down at the barn. Make sure you speak up, though, so he can hear you."

The relief in the youngster's eyes was obvious. "Thank you, ma'am. I will. Thank ya kindly."

The compassion in Hank's gaze spoke his approval. It warmed Mariah's heart.

The final man was short, stocky, and in his twenties. His name was Smith. He seemed a little uneasy when he discovered it was Mariah doing the hiring.

Smith told them he was an experienced cowpuncher, but was used to riding the larger ranches down in Texas and couldn't promise to stay on past the summer.

"That's fine, Mr. Smith. You do a good job for the Circle T while you're here and I won't quarrel when you want to go," she told him.

That night, Mariah, Hank, and Elam discussed their new additions before going to bed.

"It feels right good to see the bunkhouse full to brimming over again," Elam said.

"Yep," Mariah agreed. "How do you think Smith will take to orders under a woman?"

"Don't think he'll give you no trouble a'tall, honey, what with your husband's reputation," Elam said with a laugh.

"I don't expect the bunkhouse will brim over for long, Mariah," Hank told her. "I think Jim might just change his profession by fall."

"How do you mean? You've talked to him then?"

"Sure have. I think Jim wants to move to Denver and set up a men's haberdashery, and I think he has high hopes of taking Caroline with him."

"You don't say?" Mariah was flabbergasted, but suddenly felt very happy for Caroline. Life in the city would suit her.

Elam nodded. "That's right nice, Hank. We'll surely miss Jim, though."

"Yes," Hank replied softly. "I will too. But since I've changed my, ah, mode of existence, Jim is free to do the same."

"Is that why you wanted me to take on Randy?" Mariah asked.

"Partly. But I thought he could keep Nate and Elam company during those times when everyone else is away from the ranch buildings. He can learn a lot hanging about with those two, and it will give Nate someone to boss around," he said with a grin.

Hank said no more, but Mariah instantly took up the idea. She thanked him with her heart in her eyes. With Nate hearing less as time went on, and Grandaddy's heart in weakened health, it would be comforting to know Randy would be about in case of an emergency.

Elam, too, grasped the reasons. Not one to avoid reality, he merely said, "Thank you, son."

A week later, Mariah and Hank took a tent and supplies to last them three days and went searching for Fireball. Or so they told Elam and the rest. Actually, they rode to the Lizard's Tail and simply camped at its base for two nights. They climbed during the day, bathed together in the tiny stream, and made love in the grass, just as Hank had pictured them doing. It was a joyous, restful time.

They returned to the Circle T without Fireball, Elam noticed, but it didn't seem to him, when he watched his granddaughter and her husband that night over supper, that it made much difference. Both of them appeared relaxed and happy. He hadn't seen Mariah like that in a long time.

Late in July, a rider from town trotted into the ranch yard with a telegram for Hank.

Hank tore it open, read it, then glanced at Mariah with sparkling eyes. "That new stock I ordered will arrive tomorrow on the morning train."

"All right," she said with a smile. "You've been so all-fired excited about this new breed or whatever, I reckon we'd better get an early start in the morning."

The following morning, Elam decided to go into town with them. He'd been feeling better lately, and making more of an effort at activity.

When they arrived, they found the train was late. Hank stalked the wooden platform, his boots and spurs jingling in regular rhythm. The stationmaster finally told them he thought the train might be a full hour behind.

"Why don't you look in on Thorndyke, Hank," Mariah suggested. The deputy had just returned from a trip south, checking on the rumor of rustlers. Hank always wanted to know what was happening around them.

"Yes, that will fill my time. I'll meet you back here in about an hour."

Mariah decided to pick up their mail at the post office. She left Skedaddle hitched beside Patches at the station. Grandaddy, having brought the buggy into town, dropped her in front of Morton's before going to call on Mrs. Kelly.

Mariah talked to Mr. Morton a moment, then wandered toward the postal boxes. There, she ran into Caroline.

"Oh, hello, Mariah." Caroline's color heightened and she hastily set aside a catalog she'd been fingering.

"Hello, Caroline." The catalog, Mariah couldn't help but notice, was one for men's fine clothing. She wondered if Caroline was reading up on the kind of merchandise that Jim hoped to stock in his store. "How are you?"

"I'm very well, thank you." Caroline dropped her gaze. "I . . . I . . . suppose you're very busy these days out at the Circle T. . . ."

"Yes, we are. But the work isn't nearly so demanding since we hired the extra men."

"Oh. That's nice."

Mrs. Benton was on the far side of the store, chatting with another customer. Caroline glanced over her shoulder, then lowered her voice. "I suppose Jim is . . . is . . . well?"

Something about Caroline's unusually retiring attitude caused Mariah to be suspicious. She lowered her tone to match Caroline's. "Caroline, Jim just returned from Denver. Didn't he tell you he was going?"

Caroline shook her head, looking miserable. "I guess I couldn't have expected him to. We . . . we had a quarrel, you see. And Mama . . ."

So that was it. Mrs. Benton had been putting her spoke between Caroline and Jim. Mariah laid a gentle hand on Caroline's.

"Why don't you come out to supper tonight," Mariah asked in sudden generosity. "Then Jim can see you home. You can make it up with him then, without a lot of . . . extra eyes around."

"Should I? Without an invitation from him? Oh,

Mariah, it might look . . . very bold. It would be improper."

Mariah tamped down her irritation. "Caroline, for once in your life, *be bold*. If you're there, Jim will know you care about him. Besides, I invited you. And I'm a respectable married woman now."

Caroline glanced over her shoulder again. Her mother was moving toward them. "All right. I will. I'll be there for supper. Thanks, Mariah."

Caroline walked away quickly and Mariah turned to their letter box and took out a handful of mail. They had something almost every week, now. Hank carried on a lot of correspondence.

In the distance, she heard the train whistle. Hurriedly, she shuffled through the pieces, watching for the letter Grandaddy was expecting from his sister. Then one letter caught her gaze. It was addressed to Hank, in the feminine hand of the Eastern girl he'd known before coming here. Edith . . .

Mariah stared at the letter for a full minute. It was ridiculous to be jealous. Of course it was.

She bit her lip, wondering if she could just throw it away. She wanted to, but lectures about honesty and minding her own business drilled into her from knee-high put up a mountain-sized resistance.

The train whistle blew again and she knew the train had arrived. She had to be on her way.

"Oh, hel—" Mariah started to mutter, in total disgust with herself, then looked up and found herself staring straight into the cold blue eyes of Myrtle Alice. "—looo . . . Nice day, isn't it? I must run. My husband expects me, you know."

Clutching her mail, Mariah strode out of Morton's and turned to walk down the road. There seemed to be a number of people heading that way.

"Hey, Jake," someone called. "Someone's unloadin' sheep off a' them cars."

"Sheep? What the hell . . ." responded the man named Jake.

"Would you look at that? White woollies."

A couple of cowboys left The Nugget saloon and mounted their horses, heading toward the train. Another man hurried in the same direction on foot. A saloon girl leaned against the open door of her establishment to watch. Excitement seemed to roll up the street like a steam engine.

Then the awful, sudden suspicion crept into Mariah's mind. Hank had talked of special stock. He had been waiting patiently to fill up the new section of land with it. He had even calculated the days . . .

No, it couldn't be. Hank knew this was cattle country.

Mariah lengthened her stride. She heard a bleat, then several. Far down the road, she saw the bobbing herd of dog-sized white bodies.

There was no mistake—a flock of sheep was trailing up the middle of Mead's main road.

The sheep couldn't be Hank's new stock, could they?

They could be, an insidious voice declared.

But . . . Hank *knew* this was cattle country. Cattlemen hated sheep. *She* hated sheep.

Mariah felt her breath grow short. She had to stop this. The town would be up in arms. The county would be tearing mad. Grandaddy would have another heart attack.

Oh, Hank!

They would shoot him. Or hang him. Oh, Lord, please . . .

In the middle of her stride, she heard his voice.

"I say, miss. Could you direct me—"

22

The plummy voice sounded like Hank, yet there was something wrong in what he said. It caused her to pause. What had he said? She turned in puzzlement.

Mariah stared up into the misty gray eyes of a tall man. He wore a bowler hat and he was garbed in a finely tailored dark suit. He looked just like Hank.

"I beg your pardon, miss. Could you direct me to—" Mariah blinked. "Hank?"

She heard her name called from far up the street and half turned to see who had summoned her. Her grandfather drove toward her in the buggy.

Closer now, from the opposite end of the road, came the bleating woolly animals that most of the territory despised. She glimpsed two dogs darting after a ewe that had strayed onto a portion of wooden sidewalk belonging to The Golden Rose. The saloon's barman snapped a white cloth at the animals as he

shouted for them to get off. The flock came on amid a
babble of agitated voices.

Three mounted cowboys began to hoot and call
names at the sheep and drover, cursing roundly as
they rode their horses around the flock. It caused a
general panic among the small animals. The sheep
bleated the harder, the dogs barked louder, and
Mariah heard Hank's voice shouting from the middle
of the hubbub.

Dust was everywhere. It rose six feet high, sending
the odor of sheep to permeate the air and virtually
screening from her sight a lot of what was happening.
Mariah squinted in an effort to see.

"What on earth—" A gust of dust hit her, filling
her mouth and making her cough. She brought her
kerchief up to cover the lower half of her face.

"It must be market day. Come, miss," said the
voice that sounded like Hank's next to her ear. "We
must get away from this. Let us retire into this establishment until the sheep have passed."

They stood in front of the bootery. A man shoved
them in order to join the growing crowd.

Mariah tipped her head. Her eyes watered with the
dust, but she could see a kind concern in those gray
eyes. She must be either dreaming or falling off the
edge of reality, she thought wildly. Even the arch of
his brow and the curve of his mouth was Hank's. His
lips parted in a sudden grimace against the noise and
dust.

And all at once, Mariah knew. The man in front of
her had to be Hank's brother. He looked and sounded
exactly like her husband, except that his teeth were
absolutely straight.

Not wanting to shout over the noise, Mariah
merely shook her head to the stranger's suggestion.

Instead, she shoved her mail into her vest for safe-keeping, then grabbed the man's coat sleeve and began to drag him along behind her.

The street became even more jammed. She was worried about Grandaddy. She couldn't see him in all the mess. She hoped he'd had the good sense to park the buggy and stay put.

"I say— Uh, miss, please—"

Mariah held tighter as she waded through and around the sheep toward where she thought she had last heard Hank. There weren't that many of them in the flock, Mariah realized, only about fifty or sixty, but with all the churning and confusion it was difficult to get to Hank.

A horse whinnied and she glanced aside. Her reaction was swift; she yanked hard on the stranger as a horse reared and came down again very close to them. The man stumbled into her, almost knocking her down.

"Mariah!" Hank shouted once more. "Help me get them out of town. Turn them in to the countryside."

The stranger's head whipped around. "Henry, is that you?"

The dust thinned a little and Mariah spotted Hank. He came forward with wonder written all over his face. "Tony! Good Lord, what are you doing here?"

Hank grabbed his brother's hand in a hard grip.

"I came to see you, of course. I must say, this is a bit more than I expected."

Hank laughed. "I reckon it is, at that. Come, help me get these creatures out of town. Then we can talk."

Tony raised a brow and chuckled. "You want me to become a shepherd? Well, I suppose it is appropriate."

Hank took Mariah's arm. "Honey, let's get these animals on their way before you meet my brother."

"You mean before someone starts shooting."

"Shooting?" Tony asked, incredulous. "You mean shooting the sheep?"

"Yep. Either the sheep or Hank. Or you."

Behind her, another jubilant yell rent the air. Hank looked past her, then let go of her as though she were a white-hot brand, and began to run. "Hey, you! Stop that!"

Mariah spun around. One of the mounted cowboys was lassoing one of the rams. It resisted, bleating frantically.

"That's the ticket," shouted one of the others. He laughed uproariously and hauled out his own lariat.

"I said, stop it!" Hank demanded, as he halted within a few feet of the fat cowpoke who held his rope taut against the struggling ram.

The man stared at Hank in disdain.

"Ya ain't oughta bring them sheep around here, mister."

From the edge of the crowd, someone agreed. "Yeah. Git them sheep outa here. This's cattle country."

"Get your rope off my animal," Hank commanded. His hard gaze never left the man holding the roped ram.

"You gonna make me?" was the snarled reply.

"If that's what it takes, you lop-eared jackass."

Mariah's nerves tightened and she moved to stand by Hank. She'd never seen him so angry.

She recognized the fat cowboy as one belonging to Brill's Triple Bar X's outfit that had given Grandaddy so much trouble over the last few years. She couldn't remember his name, but he was a hateful bastard of the same cut as Kasey.

Where in blue blazes was Sheriff Tinsdale, or Thorndyke? Mariah fumed. The crowd had thickened, and though she saw faces she knew, she wasn't sure any of them would back Hank in a fight to protect his sheep.

Hell's bells, she wouldn't either if Hank wasn't her husband. She'd been raised to respect cattle and hate sheep.

The Triple Bar X cowboy's face turned ugly. "Who you callin' a jackass?"

"I will do more than call you a jackass if you haven't removed your rope from my animal by the count of three."

Mariah recognized the way Hank stood, but she thought the cowboy did not. Hank's body was on attack alert. Though his fists were loosely balled, Mariah knew that in scant seconds, they could become weapons of which to be frightened. Anyone who'd seen him box knew it, too.

Still, she and Hank were outnumbered. More of the crowd jeered at them, their mood growing dangerously closer to mob thinking. Her face set, she turned to face outward, her body at a right angle to Hank's. If they were to be attacked, she would be able to protect him from this angle.

Tony stepped forward to address the cowboys. "Now see here. We only want to pass peacefully. Surely there can be no objection—"

"Shut yer face, greenhorn."

From the corner of her eye, Mariah saw the shock that came into Tony's face at being addressed so rudely. Then she saw her grandfather pushing his way through. "Grandaddy," she frantically called. "Stay back. Go find the sheriff or the deputy."

Mariah felt a great relief when Elam turned toward the opposite end of the town, where the sheriff's office was located.

"Your time's up, cowboy," Hank said roughly as he bent to free the ram.

In that moment, the Triple Bar X man launched himself from his saddle onto Hank's back. Mariah heard Hank's grunt of surprise as the two of them hit the ground, rolling among the sheep.

That did it. She worried not one iota about Hank being able to take care of himself against the cowboy, but it was going to be hell to pay with the sheep. Because however much the drover attempted to keep them together, sheep began to scatter in little bunches. They went everywhere.

All at once, Mariah felt totally incensed. How dare this trio of flea-bitten coyotes cause such a ruckus and with harmful intentions toward defenseless animals!

The two other mounted cowboys began to laugh and hurl invectives about. The one that had his lariat in hand began to twirl it over his head, aiming at a bleating ewe.

In a fury, Mariah threw herself forward and grabbed the rope in midair as it began its descent. Instantly, she yanked with all her might. It caught the man by surprise, and he tumbled from his horse and hit the ground with a thud. In a flash, she looped and tied the man's hands, then his feet, as she would have done a calf.

She left him there, ignoring the man's screaming curses. The crowd roared with laughter.

"Thataway, Miss Mariah!" someone yelled.

She spun on her heel just in time to see Hank lay a powerful right hook on the Triple Bar X man's jaw. He went down in a heap.

She spun again, looking to see how Tony was faring. It appeared to her that her brother-in-law was attempting to reason with another of the protesters, another neighboring cattleman, by the cut of him, although he was on foot. Tony was having no success. Mariah couldn't hear the words, but she could see the outraged anger in the cattleman's face.

Bless the Lord, it seemed Tony didn't have any better sense than Hank did when he'd first arrived. A pure flat-out tenderfoot. He didn't seem to realize he was in big trouble.

Pushing a ewe from her path, she started toward her brother-in-law just as a second man approached him from the other side. Mariah felt another wave of urgency. The new greenhorn was about to get pounded into the ground. She had to reach him, before . . .

Mariah tried to run to Tony's aid, stumbling over sheep and road ruts while the dust swirled into her nostrils and eyes. "Hank," she screamed for assistance.

She was seconds too late. Suddenly, the cattleman gave Tony a mighty shove. Taken unawares, Tony's expression held blank surprise. He staggered, but didn't fall.

But Mariah needn't have worried, because the next moment brought a reaction from Tony that would rival any coiled rattler. Just as the cattleman was about to hit him, Tony's fist connected with his jaw in a lightning strike. The man crumpled and lay still. Tony spun and faced the second man, who quickly backed away.

Stunned, Mariah halted and stared.

Across the space that separated them, she heard Hank call. Swiftly, she looked at him through the haze. He didn't seem any worse for wear, although he was breathing a little hard.

Hank's glance ran over her, ascertaining her well-being, then flew toward Tony. He grinned at his brother, then at her. The three of them stood amidst a mob of bleating sheep, barking dogs, whinnying horses, and a cheering, yelling crowd. And they were nearly choking on the dust.

Mariah couldn't help herself. Hank's humor infected her like measles. She started to laugh.

The fight was over. The Triple Bar X man climbed to his feet looking totally dazed, remounted his horse with slow effort, and wheeled him in a circle. Mariah thought he wasn't exactly sure of what had hit him or what he was doing.

Thorndyke sprinted into the middle of the hubbub, forcefully shouting for everyone to break it up.

"That's enough. Here," he said to the mounted cowboys who had started the fracas. "You men clear out or I'll arrest you." Then he turned to Hank. "Hank, get your damned animals out of the road. Who tied this man up?"

Someone yelled, "She did it! Mariah!"

Thorndyke looked at her incredulously for a moment. "Mrs. Ackerley . . . aw, hell. Never mind." He shook his head, then rapped out orders.

"You." He pointed to a man in the crowd. "Haul this no-good's carcass over to Doc's until he comes to," he said, referring to the man Tony had flattened. "And Truit, you set this one loose," referring to the man struggling against his binds, "and send him on his way."

Mariah noticed Elam on the edge of the dispersing crowd and hurried toward him. He looked pale, but otherwise all right.

Sheep were still bleating, everywhere.

"Hank, you gotta get these damned . . ." Thorndyke

began in disgust. Turning to the crowd, he said, "Somebody, help get these sheep corralled."

"Here, I'll help," said Billy. He herded two ewes before him, let the dogs take over, then ran after a set of three sheep hovering in the corner near The Nugget's door.

Mariah made sure her grandfather was all right, then gave her best effort to getting the sheep back together in one flock. All in all, it didn't take that long.

When the flock was together, the sheepherder and the dogs took them through an empty lot, and they were into open land.

Hank gave the drover directions to the Circle T. "I'll help ya get 'em home, Mr. Ackerley," Billy offered. Hank nodded his thanks.

After watching the flock move nearly out of sight, they all looked at each other. Mariah was covered in dust and when she stared at Hank and his brother, she saw that they looked no better.

"Hank, I think you've plumb flat-out lost your mind," Mariah said on a soft sigh. "How could you do it? You dad-blasted greenhorn! I told you this was cattle country."

"Now slow down, there, Mariah. I explained—"

"I never once heard the word sheep. Stock. Stock is what you said."

"You never asked, either. The sheep will graze the new section, and there's government land beyond."

"You think we're going to take sheep onto that government land? You're loco. We'd be fighting every king-sized to small cattle rancher in the territory. And it won't be only a shouting-and-shoving match. It's likely to be with guns."

Mariah's distress was real and soundly based.

Hank strode toward her. He bent at the knees to stare into her face. "We'll fence and expand slowly. We'll hire more men if need be."

"Hank, fencing costs money." Her eyes were pleading with him to back down and say they'd get rid of the sheep. "That's what put Grandaddy in such a bind before."

"We'll do it as we can afford to, honey." He slid an arm around her. "I have resources I haven't yet tapped, and I promise you . . . we won't let it get to a fight. Meanwhile, we won't push beyond this small start. People will get used to the sheep in time. Especially when they see that they make money."

Mariah shook her head. "Oh, Hank. I don't know anything about sheep."

"Neither do I, love. We'll learn together. It will be a great adventure."

Tony watched the quick exchange in amazement, his gaze bouncing between the two as though his neck had springs. Was this dusty, gun-toting cowboy his ne'er-do-well brother of impeccable dress? The jaded one who had been immune to the charms of some of England's most noted beauties?

Tony looked Mariah over carefully. The young woman was slight of build, and dressed almost masculinely in a split skirt, boots, vest, and broad-brimmed hat. Yet he thought she might be rather attractive if it weren't for all the dirt.

Even beyond the dusty film that covered her skin, Tony noted the clean lines of her face and finely shaped eyes. They sparkled with spirit. He remembered that the girl had stood between him and Hank and fought like a tigress.

Tony watched as Henry brushed tenderly at a stray wisp of hair against her face and attempted to coax

Mariah into accepting the sheep. Her softening mouth took on a pensive curve.

Oh yes, Tony could see that Mariah, like other women before her, had succumbed to the Ackerley family charm. And everyone in their English circles knew, of course, that Henry had inherited a double portion of it. But he had an unprecedented hunch that this slight woman would bring Henry around if he got too far out of line, for he had never observed just that patience and sweetness in Henry's expression before.

The wonder of it all gave him much to ponder, Tony conceded, and there were many questions he had yet to find answers for. He would have to reserve judgment and see what developed. But there was one burning bit of curiosity he could address immediately.

"Ahh . . . pardon me. I don't exactly understand this objection to sheep. Can someone explain it to me, please?"

"Tony." Hank turned to his brother, drawing Mariah along with him. He teased, "It looks as though your timing is perfect, as usual."

"What?" Tony raised a brow in question, just as his brother did. The gesture was a master stroke of communication, one of unperturbed subtlety. "Do you mean my being landed in the middle of a town brawl led by you? Really, Henry . . . I thought you had outgrown schoolboy pranks."

Hank laughed. "Mariah, my darling, let me present you. This is my brother, Anthony."

Mariah couldn't help herself. She stared at Tony in unabashed astonishment. "You didn't tell me he was your twin."

"Alas, no. . . . We have been trying to convince the world that five minutes' difference in birth truly sets us apart. Other than looks, we are nothing alike."

Remembering the man that went down under Tony's mighty fist, she said, "Uh, if you don't mind, I think I'll wait and see how true that is."

Elam drove up to them in the buggy, with Skedaddle and Patches tied to the rear. He stared at Hank and Tony.

Hank made brief introductions.

"Hank, Thorndyke advises us to stay with our herd . . . er, flock," Elam said hurriedly. "That scoundrel Kasey . . . he was seen with them fellas that started the trouble back there, just before the dust-up. That one that Mariah tied up let it slip that Kasey paid 'em to stir things up."

"Kasey, huh?" said Hank, a scowl in place. "He certainly kept himself out of sight. I wonder . . ."

Mariah had kept a close watch on her grandaddy as he spoke. He appeared pale and agitated; she remembered that the last time his heart had nearly given out was when he thought her nearly drowned. Her own heart pounded in worry.

"Hank . . ." she murmured.

Hank flashed her a quick glance of understanding. "Elam, I wonder if you would be so kind as to let Mariah ride home with you so that Tony can ride Skedaddle. We'll just hang back a bit so that we can make sure we're clear of trouble."

"Why, sure, son, if you think that's the thing to do."

Mariah climbed into the buggy and gently took the reins.

Hank handed Tony the reins of the roan, quickly lengthened the stirrups, then leaped into his own saddle.

23

After a quick consultation, Hank and Tony disappeared into a wooded area along the side of the road. As boys they had played robbers and sheriff in their woods at home, and now it seemed natural to follow an old pattern of action. By the time two horsemen trotted by, with one straining to see what was ahead while the other nervously looked over his shoulder, the scene appeared quiet and serene.

"Reckon they already reached the Circle T?" queried the fat cowboy Hank had knocked down earlier. "Be harder ta do sompthin' without 'em figurin' out it was us, if they done got home with them sheep."

"Well, if you'd stirred up more of the cowhands in town like I told you, we wouldn't be trailin' them now," Kasey said, his voice full of malice. He wasn't dressed as fine as when Hank first met him; he was unkempt and needed a shave.

"Wasn't 'nuff time."

"Coulda turned out more like I hoped," Kasey continued, ignoring his companion. "Thought those sheep woulda got shot to pieces by some of the cattlemen before they got outa town," he said in a wishful tone. "If it'd gone like I figured, nobody woulda known we started the fracas. And we'd have put paid to the dude."

"Kasey, why don't ya let it go, now . . ."

"One more try, Elroy, just one more try."

"Whut c'n we do after they're home?"

"I'm thinking on it," Kasey said. "We c'n watch for our chance."

Elroy shook his head. "Attackin' a man on his own land might stir up more'n a ordinary fight, Kasey. Steppin' over the line, ya know. Folks round here like old man Taggert. Some of 'em even like the dude. He ain't likely ta put up with anything done on the sneak like the old man has."

"You've done some sly work for your Triple Bar X boss, haven't you, Elroy?" Kasey narrowed his eyes. He'd been saving up this tidbit of information for just such a need. "Breaking down fence and driving Circle T cattle into the thickets and such. Finding new mamas for some of their calves, too."

Elroy paled as sweat beaded down his temples. He thought nobody knew what he'd done for his old boss.

"How did you—"

"You spill your guts when you get drunk, you know that, Elroy?"

Elroy halted his mount and stared at his partner, his mouth set in a mutinous line. Kasey turned his horse to face Elroy's, and his hand covered the butt of his gun.

This whole thing had gone pretty sour as far as

Elroy was concerned, and he was sorry he'd gotten mixed up with Kasey. His head still rang with the punch he'd taken from the dude and he had no hankering a'tall to tangle with him again. But now Kasey was blackmailing him over some of those picayune jobs he'd done for Brill.

"Now I just wanta make it tough on that damned Englishman, that's all," Kasey said.

"Fer a man whut wants ta git a little revenge, ya sure have a way of makin' yourself scarce when it comes ta the action," Elroy said.

"You calling me a coward?" Kasey caressed the Remington .44, sliding a finger close to the trigger.

"Uh, no . . . no, 'course not." Elroy backed down quickly, though he thought that Kasey was the head honcho of sneaks. He didn't have no personal gumption a'tall unless he was half drunk and pushed into a corner, Elroy thought. Kasey was happiest when he could get someone else to do his dirty work for him.

Elroy also knew that Kasey would stab or shoot a man in the back if he thought he could get away with it.

He decided he'd had about all of Kasey he could stomach.

"See here, Kasey. If I stick this here thing out to the end, I want my money now. I'll haveta hightail it into Kansas or down South afterward, mebbe."

"You'll get your money," Kasey said. "How come you've turned chicken-livered all of a sudden?"

"Don't want no trouble with the law, Kasey," said the heavy rider.

"It is a point you should consider, Kasey," Hank said, easing Patches forward out of the woods with his rifle held loosely across his saddle.

Elroy's jaw dropped. Kasey's head jerked around to face Hank, his expression ugly. "You!"

"Move your hand away from that gun," Hank ordered, "or I'm likely to hit more than your dealing hand. Or if you prefer, we can have another go with the fists."

Kasey's face was a mask of hatred. "You think you're big stuff, don't you, Englishman, with your fancy boxing an' all those special rules. You took me easy. Well, this time there's two of us to one of you. Get him, Elroy."

"I believe you have miscalculated the situation, sir," said Tony. "There is more than one of us. But surely we can settle this dispute peaceably. . . ."

The voice came from the other side of the road. The Englishman's voice. Kasey whirled to face it. A man stepped out of the woods, an identical image of Kasey's hated foe. He held no gun, but his very presence was threatening.

Kasey's eyes bulged. "What the hell is this? Two of you?"

"Really, sir—"

"Forget it, Tony. This is one time when your sensible approach has no effect. Kasey finds insult in everything. He understands only force. Now," Hank reminded Kasey, "the gun."

Instantly, Kasey yanked his hand clear of the gun. He looked sick.

Frowning, Elroy eased back in his saddle and inched his hand closer to his six-shooter.

"Don't move, Elroy," Mariah said as she rode forward from behind a huge boulder on Flirt. She had never aimed a gun at another human being in her life, but now her gun was carefully trained at his chest.

"Don't shoot, ma'am." Slowly, Elroy raised his hands. "Don't shoot, please."

"I'm glad to know who has been responsible for making trouble on the Circle T's fence line, Elroy," Hank continued. "I would advise you to take that trip south, pronto. But before you go, you might tell the Triple Bar X boys to stay clear of the Circle T property line. You aren't dealing with just a couple of old men and a lone woman, now."

"Sure thing, Mr. Ackerley. Anything you say. Can I go now? I'll do just as you say, I sure will."

Thorndyke rode up from a nearby gully. He stopped a few feet from the scene, glancing at each of them as he started his slow drawl. "Aw . . . there you go, Hank, keeping my job interesting for me. You and Miss Mariah here, er, pardon me, ma'am, I mean Mrs. Ackerley . . . well, you sure do have an odd effect on people. What's been going on?"

"We were merely having a little chat with these men, Thorndyke. Before they move south."

"Uh-huh. Well, Kasey," said Thorndyke. "Looks like your luck is holding this time. If I had found you first, you'd be in jail quicker'n you could shake a lamb's tail." He chuckled at his own joke, then continued. "But if you're gone within the next hour, I won't arrest you."

"Arrest me for what?" snarled Kasey.

"Disturbing the peace, causing a ruckus in town, and . . . let's see, hiring Elroy and those other hombres to damage the Circle T's property—let me know, Hank, if any of your sheep got lost or damaged in all that mess—and, what else? Oh, yeah. Making a nuisance of yourself."

"You can't arrest a man for that," Kasey protested.

"You've worn out your welcome in Mead, Kasey, and for ten miles around. Hell, I think you better quit

Colorado altogether. If I see you again anywhere, I might shoot first and arrest you later."

Thorndyke turned his stare on Elroy.

"I'm leavin', deputy. I'm leavin' here for good," Elroy babbled.

"Yep, you are. But don't linger to deliver that message of Hank's. I'll do the honors."

"I will." Elroy bobbed his head, then wagged it back and forth. "I mean I won't."

"Well, folks, I reckon I'd better trail these two. So long, ma'am." Thorndyke tipped his hat and motioned for the men to go before him.

Mariah, Hank, and Tony watched the deputy herd the two men away. Then Tony retrieved Skedaddle from the woods, and they rode toward the Circle T.

"Is Elam all right?" Hank asked Mariah.

"Uh-huh . . . as good as could be given the shock of finding sheep on the Circle T. And naturally, those sheep have plumb caused an uproar. I had Chad direct the shepherd and the flock into the east pasture for now, but he's none too happy about it. We could lose a couple of the new men over this."

"Never mind, darling. If they quit, we'll hire others."

Mariah sighed and shook her head. "Hank, you just don't know . . ."

"Master Anthony!" Jim, usually so circumspect, was caught by surprise. He broke out in a pleased smile when he saw Tony dismount in front of the barn with the others, and hurried forward, his hand outstretched. "Oh, my! It's good to see you, sir."

Tony returned the greeting enthusiastically. "How are you, James?" He shook James's hand. It was the first time he'd ever done so, but he was discovering that he didn't necessarily dislike this American penchant for equality. "You are looking well. I see you've succumbed to this cowboy thing, also."

He was referring to James's mode of dress, which was almost identical to Henry's. While speaking, he glanced about him. There had been recent repairs made to the barns, he saw. New wood stood out against old, weathered boards, and beyond, the corral had new rails, the peeled logs looking yellow against the aged brown-gray. This must be where Henry was pouring his money.

He wondered what the house was like. So far, the ranch resembled the neat English farms only in purpose.

"Quite, sir," James answered. "I have, um, prospered, you could say. What is the news from home? And, might I ask . . . have you come alone, Master Anthony?"

Hank, seeing Mariah's curiosity rising and her gaze flashing between his brother and James, attempted a delaying tactic to what he knew was coming. "Let us proceed to the house, please. Tony, you have taken us by surprise."

Tony gave Hank scant attention as he answered James. "Oh, do you mean have I brought Harding? Well . . ."

Elam hailed them from the path to the house and Nate popped out from the barn. Randy, drawn by the excited voices, emerged from the cookshack, with Brown right behind him.

"What happened?" Elam asked. "Mariah, you all right?"

"I'm fine, Grandaddy."

"What's agoin' on, anyway? Mariah, you went

tearin' in an' outa here like a whirlwind," Nate complained in his loud voice.

"We had to take care of Kasey, that was all."

"Kasey!" yelled Nate. "That dad-blamed skunk. What trick is he up to this time?"

Hank turned to assure Elam that they were unhurt, intending to point them all in the direction of the house before they got into explanations. But Elam and Nate were full of questions. No sooner did he answer one than there were two more to address. He was aware of Mariah staring at his brother, however.

"Who's Harding?" Mariah asked Tony.

"Why, he's James's cousin. My valet."

"Valet? James's cousin?"

"Yes. Like James is Henry's. The Hardings are the distaff side of the Moore family. They have been with the Ackerleys for generations, my dear," Tony explained. He turned to James. "I believe your great-grandfather was the first to serve with us, wasn't he, James? He started with the second duke of Stroud?"

"That is correct, Master Anthony."

Funny, Mariah thought with one part of her mind while another assimilated the deeper truth of what Tony was saying, how Jim had reverted to that stiff way he'd had when he first came to the Circle T. His smile had faded, and while he still seemed genuinely pleased to see Hank's brother, his more relaxed expression was gradually replaced by an almost sober blankness.

The seat of Stroud . . . an English estate. Her brother-in-law continued to relate the family history. Part of her listened to the story of how, generations back, there was a connection to . . . Charles.

Mariah felt blank, overwhelmed. One of England's kings!

Oh, the tie was a remote one, to be sure, Tony went on, but tracing family history was a passion for him and he quite liked the idea that the Moores and Hardings had been with them for so long.

Mariah tipped her head and looked up at her husband from beneath lowered lashes. She assessed him anew. He was tall . . . she often stood on her toes to kiss him. His gray eyes were gentle, most of the time. Easily amused, his mouth frequently curved into a smile. He was the epitome of refinement, as Caroline would say.

Yet she knew there was a wild streak that ran through Hank's veins. While he looked handsome and urbane in his Eastern clothes, and his manners were a perfect tribute to his training, he appeared far more virile in his Western clothing.

Now he was patiently explaining their run-in with Kasey, and how they and Thorndyke had handled the situation, to Grandaddy, Nate, Randy, and Brown. He hadn't been gentle then, or when he fought. . . .

Her husband, Hank. She'd known him first as Henry Clayton. Gambler. Adventurer. Charmer.

Liar!

Henry Clayton Ackerley. Did she really know him?

Only days before they'd married, he had told her the rest of his name. Weeks afterward he had told her that he had a little money, legitimately, and that he didn't earn his living solely by gambling. Only now did she understand the full impact of all his secrecy.

He liked playing cowboy. She'd known that from the first. But for how long? How long would he stay at the Circle T? How long would he stay with her?

The duke of Stroud . . . That must be the older brother, Robert. The Ackerley family . . . Hank had probably told her the truth when he said he was a third son, by the grace of being born five minutes after Tony. He just hadn't told her his family was part of the English aristocracy.

The Circle T must look like a toy to Hank, she thought ruefully.

From somewhere far off, she heard a bleat. Flirt nosed her shoulder while Patches, his reins trailing, walked a few steps to pull at a tuft of grass at the corner of the barn.

"I'll take care of the horses," she muttered. Her chest felt as if it wanted to explode; it must be her heart breaking, Mariah thought in fuzzy confusion.

Billy rode into the barnyard, scattering a rooster from his path as he came. "Mr. Ackerley," he reported, his breath short with excitement. "We got them sheep in the yonder pasture like you wanted. But that fella Smith is boilin' mad and threatenin' to quit. Says he ain't panderin' to no sheep."

Hank broke away from Elam. "Thank you, Billy. I'll take care of Smith."

"If you come up short a man over this, I'd like to sign on with ya."

"That's fine, Billy," Hank responded. He turned toward the east pasture.

Grabbing up the reins of the three horses, Mariah led them to the barn opening. Almost blindly, she unbuckled her cinch, pulled the saddle and blanket free of Skedaddle, then threw them onto Flirt. Ignoring the hubbub of excited males, she stripped the others of their gear, turned them in to the corral, swung up onto the back of the small brown horse and pointed her nose out of sight around the barn corner, then headed toward the Circle T's far section.

Behind her, no one questioned where she was going. She left the all-male company gladly. They were engrossed in the care of sheep or tales of adventure or family history. She didn't care what they did or said.

She rode a full mile before she dismounted and resaddled Flirt. The horse had ridden skittishly. Mariah gritted her teeth, muttering under her breath as she straightened the blanket and shortened the stirrups to fit her.

"You're a danged fool, girl. A stupid, blind, know-nothing. Falling in love with a man who fills you with sweet lies. . . ."

Mariah cinched the saddle more carefully this time. Just because she was upset, she couldn't allow the horse to suffer.

"Sweet lies and promises . . ." Did those promises mean anything at all?

Behind her she heard faint hoofbeats. Now what? It could only be Hank. She didn't want to talk to anybody, least of all her husband, until she'd had more time to think. And she sure as shootin' would fold herself into his arms if he gave her one of his melt-an-icicle smiles.

"C'mon, girl," she muttered, "let's push on." Mariah vaulted onto the saddle and heeled Flirt into a gallop, away from the oncoming rider.

24

Mariah came up on the ranch buildings from behind the house. She really wasn't ready to come home, but the sun was low. It was close to supper time and she had no intention of worrying Grandaddy by staying out any longer. Mutinously, she hoped Hank had worn himself to a nub looking for her.

When she came around the corner of the house, she spotted a strange buggy in the drive. It must be one rented by her brother-in-law, she thought—before she recognized the Bentons' swaybacked nag.

Mariah squeezed her eyes tightly shut for a moment and sighed. Caroline! She'd gone and invited the girl to supper, then forgotten all about it. She figured the August sun must be softening her brains.

The day had been a walloping doozy. Mariah hoped never to have another like it. And it wasn't over.

She wondered if Hank had returned yet. What was that very correct English brother of his thinking about now, with a sister-in-law who went running

wild over the countryside without a by-your-leave?
Grandaddy was used to her sometimes needing a soli-
tary ride, but Tony must find it odd, she mused.

And Hank . . . Her mouth set tight and her chin
pushed out. She was still up-in-the-air, mad-as-fire angry
with her husband. He hadn't been honest with her about
his family's extreme wealth or social position, and it left
her feeling newborn-stupid not to have known.

Hank's family must be terribly upset with him for
having married a little nobody, Mariah thought to
herself. Now, his brother was here to look her over.

She'd never measure up. How could she, when
even half of Mead hadn't approved of her until she
married Hank? She had no polish and often didn't
conform to what society expected of her.

Idly, Mariah leaned forward and patted Flirt's
neck. She'd given the little horse a real workout while
she'd done the same with her thoughts. But during
her ride, she'd figured some things out.

Hank hadn't told her everything about himself, and
she didn't understand all his reasons for it, yet. Part of
her heart questioned if Hank would have married her
at all if she had given in to their passion beforehand.
But the facts remained—even though she was no town
flower, Hank had wanted *her.* She and Grandaddy
had nothing but the Circle T for a dowry, yet Hank
had married *her.* He hadn't left her side since, and he
showed no signs of getting ready to leave.

A warm glow stole up to swell Mariah's heart. He
had shielded and protected her from harm, and
courted her with all the love and affection a wife
could ask for. She should stop her silly blathering
about would he stay or go, she scolded herself.

The important conclusion she'd come to wasn't
exactly a revelation—that she loved Hank with every

fiber of her being. Looking back on it, she thought she fell in love with him that first day. She'd just been too mixed up to know it.

No, loving Hank didn't surprise her. It was the depth of her emotions which shocked her. For Mariah knew now that if Hank became restless on the Circle T, and wanted to go adventuring, then she'd let him go and count herself lucky to have had him for a little while.

Meanwhile, there was the here and now to deal with, and somehow, she had to teach him not to play the wrong kind of games with her, or keep secrets. Buying sheep without telling her . . .having a family that rubbed elbows with Queen Victoria . . .

First, she had to get through supper. Sighing, Mariah dismounted, ground-reined her horse, and stepped through the door. Caroline and Grandaddy were sitting at the kitchen table. Caroline clearly was attempting to keep a cheerful face, but Mariah saw a flash of misery in her eyes before she lowered her lashes.

Mariah's heart went out to the other girl. She wasn't the only one who had had a troublesome day. And all on account of those dad-gummed *Englishmen*, she thought with another flare of temper.

"Sorry I'm late, Caroline. I, um, had to check on the cattle. Where is everyone, anyway?"

"Well," Grandaddy began, "Tony went back to town but said he'd return by supper time. The men are getting washed up, I reckon. Don't know where Hank got to, exactly."

"He'll be along soon, I think. Um, Grandaddy, would you do me a favor and walk Flirt down to the barn while I clean up? Have one of the hands unsaddle her and brush her down, please. And tell Brown to delay supper for about thirty minutes. I must be wearing a pound of dirt."

"Sure, honey," Elam answered. He wasn't sure what Mariah was up to, but he'd seen that look of stubbornness in her eyes more than once. It probably had something to do with Hank bringing in the sheep. She was going to hit the ceiling when she found out he'd approved Hank's plan.

"Mariah . . . maybe I should just go home," Caroline said on an unhappy note after Elam left. "This has been a . . . a . . . an unusual day, and with all that's happened . . ."

Mariah plopped down in the chair Elam had vacated and sighed. "Oh, Caroline, please stay. I, um, could use some female company. Did you meet Hank's brother?"

"Yes. Your grandaddy introduced us. Mariah, I have to ask you . . . did you know all this time that Hank came from a titled family?"

"Nope."

"Then you didn't know that Jim . . . James is a valet?"

Mariah shook her head.

Caroline looked at her hands, twisting them into a knot in her lap. It was clear she was distressed. "Mama will be furious."

"You mean because Jim's a valet?"

"Yes, that, and . . . and she already thinks I would be marrying beneath me. You know Mama's pride."

"Caroline, does it make any difference? You love Jim, don't you?"

"Oh, *yes!* But everything was already at odds and now it will be even worse. Mama will say Jim lied about who he was and . . . you know . . . ."

The door swung open with a sudden whoosh and Hank strode through the door. Behind him were Tony and Jim.

Hank halted abruptly when he saw Mariah calmly sitting at the kitchen table talking with Caroline.

"I am glad to see you at home safe and sound, Mariah," he said on an even tone, despite his clenched teeth. "I was about to form a search party."

"Why would you do that? I wasn't lost."

"But you didn't let anyone know you were leaving. Where were you?"

"Around. Why do you want to know?"

"Because I was worried about you. You must know that."

"The Circle T is like my backyard, Hank."

"I understand that!" He glared at her. "But it's a big, untamed play yard with lots of possible dangers. You should *tell* someone what your plans are. . . ."

"Exactly. Shared plans and knowledge are normal with married couples, aren't they, Hank? A responsibility everyone should practice. And since you make such a point of it, I will tell you now that I am going to get cleaned up for supper, in *my* bedroom. Caroline will keep me company. After all, Caroline and I have *no secrets* from each other. *You* may find soap and water in the bunkhouse."

Hank's brows shot up. Behind him, Jim looked quizzically at Caroline, who sniffed and raised her chin. Tony's eyes took on some of Hank's habitual amusement.

"Oh, and by the by, Hank, here's your mail." Mariah shot her husband a speaking glance as she pulled the several envelopes and fliers from her vest and tossed them on the table. Feminine handwriting showed on the top one. "See you later, gentlemen," she said airily. Then she turned on her heel and climbed the stairs, with Caroline trailing behind.

An hour later, Mariah strolled down to the cook-shack dressed neatly in one of the new white shirtwaist blouses and print skirts, her still-damp hair curling down her back, tied with a blue ribbon. She looked what she was, she thought: a simple, hard-working ranch wife about to entertain guests.

She had, however, added Granny's brooch to her collar and wore the gold-and-diamond ring that Hank had given her on their wedding day. Her ring usually sat in a little glass dish on their dresser.

Her feelings were buoyant. Mariah didn't examine them too closely, but she thought it had something to do with feeling comfortable about who she was. She didn't have to be what anyone else expected her to be, and she'd even discovered she liked Caroline because . . . Caroline was Caroline.

She had loosened her blonde tresses and, at Mariah's urging, had let a saucy curl dance against her nape. Surely Jim would appreciate the effect.

As soon as the girls entered the cookshack, the men jumped to attention. Mariah smiled at each in turn. Hank pursed his lips slightly and lifted a brow over his glinting gray eyes. She thought he didn't know whether to take her new attitude with amusement or to be wary.

Tony, trying unsuccessfully to hide his avid curiosity about her, smiled and bowed. The cowhands, in various stages of patience regarding their hunger, fidgeted with the unusual formality. Other than Smith, who was decidedly still on the boil over the sheep, they had slicked back their hair and changed into clean shirts as if for a party.

Mariah noticed a new face, and Jim introduced his cousin Harding. Jim was watchful of Caroline's expression, Mariah noted, as he explained that they were cousins.

Grandaddy said little beyond "at last" from where

he lounged in his chair at the head of the table, but Nate did.

"Whut took ya so long, Mariah?"

"Just wanted to make myself presentable, Nate. It isn't every day we can welcome relatives who have come from so far."

Mariah tried to see the room and the meal through her brother-in-law's eyes. And her husband's.

A second table had been added to their usual one. A dozen places were set with the new, plain white tableware Hank had bought. To Mariah, the table looked inviting and pleasant in its simplicity. Brown had even gone to the trouble of putting a cup of wild-flowers in the center.

Supper was the usual fare they'd been having since Brown had joined them: steaks, fried rabbit, biscuits, baked beans, green beans, stewed dried apricots, and blackberry pie. And gallons of coffee.

Perhaps it wasn't as fancy as Powell's dining room, and certainly it wasn't as elaborate as what she'd heard about big city offerings, but Mariah was proud of it nonetheless.

Most of the men were used to eating without much conversation, and tonight was even quieter than usual. Randy was naturally bashful in Caroline's presence, Mariah thought; Smith was clearly still disgruntled; Chad kept his own thoughts; and Jim was trying hard to make Harding feel more at ease in strange surroundings. It suddenly dawned on Mariah that the poor man had probably never eaten a meal at the same table as his employer.

Her glance shot to Tony, whose expression was carefully controlled. She couldn't guess at his thoughts. If he was affronted, his good manners wouldn't allow him to show it.

Mariah wondered how Hank had felt about sharing meals and work with Jim on an equal footing all these months. He hadn't seemed unduly bothered. In fact, she remembered the camaraderie that seemed to flow between them. But that may have been because Jim was secretly still in his employ and taking his orders.

A good many ranch families did eat separately from their hands, Mariah realized; most Western men didn't want their wives or daughters fraternizing with rough, crude cowhands, and many of the women agreed with that point of view. But their arrangements for communal meals were for practical reasons and she'd be danged if she would defend them, give reasons for them, or try to make her ranch family something it was not.

Which reminded her: she was still angry with Hank. When she caught him staring at her, he gave her a wink while a corner of his mouth twitched suspiciously. She jerked her gaze away and raised her chin. He wasn't going to charm his way out of this one.

As soon as Grandaddy said grace, Mariah began a conversation with each of the men in turn, asking about the work they'd done during the day and politely including Harding in the talk. She then told them about the trouble they'd had in getting the sheep out of town and the run-in with Kasey they'd had on the road. Though she knew they'd already heard the story by now, she counted on the fact that they would be too polite to say so.

Slowly, the men began to thaw. Nate started a story about the early days on the ranch when they had yearly visits from a small tribe of Shoshone Indians, to which Harding and Randy both gave particular attention. Tony asked Grandaddy about the current

Indian wars, and Caroline entered into a whispered interchange with Jim.

Mariah drifted into silence.

His wife was certainly angry with him, Hank mused. Probably with just cause, he admitted to himself, because he'd sprung the sheep on her unknowingly. But he wasn't about to allow her to start a rift between them.

"You haven't asked about the flock, Mariah."

Hank made it a pointed statement, for in spite of her dislike for sheep, he knew Mariah cared deeply about every animal she owned. Her curiosity about the sheep would get the better of her eventually, so the sooner they hashed out the problems, the better. They could have their fight and get it over with. He certainly didn't intend to spend the night facing her back.

"How have *your* sheep fared?" Mariah asked coolly.

"*Our* sheep have come through very well, considering. I must say our shepherd was a bit shaken, though. I asked Billy to stay with him tonight to ease his fears."

"That was thoughtful of you, Hank. I wondered what had happened to Billy. "

"Merely expedient, my love."

"Have you taken Billy on permanently, then?" A touch of asperity laced her tone.

"Yes, I suppose *we* have." Hank answered in firm good humor and glanced at Mariah from the corner of one eye. "He said he had quit his other employer and didn't mind 'ridin' herd' on sheep."

Mariah pushed a bit of stewed apricot around her plate.

"Hmm . . . It's more likely he has a bad case of hero worship where you're concerned. He was awestruck by your, um, boxing thing," she said, spitting it out.

Hank casually leaned back in his chair, his good humor draining away. "I assume you mean by that, that Billy is impressed with the sport?"

"Reckon so. Sometimes he can be dumber than a fence post. . . ."

"Are you implying he is stupid to be interested in boxing, or that I am?"

Mariah took a deep breath, embarrassed at her own thoughtless words. But she would not take them back. Suddenly, in spite of all her reasoning with herself this afternoon, her emotions began to creep out. "Reckon you can take it any way you want."

Mariah turned to the company at large and refused to look at him again, instantly sorry that she'd been quick-tempered, yet feeling no relief from having vented her displeasure.

Hank, usually so ready with soothing words, was silent. He rightly guessed that Mariah's sharp remark covered more than her dislike of boxing.

"That is quite some horse you brought in today, Mr. Ackerley," Chad commented to break the lull. "His bloodlines must be from some top breeders."

"They are indeed, Chad," Hank answered. "It was good of Tony to bring Ebony over from England for me. He's the last of my stable there."

Guiltily, Mariah's interest sparked. What horse was this? She hadn't been to the corral or barn all day and obviously had missed seeing the horse under discussion. She peeked at Hank's face as he extolled the virtues of Ebony's dam and sire. There was such pride there.

Hank paused for a moment to sip his coffee, aware of Mariah's gaze, and then went on. "There is a wonderful gray stallion that roams among the wild mustangs above the Circle T's north border. Fireball. A mixed breed, of course. He's as different from Ebony as night from day, yet he's an intelligent beast. He has spirit and stamina. I want to put him to stud with Ebony. Mariah and I are going after him sometime soon."

Underneath the table, he took her hand. When she made to pull away, he held tight.

Supper ended soon after that. Jim escorted Caroline, her eyes shining, up to Mariah to say her good nights before taking her home. Her friend gave her a lovely, grateful smile. "It's all going to work out, I'm sure, thanks to you. I'll talk to you again soon, Mariah dear," she whispered as they left. Mariah noticed how both Caroline and Jim seemed to be full of eagerness to be alone.

For the moment, Mariah wanted to be in the same state of existence. To be alone. As the cowboys dispersed to their various duties, she said a polite good night to Tony, and left the cookshack, while Hank and his brother stayed to talk.

Though it was late, Mariah heard Hank climb up the stairs. Their room was dark, lit only by the light of a half-moon streaming through the windows. He didn't light the lamp. A moment passed before he slid into bed beside her. She lay still, pretending to sleep.

Her pretense didn't take her far. He immediately gathered her into his arms and pulled her back close to his chest, curving his long body around hers. He felt warm and comforting and she struggled to maintain a remnant of her righteous anger.

"Hank, I'm tired. It's been a long day." But he wouldn't let her go.

"Hmm . . . me too," he murmured near her ear, pressing his lips against the sensitive skin just behind it. "It has been a rather stressful day, all in all. I don't want to make love at the moment, Mariah, darling. You must rest. But I do think we should talk about it."

"Talk about what?"

"The sheep. The unfortunate timing of Anthony's arrival. Whatever is making you angry or hurting you."

"You . . . You!" She sat up and faced him. She was perturbed that he always knew how she was feeling, while he was so adept at keeping secrets from her. "You bring a flock of sheep into cattle country, knowing we'll have to watch over them closer than a hawk watches a baby chick, and you expect me to be happy about it?"

"I know you need time to adjust to raising sheep, Mariah, but I don't think that is all of what is causing you distress."

"And you didn't tell me. . . ."

"Now we're getting to it. I suppose I should apologize for that. And I solemnly promise to tell you of major decisions in the future."

"Or even talk to me about it. . . ."

"I didn't advise you of it beforehand because I wanted you to see the sheep first, to give them a chance. Your grandfather has dealt only in cattle, yet when I put the plan before him, he—"

"Grandaddy knew?"

"Yes. He willingly agreed to the experiment."

"The experiment of what?"

"Of putting sheep and cattle on the same range. Eventually."

"Ohhh," she groaned, knowing she had been out-gunned. Part of her was delighted that Grandaddy trusted Hank so, but it left her feeling she had to contend with the two of them. "Hank, how will I ever manage it all after you leave?"

She hadn't meant to say that, exactly. She hadn't wanted to let him know of her deeper fear.

He looked at her in puzzlement. "I am not going anywhere."

She dropped her gaze. "Oh, well . . . I meant . . . well, someday . . . you might."

"Someday? Of course, someday I might need to travel for the sake of business. Or we might still have a journey to one of the big cities. I would like you to see Paris and"—he grinned impishly—"the so-o-o divine San Francisco. And, naturally, I wish to take you home to England for a visit in a year or two."

"You do? Oh, I . . . I didn't know . . ."

"What did you think, Mariah?" He lifted her chin. Whatever expression the moonlight revealed, he wanted to see. "That I would leave you behind?"

"Well, yes, I reckon I did." Her admission was a whisper, but what it told him hit him with the force of a shout. "It's all right, Hank, really. I . . . I would never hold on to you if you wanted to leave."

"That is what's really bothering you, isn't it? You think I will someday leave you. . . ."

"You must admit, Hank, you were born to a different life than what you find here. Your family obviously expected you to make a humdinger of a connection. A society marriage with a lady who knows all the rights and wrongs in those circles. You probably should've married that Eastern girl. Edith."

Hank snorted. "Edith! I couldn't abide Edith when I met her. She hasn't half your spirit, nor a quarter of your sweetness. For your information, I threw her letter into the stove unread."

A smile began to curve her mouth. It was the first time she realized Hank admired her spirit. As to her sweetness, she would have to think about that. Maybe he equated the term with something different than she did.

"You couldn't? You did?"

"Yep, by gum." He teased her, as he sometimes did, with an attempt at the local vernacular.

"Then why . . ."

"Why?" he prompted.

"Why didn't you tell me the complete truth about your family?"

He got out of bed and walked to the window. He stared out a moment, seeing the faint outlines of the barn and bunkhouse, and farther, the stable and corral. He had loved this place almost as instantly as he had Mariah. Beyond what he could see in the dark were the mountains. But he didn't need to see them to know they were there, to feel their mighty presence.

Slowly, he began to talk, to try to express the inner change he had undergone.

"Mariah, you and I share a common trait. Inside, we are both somewhat rebellious. But unlike you, I seldom cared about hurting anyone with my behavior. Always, it seems, I have been rather self-centered. I hated it when Tony was always the good lad, the one who rarely got into trouble and got his pats on the head for it, while I seldom could stay out of it. And so, I learned to take my licks without a fuss. I suppose over time I grew not to care when first my father, then my brothers remonstrated with me to have a thought to what I was doing. I just didn't care.

"Finally, after my parents died, I made up my mind to settle down and marry. To please the family, of course, and yes, to a proper bride. But I had not once thought of loving . . . Then I met you."

He turned to stare at her. "You, Mariah. I fell in love with you so hard I didn't know if a mountain had fallen on me or the earth had swallowed me. But you were different. The rules . . . you played by honorable rules even while frequently thumbing your pretty nose at society."

Hank's voice grew constricted. His emotions had never felt so completely raw. He cleared his throat and went on.

"And all I knew was that I wanted you, and this life. And then another revelation hit me. The biggest thing I ever felt in my life was that I desired more for you than I did for myself. I wanted . . . I still want to protect you, give you everything."

"Hank . . . love," she whispered. Joyful tears rolled down her face. She didn't care anymore that he had kept secrets from her. His soul-deep declaration would fill her heart for a lifetime.

She rose and went to him. This time it was she who wrapped herself against his back. She pressed her face into his muscled shoulder.

Hank took one small hand from his waist and raised it to his lips. "Mariah . . . if I had told you where I came from, of my family, you would have run scared . . . I love the freedom between us, and if I had told you everything, you wouldn't have given me any more chance at winning your love than you were willing to give those other poor sheep when you saw them this afternoon."

"I'm sorry, greenhorn. . . ."

Against her face, his muscles eased. He turned to her. "Admit it, love. You made me work hard at leaping over your fences."

Mariah chortled, between tears and laughter. If he only knew. "A girl has to protect herself the best way she can."

His hands spanned her waist. "Mmm . . . Will you forgive me?"

"I suppose, under the circumstances, I must, mustn't I?" Mariah said, trying to make him laugh with her best imitation of his English speech. "After all, we are in this together."

"Yep, ma'am, we sure 'nuff are. Partners."

"Partners, Hank?"

"Yes, darlin', partners," he said, raising his right hand as though swearing in a court of law. "Everything we do from now on we will do in a straightforward manner. No more secrets."

"In that case, anything we don't agree on has to be, um, negotiated, right? Not just for the Circle T. Between you and me, too."

"Most definitely, between you and me."

"Then I want to make a . . . um . . . trade. I will say no more against the sheep if you'll . . . give up your boxing."

"The boxing! I knew you didn't like it. I don't know. I'll have to think. . . ."

She punched him lightly in the ribs.

"All right, darling, if you're that serious about it."

"Good! If we have anymore run-ins like we did today, you won't miss it much."

"Hmmm. Now I have one for you."

"What is that?"

"You must promise to give up kissing strangers."

"Oh . . . well, I suppose . . . if you insist. . . ."

Hank pulled her up hard against him. "I do. I most certainly do."

Epilogue

August 18, 1880

To Robert Ackerley, the Duke of Stroud
Ackerley Hall, Surrey, England

Dear Brother,

I take pen in hand at my first opportunity to inform you of the situation here with Henry. First, let me assure you he is well. Quite well, in fact. Henry appears extremely healthy and fit; he has taken on the look of an outdoorsman. Also, you may inform the below-stairs family that James, too, is well.

As to Henry's marriage . . . A simple, binding ceremony took place at the local Methodist church sometime in June between Henry and a Miss Mariah Taggert. It was witnessed by James Moore and Elam Taggert, Miss Taggert's grandfather, and several local citizens.

Our estimation of the girl's background was a correct one. We know little of her family history other than what her paternal grandfather can relate to us. However, I must tell you that Elam Taggert is a fine, honest man who has a native wisdom with which you would feel comfortable. Now I will relate to you my assessment of Henry's bride.

Mariah has an unusual type of beauty, one of unstudied grace that reminds one of a mischievous elf caught in a woman's body, and although she is nothing like the women with whom he has previously associated, one can easily see why our Henry was attracted to her. Furthermore, she seems to have no womanly guile. That is to say, she does not posture or pretend to be something she is not. Yet there is an unmistakable connection between her and Henry which—perhaps only I, being Henry's twin, can see clearly—seems often to be a silent communication of . . . playful allurement.

Mariah has little in social skills that would cause her to be thought of as a successful English hostess, nor does she have much polish. But I must say, Robert, that Mariah, like her grandfather, has a great deal of natural intelligence and seems—I know you will find this amusing, Robby—she seems to pull from Henry a commonsense approach to life which he seldom displayed for the benefit of his family and friends at home. Now, here in Colorado, and for the benefit of his bride, he is eager to set the events of his life into a sensible balance. Whatever capriciousness he formerly followed seems tempered with a deep need to protect his wife.

The Taggert property, a ranch called the Circle T, will remain, as I understand it, in Mariah's ownership, or in that of their offspring. However, Henry has agreed to expand it and help to manage it. Hence his request for sheep, an undertaking which I foresee could indeed be successful. It is a rugged land, part prairie, part mountains, with much still very wild. That, I am sure, has been its lure to Henry.

All in all, Robert, I think we may rest easy with Henry's choice of a bride. It is a bit of a stunner, of course, to realize Henry has chosen to leave England for a simpler life here, but I can understand his decision. And while Mariah is definitely not a milk-and-toast English Miss, she has attributes which are unique, and any young woman who can tame our Henry deserves our praise. High praise, indeed.

Now, about my return. I rather think I shall extend my stay here, at least into the fall. The autumn color is striking in the mountains, I am told, and I find my experience of life in Mead and on the Circle T both a fascinating and a broadening study of man. And there are one or two excursions planned in which I wish to participate. One is to make a wild-horse hunt . . .

AVAILABLE NOW

THE COURT OF THREE SISTERS by Marianne Willman
An enthralling historical romance from the award-winning author of *Yesterday's Shadows* and *Silver Shadows*. The Court of Three Sisters was a hauntingly beautiful Italian villa where a prominent archaeologist took his three daughters: Thea, Summer, and Fanny. Into their circle came Col McCallum, who was determined to discover the real story behind the mysterious death of his mentor. Soon Col and Summer, in a race to unearth the fabulous ancient treasure that lay buried on the island, found the meaning of true love.

OUTRAGEOUS by Christina Dodd
The flamboyant Lady Marian Wenthaven, who cared nothing for the opinions of society, proudly claimed two-year-old Lionel as her illegitimate son. When she learned that Sir Griffith ap Powel, who came to visit her father's manor, was actually a spy sent by King Henry VII to watch her, she took Lionel and fled. But there was no escaping from Griffith and the powerful attraction between them.

CRAZY FOR LOVIN' YOU by Lisa G. Brown
The acclaimed author of *Billy Bob Walker Got Married* spins a tale of life and love in a small Tennessee town. After four years of exile, Terrill Carroll returns home when she learns of her mother's serious illness. Clashing with her stepfather, grieving over her mother, and trying to find a place in her family again, she turns to Jubal Kane, a man from the opposite side of the tracks who has a prison record, a bad reputation, and the face of a dark angel.

TAMING MARIAH by Lee Scofield
When Mariah kissed a stranger at the train station, everyone in the small town of Mead, Colorado, called her a hellion, but her grandfather knew she only needed to meet the right man. The black sheep son of a titled English family, Hank had come to the American West seeking adventure . . . until he kissed Mariah.

FLASH AND FIRE by Marie Ferrarella
Amanda Foster, who has learned the hard way how to make it on her own, finally lands the coveted anchor position on the five o'clock news. But when she falls for Pierce Alexander, the station's resident womanizer, is she ready to trust love again?

INDISCRETIONS by Penelope Thomas
The spellbinding story of a murder, a ghost, and a love that conquered all. During a visit to the home of enigmatic Edmund Llewelyn, Hilary Carewe uncovered a decade-old murder through rousing the spirit of Edmund's stepmother, Lily Llewelyn. As Edmund and Hilary were drawn together, the spirit grew stronger and more vindictive. No one was more affected by her presence than Hilary, whom Lily seemed determined to possess.

COMING NEXT MONTH

FOREVERMORE by Maura Seger

As the only surviving member of a family that had lived in the English village of Avebury for generations, Sarah Huxley was fated to protect the magical sanctuary of the tumbled stone circles and earthen mounds. But when a series of bizarre deaths at Avebury began to occur, Sarah met her match in William Devereux Faulkner, a level-headed Londoner, who had come to investigate. "Ms. Seger has a special magic touch with her lovers that makes her an enduring favorite with readers everywhere."—*Romantic Times*

PROMISES by Jeane Renick

From the award-winning author of *Trust Me* and *Always* comes a sizzling novel set in a small Ohio town, featuring a beautiful blind heroine, her greedy fiancé, two sisters in love with the same man, a mysterious undercover police officer, and a holographic will.

KISSING COUSINS by Carol Jerina

Texas rancher meets English beauty in this witty follow-up to *The Bridegroom*. When Prescott Trefarrow learned that it was he who was the true Earl of St. Keverne, and not his twin brother, he went to Cornwall to claim his title, his castle, and a multitude of responsibilities. Reluctantly, he became immersed in life at Ravens Lair Castle—and the lovely Lucinda Trefarrow.

HUNTER'S HEART by Christina Hamlett

A romantic suspense novel featuring a mysterious millionaire and a woman determined to figure him out. Many things about wealthy industrialist Hunter O'Hare intrigue Victoria Cameron. First of all, why did O'Hare have his ancestral castle moved to Virginia from Ireland, stone by stone? Secondly, why does everyone else in the castle act as if they have something to hide? And last, but not least, what does Hunter want from Victoria?

THE LAW AND MISS PENNY by Sharon Ihle

When U.S. Marshal Morgan Slater suffered a head injury and woke up with no memory, Mariah Penny conveniently supplied him with a fabricated story so that he wouldn't run her family's medicine show out of town. As he traveled through Colorado Territory with the Pennys, he and Mariah fell in love. Everything seemed idyllic until the day the lawman's memory returned.

PRIMROSE by Clara Wimberly

A passionate historical tale of forbidden romance between a wealthy city girl and a fiercely independent local man in the wilds of the Tennessee mountains. Rosalyn Hunte's heart was torn between loyalty to her family and the love of a man who wanted to claim her for himself.